Spirit of the Sea Witch

Keepers of the Stones, Book Two

Tara West

Copyright © 2018 by Tara West

Published by Shifting Sands Publishing

First edition, published January, 2018

Edited by Theo Fenraven.

Artwork by Bob Kehl.

Dedications

To all of my readers who waited patiently for this book, thanks so much for your support. I hope the wait was worth it.

Bob, your artwork was brilliant. I have received so many compliments on this cover. You captured Eris and Naamaku perfectly. Thank you!

Thanks to my awesome beta team, Alan, Ginelle, Sandy, Sheri, and Suanne, for catching so many of my oopsies.

Special thanks, as always, to Theo, God of Grammar, for trudging through this muck and cutting 10K of unnecessary rambling.

Spirit of the Sea Witch
Keepers of the Stones, Book Two
Tara West

A SCORNED WOMAN'S REVENGE burns hotter than a pyre. The vengeance of a goddess is more destructive than a thousand fires.

DESPERATE TO ESCAPE the wrath of the vengeful Sky Goddess, Madhea, a group of brave young explorers flees to the sea in search of safe haven for their people while the apprentice witch, Dianna, steals away Madhea's dragon to the Shifting Sands. Though they are an ocean apart, the future of humanity lies in their entwined fates. Before they can defeat Madhea, they must stop Eris, the vindictive Sea Goddess, from destroying the world.

Foreword

THE ELDERS HAD WARNED Khashka not to hunt the beasts. They had told him to net the fish at the mouth of the river—those ugly soaring salamin, the staple of Aloa-Shay. Salamin for breaking fast. Salamin for the noonday meal. Salamin for supper.

Except on the days when low tide kept the salamin from entering the harbor or when a brutal thunderstorm left the water murky for days.

Then Khashka and his family had to subsist on riverweed for nourishment. Having been deprived of her mother's breast milk, his daughter, Mari, had been a sick infant and a fragile child. She needed more nourishment than riverweed could provide. Khashka was tired of depending on the salamin harvest, so he did not listen to the village elders when they warned him of Eris's wrath—not when one sea beast could sustain an entire village through the wet season.

"I have a bad feeling about these monsters, Uncle Khashka." Tung clutched the sides of the boat, his matted locks of dark hair sticking to his bronzed skin as the afternoon sun beat down on his face. The boy's gaze darted from the pale horizon to the smooth waters and back again.

Khashka chuckled softly to himself. At only five and ten summers, his nephew was still easily misled by superstition. Khashka shielded his eyes with a hand and cast his gaze to the sky. "The sky is cloudless. Unusual for the wet season. It is a good sign." They were meant to kill a whale this day.

When Khashka leaned over and gripped his nephew by the shoulder, he was surprised at how the boy trembled beneath his touch. At that moment Khashka was reminded of his nephew's insecurity. Khashka had not been a good guardian since Tung's parents had died two summers past from a sickness that had claimed Mari's sweet mother and almost half the village. He reminded himself he'd need to try harder to help the boy learn to become a man. Harvesting a broot whale would be a fine start.

The horned whales were every bit as beautiful as they were deadly. Nearly half the length and girth of a trading vessel, they had toppled more than one wayward harbor boat in Khashka's lifetime.

Though the villagers had long ago given up hunting broots in favor of netting salamin, Khashka remembered his grandfather's tales of the village fishermen hunting these magnificent creatures. Grandfather had said the meat was sweeter than any sugar cane and one slab of broot was more filling than a dozen salamin.

Tung gnawed his bottom lip. "I keep thinking about what the elders said about the young broot and the deadly storm."

Khashka let out a frustrated breath. When Khashka's grandfather had been a child, a brutal storm ravaged their village after they'd harvested a juvenile whale. Nearly a third of all the people perished, and the body of the uneaten broot had washed back into the sea. The elders believed Eris was displeased with them for killing one of her water giants, and so the sea goddess had inflicted the storm as punishment. Khashka stifled a groan as he looked into his nephew's frightened eyes. "That storm was an act of nature, Tung. People were not meant to subsist on flimsy fish and riverweed."

Despite objections from the elders, Khashka had rallied enough men to form a party of four fishing boats. He'd been insistent that his timid nephew attend the hunt as well. Tung had been terrified of the water since he'd nearly drowned as a toddler, but Khashka would tolerate no more of his nephew's foolishness. Together they would bring down a beast with net and spears, and the village would hail Khashka, perhaps even Tung, as a hero.

"Look, Uncle!" Tung came to his knees and pointed toward a bubbling in the water beyond their boat.

A pod of broots surfaced, sprouting water high into the air through the holes on top of their heads. Khashka covered his face as water rained down on him and then signaled to the oarsmen to row toward the monsters.

"Great Goddess!" Tung exclaimed with a shaky breath. "How many are there?"

Khashka let out a low whistle at the sight. This was by far the largest pod he'd ever seen, with over a dozen broots. How could he possibly hunt them with such numbers? If one broot was lethal, Khashka did not wish to invoke the ire of several.

"Hold your weapons," Khashka said to the other men in their fishing vessel. "We must turn back. Their numbers are too many."

As Khashka stood and raised his hand to call back the other boats, a spear was thrown, followed by another and another. Khashka let out a strangled cry when all three spears lodged in the flesh of a small whale. Blood pooled around the beast as it bucked against the water. Khashka fell to his knees and gripped the sides of the boat when the rocking waves threatened to topple it. A low, dark cry sounded from somewhere beneath the surface of the water. Khashka had only a moment to glance at the wide eyes of his nephew before the boy was thrown from the boat with a splintering crack.

Khashka was vaguely aware of men calling to him and slapping against wooden planks as he was lifted into the air. In the distance he heard blood-curdling screams, followed by violent splashing and low, ominous moans.

There was a burst of light, followed by the swell of a woman's breast, dark, flowing hair, and the flick of a long serpent tail. "Just as you have taken one of mine, I shall claim one of yours." The voice resounded in his skull with a sibilant hiss.

Then his world darkened.

Chapter One

A Dragon's Grudge

"I DO NOT LIKE THIS place."

Alec opened his eyes to see Des staring at him. Errant strands from the boy's mop of hair cast shadows over his dark eyes.

"Nor do I, Des," Alec whispered in what he hoped was a soothing tone, "but Ryne says only a few more days until we pass through the forest."

Alec and Des had set off with the ice dwellers, Ryne and his party, in hopes of finding a safe haven near the sea, somewhere far from the eye of the vengeful sky goddess, Madhea.

The Werewood Forest was so thick with foliage, it was perpetually dark, even during midday, when the sun would cast only a few slivers of light through the heavy pine branches. The farther they delved into the belly of the woods, the stranger the creatures they found, from little winged fairies with sharp fangs no bigger than Alec's thumb to monster plants that had thrice tried to swallow young Des and their two canine companions. Much of the vegetation was poisonous, such as stinkweed that created a smell toxic enough to leave a hapless traveler sick for days.

Alec repressed a shudder as a howl pierced the cool night air. He did not wish the boy to know this strange place frightened him. Alec was only glad they were traveling with Ryne and his hunting party. Ryne's large, furry hound, Tar, had proven to be an excellent watchman, scaring off more than one creature each night, which was far better than Brendle, Des's mangy little black dog that looked part rodent and spent most of his time cowering between Des's legs.

"Where do you think my sister is now?" Des asked for at least the hundredth time since they'd left their mountain home of Adolan over a fortnight ago.

"Dianna should have made it to the Shifting Sands," Alec answered evenly.

Des's features scrunched. "Will she be safe?"

"I should say so." Alec chuckled. "She's got a mighty protector." The sky goddess's dragon, Lydra, had turned against her and now served Dianna. The pair had flown to the Shifting Sands in hopes of finding a safe haven for their people, should the goddess decide to extend her wrath to the mountain's inhabitants.

The boy's lower lip trembled. "I miss them."

A pang sliced through Alec's chest as he thought of his brother, Markus, who had stayed behind with the ice dwellers.

"I know you do, lad." Alec clasped Des by the shoulder. "In time the pain will ease. You shall be reunited before you know it. Imagine the stories she will have to tell next spring." He smiled at the boy and ruffled his hair. "Imagine the stories *you* will have."

A wide grin split Des's face. "I cannot wait to see the land of limitless water."

Alec smiled at the thought. Ryne had told them that he'd never felt so alive as when he had visited the warm ocean village of Aloa-Shay. Alec thought back to the time when his lungs had burned with pain at every strained breath—back before Dianna used her magic to heal most of his sickness. Though Alec grew stronger with each passing day, there were times when he still had the urge to cough. He hoped the ocean air would be just what he needed for a full recovery.

"Neither can I, lad. Now go to sleep. We have a lot more walking to do tomorrow."

It did not take long before the boy curled up with Brendle, falling into a pattern of slow and steady breathing. Though Des was not a brother by blood, he had become more than a brother to Alec. He'd vowed to Dianna that he would protect the boy, just as he had vowed once before that he would give his last dying breath to protect his brother, Markus. Perhaps this was why it was so difficult for Alec to fall asleep most nights—worry over Des. And though he was loath to admit it, Alec knew there was another reason he spent many nights awake. Dark thoughts troubled him—memories from his past that resurfaced in his nightmares, especially of that fateful day he'd plunged a knife into his abusive father's back.

Alec jumped out from under his furs at the sound of a familiar scream. Across the campfire, Ryne was pushing his furs aside, spear in hand. Ryne's furry hound was already on all fours, growling low, his snout pointed in the direction of the screams.

Ryne's blue-tinted skin glowed eerily in the firelight. Alec looked for the other three hunters in their party, but only two men, Luc and Filip, emerged from their bedrolls. Ven was missing.

"Ven!" Ryne cried.

Alec slipped on his soles and reached for his bow and arrows. Des looked up at him through half-lidded eyes, his little mutt whimpering beside him. "Stay here," Alec commanded and followed the bobbling torchlights of Ryne and the other hunters.

IT WAS NOT HARD TO find Ven. All they had to do was run in the direction of the loud booms that shook the ground beneath their feet, sounding as if trees were being uprooted from the earth.

"Giant," Ryne growled under his breath.

Alec prayed there wasn't more than one.

As the fervor and pitch of Ven's screams intensified, Ryne held out a staying arm, waving the party back with his torch. Though Ven needed them, Alec knew it would not be wise to rush head-on into a gathering of giants.

Alec followed Ryne, sidestepping strangling ivy and mollusk hives to the small clearing ahead. The ground shook with such intensity, Alec thought his skull would snap in two. Tar growled beside Ryne, the silver fur on the back of his neck standing on end.

"Easy, Tar," Ryne warned.

Alec hoped the dog listened. He would not wish their protector to be trampled.

"Play Gorpat!" a deep voice bellowed.

"Nooooo!" Ven hollered. "Help!"

It was then Alec spotted the beast, her wide, flattened nose and droopy eyes eerily lit beneath the glow of the full moon. She was at least eight men in height, with legs thicker than towering pines. Though most giants had unshorn hair, this monster wore a billowing dress and two long, symmetrical braids tied with yellow ribbons.

Before this night, Alec had thought the tales the trader Zier had told him about giants were fables. Odd how Zier's stories always depicted giants in animal hides or nothing at all. Perhaps they could reason with this beast, as she appeared to be more 'human' than the others.

She swung poor Ven into the air, catching him by the leg as he was about to land on his skull. "Play Gorpat!" she bellowed, stomping a foot.

Alec bit back a curse when he realized he wouldn't have time to reason with the giant. If she continued to 'play' with Ven this way, he'd be dead within the hour. Just as Ryne stumbled and fell back, Alec unleashed an arrow. It went straight into the giant's arm.

The beast released Ven with a howl. "Owie!" she cried. "Dada!"

Alec's limbs trembled with fear. "Dada? We have to get out of here!"

Ven was already crawling away from the beast, but Alec could tell he was injured.

Ryne tossed his torch into the wet moss and advanced toward the giant, spear raised. He called to the others in their party. "Get Ven!"

As the crying giant fell to the ground, Luc and Filip grabbed Ven and pulled him to the edge of the clearing. Alec and Ryne had their weapons trained on the giant while Tar growled menacingly at the beast. She paid them no heed while picking splinters of wood out of her arm.

Ryne spoke to Alec out of the corner of his mouth. "Slowly back away."

Alec did not need to be told twice. He backpedaled toward the forest. Ryne whistled to Tar, but the dog held his ground, teeth bared and ears flattened against his skull.

"Tar!" Ryne hissed. "Back!"

The giant lifted her massive head and bellowed into the night sky, "Dada!"

Alec did not know which shook more, the branches on the nearby trees or his quivering innards. One thing he did know—if they did not make haste, they would be reduced to nothing more than splat beneath the monster's foot.

"Tar!" Ryne pleaded urgently.

Much to Alec's relief, Ryne's dog slowly backed up until they were all, once again, shrouded by the canopy of dense forest. Alec turned to the others. Ven was vomiting onto a nearby patch of stinkweed. The pungent odor of Ven's vomit, mixed with the poisonous gasses from the hostile plant, was nearly enough to make Alec faint.

"Come on!" he commanded.

Alec kept throwing anxious glances behind him as they made slow progress back to camp. Luc and Filip had to practically drag Ven as vomit ran down the side of his mouth.

Once they reached camp, they made quick work of putting out the fire, rolling up their sacks, and making a litter for Ven out of spears and furs, but Alec feared they wouldn't be fast enough. There was no way their party could outmatch a giant's long strides.

By the time they set away from camp, Alec's heart was pounding out a wild staccato in his ears. Tar trotted in front of him, whimpering as Ryne cut through overhanging snake moss with his blade. Only after the giant's cries had gone from a booming echo to a distant, muffled sob, did the tension coiled around Alec's spine unwind.

Ryne stopped for breath, wiping a bead of sweat off his brow and turning to the others. Ven was still not well, alternating between moaning and heaving.

Alec, who'd brought up the rear with his bow in hand, looked at Ven's trail of vomit, eyeing it with a scowl. "Do giants have a good sense of smell?" he asked Ryne.

Ryne shook his head. "Not that I'm aware of, not when their noses are so far from the ground."

"Good thing we are not running from dwarves," the boy, Des, said with a sideways grin.

Alec peered at the boy. "This is not a time for jests. That giant could have killed us all."

Des nodded solemnly. Alec ruffled his dark mop of hair.

Their tender moment only served as a reminder that they needed to put more distance between themselves and the giant. Alec had to find a safe haven for his people before the glacier melted and all of Adolan was underwater. Ryne's kingdom was relying on him to find safety for their people as well. Sudden booming sounds unnerved Alec to the marrow of his bones. It was a giant to be sure, perhaps more than one, and they were running toward them.

"Move!" Ryne commanded.

Ryne hacked feverishly through the moss as Alec and the others followed swiftly. As the booming drew closer, shaking the ground beneath his feet. Alec's heart thumped against his chest even harder than before and nervousness made him itch. Any moment and the giants would be upon them.

And then what? How could a small party of mortals and two dogs defend themselves against giants? If they didn't find a means of escape, they were all doomed.

"WE MUST FIND A PLACE to land."

Dianna shielded her eyes from the wind and sand that pelted her and peered over Lydra's back. Nowhere in this cursed desert was there a good place to land, but she could tell by the arrhythmic flapping of Lydra's wings that the dragon needed rest and water. They had been flying for weeks with little sleep or nourishment, because Dianna was anxious to be far away from the vengeful goddess, Madhea.

Dianna and her dragon had flown across great mountains and valleys, then farther still over a limitless sea. When they'd reached the shoreline, Dianna and Lydra had had little time to find water or food before the villagers, armed with spears and bows, had driven them into the desert.

Dianna smoothed her hand across the dragon's cracked scales. Flakes of iridescent hide broke apart in her fingers. This was not good. Lydra was an ice dragon. She thrived in cool air, but there was not so much as a breeze in this parched wasteland. They would be lucky to find a small stream in the never-ending sea of dust, much less a body of water large enough to quench her dragon's thirst.

She fumbled for the stone in her pocket, gliding her fingers across its even surface. This magical stone, that her brother Markus had given her, encased the spirit of her ancestor, a woman named Sindri, who could speak to Dianna through it. She'd guided Dianna and her dragon to the Shifting Sands, but Dianna worried the stone was a trick, mayhap an enchanted rock planted by Madhea to fool Dianna into coming to this cursed wasteland. Even more suspicious was that Sindri had been silent the past several days. She usually spoke to Dianna in thought whenever she rubbed the stone. Where had Sindri gone, and why would she abandon Dianna in her time of need?

She leaned over and patted Lydra's side, alarmed as more bits of scale flaked off. "Forget landing," she called against the wind. "We must find you water."

The dragon grunted her understanding and continued the slow flap of her wings. Dianna hoped they would find water soon. She did not know how much longer Lydra could withstand the heat.

Chapter Two

"YOU SHOULD BE ASHAMED of yerself for shootin' an innocent wee lass!"

Alec's mouth hung open as he looked down at the irate dwarf, whose flushed rounded cheeks and bulbous nose resembled three overripe apples. The little man squinted at Alec from beneath bushy graying brows and pointed a finger at his chest.

Alec held out his hands and backed up, glancing at Ven, who was lying supine on the litter, flanked by his two kinsmen, whose spears were poised at the giant. This was not good. Alec had heard tales of giants taking out entire villages. These ice dwellers wouldn't stand a chance.

Though Ven had stopped heaving, his blue-tinted skin was a pale shade of sickly green. Alec turned back to the dwarf, hating the pleading tone that slipped into his voice. "I'm sorry, but she would have killed our companion."

"My pearl?" The dwarf gasped. "Hogwash!" He squinted at Alec again and waved a fist at the crying giant. "Look at what you done to her arm!"

The beast sat on her haunches, leaning against a pine and clutching her injury. The light from the full moon made her ruddy cheeks glow like twin suns. She sniffled loudly, long, sticky pendulums of snot hanging from her nose.

Alec repressed a shudder as she dragged the back of one hand across her nose and then flung the snot all over the forest floor. Collective swearing ensued as everyone in the party got slimed. Bits of goo was slung across Alec's boots, and several large chunks pelted the dogs' fur. The dogs whimpered before shaking. Ryne and the other hunters swore again when they were sprayed with more goo.

"Ew! Giant boogies!" Des squealed, pulling a tendril of snot from a wild, dark lock of his hair.

Alec stifled a groan. "Look at my friend. He still cannot walk!"

Alec pointed to poor Ven, who had been slimed with a majority of the giant's boogers, so much in fact that the stuff coated him in a clear cocoon, making Ven look like the larvae of a bug. He was leaning over the litter again, vomiting bile. His companions grumbled and cleaned slime off their spears.

"Serves him right." The dwarf chuckled, seemingly heedless of the clumps of snot clinging to his matted beard. Then his laughter died, and his smile thinned. Storm clouds brewing in the depths of his eyes, he pointed a finger at Ven. "How long was he alone with my daughter? Did he violate my pearl?"

"What? No!" Alec shrieked.

Beside him, Ryne grumbled louder, his blue cheeks turning violet.

The dwarf bridged the short distance between them and puffed up his chest, glaring up at Alec with a look so earnest, it could only be described as comical. "How can I trust you?"

"Because your pearl is a beast!" Ryne's hands were clenched by his sides while he scowled down at the dwarf.

The dwarf turned to Ryne and jutted one leg forward, raising stubby arms. "You ugly blue *gnaz!* You dare insult my child?"

Behind them, the giant sniffled loudly. "Gorpat not beast. Gorpat friend. Friend play."

Alec instinctively ducked when the giant lifted the hem of her dress and blew her nose into the fabric.

The dwarf beamed up at his daughter. "You want to play, my pearl?" He waved at Ryne. "Play with this young man."

Ryne had only a moment to gasp before the beast jumped to her feet and excitedly scooped him up.

"Oh, no!" Ryne screamed and pounded on her finger. "Put me down!"

"What's that?" The dwarf leaned forward and put a hand to his ear. "Play harder?"

Gorpat smiled down at her father before tossing Ryne into the air. He spun like a lifeless rag doll, nearly hitting the ground before she caught him by the legs and spun him again.

The dwarf turned his scowl on Ryne's companions when they raised their spears. "Put those down, you fools. Your puny spears will only anger my pearl."

Alec held up a staying hand, "He's right. Lower your weapons. We don't want her dropping Ryne."

Luc and Filip reluctantly lowered their spears, but Tar refused to back down. The dog ran to the giant, barking and nipping at her massive bare toes. The beast frowned at Tar and tried to stomp him, but the dog proved too fast. He continued skirting the giant, nipping and barking. Ryne struggled in her grasp while she was distracted with Tar.

Alec scowled at the chuckling dwarf. "Please stop this," he implored. "She will kill him."

The dwarf gave Alec a sideways look. "Serves him right for calling my daughter a beast."

"I'm sure he did not mean it," Alec lied, desperate to free his friend.

The dwarf laughed. "I'm sure he did."

Alec squared his shoulders, determined to make the dwarf listen to reason. "If my friend dies, your daughter is a murderer. Then she will certainly be labeled a beast, sir. Is that what you want?"

The dwarf's eyes widened. "Very well." He crossed his arms, looking like a petulant child. "Gorpat! Hold the boy."

"Yah, Dada," she said, gazing at the dangling, cursing Ryne.

Ryne had managed to dislodge a blade from his boot, and Alec feared the giant's retaliation would be deadly if his friend attacked.

The dwarf cupped his hands around his mouth, hollering up at Ryne. "Are you prepared to apologize to my pearl?"

"Beast!" Ryne wailed, and Gorpat flicked the blade out of Ryne's hands.

The dwarf flashed Alec what appeared to be a cross between a smirk and a grimace, and hollered again. "Play, Gorpat."

The monster giggled and tossed a screaming Ryne back into the air. Tar continued to bark, and Brendle cried, his bony limbs trembling as he tried to hide behind Des's legs.

Des fell to his knees, tears streaming down his dirt-stained cheeks. "Please, sir," he turned imploring eyes to the dwarf, hands clasped in a prayer pose. "Don't let her kill him."

The dwarf gaped at Des, who was at eye-level with the dwarf while on his knees. The dwarf grumbled, the coarse curtain of his moustache falling around his mouth. "Gorpat!" he finally called. "Put him down."

When the giant fell back on her haunches, Alec nearly toppled as the ground bucked beneath his feet. She unceremoniously dropped Ryne on his back, and Tar raced to his side to lick his face, once a luminescent blue and now a sickly white. Ryne turned over on his side, moaning and bringing his knees to his chest.

"You are lucky I have a soft spot for children." The dwarf chuckled and patted Des on the shoulder.

When Des jumped to his feet, Alec grabbed his arm, pulling him to his side while Luc and Filip sat Ryne up and examined him for injuries.

Des looked at Alec with a trembling lip. "Is Ryne going to die?"

Alec solemnly shook his head before wiping a stray tear off the boy's cheek. "He'll survive. Ryne is strong."

The dwarf scowled at Des and Alec. "You are too young to be his father."

Des stiffened, turning up his chin. "My parents are dead. Alec takes care of me now."

The dwarf's eyes lit up. "My Gorpat was orphaned when she was a wee tot. Poor baby would have starved if I hadn't taken her in."

Alec had to bite his tongue. He didn't think a 'wee tot' giant would be hungry for long. She'd probably been the size of a snow bear and could easily crush a full-grown stag in her grip.

"Looking back on that night," the dwarf continued, beaming up at his child, "I don't think it was me who saved her. No, she saved me. My life was dull and gray before my pearl found me. I thank the Elements for each day we have together."

The giant sniffled, then scooped her father into her arms, cradling him as gently as if he was a fragile, newly hatched chick. "Gorpat love Dada."

The dwarf frowned at Ryne, who was still crouched in a fetal position, clutching his stomach and moaning. "She wouldn't intentionally hurt no one." He patted his daughter's grimy finger. "She's a lamb, not a beast."

Again, Alec had to bite his tongue as Ven vomited into the grass. Though Alec desperately wanted to contradict the dwarf, he preferred that his supper remain in his stomach.

DIANNA SQUINTED INTO the setting sun, breath hitched as she gaped at the towering wall of what appeared to be an ashy cloud, swallowing all sight and sound as it swept over the barren landscape. It had materialized so suddenly, she barely had time to comprehend their perilous situation.

"Turn, Lydra!" she hollered, hunching over the dragon's neck and clutching her scales as Lydra spun mid-air with a grunt.

Dianna's heart quickened as she looked over her shoulder at the wall of sand that barreled toward them with alarming speed. Lydra whimpered, beating against the air as if each slow flap of her wings pulled them backward in time. Dianna's heart slammed against her chest when she realized it would do no good to try to flee the storm. She pointed at a cluster of sand dunes that looked like a pattern of jagged waves upon the sea.

"Land there!" she yelled.

The dunes hardly served as a shelter, but they would have to do. Lydra could not outpace the storm, and Dianna feared they would be swallowed by the tempest.

Lydra grunted her understanding, then dove for the ground, crashing with a hard tumble before smashing into the peak of a soft dune. Dianna screamed as she was thrown from the dragon's back, landing on her stomach and choking on a mouthful of sand.

Lydra scooped Dianna into the crook of her wing, shielding her from the sandstorm. Debris pinged off her scales, and the deafening wind roared around them. Dianna couldn't contain her tears as she cupped Lydra's jowls. The dragon's glowing red eyes dulled like the wick of a candle that had receded until there was naught left but a pool of hot wax and a flickering ember. Dianna felt Lydra's life force slipping away, and she knew it would be a miracle if her dragon managed to survive this storm.

WITH RYNE TOO SICK to stand, Alec had taken control of their party, dictating where to set up camp. After they found a clearing alongside the shallow bank of a wide stream, much to their dismay, they discovered the dwarf had chosen to set up camp beside them. Though the ice dwellers grumbled and swore, nobody was brave enough to send the father and his monster child away. Alec sent up a silent prayer to the Elements that the giant wasn't a fitful sleeper. He had no desire to be crushed in his sleep.

When the dwarf unpacked a sack full of sweetmeats and tarts, slipping two berry tarts to Des, Alec decided their party could tolerate one night with their unwelcome visitors. Even Tar had forgiven the father for his daughter's transgressions, leaving the side of his sick master to drool at the dwarf's feet. The dwarf slipped a bone into the dog's mouth, then shooed him away. Tar happily trotted off, tail spinning like a cyclone before he perched on a secluded rock overlooking the camp. Seeing Tar rewarded with food, Brendle discovered his courage, slinking up to the dwarf with his bushy black tail tucked between his legs. After he, too, was rewarded with a bone, he crept into the night, disappearing behind thick bushes.

Luc and Filip checked on their friends one last time, then warily eyed the giant before tucking into their bedrolls.

Alec sat cross-legged beside Des, slanting a sideways smile as the boy greedily ate his pies.

The giant grunted and rolled on her side facing their campfire, yawning and then expelling a hot, rancid breath that blew embers on Alec's bedroll.

Scowling, Alec hurried to put out the sparks, realizing he wouldn't be sleeping this night.

The dwarf sat on a log beside the fire, his back to his daughter, seemingly unnerved by the whistling sound coming from her nose or the gusts from her blubbering snoring that whipped the hood of his furry cape against the back of his skull.

He leveled a pointed stare at Alec, his beady orbs assessing, as if he was trying to measure his worth. "So what is a party of ice dwellers doing so far south?"

Alec arched a brow. "You know of the ice dwellers?"

The dwarf slipped a flask from his leather vest and took a long drink. "I know many things." He grimaced as if he'd swallowed pig swill, then corked the flask and wiped his glistening beard with the back of his hand.

Alec straightened. Perhaps the dwarf would be able to help. "We are searching for the cause of the melting glacier."

"*Hmph.*" The dwarf crossed his arms over a barrel chest. "Eighty summers I have lived on this earth, and with each spring thaw, the river's path widens."

"We know," Alec said wryly. Hence the reason they were on this quest.

"You think a party of insolent lads can stop it?" The dwarf waved at the ice dwellers, who were glaring at him and his daughter from under their furs.

"We cannot stop it if we don't at least try to understand its cause."

"I can tell you the cause." The dwarf leaned back, crossing stubby legs at the ankles. "Madhea's power is waning while her sister's power grows."

Alec gaped at the dwarf, feeling like an insignificant river mite whose hill of pine needles and clay had been swept away by a raging flood. That was all he and his people were to the goddesses—mites, easily overlooked while swept away in the tempest of their foolish warring. Though his brother, Markus, had told him of Madhea's cruelty, Ryne had said her sister the sea goddess was even more vengeful, having washed away entire seaside villages with monster waves if even one villager displeased her.

"How do you know this?" Alec asked.

"As I've said." The dwarf chuckled before tossing his flask over the fire into Alec's lap. "I know many things." He nodded to Des, who was licking sticky sugar off his fingers. "You and the boy aren't ice dwellers. Why help them?"

Alec looked at the leathery bottle. Even though it had been capped, the smell from the flask was strong, hitting Alec like the time his father had smacked his nose with the flat side of a shovel. Though he was in no mood to partake of alcohol, he didn't wish to offend his guest. He uncorked the flask and quickly swallowed a mouthful, nearly retching as the rancid, hot liquid burned a hole to his stomach.

He sputtered and coughed and finally managed to take a deep breath. "You ask many questions, sir," he said with a wheeze as the fire raced back up his throat. He was suddenly struck by the notion that the dwarf's potion had turned him into a fire-breathing dragon.

The dwarf laughed out loud, slapping his knee. "How else can I know so much? I am Grimley." He jutted a thumb in his chest and nodded at the giant behind him. "And you have already met my pearl."

Though the thunderous rattle of her snores still shook the ground beneath Alec's arse, the giant opened one eye, looking around the camp before focusing her unnerving orb on Alec.

Alec avoided her gaze. "Gr-Grimley?" He sputtered again as more fire rose in his throat, and his world tipped slightly to one side. What was in that flask?

"Aye, but you may call me Grim." A wide smile split the dwarf's round face. "That's what my friends call me."

Friends? Alec was taken back by the dwarf's good nature, especially when he compared this father to his own. Since Alec's world was off-kilter, he decided he'd had enough of the dwarf's draught. He didn't trust his aim, so he handed the flask to Des.

"Pass this back to him," he whispered.

The boy jumped up and ran around the fire, handing it to the dwarf, then squealed when he was rewarded with another pie. He sat down beside Alec, happily gorging on his food. Despite earlier events, Alec was growing fond of the dwarf. Mayhap not his adopted child, though, as she still stared at him with one wide eye.

Alec withdrew a meat stick from his sack, hoping a little nourishment would ease the spinning in his skull. "You're too jovial to be Grim."

Merriment danced in Grim's eyes. "There's the joke of it, you see?"

"I am Alec, and this is Desryn." Alec nodded at the boy beside him, then bit into the leathery meat.

The boy sat up, a mouthful of crumbs spewing down his tunic as he spoke. "You can call me Des."

Grim answered the boy with a wink. "A pleasure to make your acquaintance, young Des."

Des flashed a smile full of chewed fruit and crumbs before returning to his pie.

"We are from Adolan," Alec added, picking a piece of meat from between his teeth.

Grim's eyes widened, then narrowed. "So Alec of Adolan, why do you care to help these blue-skinned gnazes find the cause of the melting glacier?"

Alec did his best to ignore the grumbling coming from his companions' bedrolls. He'd suspected they hadn't fallen asleep. They probably didn't trust the snoring giant either.

"Because we share a common interest, which is seeking safety for our people."

Grim arched a bushy brow. "Think you that Adolan is unsafe?"

Alec swallowed a lump of dry meat. "None of the world will be safe once the glacier melts."

The dwarf took a swig of his fiery drink, then coughed while pounding his chest, his nose and cheeks turning even redder. Alec wondered why Grim drank that poison if it made him sick, but then he was reminded of his father, always with a tankard in hand. Mother had said that his father drank to forget the past. Perhaps Grim had memories he was trying to bury, too.

Grim cleared his throat before capping the flask and slipping it back inside his vest. "Aye, there is truth in that, for then the sea witch will have all the power."

Gorpat snorted, then her other eye flew open. Her brow drew down, the heavy folds nearly falling over her eyes. "Don't say 'witch,' Dada."

The dwarf looked over his shoulder at his giant daughter's scrunched features. "Sorry, my pearl." He turned back to Alec, pulling a cloth out of his vest and wiping glistening drops of sweat off his brow. "Her ma don't like me speaking of the demon fish so."

"Demon fish?" Alec was confused. Was he speaking of the Sky Goddess's sea-dwelling sister?

Grim solemnly nodded. "The torso of a beautiful maiden, the tail of a fish, but the heart of a serpent."

Alec rubbed his chin, sharing a puzzled look with Des. "You are speaking of the sea goddess, Eris?"

The dwarf frowned. "Aye, 'tis the same bitch," he mumbled, casting a wary glance over his shoulder.

The giant's eyes nearly crossed as she frowned at her father.

"I'd no idea she had a fish's tail. Is she a siren?" As far as Alec knew, the Sky Goddess Madhea had no tail, though his brother had told him she had wings that buzzed angrily like demonic little pixies. How strange her sister would be so different.

"Nay, she is no siren." The dwarf shook his head, snickering. "The sirens are angels in comparison."

He snorted. "I find that hard to believe." Alec had heard too many tales of sirens luring ships to the rocks and then baring rows of shark-like jagged teeth and feasting upon shipwrecked sailors as they screamed for mercy.

The dwarf's eyes hardened. "Then let us hope you never meet Eris and find out for yerself."

"Sing the song, Dada," the giant pleaded, nearly knocking Alec back with a wave of her hot breath.

Grim looked over his shoulder at the girl, shaking his head. "Nay, my pearl. 'Tis too sad."

"Sing, Dada. Pur-lease."

He flashed her one more doleful look. "Very well." He cleared his throat, straightened his shoulders, and began with a soft hum.

Alec had to strain to hear at first, but then Grim's voice grew so deep and strong, it filled Alec's bones with the reverberations of a snow bear's roar.

"Goddess of ash and sea." The dwarf's tone was so rich and pure, Alec's heart nearly broke from the beauty of it. "Please return my child to me. Though 'tis four score since she wandered this shore, my spirit doth cry Annalie... Annalie... Annalie."

Alec stared at the dwarf through the campfire's dancing flames, struck dumb for a long moment before he realized his blurred vision was not from the smoke or fiery drink, but from his own sheen of tears. He looked at Des, who was drying his eyes as well.

Alec didn't know if Grim's beautiful voice or the song's sad story had stirred these emotions, but sadness soon turned to fear, an icy tendril coiling around his spine like a serpent threatening to choke his last thread of sanity. Realization soured his gut. "Eris steals children?"

Grim leveled Alec with a sinister glare, the reflection of the fire dancing in his haunted expression. "Laddie, the witch takes anything she damn well pleases."

Chapter Three

DIANNA COULD SCARCELY believe her eyes, for after the storm passed, they awoke to find the desert landscape as smooth as the icy shield that blanketed the lakes in Adolan during a winter's frost. Not a stone marred the sand's slick perfection, though there was something on the horizon that appeared out of place.

Could it be water? No, she'd been fooled too many times before, urging Lydra to fly toward the evaporating ripples upon the desert, a trick of the eyes that disappeared before they reached their destination. But this looked different than the illusions from before, and was it her imagination, or did she *smell* water?

The wind stirred, kicking up a cloud of dust at her feet.

Sssanctuary. Go.

Dianna jerked back at the sibilant hiss in her ear. Had the wind just whispered to her? The serpentine voice didn't sound like Sindri's deep lull. Surely the desert's relentless heat was driving Dianna mad.

Lydra's nostrils flared as she pointed her snout in the air and inhaled.

Dianna placed her hand on the dragon's cracked scales. "Do you smell water, too?"

Her dragon answered with a grunt and stumbled to her feet. She took hold of the crude rope tied around Lydra's neck and hauled herself up, sitting in the crook of the dragon's wings. "Go, Lydra."

The dragon stumbled and then took off, her wings flapping arrhythmically. It was then that Dianna noticed a tear in Lydra's wing.

She sent her thanks to the Elements when Lydra landed on the edge of a cliff overlooking what had to be a dream. She heaved a sigh of relief, the tension that had been a noose around her neck slowly uncoiling, like a serpent slithering off her shoulders.

They'd happened upon an oasis, a waterfall pouring into a lush pond surrounded by leafy green plants and colorful flowers.

The dragon roared her delight, and before Dianna could catch her breath, Lydra jumped from the cliff, diving straight for the water.

She shrieked, then laughed, as she was sprayed with water deflected by Lydra's wings. She let go of the dragon and bobbed on the surface when Lydra dove down. The water's temperature suddenly shifted. Though Dianna's magical blood protected her from the Elements, she feared she'd soon be trapped in a block of ice. She swam to the shoreline before Lydra resurfaced, blowing water into the air like a spouting geyser. The water crystalized, turning to ice before it hit the surface. The water around the dragon began to solidify.

"Hang on," Dianna called. "Let me get a drink before you freeze everything."

She waded knee-deep back into the water and drank several mouthfuls. *Ahhh.* It felt good to quench her thirst. Her mouth had been as dry as the desert. She hadn't realized how thirsty she was.

Once she had her fill, she filled the doeskin bladders and climbed out of the pond, resting on the shore.

Lydra turned the desert oasis into a glittering spectacle, coating the pond in a layer of ice thick enough to hold her weight. The red glow returned to the dragon's eyes, and her wind-chapped hide was already healing as she let out a deep chuckle some would say sounded like the sinister call of a demon. The monster skidded across the ice, an explosion of crystal shards erupting from her jowls as she turned the waterfall into a frozen curtain. The beautiful greenery along the shore was coated with frosty crystals, their vibrant colors muted beneath their wintery coat.

The stone in Dianna's pocket warmed, its bright red glow pulsing beneath the fabric of her heavy vest, making it look as if she had stuffed a hot coal in her pocket.

Beware, my mother's guardian approaches. Sindri's deep voice rattled in Dianna's skull.

Her mother's guardian? "What?"

Dianna looked up when her environment shifted. She had been with Lydra long enough to know the long shadow that blanketed the ground like a heavy shroud and blotted out the sunlight was no bird.

She barely had time to suck in a scream before the dragon's powerful roar nearly flattened her to the ground. She shook when the terrible golden monster, with a wingspan twice that of Lydra's, sprang from the cliff and landed on her dragon with an earth-shattering thud.

The ice beneath them exploded. Dianna fell to the ground when shards as big as daggers flew through the air while the dragons wrestled and roared, a ball of flame consuming them. Lydra flapped backward, flailing in the water and blowing a curtain of ice at her nemesis. But Lydra was no match for the behemoth dragon, who melted her ice with his scorching breath, his fire lapping at Lydra's jowls and causing the ice dragon to howl in pain.

The golden monster puffed out his chest, his wingspan extending the entire width of the pond. Dianna knew the flame dragon intended to destroy Lydra.

Instinct fueled her movements as she jumped to her feet, not knowing what to do but knowing she needed to do something. Sindri's stone pulsed in her vest, sending ripples of warmth through her that made her blood pump faster. Fire raced through her veins, and energy pooled in her palms. She pointed her fingers at the golden dragon and screamed, "Stop!" and was knocked backward when bright bolts flew out of her hands.

A hush fell, as if all sound had been sucked from the air by a giant vortex. Dianna sat up, dizzy, trying to uncross her eyes.

The fire dragon was on his back, wings flattened against the ground, golden eyes staring at the sky, his jowls hanging open as if he was suspended in shock. Only his tail moved, twitching like a headless serpent, indicating threads of life still flowed beneath the massive scales.

Had Dianna done that? Had she disabled a dragon? Had it been her magic or the stone's?

Lydra swam to shore, crawling toward Dianna. With a sigh and a shudder, she fell by Dianna's side.

Dianna wearily eyed the golden dragon, smoothing a hand across Lydra's burned scales. "Are you okay, my friend?"

Lydra answered with a grunt, nuzzling Dianna's neck with her cold snout.

Dianna didn't know how long the golden dragon would be disabled, but they wouldn't be safe there for long.

Lydra's wings were blackened with soot and sticky with blood. Would her friend be able to fly them to safety before the golden dragon recovered? If not, would Dianna have the strength to battle the golden dragon again? The stone in her vest had gone eerily still and cold, as if all of its magic had been drained, though she still wasn't sure if it was the stone's magic or hers that had disabled the dragon.

She looked at her fingers, which were throbbing and charred at the tips. Never before had she been able to shoot bolts out of her fingers. Then again, never before had she needed to break up a fight between two dragons. Dianna rested her forehead against her dragon's chest. "Oh, Lydra, what do we do?"

She jerked back at Lydra's low growl, spinning around in time to see the golden dragon shudder. His wings struck the ground, then he jumped to his haunches with a roar that reverberated through Dianna's bones. His giant eyes darkened as they narrowed on Dianna, and he roared again, his powerful breath hitting her from across the pond like the hot currents of a wind storm.

Great goddess! That was one angry dragon.

Lydra's growls intensified, and Dianna feared her dragon was not strong enough for another battle. Her knees nearly gave way when the golden dragon's chest swelled as he sucked in a breath. She knew without a doubt he could burn her from across the pond. Though she had always been impervious to the Elements, she realized her magic may not be strong enough to repel dragon fire.

She lifted her trembling hands, her confidence waning as she tried to channel her energy and strike the dragon again. *Please help me, Sindri.* But the stone was silent.

"Tan'yi'na, no!" someone screamed, and a thunderous boom knocked her down on her hands and knees. Lydra groaned, rolling onto her back and cradling her injured wing.

Spitting out a mouthful of sand, Dianna turned to see a group of robed women. Three tall, young women with beautiful long, dark, braided hair, rich, bronze skin, and tapered amber eyes flanked a much smaller and older woman, who clutched the head of a gnarled cane. The old woman reminded Dianna of the prophet Dafuar, who had so many lines and wrinkles, her face resembled the tributaries of an ancient, weathered map.

"This witch is not Madhea." The old woman gestured at Dianna, her voice crackling. "She does not have wings."

The fire dragon the old woman had called Tan'yi'na sat up, shaking golden specks off his wings.

It is a trick. The deep, thunderous voice ricocheted in Dianna's skull.

Her hand flew to her throat. Had she heard Tan'yi'na's thought? "I am not Madhea, I swear." She sank to her knees and stuck a prayer pose, turning pleading eyes to the dragon, then the old woman. "We have come seeking sanctuary."

How does Lydra follow you when she is bound to the sky witch?

No doubt about it now; she could hear Tan'yi'na's thoughts in her mind. She spun toward him, doing her best to keep the fear from her voice. "I have freed her from Madhea."

Tan'yi'na's hooded eyes narrowed. *Who are you? One of Madhea's worthless Elementals?*

Lydra let out a warning noise and flashed sharp fangs, her glowing, red eyes tunneling on the golden monster.

Dianna placed a hand on Lydra's neck, wincing at the pain in her charred fingers. "Easy, girl." She had no wish to break up another dragon battle. She rose to her feet, doing her best to summon a courage she didn't feel. "No, I am Dianna."

He extended his elongated neck. *There is more. Do not lie to me, witch.*

"My father was a mortal. Madhea is my mother. Please," she said, hating that she had to beg. "We mean you no harm."

Judging by the fire dragon's ominous response, Dianna knew he didn't believe her. Behind her, the women's whispers sounded like hissing snakes.

Dianna arched back when the wind blew, twisting the old woman's robes around her knees and blowing back her hooded cape, revealing a long braid of stark, white hair. One of the young women stepped forward, drawing the hood back over the old woman's hair.

What little moisture Dianna had left in her parched throat evaporated when the old woman pointed a crooked finger at her. "This girl speaks the truth."

Do not trust her, My Deity! Tan'yi'na's warning roared in Dianna's skull.

Dianna looked at the old woman. She was a goddess, like Madhea?

The old woman turned up her chin, eyeing the dragon with a smirk. "I trust in the Elements, Tan'yi'na." She leveled Dianna with a stern look. "Your dragon is injured. Will she harm my healers?"

Relief swept through her as she turned to Lydra. "Please don't harm them," she beseeched, smoothing a hand down her snout.

Lydra answered with a knowing grunt, followed by a heavy sigh. She focused on Tan'yi'na, who was crawling toward them, his golden eyes turning dark chestnut. A low rumble escaped from his throat while he slithered behind the deity.

Dianna bowed her head to the woman. "I thank you. She will not harm them." Dianna cast Tan'yi'na a wary glance. "Will he try to hurt her again?"

The old woman's lips twisted, and she craned her neck toward the golden dragon. The dragon cowered.

The deity slowly turned around with a confident smile. "No, he will not." She nodded at one of the young women flanking her side. "See to the dragon's injuries." She held out a hand to Dianna, flashing a toothless grin. "Come, let us go to my underground city of Kyanu. You must be in need of rest and nourishment."

She took a hesitant step back, pressing up against Lydra. "Thank you, but I cannot leave her."

Tan'yi'na opened his wings, casting a shadow over the robed women, and stretching his neck until his massive head nearly pressed down on the deity's tiny frame.

The old woman scowled up at him, shooing him away as if he was a fly buzzing about her head. "Your breath is too stifling. My breasts do not need another excuse to stick to my stomach, Tan'yi'na. Please assist the healers with Lydra."

The massive dragon shrank back as if he'd been slapped, then he dropped his gaze to the ground when the old woman wagged a finger in his face, clucking her tongue. "Do as I say!"

She turned to Dianna with a sweet, grandmotherly smile. "She will not be harmed, child. You have my word."

A light breeze tickled the nape of Dianna's neck. *Trussst,* came a soft whisper in her ear.

She looked around for the owner of the voice. Could the Elements be speaking to her? They wanted her to trust this old woman, whose dragon had nearly killed them? She had to be mad to be contemplating the advice of an unknown voice. But what choice did she have? Her dragon couldn't fly with so many injuries. Dianna knew neither of them would survive the desert's hostility much longer.

She kissed Lydra's cold scales and whispered soothing words into her ear, promising to return swiftly. Then she took the deity's outstretched hand, sucking in a hiss when the old woman squeezed her burned flesh. She did her best to keep her knees from giving way as they walked hand-in-hand beneath the stifling shadow of the fire dragon.

She had completely given over Lydra's life and hers to the fate of these sand people and their monster, blindly believing in the whispered promise of the wind. Elements save them all, she hoped she wasn't walking into a trap.

"YOU'RE AWAKE." ALEC knelt beside Ryne, handing him a cup of black coffee, praying to the Elements that Ryne had recovered from his sickness.

"Yes," Ryne grumbled, clutching the tin cup and blowing the steaming liquid.

Alec cast a wary glance at the giant, who was giggling like a tot while splashing in the river, soaking his grumbling companion's bedrolls.

"Do you feel well?" he asked Ryne, inwardly cringing when his friend glared at the giant.

Ryne turned his gaze back to the cup, frowning. "As well as can be expected."

Tar bounded up to his master, soaked to the bone and tail wagging like a cyclone. Ryne smiled when his companion licked his face, then swore when he shook water all over him.

"Shoo!" Ryne hollered, sloshing coffee on his legs and waving off his dog. "Bad boy!"

Tar whimpered and scurried off, tail between his legs, seeking comfort with the dwarf Grim, who fed him a scrap of meat, leveling Ryne with a glare.

Ryne returned the dwarf's glare, making Alec shift uncomfortably. When Ryne turned back, Alec could read the simmering rage in his pale orbs.

"How many days until we reach Aloa-Shay?" Alec asked, hoping to divert Ryne.

Ryne swallowed several gulps of coffee, then wiped his mouth with the back of his hand. "Another week at best."

Alec swallowed, bracing himself for Ryne's reaction. "Grim says he knows a shorter route."

Ryne arched a brow. "Grim?"

"The dwarf." Alec swallowed, averting his eyes. "He travels in that direction and has agreed to take us to the neighboring village."

If it was at all possible, Ryne's cold features hardened even more. "We are not traveling with them."

"Why not?" Alec straightened, gesturing at the giant as she stomped through the river, no doubt crushing every hapless fish that swam downstream. "Can you think of a better protector?"

Ryne nodded to his mutt, who was begging the dwarf for more scraps. "We have Tar."

"A dog?" Alec snickered. "He cannot compare to a giant."

Ryne's voice rose as crimson flushed his blue-tinted face. "Have you forgotten she almost killed Ven and me?"

"I have not forgotten, and Grim promises she will not hurt you again."

"You expect me to take this dwarf's word?" Ryne's scowl deepened as he nodded toward Grim, who had enlisted Des to help him unwind a long trapping net on the shoreline. "He could be leading us all to his daughter's giant cauldron. Did you not think he's only being friendly because we're her next meal?"

Alec refused to believe it. If the giant wanted to eat them, she could have easily done so while they slept. "If you have no faith in my judgment, then look at the dogs." Tar and Brendle were happily sitting at the dwarf's heels. "You yourself said dogs are excellent judges of character."

"Yes." Ryne laughed. "When they're not begging for scraps."

But the dwarf's kindness toward the dogs was a testament to his character. Not only had he given the dogs their fill of scraps, but he'd also shared several pies with Des. Above all, Grim's love and adoration of his beast of a daughter said more about the man's heart than anything. Grim was a good man and a good father—the complete opposite of the man who'd sired Alec, which made Alec even more inclined to trust him.

Alec crossed his arms, watching Grim hand the net up to his child. "The dwarf promises a safer route, and with a giant as a companion, I can't think anyone would attempt to do us harm. Ryne, I have more than just my safety to consider. I have to think of Des." Alec had made a promise to Dianna to keep Des safe, and he had every intention of honoring his word. He braced his legs apart, forcing himself to meet Ryne's glare. "You and your men may take your route, but Des and I follow the dwarf."

Ryne threw up his hands. "Perhaps I should turn over the entire expedition to you then?"

Tar and Brendle started barking, running up and down the riverbank as if their paws were on fire. Des let out a squeal, jumping up and down as the giant hauled up a net of at least fifty flopping fish and tossed it on the shore.

Grim bowed, sweeping his hand at the feast. "Breakfast is served, lads."

Alec clapped his hands, offering the giant a warm smile. "Well done, Gorpat." He turned to Ryne, his tone as firm as his spine. "My decision is final, Ryne. I have fish to fillet." Ignoring Ryne's grumbling, he unsheathed his boning knife and walked away.

Luc and Filip had forgotten their previous grudge against the giant and were happily whistling while stoking the campfire and pulling pans and spices out of their sacks. Only then did the weight of worry lift off Alec's chest, and he knew the ice dwellers would follow his lead.

Chapter Four

THE OLD WOMAN LED DIANNA across a field of cracked soil to the wide mouth of a cave, where a dozen armed guards were waiting. Though what use were the guards when the deity had a fiery dragon at her disposal? Tan'yi'na followed them, keeping just close enough that Dianna felt his hot breath at her heels. He crept on all fours like a cat toying with a mouse, and Dianna suspected he was trying to frighten her into believing she was one snap of the jowls away from being his next meal.

His plan worked. Dianna's knees quaked with each step, and her gut churned. Fortunately, the cave did not look wide enough for him to fit through, and Dianna would soon rid herself of the menacing dragon.

As she approached the guards, she noticed they, too, were dark-skinned, like the robed healers who'd stayed behind to tend to Lydra. These men had broad, barrel chests, long, matted locks of hair, and gold bands encircling wide, muscular arms. What was more disturbing than the long bronze spears they carried was their obvious lack of clothing. Their tattooed chests were bare, and their loins were covered with slips of golden cloth that exposed their thick thighs. They were magnificent. She only wished they'd cover themselves more.

The deity, as pale as a sheet of ice, looked nothing like her people. During that brief moment when her ivory head had been exposed to the scorching sun, Dianna feared the old woman would shrivel up like over-ripened fruit. Surely the deity had not been made for this climate, yet here she was, a goddess among the desert people. She was sure the woman's origin had to be a fascinating tale.

Fortunately for Dianna, the cave opening was too narrow for the dragon. As Dianna was about to cross the cave's threshold, the beast shot into the air, raining dust down on all of them as he shook his massive wings. The old woman jutted a fist up at him, a litany of unfamiliar words pouring from her mouth as Tan'yi'na circled above them like a hawk looking for his next meal.

Dianna was glad to be free of him. She breathed a sigh of relief when the guards flanked her back. She'd take bronze spears over hot dragon breath any day.

"You must forgive Tan'yi'na," the deity said, pulling Dianna to a halt. "An old grudge festers deeper than an open wound."

She winced when the old woman squeezed her sore hand.

"You've burnt yourself, child." She smoothed bony, crooked fingers over Dianna's.

Much to her amazement and delight, a soft, white glow pulsed between their joined hands, and soon her charred fingertips were as smooth as a babe's.

She squeezed her hand shut, amazed when she didn't feel the slightest bit of pain. "How did you do that?"

The woman patted Dianna's hand before linking arms. "A little healing spell my father taught me years ago."

She barely felt the weight of the old woman as she leaned into her. When the deity traced Dianna's vest pocket, she pulled away, fearing the woman was trying to discover her stone. But how would the deity have known about Sindri?

"I didn't hear you recite a spell," she said, unable to keep the mistrust out of her voice. Why had the old woman touched her pocket? Did she know she kept the stone there?

"Oh, I used to," the deity said casually as she took the arm of a nearby guard, letting him lead her to a set of stone stairs that descended into a dark cavern. "But now it's become second nature. All I have to do is think of the spell I wish to invoke, and the magic comes to me."

"You are lucky your magic does your bidding," she said, warily eyeing the stairs. They were narrow and slick, vanishing into a black abyss.

"Why wouldn't it?" The old woman stopped, turning to Dianna and looking at her as if she'd grown a second head. "'Tis *my* magic."

"Yes, of course." She forced a laugh. Perhaps she didn't want this woman knowing she didn't have that kind of control over her magic, just in case the old woman's kindness was a ruse. Yes, Dianna had healing powers, and she was getting better at manipulating the Elements. However, her magic was nothing compared to the old witch's. She could heal small wounds, though it took hours to coax her magic into doing her bidding. Dianna's healing skills were with herbals and brews. What this witch had done required no brewing, and it appeared to take little effort. She had an insane notion the deity could teach her how to wield her magic, but why would anyone want to help Madhea's daughter become more powerful?

They navigated a maze of tunnels and cool stone stairs that spiraled steeply downward. The pungent air was heavy with moisture and smelled faintly of fungi, molds, and other strange scents. Traversing the wet and sometimes slippery stairs took far too much of concentration. She almost lost her footing three times before a guard took her by the elbow, leading her the rest of the way. She was ashamed. Despite the old woman's cane, she navigated better than Dianna, and the guards floated down the steps as if they were made of smoke.

They ended up in the center of a cavern large enough to fit several dozen Tan'yi'nas, dimly lit with wall sconces whose flames reflected off the damp walls and cast an eerie glow resembling millions of tiny stars dancing across the ceiling. The room was humid yet not as stifling as above. More unnerving than the cavern's size and space was the swarm of people that easily numbered in the thousands, all standing below the stone dais which Dianna found herself upon. They glared up at her.

They were dark-skinned and decorated with jewels and gold. Many women carried babes on their backs or hips, and their thick, dark hair was piled in intricate weaves on top of their heads. The men were strong and muscular, barely clothed like the deity's guards. Their expressions communicated hatred and mistrust, their full lips twisted into angry scowls. Dianna move closer to the deity.

The old woman must have sensed Dianna's unease, for she took her hand and squeezed, her golden eyes shining as she smiled. "Do not fear, child," she said with a wink, flashing a toothless grin. "These are my people, the Kyanites."

Kyanites? She surmised they must have been named for their dead goddess, Kyan, and she wondered how many among them had inherited magic.

The deity held up their entwined hands. "Children of Kyanu, I present to you Dianna, daughter of Madhea—"

The crowd collectively gasped. Children hid behind their mother's skirts, and men and women unsheathed knives.

"Put down your weapons!" The deity squeezed Dianna's hand so hard, she feared her fingers would snap. "The Elements have spoken. She means us no harm. Dianna is a powerful witch, but she is not responsible for her mother's sins. She and her dragon have come seeking sanctuary from Madhea's wrath, and we shall treat her with kindness."

Dianna swallowed a lump of unease as the grumbling Kyanites sheathed their weapons. She sent up silent thanks to the Elements for speaking to the deity on her behalf. She only hoped the old woman's forgiving nature would last, for she knew without a doubt, the deity's followers would not hesitate to slash her throat.

DIANNA WAS LED TO A small chamber that reminded her of a temple, beautifully painted with several seven-pointed stars. Vivid green moss and intricate tapestries covered the walls, and flowery plants hung from roots that grew from cracks in the ceiling, twisting around each other like a natural trellis.

Two young servants helped the deity out of her cloak and into an ornate wooden chair that resembled a fairy throne. Carved into the back of it was a seven-pointed star with the words, "The light from a falling star illuminates the path for others."

She couldn't help but notice the old woman's thin arms poking out of her soft, pale gown, reminding her of brittle, frost-covered branches of a dying tree. The deity looked even older than the prophet Dafuar, who was rumored to be hundreds of years old.

Knowing it was rude to stare, she gazed at the raised pool in front of them. Carved of stone, it resembled a volcano, with swirling mists pouring out of the funnel and fanning out across the floor, obscuring her feet in wispy clouds.

The deity motioned to a wooden table between them laden with breads, fruit, cheese, and drinks. "Please have some wine and bread. I'm sure you're hungry."

A young, pretty serving girl handed Dianna a goblet filled with red liquid. She thanked the girl and greedily drank the wine. It was refreshingly cool and slightly sweet, with a hint of spice. She finished and set the goblet down, pleased when the girl refilled it. She knew her head would swim if she drank another glass, but it quenched her thirst and washed away the bitter dust that had coated her mouth for weeks.

By the time she finished the second cup, her world tilted to one side. She piled a wooden plate high with food and greedily ate. The brightly colored fruits were tangy and sweet, and the breads and cheeses had the same subtle hint of spice as the wine, a pleasing foreign taste that lingered on her tongue long after she swallowed the last bite.

She took one more swallow of her third glass of wine and then sat back in her chair, burping into her fist. "Thank you." She paused, smiling at the deity. What was she supposed to call her? *My deity? My queen? My holiness?*

As if the old woman sensed her hesitation, she flashed a toothless grin "Feira. You may call me Feira." She patted Dianna's hand. "We are cousins, after all."

Her world tilted to the other side as she clutched her goblet to her chest. "We are?"

Feira nodded, the reflection of the swirling mist dancing in her eyes. "The benevolent goddess, Kyan, your mother's sister, was my grandmother."

"Oh, I-I didn't know." Unease hardened her veins as realization settled in her brain like a thick fog. *My mother murdered Feira's grandmother.*

"Well, of course you didn't." The old woman winked, holding up her goblet so a serving girl could fill it. Then she waved the girl away. "You will forgive Tan'yi'na for attacking you. He served my grandmother before me, and as you may have heard, Madhea murdered Kyan and her daughters." Feira fixed Dianna with a steady gaze, taking a long, slow sip of wine.

Dianna set her goblet on the table beside her with a trembling hand, recalling the prophet Dafuar sharing her campfire one night and telling her the story of how Madhea had turned the goddess Kyan and her daughters to stone. She had thought the story only fable until she discovered the warming stone with the spirit of a girl named Sindri, who claimed to be her cousin, trapped inside. As if Sindri sensed Dianna was thinking of her, the stone warmed her vest pocket, throbbing like a heartbeat. She tried to ignore the sensation. She did not trust Feira enough to reveal her magical stone and quite possibly the source of her new-found power.

She folded her hands in her lap, trying to stop them from shaking. "I am truly sorry for the loss of your family. I have heard the tale from the prophet."

Feira arched a white, bushy brow. "Dafuar or Odu?"

Dianna swallowed a lump of granite. This old woman knew of the prophets? What else did she know? "Dafuar," she managed to say, though her chest tightened with unease.

Feira leaned closer, her eyes narrowing to slits. "And what of his brother, Odu? Do you know him as well?"

The air between them grew stagnant. The look in her eyes reminded Dianna of the wonderment in her young brother Desryn's eyes whenever she carved him a new wooden toy.

She shook her head, feeling the keen stab of Feira's disappointment as if it was her own. "No, he dwells with the Ice People, but my half-brother Markus has met him."

Feira sat back, smoothing the wrinkles in her gown and staring at her bony fingers. "And how fare the prophets?"

She knew the old deity had a special connection to these brothers, particularly Odu. Had he been a lover? "Old and somewhat perplexing," she answered honestly, then cringed, regretting her choice of words.

Feira broke into cackling laughter that startled Dianna. She slapped her knee, flashing a sideways smile. "Then they haven't changed much these three hundred years."

Her jaw dropped. "You are three hundred years old?"

"Child." Feira wagged a finger, laughter still twirling in her eyes. "Do you not know it's rude to ask an old woman her age?"

"Forgive me." She bowed her head. "I did not mean to offend."

"No offense taken." Feira waved off her words with a flick of the wrist. "But how kind of you to worry." She took another sip of wine, then wiped her red-stained lips with the back of her hand. "Are you sure you're Madhea's child?"

There was no mistaking the sarcastic humor in the old woman's tone. It was then she realized how much she liked her cousin Feira.

"Unfortunately, yes." She leaned back in her chair, the warmth from the wine seeping into her bones and making her feel more at ease than she had in weeks. "I was not raised by her and have only just learned she was my mother."

"Who raised you then?"

She swallowed a lump of emotion as she thought of the kind mortals who'd raised her. They'd been killed two winters past, leaving Dianna alone to care for her brother. With no one else to rely on, her magic seemed to bloom out of necessity. If only her magical powers had been strong when her parents were buried by that avalanche, she might have been able to save them.

She choked back tears of regret, clearing her throat. "My foster parents were villagers of Adolan, a city below Madhea's ice mountain."

Feira's eyes widened. "I know of Adolan. I cannot believe Madhea would give a child of such magic to mortals."

"She didn't give me to them," she explained. "The Elementals switched me at birth with a mortal child, tricking both my foster parents and Madhea, because they were afraid Madhea would use my magic for evil."

"They were right, and it bodes well that your sisters still try to contain your mother. And what of this mortal child given to Madhea?"

"Her name was Jae." Guilt washed over her as she twisted a strap of her worn leather vest around her finger. "Madhea has already killed her."

"Sickening, but I'm not surprised." Feira let out a heavy sigh and sank back in her chair. "Your mother has no respect for human life."

Dianna agreed, though it took her a few moments to gather her composure, her throat still feeling constricted. Though she'd never had the opportunity to meet Jae, she knew the girl must have had a loving heart, like her birth parents, for she'd sacrificed her life to save Markus from Madhea. Had Jae survived, Dianna knew she would have loved the girl like a sister.

Feira tapped a finger to her lips, lost in reflection. "Why did she kill her? Was she a sacrifice?"

Was it a common thing for goddesses to sacrifice mortals? She certainly hoped not. The thought of one of her brothers on a sacrificial alter made her stomach sour.

"A sacrifice? No." Dianna wished she could put distance between herself and the disturbing look in her cousin's eyes. "My brother told me it was because Jae betrayed Madhea."

"Ah, I see." Feira rubbed her temples, her voice deflating like she'd run out of breath. "Tell me about Madhea's pixies."

Pixies? First human sacrifices and now pixies? She wondered where these questions had come from. "I know nothing of the pixies, other than they delivered Markus safely back to Adolan after his confrontation with Madhea."

Feira's jaw dropped. "Why would they do such a thing?"

This old woman's questions were becoming more perplexing. Dianna tried to recall what Markus had told her. "Because the Elementals told them to."

Feira clenched the gnarled armrests of her ornate chair, her knuckles cracking against the wood. "So these pixies obey both Madhea and the Elementals?"

"I believe so." Dianna was unnerved when the gleam in Feira's eyes intensified. "Why?"

Feira rubbed her hands together. "This gives me hope, child."

"Hope for what?"

"Hope for humanity," Feira said in a knowing tone. "Did you not try to control the pixies?"

"No." She frowned. What would she have done with thousands of little winged demons with razor sharp teeth? "After they delivered Markus, they flew back up Ice Mountain."

Feira's thoughts seemingly wandered again as her eyes glazed over. "Tell me about the ice dragon."

She coughed into her fist, then gazed upon the swirling mists on the floor. "Madhea turned Lydra upon the people of Adolan, which is why I had to steal her away."

Feira arched a pale brow. "So you left your family behind to bring the dragon here?"

"My parents are dead. One brother has returned to his friends in Ice Kingdom, and my other two brothers travel to Aloa-Shay in search of a safe place for our people." Her stomach churned, making her feel as if she'd swallowed a bucket of rocks. She worried over her brothers, especially Des, who was barely ten summers old.

Feira shook her head, clucking her tongue. "My dear, Aloa-Shay is no safer. Madhea's cruel sister Eris rules those waters."

She jumped from her seat, the wine swimming in her head nearly making her topple forward. She pressed a hand against her spinning skull. "I must fly to them." She'd never be able to live with herself if her brothers perished.

Feira rose, latching onto Dianna's wrist with a firm grip. "And risk Eris capturing your dragon?"

She pulled away from Feira and paced, the mist swallowing up her feet. "Then what do I do?" She turned to Feira, throwing up her hands. "I can't do nothing."

Feira leaned against her chair, groaning as her knees made sickening popping sounds. "My dear, I didn't expect you'd do nothing, but you will need training if you are to defeat two goddesses."

The food roiling in her stomach practically catapulted into her throat. Was Feira in earnest? Did she expect Dianna to wage war against two powerful and vindictive goddesses? "I'm not trying to defeat them, only to find safety for my family and friends."

Feira smoothed her hands over her knees, seemingly oblivious to Dianna's dilemma. "They shall never be safe as long as evil rules our earth."

Oh, heavenly Elements, Feira has to be mad! "My magic is not strong enough to take on two goddesses."

Feira flashed a crooked smile. "Perhaps not *your* magic, but you have another power at your disposal that they do not."

She froze. Had Feira known about Dianna's magic stone all along? "W-What?" she asked, though she feared she already knew the answer.

She flinched when Feira placed a hand over her heart.

"This," the old woman said with a wink. "As long as you have love in your heart, there is hope for humanity."

She stepped back as the stone warmed her chest. "Love will not overcome Madhea's thunderbolts."

Feira opened her mouth as if to speak, but then she smiled at something beyond Dianna's shoulder.

"Grandmother, is it true Madhea has come with her ice dragon?"

When Dianna turned at the sound of a man's booming voice, the rocks in her stomach turned to butterflies, spinning circles before fluttering all the way to her heart.

The bronze-skinned man approaching them had to be the handsomest person she'd ever seen. He was tall and muscular, like the other sand dwellers, and his dark hair was woven into a thick braid that hung down his back. But whereas their faces were made of severe, hard angles, he had a mischievous tilt to his full lips and a wicked gleam in his golden eyes that turned Dianna's knees to jelly.

"No, not Madhea." Feira heaved herself into her chair, her knees cracking again. She waved at Dianna with a casual flick of the wrist. "Her daughter, Dianna. She means us no harm. She is a guest here and will be treated as such."

Something flashed in his eyes before the man broke into a wide grin. "Yes, Grandmother."

He turned to Dianna with a graceful bow, and she thought she heard her heart hit the floor. Why did he have this effect on her? She had many suitors in Adolan and the neighboring village, but no other man had made her heart race and her knees weaken before.

Feira raised her chin. "Simeon, my grandson many times removed." The old woman's pride in him shone through a grin that nearly stretched ear-to-ear.

Dianna pulled back her shoulders and cleared her throat, doing her best not to sound like a cooing, love-struck bird. "Hello, Simeon."

"Welcome to the Shifting Sands, my lady." He bowed, reaching for her hand.

She instinctively stepped back, putting enough distance between them that he couldn't touch her, despite how badly she wanted him to take her hand. "Dianna will do."

He straightened, flashing a grin that would rival the wickedness of Madhea's pixies. "Very well, *Dianna*."

When her name rolled off his tongue in a soft purr, she knew this man was trouble. But her brothers were in danger, and she had no time for flirting, no matter how much those butterflies in her heart revolted.

"Simeon, will you kindly show our honored guest to a chamber?" Feira batted her eyes, biting her lip like a love-struck girl. "I'm sure she would appreciate a bath and fresh clothes."

"Of course, Grandmother." He bowed to the old woman, then held out his arm to Dianna, the gleam in his eyes reminding her of a hungry snow bear stalking his prey.

"Do not fret, child. You will be safe with Simeon," Feira said with a knowing smirk.

She wasn't so sure, but she joined him anyway.

"Certainly she will be. I do not bite." He flashed a sideways smile before whispering in her ear. "Unless you ask me to."

She jerked away, scowling even as his smile widened.

He let out a low chuckle and held out his arm, obviously unnerved by her scowl. "Come with me, please."

When Dianna hesitantly slipped her hand through the crook of his arm, she felt as if she was being pulled into her own, personal hell. What power did this man have over her, and how had her foolish heart easily succumbed to his command? Simeon was far more lethal than any dragon.

SIMEON LED DIANNA THROUGH a winding maze into the bowels of the underground caverns. The farther they descended, the cooler the dark air became, for which Dianna was grateful. Though she was impervious to the Elements, she preferred the feel of a soft breeze tickling her nape to the trickle of sweat. She managed to touch a few stones along the the way. They were damp and cool. There must be a water source nearby. Their route had twisted and turned so many times, perhaps they were now under the pond where she and Lydra had played.

Men and women walked past them, some balancing baskets laden with food and wine jugs on their heads. They were dark-skinned like Simeon. The women had long, lean legs and beautiful, smooth skin. The men had broad backs and barrel chests. They were built like warriors, which was good should the evil goddesses ever send her army to attack.

As she and Simeon walked arm in arm, Dianna couldn't help but be unnerved by the glares from the sand dwellers. The women were the worst. Though they bowed their heads, they glowered at her from under their lashes, their mouths tight, as if they'd just eaten sour meat.

Did they despise her for her lineage or something else? When the women alternated between scowling at Dianna and swooning over Simeon, she realized they were jealous of her.

"Hello, Simeon." A group of girls giggled behind their hands before shooting mean looks at Dianna. One girl even spit precariously close to Dianna's feet.

She did her best to ignore them. It was too soon to make enemies, though it took all of her restraint not to lash out when magic tickled her palms. How she'd love to knock the girls back on their arses, like she'd done with Tan'yi'na.

"Ladies," Simeon said to another group of girls who stood in their way.

They swooned, then shot eye daggers at Dianna. What did she care about them anyway? She had powerful magic and her own ice dragon. She could freeze them in blocks of ice should they look at her sideways again.

Careful, Dianna. You sound like your mother.

She flinched and nearly tripped over her own feet at the sound of Sindri's admonition echoing in her head.

"Easy." Simeon laughed, tightening his hold on her arm. He led her toward an open archway carved into the stone walls.

Dianna paid Simeon and her surroundings little heed. Sindri was right. She had sounded like the evil sky goddess. What had come over her?

A pretty, slender girl with skin the color of polished onyx ducked under an overhang of jagged rocks and smiled brightly when she saw Simeon approaching.

Dianna tensed, squeezing Simeon's arm harder and feeling the barbs of jealousy pierce her heart.

The girl strode up to them, swaying her hips, a basket of brightly painted fabric balanced on her head. "Is that a new tattoo, Simeon?" she asked, ignoring Dianna and running a palm down Simeon's thick biceps.

He released Dianna to flex his arm for the girl. "It is. Do you like it?"

She couldn't help but gawk at the gold ink that formed a seven-pointed star over the bulge in his arm. She stood aside, instantly missing the smell of

Simeon's warm musk. When the girl ran long fingers down his arm, Dianna repressed a curse.

"Eris and her daughters, I love it. I have a new tattoo as well," the girl whispered loud enough for Dianna to hear, smirking at her before turning her doe eyes back to Simeon. "I cannot show you here." She trailed fingers down his arm. "Perhaps if you visit my chamber later."

"It would be my pleasure," he purred.

The girl giggled, then strode away, exaggerating the sway of her hips.

Stinking siren, she thought.

Easy, Dianna, Sindri warned.

She did her best to ignore her cousin, thinking perhaps she'd toss the stone in the pond when she visited her dragon. She inwardly smiled when Sindri's gasp ricocheted in her head.

Simeon pushed open the heavy wooden door to a lavishly decorated chamber, and she paused on the threshold, amazed. Never before had she seen such a stunning room. It was far more extravagant than anything she was used to. The stone walls were hidden behind colorful tapestries, and rugs of the softest fur covered the floors. In the center was a canopy bed, decorated with dozens of fluffy pillows. Beside the bed was a beautiful dresser that appeared to be chiseled from white stone. But most impressive of all was the pool—a shallow well carved into the floor with steps that led to a deeper end where a waterfall cascaded down the uneven stone walls. Finely woven towels and bars of soap had been set at the edge of the pool. Was this some sort of heavenly bath? It was large enough to fit a dozen people.

She was so enamored with the room, she almost forgot her annoyance with Simeon's admirers. Almost. The giggling outside her door was a nagging reminder that he was only a breath away from incessant flirting. She'd never seen girls with such lack of self-control. And the people of Adolan had chastised her for wearing men's breeches. That was nothing compared to the wild behavior of Shifting Sands women. They acted as if Simeon had magically charmed them into behaving like fools.

A thought struck her. What if he *had* used magic to charm them? 'Twould explain Dianna's jealousy, for she'd never felt so possessive of a man before. If Simeon had the magical ability to charm, he was indeed far more dangerous than Tan'yi'na.

I was wondering when you'd figure it out, cousin, Sindri echoed.

Dianna blew out a frustrated breath. *Stay out of my head, Sindri.*

The stone had been quiet for weeks, only making an appearance to chastise her or confirm she'd been acting like a fool. And now she felt like one, to have fallen for Simeon's magical charms. Well, she wasn't going to fall for him any longer.

"Do you find your chamber suitable?"

Simeon sat on the edge of her bed. He'd kicked off his sandals and was looking at her with that wicked gleam in his eyes.

She turned up her chin. "Yes, quite suitable." She jutted a finger toward the door. "If you don't mind, please leave."

He patted the bed. "But we haven't yet gotten acquainted." He leaned back on his elbows, flexing chest muscles.

When he tossed a long braid behind a toned shoulder, winking up at her, her admiration for Simeon turned to irritation. He was preening like a bird ruffling his feathers. He must have taken her for a simpleton.

More nauseating giggles could be heard outside, followed by Simeon's name being whispered over and over. Dianna tried to suppress her annoyance, ignoring the heat that flamed her chest and face. The laughter continued, and it took all of her willpower not to blast the heavy door off its hinges. She balled her hands into fists, magic pulsing in her fingers.

"You are quite popular among the ladies," she said through clenched teeth, trying her best to sound indifferent and failing miserably.

He arched a thick brow, flashing a wolfish grin. "You noticed?"

"Even a blind woman would notice." She frowned at the door. They were scratching on it now like mongrels, begging to be let inside. "They swarm you like flies to a rotting carcass."

"A rotting carcass?" He shot up, his wide eyes reminding her of Desryn's contrite dog after he'd been caught trying to steal her food. "Surely you could think of a better comparison than a pile of putrid meat."

She jutted hands on her hips, blowing out a frustrated breath. "No, not really." Sindri's soft laughter reverberated in her head.

The door squeaked open, and a cluster of young women barged inside, carrying baskets of wine and richly colored fabrics.

"Who are they?" Dianna demanded as the women glared at her, then preened for Simeon.

One woman said, "We are here to attend you."

She studied her. Unlike most of the other sand people, her eyes were dark. She had a long, jagged scar from ear to temple. Dianna wondered if the scar had been made by a powerful magic too strong for Feira or her healers to treat.

Dianna shook off another woman who tried to remove her vest. "I don't need anyone to attend me."

"It is a big bath." Simeon chuckled, pushing himself off the bed. "You may need help."

She backed away from another girl who reached for her hair. "I can assure you I don't."

Simeon stepped closer, ignoring the girls who sighed when he brushed past them. "If you have an aversion to women," he whispered in her ear, toying with the leather fringe on her vest, "perhaps I can be of assistance."

"I especially don't need help from you."

She pushed him perhaps harder than she'd meant to, but she achieved the desired result. He looked at her with comical horror before falling into the gaggle of girls.

Was he in earnest? No man could possibly be so wounded over a woman's scorn.

The girls helped lower him on the bed, fawning over him as if he'd been struck in the chest with a spear. Tears welled in their eyes as they smoothed his brow.

She didn't know if she should laugh or cry at the way Simeon draped a hand across his eyes and let them baby him. Great goddess, Dianna wanted to give them all a good slap.

She threw up her hands. "Have all of you gone mad?"

Simeon let the girls pull him to his feet.

He brushed himself off as if he'd been pushed in a nest of swarming mites. "They have never seen a woman reject me before." His lower lip hung down in a dramatic pout. "Neither have I."

She couldn't help but laugh. "Get used to it."

The girls gasped again.

"Out!" she yelled. "All of you!"

The girls squealed and draped their arms around his shoulders, practically carrying him out of the room.

She stared after them, wondering if Simeon was only jesting or if he truly was a big man-child in need of a strong tincture of reality.

She fell on the bed with a groan, burying her head in her hands. What had she gotten herself into? She'd come here seeking sanctuary and instead found more madness. How could she possibly stay in this place, with a man who both tempted and infuriated her? With women whose expressions told her they'd gladly slit her throat while she slept?

She jumped up and strode to the door, no longer trusting in the hospitality of the Kyanites. She had to check on Lydra to ensure she was safe. Elements save them all if they'd done her dragon harm.

Chapter Five

ALEC DID HIS BEST TO ignore Ryne's incessant grumbling as they trudged through the forest. The sky was getting darker, and the weeds and brush were getting thicker, but the giant cleared a path for them, so Ryne had little to complain about. Still, he moaned about everything. True, the swarms of flying mites that pricked their skin were bothersome, but as the sun set behind the canopy of trees, the sweltering heat was slowly replaced with cool air, fragrant with the scents of pine and forest flowers. Grim had promised to cut four days off their journey, plus they had a giant's protection. Still, Ryne refused to look at the positives. Even Ryne's dog was growing tired of his complaints, preferring to trot at Grim's heels. Though Ryne argued that Tar was only looking for scraps, the dog continued to shadow the dwarf even after he'd given Des's dog the last crunchy fish tail.

Ryne's blue-skinned companions seemed to grow weary of his complaints, too, exchanging sideways looks whenever their friend launched into another tirade.

The giant had just tossed a fallen log to the side when the dogs suddenly launched forward, jumping over Gorpat's feet and disappearing down an incline, the sound of their wild barking reverberating off the trees.

"Tar!" Ryne screamed. "Get back, you blasted mongrel!"

"Brendle!" Des cried and ran after them, leaving Alec with no choice but to follow Des.

"Wait, Des!" Alec hollered. Though he'd much recovered from his childhood infirmity, Alec sometimes still became breathless. He only hoped he could keep up with the boy. Dianna would never forgive him if he lost him to the dark forest.

"No, doggies!" Gorpat tossed logs and knocked back brush, but the dogs were long gone, their barking distant echoes.

"Elements curse those stupid slogs!" Ryne groaned. "Hurry, before the sun sets, and they're lost for good!" he hollered up at the giant as she shoved more limbs out of the way.

Alec tensed when Grim turned on Ryne, pointing a stubby finger at him. "Mind how you address my pearl. She's doing all she can."

Ryne threw up his hands. "Well, it isn't enough."

Gorpat let out a sound that reminded Alec of a dragon's roar, so powerful it shook the marrow of his bones. She charged the trees like a territorial goat preparing to butt horns with another, flattening a wide path.

"My pearl!" Grim's hands flew to his mouth. "You'll tear down the whole forest."

Ryne brushed past Grim and chased after Gorpat, cutting down the few plants that had miraculously survived the giant's assault. Alec followed close at Ryne's heels, though his lungs strained for breath.

By the time they reached the bottom of a clearing, Alec was surprised to find the dogs sitting in front of a warm campfire, happily devouring scraps of meat tossed to them by a company of at least two dozen dwarves. Gorpat was sitting on a large overturned pine beside the fire, laughing with the dwarves as if they were old friends. Ryne was keeping his distance from the group while trying to no avail to call Tar back to his side. The rest of their company still hadn't caught up to them.

When Alec halted to catch his breath, chest heaving from over-exertion, a familiar-looking dwarf stood and turned toward them. Alec recognized the dwarf's tall pack, which was laden with goods, leaning against a nearby tree. Zier the trader traveled through Alec's village every spring and fall. His family had known Zier ever since he could remember. The trader had given their father many pints of strong brew in exchange for the animal pelts from his brother Markus's hunts.

Grim, Des, and the others barreled into the clearing, stopping as if they'd struck an invisible wall, gaping at the campfire.

"Cousin!" Hunched over, as if he still wore that heavy pack laden with pots, pans, and furs, Zier wobbled toward Grim.

Alec noted how Zier's once vibrant red beard was now peppered with strands of gray, and his eyes had more creases at the corners. The man looked like he'd aged ten years since he'd last seen him. What could have caused this?

After Grim and Zier exchanged hugs, Zier turned to Alec, his jaw dropping. "Alec Jägerrson is that you?"

Alec dropped to one knee, coughing into his fist and then offering the trader a warm smile. "It is, sir."

Zier came up to Alec, grasping his shoulders. "Lad, I hardly recognize you. You look so hearty."

"Thank you." The last time he had seen Zier, Alec was living with Dianna and still recovering from his sickness and the injuries sustained by his father's abuse. Zier had promised to take Alec to Aloa-Shay once he'd fully healed.

Zier's mossy green eyes searched Alec's. "What miracle is this?"

Alec smoothed a hand down his chest. Not long ago his lungs felt as if they were buried under the crush of an avalanche. Now, his sickness hardly pained him. "Dianna cured me." He turned his head to cough. "Well, for the most part."

"Dianna, eh?" Zier rubbed his bushy beard. "I always figured her for a witch."

Des stepped forward, a wild, dark curl falling over one eye as he puffed up his chest. "A good witch."

"Of course, of course." Zier chuckled, waving away Des's concern. "They can't all be like the sea siren and the ice bitch. At least," he added with a sly smile, "I hope not."

Gorpat stomped up to them, making Alec's brain rattle in his skull. She frowned down at Zier, her big, bulging eyes nearly crossing. "No say bad words, cousin. Ma put soap in mouth."

Zier grimaced, his cheeks turning a ruddy red. "Sorry, my dear." He patted Gorpat's big, grimy toe as if he was soothing a baby.

Gorpat smiled at Zier, stroking his head with a finger, like she was petting a mouse. "It okay, cousin." Then she let Grim lead her back to the campfire.

The old dwarf hollered and hooted, clasping hands and embracing his kinsmen. The other dwarves took turns welcoming the giant into their circle, treating her as if she was their little sister. Alec imagined they found great comfort in claiming such a powerful protector as one of their own.

Des cleared his throat, clenching his hands by his sides. "My sister's the best witch and the best person in the whole world."

Alec repressed a chuckle. Des obviously wasn't about to forget Zier's slight. He admired the boy for his loyalty. It was one reason why he didn't have the heart to tell the child Dianna wasn't his blood sister.

"Easy, lad. No offense meant." Zier ruffled Des's mop of hair before magically producing a small pie out of his vest pocket. "Desryn, is it? I traded with your parents years ago." He handed the pastry to the boy. "You're a long way from home, son."

When Des greedily took the offering, Alec wondered how these dwarves came by so many pies. It was almost like currency to them or a means of winning over children. Alec remembered with fondness Zier slipping a few pies to him and Markus when they were younger.

"Thanks!" Des said around a mouthful of crumbs. "I'm going on a quest with Alec."

"Are you now?" Zier patted Des's head once more before turning to Alec with a sullen expression. "Alec, I'm sorry about your brother." He squeezed Alec's shoulder. "I know the two of you were close."

Alec remembered Zier had been the last person to see Markus before his brother had fallen into Ice Kingdom, the last person to witness Markus being pursued by the ice dragon, Lydra.

Alec stood, dusting dirt off his knees. "My brother is fine, Zier. He's dwelling with the Ice People."

The dwarf stumbled back, looking as if he'd been struck in the chest by an invisible mallet. "Well, I'll be a gnaz's hairy ass. Last I saw him he had a dragon pursuing him. How did he escape?"

"Pure dumb luck." Alec couldn't help but laugh as he recalled his brother's story about the dragon getting stuck beneath an avalanche while he tried and failed to climb Ice Mountain. If it hadn't been for the girl, Ura, who found him with a broken arm and bruised skull, Marcus would have died.

Zier squinted at Alec, then shot Des a questionable look, at which the boy shrugged.

Zier shook his head. "And here I thought the Ice People only fable."

Ryne, who'd tried and failed to lure Tar back to his side, stomped up to them, pounding his chest. "Do we look like fables?"

"Great goddess!" Zier's gaze traveled up the length of Ryne's body. "No, you do not."

Alec motioned to his scowling blue friend, whose cheeks were turning a soft shade of purple. "Zier, this is Ryne and his companions, Ven, Luc, and Filip."

"It is a pleasure to meet you all." Zier grabbed Ryne's hand and heartily shook it. "You are truly ice dwellers?"

"We are." Ryne pulled his hand away, shaking it as if he'd been scalded.

Alec couldn't help but feel ashamed for the ice dweller. His foul mood from yesterday seemed to be getting worse.

Zier smoothed a hand down his beard as he gaped at Ryne and his companions. "Your skin is blue as in the fable."

Ryne crossed his arms. "Again, we are no fable."

"My apologies." The dwarf swept a hand in front of him and bowed, looking ready to fall face-first into the dirt as his back was already bent at an odd angle. He straightened as best he could. "My tongue wags when I'm in shock."

"I think we've all experienced that a time or two, Zier." Alec patted him on the back while shooting Ryne a warning glare. It would do no good to make enemies of the dwarves, especially not when they had a roaring fire and two boars roasting on the spit.

"Indeed." Zier beamed at Alec, seemingly unaware of Ryne's deepening scowl. "My family, from the village of Aya-Shay." He nodded to his company of dwarves.

"I have heard tales of the dwarf village," Des piped up, wiping crumbs off his tunic.

Alec had heard tales, too. Aya-Shay meant "blessing by the sea." The town had to have been blessed, for they prospered like no other. It was said their harvest was so abundant, they had enough canned goods to last a century.

"What have you heard, young Desryn?" Zier asked with a wink.

Des flashed a wide smile, his teeth sticky with fruit. "That is where the best pies and pastries come from."

Zier tilted back his head and let out a hearty laugh. "Indeed, you are correct." He patted his rotund belly. "Aya women know how to keep their husbands well fed."

Des swiped a hand across his mouth. "Dwarf pies are the best I've ever eaten."

"Wait until you taste one fresh from the oven." Zier rubbed his hands together, licking his lips. "The buttery crust will melt on your tongue."

Des practically jumped from his tattered boots. "I can't wait."

When Ryne let out a frustrated groan, Alec cringed. He was starting to regret accompanying the ice dwellers on this quest. Though he was grateful for their numbers, their leader's perpetual bad temper reminded Alec too much of his dead father.

"We head to Aya-Shay, and then travel to Aloa-Shay," Alec interjected, stepping in front of Ryne and hoping to block his dark looks and groans.

"I travel that way, too." Zier slipped his hands inside the pocket that ran across the belly of his fur-lined vest and rocked on his heels. "It's part of my trade route. Perhaps you wouldn't mind more company."

"Your company is always welcome," Alec said, then forced a loud cough when he heard Ryne grumbling behind him.

Zier peered around Alec, winking up at Ryne. "'Twould be my pleasure to learn about the Ice People. Perhaps we can even discuss trade."

Before Alec could stop him, Ryne grabbed hold of Alec's belt and yanked him backward. "Alec, a word please." Ryne growled in Alec's ear.

"Excuse us." Alec made a hasty bow before Ryne dragged him away, the other man's superior strength reminding Alec he still hadn't fully recovered from his infirmity.

Ryne grabbed Alec by the collar, hauling him close until they were nearly nose-to-nose. Alec's chest tightened, and his breaths came in shallow gasps. How many times had he been held in just this way by his father?

"You forget I lead this expedition." Ryne spoke with a jaw so tight, his lips hardly moved.

Alec jerked out of Ryne's grip, anger threatening to burst his skull in two. He let out a slow and shaky breath, knowing it would serve no one if they both lost their tempers. He turned up his chin, refusing to be intimidated. "These dwarves know the safest routes. It would be wise to accompany them."

"This. Is. Not. A. Trade. Mission." Ryne enunciated each word as if he was speaking to a child.

Alec had suffered from his father's bullying his entire life, and he refused to have his will bent by another again. "It would serve you well to make friends on this expedition." He smoothed his rumpled vest, hating the way his hands shook. "You may never know when you'll need them."

Ryne opened his mouth to speak, but Alec held up a silencing hand. He was tired of the ice dweller's incessant complaints. "Des and I stay with the dwarves. You may depart anytime if their company isn't suitable."

Ryne rolled his eyes before sidestepping around Alec. "Are you traveling straight to Aloa-Shay?" he pointedly asked Zier, his voice as rough as a boar's hide.

Zier narrowed his eyes at the blue man. "Aye, after I visit with family a spell."

"We don't have time for a spell." Ryne sneered.

Alec stifled a groan, then flashed Zier an apologetic smile.

"Suit yerself then." Zier crossed his arms and muttered under his breath. He offered Alec a friendly smile. "You may camp with us tonight if you like. Tomorrow we leave for Aya-Shay."

Alec placed a hand on Zier's back, walking with him toward the fire. "We would appreciate the warmth of your fire and the company as well. You always tell the best stories, Zier." Alec shot Ryne a dark look over his shoulder, not surprised to see his scowl had returned. He sent a silent prayer to the Elements that Ryne wouldn't say or do something to anger the dwarves tonight, though he feared his prayer would go unanswered, and he and his friends would be forced to complete their quest on their own.

DIANNA FOUND LYDRA sleeping along the bank of the pond, snoring loudly as little flecks of ice blew out of her nose.

Five female healers attended the dragon, gracefully jumping over puddles of water mixed with snow and ice and rubbing a sticky orange paste on Lydra's wounds. All the healers were tall and lanky with long, elegant necks and large golden eyes. Their skin varied from warm honey to dark ebony, and they were all pretty. Very pretty. She wondered if they, too, had fallen for Simeon's magical charms, then berated herself for caring.

At least two dozen armed guards clustered around them, standing as still as statues, tightly gripping their spears. Dianna knew they were there to protect the healers, but their presence unnerved her. She didn't want them upsetting Lydra.

She slid across a sheet of ice and placed a hand upon her dragon's neck, running her fingers down scales still charred from Tan'yi'na's attack.

"What has happened to her?" she asked a nearby healer.

The girl looked over at Dianna long enough to scowl. She then turned back to the paste she was stirring in a wooden bowl, the gold-and-silver bangles adorning her arms chiming with each stroke. "She is sleeping. We gave her a healing draught. She had many injuries." She smoothed the paper-thin membranes of Lydra's wing. "Look. We removed an arrow tip."

"Oh, Markus." Dianna ran her hand along the scar covered in dried orange paste, recalling Markus telling her he'd hit Lydra with an arrow in an attempt to slow her pursuit. That was when Lydra had been intent on turning Dianna's brother into a block of ice. "Thank you for caring for her."

The girl turned up her nose. "You do not need to thank me. I'm following my deity's orders."

Why were all the women of the Shifting Sands so intent on hating her? It seemed her only friend among them was Feira. Well, and perhaps Simeon, though he was more flirt than friend.

Magic burned Dianna's palms, making her wish she could force the girl to bend the knee instead of hovering over her like an angry raven, but she forced a smile and ignored Sindri's heavy sigh echoing in her skull. "Well, thank you for following those orders."

The breeze tickling Dianna's nape evaporated as the air behind her backside became heavy with heat.

Did you think we would harm her? a dark voice boomed in her skull.

She spun on her heel to see Tan'yi'na behind her, stretching his neck to full height. How was such a giant able to sneak up behind her without making a sound? His ominous, glowing eyes narrowed to two deadly slits, making Dianna feel like a mouse caught in a snake's den.

She forced her slackened jaw to close and stepped back until she pressed against Lydra's cold scales. She did not know if it was anger or fear that kept her from answering the golden dragon. Though her blood boiled at his unfair treatment, her knees shook at the realization the monolithic beast could easily devour her in one swallow.

Steam poured out of his nostrils. *You do not trust us,* his accusation reverberated in her head. Odd how he was able to project into her mind.

The hurt in his tone reminded her of a petulant child, and she had to refrain from rolling her eyes at his indignation. She shrugged. "I do not know you."

He folded one clawed foot over the other, his tail erratically slapping the earth, like he was a bored and pampered feline. *And we do not know you, yet my mistress has given you food and shelter, and has assigned her best healers to your dragon.* His fanged jowls hinted at a smile. *Despite what you are.*

Dianna's spine stiffened. "What I *am?*"

Spawn of a cursed bitch. The dragon scraped one long claw across the top of a discarded shield, sparks flying from the friction. *You look just like her.*

Energy crackled in her palms, and it took all her willpower not to strike the smirk off the dragon's face. "I am not her. I am my own person."

He gave Dianna a pointed look, one that said she was no more worthy of his time than the scum that collected between the pads of his paw. *You are no person. You are the daughter of a goddess, a creation of Elemental magic.*

She vehemently shook her head. "I was raised by people, loved by people." She refused to let him believe she was anything but a beloved daughter, sister, and friend.

His serpentine tongue darted out, swiping grime and dust off his snout. *But that doesn't make you human.*

"I will not let you or anyone else define me." Magic crackled when she pounded her chest. "I know what I am."

And what are you? he asked in a sing-song voice, tempting her more and more with his smug attitude. How badly she wanted to flatten the earth again and knock the bothersome dragon on his arse.

She hated the way her voice shook when she spoke. "I am Dianna, daughter to two beloved parents and sister to three brave brothers. I am alone in a strange world. I am tired and afraid, but I am determined to save my people from the wrath of two cruel goddesses, and I am *not* deterred by a stupid, menacing dragon with a misplaced grudge." Dianna took a shallow breath, fanning the cloud of thick smoke around her. "Your breath smells like pig dung."

She knew her insult had gone too far even before the healers ran behind Lydra when Tan'yi'na jumped on all fours and reared back, a glowing red ball pulsing beneath his chest scales.

Energy crackled in her palms as she prepared to strike Tan'yi'na before he unleashed his fire.

"There you are, Dianna. My grandmother is looking for you."

She was shocked to see Simeon race right under Tan'yi'na's front leg and to her side, linking his arm through hers. Simeon's smile appeared to be plastered to his face as they walked arm-in-arm around the dragon's monster tail, which broke open the earth as it lashed the ground.

"Thank you, Tan'yi'na, for keeping watch over her in my absence," Simeon shouted at the monster. "Grandmother will be most pleased to find her unharmed."

Dianna felt the dragon's hot breath on her back as Simeon practically dragged her to the cave and down the stone stairs.

As soon as they reached the first landing, he released her, slumping against the wall. He smoothed his cheeks with a groan. It was then she noticed how he visibly shook.

He looked at her with a slackened jaw. "Do you have a death wish?"

She repressed a smile as she leaned against the opposite wall. "Perhaps."

He pushed off the wall, throwing up his hands. "You are the most perplexing woman I've ever met."

She crossed her arms, pressing her back into the wet stones when he approached. "Is this about me not fawning over you or standing up to Tan'yi'na'?"

Dianna's breath caught in her throat when he stood over her, brushing a strand of hair out of her eyes and pushing it behind her ear.

He flashed a slanted smile. "Both."

She tried to think of something clever to say, but her heart pounded like a gong in her ears, making it hard to think. His amber eyes had bright flecks of gold in them that reminded her of Tan'yi'na's scales, glistening in the sun. Perhaps the gold was where his magic was hidden. 'Twould make sense, since his eyes were so mesmerizing.

"Was it true what you said back there?" He twirled the tip of her pale braid around his finger. "You care about the fate of mortals?"

She thought about escaping, but he had her trapped between his thick arms, his palms flat against the wall while he leaned far too close to her, so close the smell of his sweaty musk turned her limbs to porridge.

"Of course," she said, sounding strangely breathless. "I was raised by mortals. My brothers are mortals."

"Odd that you are so compassionate despite possessing powerful magic." His voice dripped with sweetness, like thick syrup.

Somewhere in the back of her mind, she knew he was using his magic to subdue her, and she cursed herself a fool for letting him.

She wished she could find a way to escape his spell. "You know nothing about my magic."

He arched a thick brow. "You control Madhea's dragon, do you not?"

"Yes."

"Then your magic must be powerful indeed."

He brought the tail of her braid to his nose, inhaling and then sighing. At first she was flattered by his display, but she couldn't stop thinking about his odd behavior, and she had to cover her mouth to keep from laughing. What kind of man would inhale her hair? She hadn't bathed in weeks. Between the dirt and bugs caked in her hair, and the spray from Tan'yi'na's breath, she probably smelled like a discarded animal carcass.

Disgusted, she brushed his hand away. "Can't a woman be both kind and powerful?"

"Of course, but you are a goddess, not a woman."

When he reached for her again, she brushed him away. "I can assure you, despite whatever magic flows in my veins, I am first and foremost a woman."

That was the wrong thing to say. She knew it as soon as the words had left her mouth and he flashed that wolfish grin.

"Prove it."

When he slipped a hand behind her neck and leaned into her, lips puckered, she instinctively slapped him so hard, he spun backward, the sound of her palm striking his cheek ricocheting off the walls and bouncing down the stairs.

"Is that proof enough?" She flexed her fingers, preparing for another strike.

He turned to her, rubbing the pale imprint of her hand. "No woman has ever struck me."

"I guess there's a first time for everything." She leaned into him, jutting a finger in his chest and inwardly smiling when he flinched. "And if you ever try to kiss me again, it won't be the last."

She hurried away, using the wall for support and hoping she didn't fall on her arse as she flew down the slick steps. Great goddess, everyone in the Shifting Sands was mad, and she was craziest of all for regretting the feel of the sting in her palm and desperately wishing she would have let Simeon kiss her.

Chapter Six

ALEC SAT ON A FLAT slab of stone a few paces from Zier and Grim's log bench. Des sat beside him, gorging on yet another pie. Dwarves roasted wild boars and a stag in a fire pit. Gorpat had trapped the stag in a nearby ravine. The poor beast hadn't stood a chance when Gorpat's foot crashed down on him. After Alec saw Gorpat returning to camp with the flattened stag slung across her shoulders, he was glad he hadn't made enemies of the giant or her dwarf father.

The dwarves skinned the deer and cut it up, its thin steaks hanging from the spit like wet socks. Grim assured Alec the meat would be tender. To Alec's delight it was, though he couldn't help but feel pity for the animal as he chewed its succulent meat.

Much to Alec's dismay, Ryne and his companions refused to eat or sit with the dwarves. They built their own smaller campfire, ate dried fish, and then retired early to their bedrolls. Gorpat had gone to sleep, too, lying on her back beside the fire, the suction from her powerful snores pulling down the tree branches overhead until they'd nearly plastered her face, wildly flapping and leaves fluttering to the ground with each exhale.

Grim's many cousins sat around the campfire, talking amongst themselves while casting the ice dwellers strange looks. Alec couldn't decide if they were intrigued or aggravated by their guests, but after Ryne stomped around most of the night like an angry bear, Alec suspected the latter.

Alec couldn't understand what had put Ryne in such a foul mood, other than the misunderstanding with Gorpat the day before. Would he hold on to that grudge forever? Perhaps he was angry that his furry companion had switched loyalties. Tar and Brendle had found a friendly pair of dwarves at the other side of camp, who were handing out bones.

"Masters Zier and Grim," Alec said, picking meat from between his teeth, "I thank you and your family for your hospitality. Indeed, this meat is the best I've ever eaten."

Though Alec had been trying all night to compensate for Ryne's dark mood and lighten their spirits, 'twas no lie. His sweet departed mother had been highly skilled with healing herbs, but her roasts were often tough and dry. Mayhap there was something to smashing your food before roasting it.

"Wait until you try Ma's fresh pies," Grim said before taking several hearty gulps of his flask and passing it to Zier.

"I can't wait," Alec said in earnest, not minding at all if they delayed in the town of Aya-Shay while Zier visited his family for a spell.

Des wiped crumbs off his lips, which were stained with the pie's red berries. "Me, too!"

Des was rewarded with two more pies from Grim's cousins.

"Fanks!" Des said, stuffing his face, too preoccupied with his food to pay Alec any heed when he warned the boy to slow down.

These dwarves must have a secret pastry treasure trove. Alec had thought of asking for one himself, but his belly was full of stag and boar meat.

"Have you heard of the Ash Witch poem, lad?" Zier asked.

"No," Alec answered, curiosity piquing his interest. "I haven't."

Zier puffed out his chest and recited:

"Tongue of a serpent

Beauty of a rose

Soul of a demon

With ne'er as many clothes."

When Des giggled, Alec couldn't help but laugh with him.

"We don't need to hear the next verse," Grim said to Zier, his features darkening.

"But 'tis the best part." Zier laughed, slapping his knee.

"Heart of a shrew

Eyes of a hawk

Pay the witch her due

Or she'll chop off your block."

Alec swallowed hard at that, his hand instinctively going to his neck. He hoped he'd never have the misfortune of crossing the sea witch's path.

"I know another ending." Zier elbowed Grim, then looked at Gorpat behind them. "But there is a lady present."

Alec shifted uncomfortably, thinking death by voracious siren would be a better fate than facing Eris.

Zier drank from Grim's flask before handing it back to him. "Your blue-skinned friends aren't much for company." He nodded at the ice dwellers, lying in their bedrolls, their backs to the rest of the party.

"No," Alec said on a sigh, "they aren't."

Zier leveled Alec with a surprisingly somber look for someone who'd drained his flask and half of Grim's. "How did you come to be with them?"

"Ryne's family nursed my brother Markus when he fell into Ice Kingdom." Alec frowned, his heart feeling like a block of splintered ice when he remembered how he'd almost lost Marcus to Madhea's curse. "Without them, he would have died."

Zier's coppery brows dipped low over his eyes. "So now you are indebted to this blue slog?"

Alec shrugged. "We were traveling the same direction, so...." But now he was having serious regrets about agreeing to accompany Ryne on this journey. Markus hadn't warned him the ice dweller was disagreeable.

Grim and Zier shared knowing looks. "Hopefully the rest of the Ice People are not like him," Grim grumbled.

Alec straightened, thinking about how Ryne's behavior would affect the other Ice People. If Zier refused to accompany them to Aloa-Shay, they would be on their own in a strange land. Whether Ryne agreed or not, they needed the trader's guidance and expertise.

Alec cleared his throat. "Marcus assures me they are kind. Ryne carries the weight of his people's fate on his back, so I imagine such a stress would affect his mood."

Though it was true, Alec resented Ryne for putting him in the position of having to justify Ryne's behavior after Alec and his mother had spent too many years making up excuses for his cuts and bruises rather than placing the blame where it was due, on his father.

Zier rubbed his bushy beard, snickering. "Even more of a reason to show gratitude when others help him."

Curse Ryne for making Alec look like a fool. He stared into his empty cup. He'd taken the bronze goblet, worn from years of use, from his home before Lydra destroyed it. Seeing his dull reflection in the bottom of the cup, he recalled something. Markus had given him Zier's shield, and he had yet to return it.

"That reminds me." Alec stood, stretching his legs, then walking over to his bedroll. "I am grateful to you, Zier." He slipped the heavy disk with the imprint of a rotund whale, spouting water from the top of its horned head, from the roll. Balancing the shield against his leg, he carried it to Zier and heaved it into the dwarf's arms. "This served Markus well on his travels. He asked me to give it back to you."

"Ah." Zier hugged it to his chest like a long-lost lover. "I had mourned this treasure, thinking it gone for good."

Grim slapped his knees and pointed at his cousin. "Zier has carried that shield with him for over thirty years. I can't believe he'd part with it."

Zier puffed up his chest. "Well, young Markus needed it more than I did."

Alec had to bite his tongue, for Markus had told him Zier only parted with it in a desperate attempt to keep Markus from leading the ice dragon to the village of Kicelin, where Zier's two married daughters lived with their families.

"Indeed, it is a fine treasure. Thank you for allowing my brother to borrow it. Also, there is this." Alec handed Zier a bag of gold he'd kept in his vest pocket. "Payment for the gear you gave Markus. I'm afraid his boots and gloves did not survive the journey."

Zier leaned over his shield and poured a few coins into his hand, then gave the bag back to Alec, still weighted with several pieces. "Here, my friend," Zier said. "Surely an old pair of boots and gloves wasn't worth that much."

"Thank you." Alec stuffed the coins back inside his vest, buttoning his pocket. "You have always dealt fairly with my family."

"Aye, and your mother and father always dealt fairly with me, though your father not with you so much, eh? There was not a time I didn't visit your hut that you didn't sport some new cut or bruise. I heard how Rowlen died. Can't say I blame you. I myself wanted to cut him down a time or two for his treatment of you, but I swear the man was part giant." He elbowed his cousin, gesturing to a tall tree branch above them. "I barely came to the slog's knees."

A log in the campfire crackled and split, sending a burst of embers into the air. Alec shifted uncomfortably. A strange feeling came over him, as if he was being watched, not by any living thing, but by his father's ghost. He rubbed the prickly hairs on the back of his neck, shifting again and cursing himself a fool for believing Rowlen was near. His father's spirit had probably long departed from this world, hopefully after finding a way to reconcile his cruelty in the afterlife. Of one thing Alec was certain: it would be a long while before Alec could think of his childhood or his father's ugly death with anything other than sorrow.

"I'm sorry, lad," Zier said. "I see it pains you to hear of him."

Alec struggled to speak around the lump that had formed in his throat. "Aye, that it does. I can't close my eyes at night without seeing his face. One day I will be able to bear the memory of his abuse without so much bitterness. After all, it was Madhea who put the curse on his heart, making him hate me."

Zier straightened, sharing startled looks with the other dwarves, who'd suddenly gone silent, staring across the crackling campfire at Alec.

Zier leaned on one knee. "I did not know this."

Alec wiped a bead of sweat off his brow, wishing he could move his stone slab farther from the fire. "I only just learned it from Markus."

Low murmurs spread around the circle.

"And how came he by this knowledge?" Grim asked.

Alec tapped out a nervous rhythm with his foot. How were these dwarves expected to believe him when he hardly believed the tale himself? "He learned it from the Madhea's servant when he fought Madhea in her ice palace."

Zier let the shield slide to the ground with a clank. "Your brother fought the Sky Goddess and lived to tell the tale?"

Alec scanned the attentive faces around the campfire. "He did."

Grim racked his knuckles. "Forgive me if I find this story too wild to believe."

Alec fixed Grim with a stern gaze. "He did, and when the Elementals sent him back to Adolan, her dragon came after him again. Dianna was able to stop the dragon and make it bend to her will."

When soft murmurs rose, Alec nudged Des, who had been preoccupied with his pies.

"Laddie." Grim stood, sweeping a hand across the camp. "Surely you do not expect us to believe this."

Alec's chest tightened at their disapproving looks. Ryne had already given the dwarves cause not to like them. He didn't want to give them another. "I would not believe it, either, if I hadn't seen it with my own eyes."

"I saw it, too," Des added, picking crumbs off his breeches and popping them in his mouth. "The dragon made me a slide of ice."

"Dianna has flown the dragon to the Shifting Sands, far from Madhea's eye." Alec glanced at the dark forest, knowing somewhere beyond the trees and the distant shore, his sister was alone with her dragon. "She is looking for a place for our people before Madhea's wrath comes down on us all."

"Or before the ice melts," Des added.

Grim and Zier bent heads, murmuring into each other's ears. Finally Zier turned to Alec with a drawn mouth. "This news is both fascinating and troubling. But you never told me how Markus survived a battle with the goddess."

Alec let out a slow exhale, knowing his tale was about to get wilder. "He wore a magical stone that deflected her magic."

"Where did he get such a stone?" Grim snapped, his eyes alight with mistrust.

"From the Ice People," Alec said, fearing the night was only going to get worse.

Gorpat's eyes flew open, and she jumped to her knees. "Fire! Fire!" She pointed to the ice dwellers, then lifted Ven out of his bedroll.

The blue man screamed, trying to swat the giant while dangling upside-down in the air.

Ryne jumped to his feet and kicked Ven's bedroll. A red stone rolled out, its color fading to white as it came to rest beside Ryne's foot.

"It is not a fire, you beast!" He pointed at the giant, his pale eyes lit with fury. "It is Ven's warming stone."

Gorpat's face fell, and she dropped Ven back on the ground. He hit the dirt with a *thud*, cursing as he rolled onto his side.

Zier scratched the back of his head, sharing startled looks with his cousins. "Warming stone?"

Ven stood and limped to Ryne's bedroll, scooping up the stone. "I use it to chase away the chill."

Zier turned to Alec, an excited gleam in his eyes. "Is this stone like the one Markus used to deflect the goddess's magic?"

Alec nodded, finally relieved he had proof his story was not a hoax. "It's exactly like the stone Markus used."

A chorus of excited whispers broke out as the dwarves jumped to their feet, heads bent and arms wildly waving.

Zier hobbled over to Alec, patting him on the knee. "I'm sorry for doubting you, son."

"Why do you ask?" Ryne's booming voice cut through the dwarves' chatter.

All eyes shot to Ryne, and not a sound could be heard except for Gorpat blowing her nose into her sleeve. Ryne glared at them with legs braced apart, his hand on the hilt of his blade.

Zier rubbed his beard, eyeing Ryne for a long, tense moment. "How many do the Ice People have?"

Ryne jutted a foot forward, speaking through clenched teeth. "Again, why do you ask?"

"I would gladly trade any of my goods for such a stone," Zier answered.

Ven tucked the stone back in his bedroll and went to stand beside Ryne, his youthful face transformed into a mask of hard angles. "This stone has been in my family for generations and is not for trade."

Zier rubbed his hands together. "I have spices, gold, weapons." He waddled back to the campfire, lifting the shield with a groan. "Look at this fine workmanship."

"Again," Ryne boomed as the other ice dwellers rose from their beds and flanked him, "this stone is not for trade."

"Very well." Zier heaved an overly-dramatic sigh and lowered the shield. "But if you should change your mind—"

"Our minds will *not* change." Ryne said firmly.

Alec's breath caught in his throat at the murderous look in Ryne's eyes, the same look the dwarves were reciprocating as they flanked Zier, their hands resting on the hilts of their swords. The dwarves outnumbered the ice dwellers seven to one, not to mention they had a giant on their side who could flatten them all into hotcakes.

Brendle ran behind Des, shaking as if he'd just been pulled from an icy river. Tar stood between the dwarves and Ryne, dancing on his paws.

"Come here, Tar!" Ryne growled.

Tar nuzzled Grim's hand before slinking over to Ryne, his tail between his legs.

The dog didn't want to see his master fight with the dwarves, and neither did Alec. He had to think of something, and fast, before their disagreement escalated.

He stepped between the dwarves and Ryne, holding up both hands. "Why don't we all get some sleep?" He did his best to keep his composure, despite the wild beating of his heart. "We can discuss the stone in the morning."

"Are you as daft as the dwarves?" Ryne pointed at Alec with an accusatory finger. "There will be no discussion."

"Go to bed, Ryne," Alec spoke through a frozen smile.

"Do not tell me what to do."

Ryne was either very stubborn, very foolish, or both. Either way, Alec had had enough of his temper. Balling his hands, he channeled his dead father's dark and violent moods as he stalked toward Ryne. "I said, go to bed!" He jutted a finger at Ryne's bedroll, feeling the heat creep into his chest as he and Ryne locked gazes for several interminable, thudding heartbeats.

So enraged was Alec, he was barely aware of his own shallow breathing or of Gorpat sniveling behind them.

"Friends no fight," the giant cried.

Alec couldn't let Ryne win this battle of wills. As the dwarves' grumbles grew louder, Alec knew their lives depended on Ryne backing down.

Finally, Ryne threw up his hands and stomped back to bed. "What a fool I was for allowing a land dweller to accompany us."

Ryne flopped on his bedroll, punching the ground beneath him before turning his back to Alec and the dwarves. His companions slowly made their way back to their bedrolls as well, their wary gazes traveling from Ryne to the dwarves. Alec turned to the dwarves to apologize, but their attention was locked on Ryne, their bulbous noses and round cheeks as flame red as the fire's embers. 'Twas then Alec knew nobody would get much sleep that night.

DIANNA MADE HER WAY through the labyrinth of stairs, accompanied by two guards, who promised to wait outside and escort her to supper. She didn't know if she should feel relieved or unnerved. Their spears could take down Lydra. These men were tall and muscular, like Simeon, but their eyes were dark, not bright with gold flecks. Their faces were masks of granite, impassive and unfriendly, unlike Simeon with his wide grin.

Luckily, the giggling girls in her room left her alone with a clean change of clothes, and she was able to bathe in peace. The throbbing in her fingers from slapping Simeon was starting to subside, and it felt good to wash off the sand and grit. She lingered longer than she'd intended, but the warm water was soothing.

After she dried off, she enjoyed running a brush through her hair, though it took a while to work out all the knots. Dressing was another story. She didn't wish to wear her grimy breeches, but the girls had left her only a gown. Sirens' teeth! She loathed dresses. What good were they? She couldn't hunt in one or ride a dragon without chafing her thighs.

Dianna held the fabric in her hands, so light it cascaded like water through her fingers. She supposed she'd have to make do until her breeches were laundered. The dress fell around her legs like a soft cloud. It cinched at the waist and the top with thin straps that barely covered her breasts. Never before had she gone out in such revealing clothes, but after gawking at enough scantily clad Shifting Sands women, she feared she wouldn't find anything with more coverage. She thanked the Elements the people of Adolan or her brothers couldn't see her like this. She caught her reflection in a looking glass hanging above her dresser. She could not deny the dress was radiant, a shimmery gold that reminded her of the way Tan'yi'na's scales reflected the sunlight.

What will Simeon think of my gown? she thought, then berated herself for caring. His opinion mattered naught to her. At least, that's what she kept telling herself.

She pulled her hair back, threading it into a braid with nimble fingers, a trick her adoptive mother had taught her years ago. She tied it with a leather band, wishing she had a fancy ribbon to compliment her clothing. Again, she berated herself for her foolish whims. Why did she need a ribbon when she had more important things to worry about, like saving her people?

She looked in the mirror, and a strange sense of recognition fell like a heavy stone in the pit of her stomach. She'd seen this woman in paintings of the sky goddess. With the exception of Madhea's translucent wings, Dianna looked like her mother.

She heaved a resigned sigh as she gazed at the white stone sitting on the bed. Could this be why Sindri rarely spoke to her? Did her cursed cousin resent her because she looked like the witch who'd destroyed her family? Dianna hoped the stone couldn't see her. After all, it had no eyes. But though it had no mouth, Sindri spoke to her. If Sindri was listening to her thoughts, she made no attempt to allay her worries. The stone on her bed was inert, as if it possessed no magic at all.

She heaved a frustrated breath and plopped on the bed with an unladylike grunt. *I'm not my mother,* she thought to herself. *I'm not,* she thought again, not knowing if she was trying to convince herself or Sindri.

Her stomach churned, and she realized it was most likely from hunger. Pleasant smells of roasting meat and freshly baked bread wafted into her room, making her stomach protest even more. She decided she'd save worrying over her mother's similarities for another time.

She laced up a pair of tan sandals that wrapped around her ankles, admiring her slender feet. She couldn't remember a day when she hadn't worn her boots, but the sandals made her feet look pretty. She thought of the giggling girls who'd flirted with Simeon. They, too, had worn sandals, only their toenails were painted bright colors. Dianna's toenails still had traces of grime under them, but it was not to be helped. Those girls with painted nails hadn't just ridden a dragon across the desert. She grabbed the stone off the bed and tucked it into a leather pouch, then attached it to her belt. She placed a few loose coins on top of the stone; if anyone asked, she'd say the pouch was a coin purse. She still wasn't ready to show her stone to Feira.

Dianna made it a point to not look directly at the guards when she emerged from her chamber. She felt indecent in the borrowed gown and feared the heat in her face was visible for all to see. She kept her attention centered on one guard's dark, broad back and followed him to the great hall, where he told her she was to dine as an honored guest.

The great hall was just that, a long room of dark stone decorated with a table of polished ebony wood that seemed to stretch for an eternity. She stopped counting the chairs, but estimated the table sat at least two hundred. Her mouth watered when she saw the roasted birds, jugs of wine, a variety of colorful fruit and plants, and baskets of rolls and pastries. She could almost taste the myriad savory scents. How did the sand dwellers find so much food in the middle of a desert?

The lively chatter and music died down when she entered the hall as all eyes turned to her. She turned up her chin, ignoring curious looks by focusing on the furnishings. Intricately carved flaming balls of metal hung from the ceiling, and the walls were decorated with magnificent colorful tapestries depicting seven beautiful dark-skinned women adorned in jewels. She instinctively touched the stone on her belt.

These women had to be the goddess Kyan and her daughters, for the final tapestry depicted seven pale stones surrounded by flowers, and hovering behind them was a magnificent golden dragon, a single tear dripping down his long snout.

It was then she noticed how many seven-pointed stars were woven into the tapestries and carved into the walls and table. Though she tried to ignore the Kyanite's scowling faces as they pressed against the wall, turning up their noses as she passed, she noticed seven-pointed jeweled emblems around their necks and seven-pointed tattoos on their arms. Kyan and her daughters were more than just dead deities to them. They were living memories, and these people mourned their deaths every day, all because Dianna's mother had killed them. She feared the sand dwellers would never forgive her for Madhea's sins.

Destiny is not forged in blood. It is made in spirit. Sindri's voice echoed in Dianna's skull.

"What does that mean, Sindri?" she whispered to herself as she passed more unfriendly faces.

It means you control who you wish to be, despite the cursed blood which runs through your veins. Do not let Madhea's past actions shape your future.

"Tell that to the Sand People," she grumbled. "They think I am like her."

Sindri didn't answer.

As she stole glances at the others in the room, she observed two distinct classes of people—those who wore fine clothes and held their noses high while sipping from shiny goblets and those who seemed to be servants, wearing plain clothes and stacking food on the tables.

The two guards brought Dianna to the end of the table, where Feira was waiting. The deity was seated beside a man so old and wrinkled, Dianna feared he was a corpse. The guards bowed to Feira, then backed against the wall, standing so still, they appeared to be sculpted of granite.

Feira gestured to the seat beside her, and a man stepped forward and pulled it out.

"Sit," Feira said to Dianna.

She sat in the chair, warily eyeing the decrepit man who sat across from her. His eyes were devoid of color, covered with a milky haze, and his gray flesh hung so far off his bones, he looked like a skeleton draped with an old, worn sock.

She jumped at the sound of a loud gong. The hall filled with a cacophony of scrapes as the other diners pulled out their chairs and sat at the long table.

Feira stood, holding up her goblet and sloshing red liquid on the table. "Children, please join me in welcoming our honored guest."

Dianna shifted uncomfortably, not liking being the center of attention, especially when she knew the Kyanites would rather feed her to Tan'yi'na than toast in her honor.

When Feira held her goblet in the air, the others followed suit, their expressions pained. They obeyed their deity, however.

The heat that flamed Dianna's face was discomforting. She looked into her cup of swirling red liquid, unable to keep her gaze on the long row of scowls. A quick glance revealed that Simeon wasn't present. She wondered if the empty seat beside her was meant for him.

Feira ripped open a roll and bit into one end. Then she chased it down with a hearty drink. Another gong sounded, and the music resumed. People piled their plates with food.

Dianna was glad to see her presence hadn't dampened their appetites. She was famished again, and despite the nervous roiling in her stomach, she grabbed several slices of pink meat, a few rolls, and a heaping spoonful of creamy, purple fruit.

"Where's Simeon?" Feira asked a nearby servant, then frowned when the man whispered in her ear.

Dianna fought the urge to slink under the table when Feira turned her pointed gaze on her, then flashed a rueful smile.

Feira leaned toward Dianna. "I'm afraid Simeon won't be able to join us."

Forcing a smile, Dianna infused indifference into her voice. "Oh, that's too bad." She met Feira's assessing gaze and squeezed a roll so tight, filling squirted out one end and splattered the table. "Oops. I didn't know that would happen."

Before she could clean up the mess, a servant was doing it for her.

When she thanked him, he only nodded and backed away. Dianna thought his behavior odd, though she wasn't used to servants attending her. In her town of Adolan, only a few of the very wealthy had servants, and they were generally treated as members of the families they served. When she looked down the row of people, she saw those dressed in fine clothes waving away plain-clothed sand dwellers with disdain or demanding they refill their goblets. Dianna pitied those who waited on her.

"Most of these people are my descendants." Feira waved toward the people gorging on food and giving orders to the servants. "Those with my eyes have my magic. The brighter the gold, the stronger the magic."

"Like Simeon," she breathed. For the first time, she noticed a key difference between the servants and those they waited on—their eyes. The servants had inky black eyes while those drinking wine and laughing with their friends had eyes ranging from dark amber to bright gold.

"His power to charm is indeed strong, but not strong enough to work on you, or is it?"

Dianna's jaw dropped. The old woman was flashing a toothless grin. Had she made it obvious she was attracted to Simeon?

"No, it's not," she lied. Truthfully, his magical charms had worked on her too well, and she was sorely wishing he was here.

"This is my husband, Tumi," Feira said, patting the knee of the living corpse beside her.

She thought she saw a muscle twitch in the old man's jaw, but she wasn't sure. Having gotten used to the frail and nearly deaf prophet, Dafuar, Dianna raised her voice so Tumi could hear her over the din of music and laughter. "Nice to meet you."

Feira smiled affectionately at her husband. "He can't hear you."

"Oh." Dianna plastered on a wide smile and waved at the skeletal man.

Feira wiped a trail of drool off Tumi's lip. "He can't see you either."

Dianna felt ten shades of foolish. "I'm sorry," she said to Feira. She wondered how the old relic was still alive.

"Silly child." Feira laughed. "'Tis not your fault. I'm the selfish witch who keeps her three-hundred-year-old mortal husband alive through dark magic." She affectionately stroked her husband's cheek. "He is little more than a corpse, yet I can't bear to part with him."

Dianna was at a loss for words. Feira fed Tumi a spoonful of soup. Most of the broth ran down his chin, and a servant wiped the old man as Feira tried feeding him again. Feira could have been nursing a stone statue. Forced to look away, Dianna stared at her food as her appetite vanished.

The revelry at the table continued. People gorged on food and drink, waited on by their servants, ignoring the old witch and her frail husband.

Dianna examined her golden spoon, amazed at how much it shone beneath the glow of the overhead candles. She had only ever eaten with wooden spoons. She pushed the food around on her plate, hoping her appetite would return despite the images of Tumi drooling all over himself that replayed in her mind.

"'Twill be your fate should you ever fall in love."

Feira's stare made Dianna's flesh rise. Oh, heavenly Elements, it was as if the old woman's gaze had crawled beneath her skin.

"W-What?"

"The powerful magic that runs through your veins will keep you alive for hundreds, perhaps thousands of years." Feira dropped Tumi's spoon on the table with a clatter. "There is no man on earth with magic as strong as yours, which means should you marry...." Feira motioned to her husband.

Dianna pushed her plate away. "Well, 'tis a good thing I have no intention of marrying."

She'd never given it serious thought, but now she realized, should she ever fall in love, she would outlive him by centuries. She thought of her brothers, all mortal save Marcus, who had been born with the hunter's mark. Even with his magical gift, she doubted he'd live longer than other men. She clutched her chest, feeling as if a poisoned dagger twisted in her heart. Unless she wanted to keep them barely alive like Tumi, she would lose everyone she ever loved.

She looked at Feira through a sheen of tears. "What can I do?"

Feira wiped Tumi's chin. "There is nothing you can do. There is no magic in the universe powerful enough to stop a heart from breaking." She wiped her wet fingers on a cloth before throwing it on her plate. "Believe me, child, my heart has broken for many of my people. Too, too many...."

If only this was a dream, though Dianna knew this nightmare was real by the unrelenting pain in her chest. It was as if her heart had fractured into shards of ice. How could the Elements have been so cruel as to design her this way? If they had intended on goddesses and their children living forever, they should have created mates with similar powers. She pushed her chair away from the table and stood, heedless of the looks she was getting from the Kyanites.

"Forgive me, cousin," she said to Feira. 'Twas a long journey, and I'm exhausted."

"Oh, my dear." Feira's hand flew to her throat as she struggled to stand. "I didn't mean to upset you."

"Please don't get up." Dianna swiped a stray tear, angry with herself for letting the Kyanites see her cry. "Thank you so much for your hospitality."

Dianna turned, nearly running into the broad chest of one of her guards. Had he been behind her the entire time? She briefly stared into his dark eyes before sucking in a gasp when she saw one of his long braids had fallen behind his shoulder, revealing a left ear that looked as if it had been chewed off. What little was left of it was a shredded mass. The burly man tensed and tugged his braid back over his mangled ear.

She quickly looked away, realizing she'd been rude, but she couldn't stop wondering if her guard had been born with that deformity or something more sinister had happened to him. If so, why hadn't a witch healed him?

With a resigned sigh, she let her guards lead the way out of the hall. She held her head high, ignoring the sneers and laughter of the golden-eyed witches as they watched her go and feeling more alone than she'd ever felt in her life.

Chapter Seven

ROWLEN WAS DEAD, KILLED by Alec after his father tried to murder Markus. His father's spirit should have passed to the Elements months ago, yet his memory still haunted Alec in his sleep. Alec wasn't sure if dreams of his father were figments of his imagination or something more.

Alec knew this to be a dream, but the cool mountain breeze that ruffled his hair felt real. They were sitting outside in the rocking chairs Rowlen had built for himself and Mother. Rowlen looked at Alec, a gentle smile lightening his dark, normally sullen features. How odd, for Father had once knocked out Alec's tooth for sitting in Mother's special chair. He was compelled to look away from his father's penetrating gaze, focusing instead on Mother's herb garden. Markus and Mother weren't in sight. In fact, not even a bird or squirrel crossed Alec's line of vision.

"You must trust in the dwarves."

"What?"

"They did not steal it."

"Steal what?" Alec asked.

But then, like all dreams, Rowlen faded away before Alec could ask him more questions, namely, why he haunted the son who'd stabbed him in the back. Rowlen didn't seem bent on revenge. If anything, he appeared to want to help Alec. Even though he knew his father's heart had been turned against him by Madhea's curse, it was difficult reconciling this kind spirit with his late father. He had so many questions. Why did he slip away? And what had been stolen? Alec feared the answer would come to him when he woke. Elements save them all if the stone was missing.

DIANNA TOSSED AND TURNED, getting a fitful night's sleep while alternating between wayward thoughts of Simeon's devilish grin, worrying over her brothers, the fate of humanity, and dreading the possibility of a long, lonely existence. She awoke groggy and in a sour mood to a sharp pain in her gut, as if pixies were gnawing on her insides. She sat up, tossing silken sheets off her legs and regretting that she hadn't slept with Lydra, but coward that she was, she'd been too afraid to test Tan'yi'na again. She was determined not to be deterred by fear this morning, but first, she needed to eat before those pixies in her stomach rioted.

Though there were no windows in her secluded cavern, the bright wall sconces gave the room ample light. Someone had to have lit them when she was asleep. Dianna didn't know whether to be concerned or relieved she hadn't heard anyone enter her room. She padded over to a small dining table, pleased to see a display fit for a queen. The table was adorned with a fresh vase of yellow flowers, but it was the steaming platters of food that made her mouth water. There were large rolls and fresh butter, ham, eggs, slices of colorful fruit, and a tall pitcher of a bright orange drink. She didn't know if this spread was all for her, or if she was to have company, but she didn't care. She sat at the table and ate her fill, then ate some more.

By the time she was finished, she'd eaten more in one morning than she usually ate in an entire day. She vaguely remembered the food being succulent and flavorful, but she'd ingested it so fast, she hadn't taken the time to savor it. After she relieved herself in the chamber pot—at least she'd hoped it was a chamber pot—she washed in her private pool and then dressed in the clothes laid out for her. This time she was pleasantly surprised to see a soft pair of white breeches included in her wardrobe, though they were too thin and revealing to wear alone. She had to wrap a skirt around her waist. The top was a scrap of cloth that barely covered her chest, with straps for sleeves. Again, she thought of the people of Adolan and how they'd snicker if they saw her.

She turned when the door cracked open, surprised to see a child tiptoe into her room. The girl was smaller than her youngest brother and slender, hair woven into several small braids pulled up into a single knot on top of her head and held in place by an array of beautiful leaves and flowers. Her brown dress appeared to be sewn together from patches of earth and her sandals woven from dried grass. The girl smelled as fragrant as a freshly cut bouquet, no doubt because of her earthy attire. Dianna was taken aback by the girl, whose bright golden eyes sparkled like jewels against her ebony skin.

"Hello," the child said, sitting at the breakfast table and dipping her finger in the butter before spreading it on a roll.

"Hello." Dianna pulled out a chair and sat across from the girl. "Who are you?"

"Kyani," she answered before biting into her bread.

Dianna leaned against the table, smiling. "That's a pretty name."

Kyani gulped the remainder of Dianna's juice before slamming the goblet on the table and letting out an impressive belch. "I'm named after our beloved goddess."

"So you are." She leaned back in her chair, doing her best to hide her smile.

Kyani snatched a flower out of the vase. "But you can call me Sprout. Everyone else does."

"Sprout?" Such an unflattering name for a beautiful child. "But Kyani is so much prettier."

Kyani cradled the flower in her arms as if she was holding a newborn babe. Dianna's eyes widened when the flower grew and sprouted more flowers, a long stem shooting out of Kyani's arms and wrapping around her chair. Kyani laid the bouquet on the table and took another bite of her roll. Then she grabbed another flower from the vase, and it, too, blossomed.

"Your magic is quite good, Sprout," Dianna said to the girl. The nickname suited her perfectly.

"Thank you." She slipped out of her chair and skipped over to Dianna's bed. She touched a thin trail of ivy growing up the stone wall behind the headboard. The ivy sprouted and branched across the wall, wrapping around the posters of the bed.

Dianna followed the girl, sitting on the opposite side of the bed, amazed as the ivy continued to stretch across the ceiling. "How old are you?"

"I am seven summers old," Sprout answered, twirling a dangling vine around her finger. The girl seemed unimpressed with her own magic, as if making plants grow at an alarming rate was second nature.

Desryn had been about her size when he was that age. "You are a few years younger than my baby brother."

Sprout's gold eyes dazzled beneath the glow of the flickering wall sconces. "Does he have magic like you?"

"No." She swallowed, realizing it was a bad idea to speak of Des. Memories of her brother only brought her heartache now that she knew his time on earth would be short compared to hers. "He is a mortal."

"That's too bad." Sprout coaxed more ivy to spread across the ceiling and wrap around Dianna's bed. "Is he your servant?"

"Of course not!" Dianna remembered the brown-eyed Kyanites from last night, how they must have been forced into servitude because they lacked magical powers. "Are you lost, Sprout?"

"No." She touched plants that sprouted off the ivy, coaxing little white flowers out of their pods. "Why would you think that?"

"Can I help you with something?" As amusing as this child was, Dianna needed to check on Lydra. She didn't have time to play nursemaid.

"Grandmother says Simeon is sulking." Sprout flashed a sideways smile before turning back to her flowering pods. "I'm here to take you to the gardens."

"Sulking, is he?" Did the child know more than she was letting on?

Sprout picked a flower, handing it to Dianna. "My brother's not used to rejection."

Dianna smelled the fragrant petals, looking at Sprout from beneath her lashes. "I didn't know Simeon had a sister." Hopefully, that meant Sprout was one of the few Shifting Sands girls immune to his charms.

"Twelve sisters," Sprout said, handing Dianna another flower. "We all have strong magic, like our parents."

"Simeon has twelve sisters?" And all witches, at that. Dianna had never known other witches growing up, especially since suspected witches in Adolan were sacrificed to Madhea. She twirled the soft stem between her fingers, wondering if she'd seen any of the girls before, perhaps one of the few who hadn't shot eye daggers at her yesterday. "How many brothers does he have?"

"He's the only boy in our family."

"Oh, heavenly Elements." No wonder he was so adept at manipulating females. He'd probably had plenty of practice with his sisters.

"You should be happy." When Sprout flashed a mischievous grin, the same as her brother's, Dianna expected to see devilish horns shoot from the child's head.

"Why is that?" It was hard not to punch a nearby wall. Even if she were to succumb to Simeon's charms, or any man's for that matter, their passion would be doused by time while Dianna lingered on alone for an eternity.

"That's twelve less girls you will have to fight off Simeon." Sprout giggled.

Dianna jumped up and tossed the flowers on the bed before she gave in to the urge to stomp on them. "I'm not fighting anyone over Simeon."

"Grandmother says you will." Sprout flashed a far too knowing look for a child of seven.

The flush of embarrassment flamed Dianna's cheeks like a rush of venom. "Your grandmother must be mistaken." Her humiliation quickly turned to anger. Why would Feira say such a thing after she'd warned Dianna she'd outlive any man?

Sprout vehemently shook her head. "She's seen it in the swirling mists."

Dianna paced the floor, fighting back the anger that threatened to split her skull in two. The swirling mists? Markus had told Dianna about that nonsense. The prophet used it to see into the future. Or so he said. Well, those swirling mists didn't control her destiny. She'd make sure of it. She exhaled a shaky breath and turned to Sprout. "About these gardens?"

Sprout jumped off the bed, long strands of ivy trailing after her like a toddler chasing her mother. She waved the ivy back. "Grandmother said you'd want to see them."

"That sounds wonderful." She clasped her hands together. If Sprout could control vegetation so easily, no wonder her people dined on such delicious fruits and grains. Still, Dianna couldn't get ahead of herself. Lydra had been left alone with Tan'yi'na all night. Even though the menacing dragon had given his word no harm would come to Lydra, she didn't trust him. "I must check on my dragon first."

"Okay, but Grandmother says I must accompany you so Tan'yi'na doesn't eat you."

Dianna couldn't help but laugh. "Thank you, but if he intends to eat me, I don't think you can stop him."

Sprout squinted, looking at Dianna as if flowers had budded out of her ears. "Of course, I can."

This small child against Tan'yi'na? How would she defend herself? Throw flowers at him?

Dianna held the door open, and Sprout led the way. "Forgive me if I have my doubts."

GORPAT STARTLED ALEC with a loud, blubbery snort before turning on her side and snoring in the other direction. Alec awoke with a stiff neck and a sore back, the result of a fitful night's sleep, no thanks to the giant's bear-like noises. She changed position again, kicking a tree and snapping it in two before moaning about the "bad witch." Whatever the giant was dreaming about, it certainly wasn't pleasant.

Alec let out a frustrated sigh. No use trying to go back to sleep, for it wasn't just the giant who'd disturbed his slumber. When he wasn't waking up to check on the dwarves and the Ice People, he was dreaming of Rowlen's ghost. Even as Alec looked up at the dawn's rays, peeking through the canopy of trees, he could still feel his father's haunted gaze on him. As he tried to recall his dream, he was almost certain Rowlen had warned him about something. But what? He vaguely remembered they had been sitting in rocking chairs.

Alec couldn't help but wonder if his dreams were something more, a way for his father to relay a message from beyond the grave. Whatever Rowlen had to say, Alec wished he'd get it out instead of torturing him each night.

He rubbed the sleep from his eyes and then rose from his bedroll, shaking off the morning chill. A few dwarves were up, tending the fire, and the ice dwellers still slept. Hopefully Ryne would wake up in a better mood, though Alec wasn't counting on it. He shuffled toward the fire, which had shrunk considerably since last night, leaving behind a few angry embers. He held his hands over the warmth, then rubbed his arms.

When Zier hobbled up to him, offering a hot cup of black coffee and a pie, Alec thanked him. The buttery crust, though slightly stale, was still the most delicious he'd ever eaten. The sweet fruit and nut filling inside awoke

Alec's senses, and he moaned with every bite. Grim joined them, and the trio drank and ate while staring into the pit.

Alec was wiping his hands on his vest and thanking Zier for the delicious breakfast when a commotion from the end of camp drew his attention.

Ven was kicking his bedroll and screaming wildly. "It's gone! It's gone! My stone is gone!"

Ryne jumped up and pushed Ven aside. He forced the other ice dwellers out of their bedrolls and tore through them like a snow bear mauling its prey. When he turned toward the camp empty-handed, the violence in his eyes made Alec's knees go weak.

"Thief!" Ryne unsheathed his blade, charging Zier like a warrior heading into battle.

Alec had only a second to spring into action. Ryne's blade scraped his neck when he slammed into him, pushing him back while Ryne fought to get past. Alec was hardly aware of the stinging pain or the warm trickle of blood that dripped down to his shoulder. He'd survived much worse at his father's hands. He could handle a mad blue man.

"Drop it!" Alec hollered, trying to knock the weapon out of Ryne's hands.

Ryne was far more skilled in combat than Alec, easily deflecting him and striking a painful blow to Alec's nose with the blunt end of his blade. Stars swam in Alec's vision, and he tripped over his own feet, falling hard on his arse. Luckily, Tar jumped between them, growling and making Ryne back up a few steps.

"Disloyal mutt," Ryne grumbled.

Alec sat there stunned, blood gushing out his nose. In that moment, two thoughts occurred to him. First, the pain was intense, and second, he was ashamed of having been defeated so easily. What would the dwarves think, seeing him planted on his arse? What would Des think?

Alec shut his eyes against the agony, imagining Rowlen standing over him, calling him a worthless coward. He gritted his teeth and swore, getting to his knees before rising on shaky legs. His jaw dropped when he faced Zier and his cousins, some wielding axes and blades while others held bows, their arrows pointed at their chests. Behind him, Tar whined.

"Move aside, lad," Zier said to Alec, spitting a wad of grit on the ground. He wielded an axe that was taller than him, though he held it in his beefy arms as if it was an extension of himself.

"Zier, please." Alec held out his palms, struggling to suck in a breath as he wiped the blood that trickled down his nose and into his mouth. "Let's discuss this."

Zier pointed his axe in Ryne's direction. "We were through discussing when he called me a thief."

"You coveted that stone, and now it's missing." Ryne held his dagger at the ready, clutching the hilt so tight, his blue knuckles whitened. "Who else would've taken it?"

The other ice dwellers grumbled their agreement, flanking Ryne on both sides. Had they all a death wish? Were they expecting to do battle with an army of dwarves?

Tar shifted from foot to foot, nudging Alec's hand as if expecting him to prevent a battle between two stubborn opponents.

Zier's nostrils flared, and he kicked up dirt like he was an angry bull, ready to charge. "I have no idea where yer cursed stone is, ya boar-headed son-of-a-siren!"

Not to be outdone, Ryne kicked up dirt, too, then swung his blade, poised to cut off Zier's head. "Give us back our stone!"

What a fool. Ryne had to know he wouldn't get in the first blow before he was filled full of dwarf arrows.

"I am no thief! Alec has known me his whole life." Zier's round cheeks turned crimson. "He can vouch for me. I've always been a fair trader."

Alec's nose continued to gush, and he was forced to suck in shallow, bloody breaths. Ryne had made up his mind about the dwarves and their kin, but he had to talk some sense into his foolish blue friend.

"Zier has always been honest with my family and the villagers of Adolan." Alec winced as pain shot through his face with each word. Great goddess! His nose throbbed and spurted like a damn infected boil.

"And yet the stone is missing." Ryne's gaze sharpened. "I have heard tales of how the dwarves hoard gold."

Grim cleared his throat, standing shoulder-to-shoulder with his cousin. "Aye, we do. We've earned our treasure through honest work, and we don't appreciate you insinuating otherwise."

"Yah, Dada. We dwarves honest," Gorpat chimed in, leaning against a tree and rubbing sleep from her eyes.

Alec gritted his teeth. Just great. The giant was awake. If the blue men had stood no chance before, they'd fare better against a pod of starving sirens than this lot.

Ryne waved a fist at the dwarves. "And I don't appreciate you stealing an heirloom that has belonged to my people for over three hundred years."

Zier heaved a blubbery sigh, heavy lines framing his eyes. "I'm sorry, Alec, but your friends are no longer welcome in our camp."

"We're not leaving without the stone." Ryne stomped a foot like a wayward toddler.

Zier's cousins drew back their bows and raised their weapons.

Zier held a hand to his ear, leaning toward Ryne with a crooked smile. "What was that, son? I thought I heard you say you weren't leaving, but I must be mistaken."

"You're not mistaken." Ryne widened his stance. "We're not leaving without the stone."

Grim tossed back his head and laughed, his cousins following suit. Soon, the forest was awash in the dwarves' laughter while Ryne's blue skin turned a bright purple.

"The way I see it, you got two choices," Zier said with a wink, thumbing at his armed cousins. "Leave while you still can or stay and be poked full of holes."

Alec cursed under his breath. His knees weakened at the glint of determination in Ryne's eyes as he refused to budge. The pastry in Alec's stomach threatened to make its way back up his throat. As much as he was starting to despise this ice dweller, he didn't want to see him killed. To make matters worse, a soft, strangled sob came from somewhere behind the dwarves, followed by the shrill sound of distress of another dog. Des and his mutt were awake and none too happy. What would he say to Des if the dwarves slaughtered the Ice People?

"Ryne, no." Ven placed a hand on Ryne's shoulder. "Our people are depending on us to find answers."

Keeping his gaze trained on Zier, Ryne spoke to his friend out of the side of his mouth. "What will you say to your family if you return without the stone?"

Ven shrugged. "They would rather I returned empty-handed than not at all."

Ryne's shoulders dropped. He cursed, kicking a rock toward Zier. "Ice dwellers do not forget when they are wronged, dwarf."

"And dwarves do not forget when they've been insulted."

Ryne turned his heated gaze to Alec. "Are you coming?"

Alec backed up a step, instinctively shielding his aching nose. "We're staying here."

Ryne's face fell before he plastered on a sneer. "You'd rather trust your fate to a band of thieves?"

"They're not thieves, Ryne." Alec groaned, wishing the ice dwellers would leave already. The tension Ryne had created was as thick as stale gruel, and Alec did not know how he'd ever make enough apologies to his dwarf friends.

"This is all your fault." Ryne pointed his blade at Alec's chest. "If only you hadn't insisted on following that toad and his freak child."

Alec froze when he heard the familiar *thwack* of a bowstring snapping.

Ryne cursed, jumping back as an arrow flew between his legs, coming precariously close to slicing off his bollocks.

"Fine. We're leaving," Ryne spat, motioning for his friends to retreat.

As they rolled up their packs, Tar trotted over to Alec, whimpering and licking blood off his hand. A knot caught in Alec's throat. Though he wouldn't miss the ice dwellers, he'd miss their dog. He was sure Brendle would miss Tar, too.

Alec spun around at a shrill bark. Des's dog raced between the dwarves' legs and up to Tar. They nuzzled and licked each other, making their farewells. Alec fought the urge to demand Tar stay with them. Ryne had already been pushed to the edge of madness. If Alec kept the dog, it would drive Ryne to do something epically stupid. Besides, the Ice People needed a protector after angering the dwarves.

Alec wiped away an errant tear while he bent over and scratched Tar's ears one last time. Tar licked his bloody nose, then trotted off after his master, who gave Zier one last heated look, a look that promised retribution, before disappearing into the forest. Curse the ice dweller, Alec feared he was dumb enough to seek revenge.

Alec thought the worst was over, but tension still hung in the air like a thick fog. The dwarves kept their weapons trained on the forest where the ice dwellers had disappeared.

Grim whistled up to his daughter. "Follow them, my pearl. I don't trust those blue *broots*."

"Ya, Dada." She stomped off, knocking down trees and flattening bushes.

Zier whistled to his cousins, and several of them followed Gorpat, weapons drawn.

Alec mourned the loss of his party.

Des came up to him, hugging Alec's waist. "Why did they go?" he sniffled, tears streaming down his grimy face. His little mutt cringed at his feet, staring after Gorpat.

"Because they're idiots," Alec answered, silently cursing Ryne for risking not only his life but the lives of others in his party.

Alec looked down at Zier when the dwarf joined him. "I'm so sorry for everything."

The dwarf frowned. "Nothing to be sorry about, lad." He let out a long, slow sigh. "It is I who am sorry, but this is for your own good."

"What?"

When Zier knocked Alec's feet out from under him, Brendle screeched and Des gasped.

Alec hit the ground so hard, he saw stars. "W-What did you do that for?"

"Sorry." Zier scratched the back of his head. "I forgot how far down you have to fall."

Grim and Zier shared wary looks, then Grim uncorked his flask and handed it to Alec. "Drink this," he said.

Alec tried to push away the foul-smelling drink. Dwarf whiskey this early in the morning? Alec would pass out.

He gaped at Grim. "Why?"

When Zier cracked his knuckles, frowning at Alec's bloody face, he knew exactly what the strong brew was for. His mother had set his nose enough times for him to know what was coming. Curse the Elements! Alec took several gulps and handed the flask back to Grim. Two dwarves came up behind him, latching onto his arms.

When Zier grabbed Alec's nose, he thought he'd pass out from the pain. Alec fought his captors, screaming, but those damn dwarves were as strong as boars. Zier shifted his nose once, twice, and then stars exploded in Alec's skull when the dwarf set the bone in place.

Alec gaped up at Zier. "Siren's teeth! That hurt!"

He leaned over Alec, running a finger across the bridge of his nose. "Better now than after it sets, when we'd have to break it again."

"Aye. It isss," Alec slurred, his tongue feeling too big for his mouth.

Zier flashed a crooked smile. "Do we need to give you a moment?"

He held up a hand as Zier transformed from one dwarf into two. Or mayhap he was confusing Grim for Zier. "Aye, just a moment," he said, then smiled as a pleasant tingly feeling numbed his extremities, making his arms feel like two sacks of stones. Soon the warmth spread across his chest and up to his face, numbing his nose until the painful throbbing was just a dull ache.

Alec smiled at Zier as two images became one and then broke apart again. "Thanksss, friend. Feels much better."

Zier shook his head. "Night, son."

Before Alec could answer, his eyelids fell shut.

DIANNA THOUGHT IT STRANGE how Tan'yi'na sat beside the shoreline, watching the healers apply poultices to her sleeping dragon's wounds as if he was inspecting their work. Did he care for the fate of her dragon? More likely he was only there to ensure Lydra didn't eat the healers.

As soon as he spied Dianna's party approaching, the monster reared up on all fours, arching his back and hissing like a cat, a giant fire-breathing cat with a dragon-sized grudge.

Sprout pushed ahead of Dianna and the guards, wagging a finger at the menacing dragon. "Tan'yi'na, Grandmother says you are to be nice and not eat our honored guest."

He sat down, his jowls drooping. "I am not a servant, little Kyani. I do not take orders."

Undeterred, the child placed both hands on her hips. "You will be nice, or I will have no choice but to restrain you."

Dianna pushed ahead of the guards. Why would this little girl threaten a dragon, and why weren't the guards stopping her? "Sprout, please." She grabbed the child by the shoulder, pulling her away from the rancid heat of the dragon's breath. "Don't provoke him."

She knew as soon as she'd taken hold of Sprout that she'd made the wrong move. Tan'yi'na jumped up again, letting out a primal roar, plastering her face and hair with dragon spittle and nearly causing her to fall backward.

His roar was enough to wake Lydra from her healing slumber. Her eyes shot open, red and ominous as she struggled to stand. Tan'yi'na spun around, his chest swelling as he roared at Lydra. A pestilence of pixies! Dianna was not looking forward to breaking up another dragon fight.

"Sindri, please help," she whispered, releasing Sprout.

Sprout lifted her hands, and the ground shook and grumbled, then burst open in points of light that surrounded the golden dragon. Ivy trellises as thick as Tan'yi'na's tail shot up from the earth and quickly ensnared Tan'yi'na's legs and wrapped around his jowls. The more the dragon fought against his restraints, the tighter the ropes cinched around him, pulling him to his knees until he was eye-level with Dianna, steam pouring out of his nostrils.

Lydra chuckled, licking her paw and grooming herself like a feline.

Dianna could scarcely believe that such a small child had the power to bring a dragon to his knees. Though she had a new admiration for Sprout, she also feared for the girl's safety. She couldn't contain the dragon forever, and then what? Dianna was already well aware Tan'yi'na didn't let go of old grudges.

Sprout jutted her hands on her hips. "Are you going to be nice?"

More steam poured from his flaring nostrils. He growled, then winced as his restraints squeezed his legs so tight, they looked ready to snap the dragon in two. Finally, Tan'yi'na heaved a comically pitiful sigh, then nodded.

Sprout waved her fingers in the air, and the bright ivy turned dull brown, dried out, and snapped off Tan'yi'na's limbs with ease. The dragon jerked forward with a grunt, stomping the dried foliage into the sand and kicking up a cloud of dust.

Dianna placed a protective hand on the child's shoulder, nudging her back in case Tan'yi'na paid them both back for his humiliating captivity. A dragon as proud as Tan'yi'na would not easily forget being shamed in front of the spawn of the woman who murdered his mistress.

"Thanks, Sprout," Dianna whispered in the child's ear, fanning dust away from her face and warily eyeing the dragon.

"Don't mention it." The child broke free from Dianna's grip and daringly skipped under Tan'yi'na's massive jowls, patting his neck before hugging one thick, scaled leg. Much to Dianna's amazement, the dragon nuzzled the child's head, purring like a kitten.

She supposed she should've been relieved the dragon wasn't angry with Sprout. It seemed he only held a grudge against her, though she'd never done anything to offend him other than make the mistake of being born.

Sprout waved to Dianna. "You may go see your dragon." She turned back to Tan'yi'na, shushing him when he growled.

Dianna left the useless guards behind and walked a wide path around Tan'yi'na, magic crackling in her palms as she nervously watched the golden dragon.

Lydra was sitting up on all fours, her head bobbing and her eyelids heavy with sleep. Whatever draught the healers had given to her was strong, but Dianna was pleased to see the dragon's wounds were healing amazingly fast, considering her fight with Tan'yi'na the day before.

The ice dragon slid down on her belly when Dianna approached, cooing a greeting.

"Hello, girl." Dianna leaned up and stroked Lydra's muzzle. "You look so much stronger."

Of course, she is. Tan'yi'na's admonition echoed in Dianna's skull. *We dragons are far more resilient than you weak humans.*

Ignoring him, she climbed up on Lydra's front leg and scratched a favorite spot behind the dragon's ear. "How do you feel?"

Lydra whimpered her response.

You treat her like a pet, Tan'yi'na scolded.

She glared over her shoulder. The golden dragon was hovering like a nosey neighbor. "She is not my pet. She is my friend." She caressed her ear and did her best to ignore Tan'yi'na's hot breath pouring down her back.

You ride her like a pony, the menacing dragon said, chuckling.

She suspected the dragon was provoking her and did her best to keep her composure, forcing a note of calm into her voice. "How else did you expect us to escape my mother?"

If you escaped. There was no mistaking the acidic accusation in his words.

"What is that supposed to mean?" She regretted the question as soon as she'd asked it.

Tan'yi'na's eyes widened, then narrowed, making her feel like a cornered mouse beneath his hawk-like glare.

He leaned into her, until the steam from his nostrils fogged up her vision. *It means I still do not trust that you and your deceitful mother aren't laying a trap for my people.*

Lydra's low growl reverberated through Dianna. She laid a comforting hand on her dragon. "Easy, girl. It's okay."

But it wasn't okay. Her thudding heart quickened, sounding like a gong in her ears. No other being unnerved Dianna like Tan'yi'na, not even Simeon. "I did not come here to trap anyone." She hated the way her voice shook. Though the dragon's taunts made her want to pull out her hair by the roots, she didn't want him to know how much he affected her. She forced herself to act brave, even though her limbs quaked with fear. "Feira trusts me, and that's all that matters."

His fanged jowls hinted at a smile. *No, that is not all that matters, for you still have not been judged by The Seven.*

Dianna arched a brow. "The Seven?"

The dragon's sadistic laughter ricocheted in her head. *You have not met the coven, but you are in for a shock. They will not be as trusting as my mistress.*

"What is this coven?" she asked, no longer masking her ire.

Sprout stepped from behind Tan'yi'na's legs, frowning up at Dianna. "Seven of the Shifting Sands' most powerful witches. They are the deciders of fates."

She was confused. If these seven witches were the rulers of the Shifting Sands, why did they call Kyan's granddaughter their deity? "I thought Feira ruled the Shifting Sands."

"She did," Sprout answered, "but much of her power was transferred to The Seven after the great famine."

"The famine?" Dianna recalled the magnificent feast at last night's supper and the impressive spread in her room this morning. "I don't understand. The people don't appear to be starving."

Not now, because we have Sprout. Tan'yi'na nuzzled the child's head. *But during the famine, my mistress wasn't able to make difficult choices, which was when The Seven were created.*

Dianna leaned against her dragon's cool scales. "What choices?"

"Which mortals to sacrifice," Sprout said evenly.

Dianna's knees weakened. "You killed people?" She gawked at Sprout, then the golden dragon, praying to the Elements they were in jest.

Sensing Dianna's shock, Lydra's snout whistled as she whined, but Dianna was too stunned to give her dragon comfort.

We still do, Tan'yi'na said with a gleam in his eyes, as if he took satisfaction in her horror.

"Only those who lack magic." Sprout darted behind Tan'yi'na's leg as if she were playing a game of hide-and-seek. She popped back out, giggling. "The pixies require less meat when the crops are plentiful."

"No, no," she breathed. "This can't be true."

Tan'yi'na's eyes narrowed to slits. *You are calling her a liar?*

"Tan'yi'na, do not make me restrain you again," Sprout said, then gave Dianna an innocent smile. "The pixies ate all our crops during the great famine. Our people almost died of starvation. That was when we were forced to make the sacrifices."

Her stomach churned. How could this child tell such a tale without so much as a tear? "But I've seen how you grow plants." Images of innocent people being devoured by pixies flashed in her mind. Oh, heavenly Elements, she could almost hear them screaming. "Can't you grow enough for all the people and the pixies?"

"Yes." The child heaved an overly dramatic sigh. "But now the pixies have grown to like the taste of human meat. If we do not sacrifice, they attack everyone."

"Why don't you just destroy the pixies?" Surely there had to be one person among all of Kyan's magical offspring who was powerful enough to take them down.

If it was that easy, don't you think we'd have done so already? These pixies have been flying wild for over a thousand years, ever since your mother destroyed the goddess who controlled them. Their magic is as uncontrollable as they are. They are unstoppable.

"Can't you feed them animals?" Dianna cried.

Sprout leaned against Tan'yi'na's leg. "We've tried, but it's human flesh they crave."

Dianna felt her breakfast making its way back up her throat, and it took all her willpower not to vomit. How could this sweet child seem so indifferent to the suffering of mortals, and what would it take for her to learn compassion? "How often do you sacrifice?"

"Only during full moons."

Her heart beat so hard, it felt as if her chest would explode. "But that is twelve times in a year."

Tan'yi'na snorted. *Before Sprout was born, we were feeding them twice as often.*

As if that made the sacrifices bearable? She shook her head, still hardly believing what she was hearing. "Why do you only sacrifice those without magic?"

Sprout matched Dianna's direct stare with one of her own. "Because they are less important."

Dianna pushed off from Lydra's scales, throwing up her hands. "I'm sure they don't feel that way."

The golden dragon lifted his paw, examining grime beneath his talons. *That was my mistress's argument, which is why The Seven make the laws now.*

Dianna straightened her shoulders, anger pulsing through her veins. "I wish to speak to these Seven."

Tan'yi'na sniffed the air. *They will return later today.*

"Where are they?"

He straightened his long neck, casting a foreboding shadow over her. *They prefer to bring the sacrifice to the pixies rather than wait for them to come to us.*

"The pixies live several miles below the earth. It takes days to get there, but you don't need to worry." Sprout flashed a wide grin. "Your magic is too strong. You will never be sacrificed."

As if that made it all better? Then a thought struck her. Dianna had been hoping to find sanctuary for her people among the Shifting Sands, the one place she hoped would be far enough away from the Sky Goddess's wrath, and the one place she now realized was even more dangerous for mortals than living beneath Madhea's mountain. How could the descendants of the benevolent goddess Kyan send their own people to be slaughtered by vicious demons? More importantly, how was Dianna going to stop them?

Chapter Eight

ALEC WAS SURE HE MUST have died, for when he awoke, he was floating above the trees, traveling across the wind as if by a heavenly carriage. He squinted up at bright lights, stretching his fingers toward the sky and wondering why the clouds seemed within reach yet he couldn't touch them. He rolled over on his springy bed, looking down at thick, dark strands of dead grass. He sat up, rubbing the sleep from his eyes and instantly regretting the throbbing pain in his nose that shot through his skull like an arrow.

If he was dead, how was he still able to feel pain? And why was he floating through the sky on a patch of dead grass? He tried pulling the grass and was rewarded with an ear-splitting howl. The breath whooshed from his lungs as a giant hand sent him flailing through the air. He was deposited on his arse with an unceremonious *thump*. He looked up at Gorpat, whose eyes were crossed.

"Friend hurt Gorpat," she scolded.

"I'm sorry." He scratched the back of his head as realization dawned. "I didn't realize that was your hair."

Zier hobbled up to Alec. The giant pack on his back, clanging pots and various goods dangling down the sides, looked as if it had been strapped to a tree trunk with bent branches. "Glad to see you awake, son." Zier offered him a hand up.

Alec was surprised when the smaller man yanked him to his feet. He stumbled like a drunk, his world tilting from one side to the other, making him wish he was back on top of the giant's head.

"You okay, lad?" Grim steadied him with a strong hand.

Alec shook his head, trying to clear it of the thick fog. "I'm not sure."

"That was a heavy blow you took," Zier said as he steadied Alec. "Perhaps you should rest on Gorpat a little while longer."

Alec looked up at the pouty giant. As kind as the girl was, he still didn't trust her enough to be carried on top of her head without accidentally meeting a bloody and grim death. All he had to do was remember that flattened stag to know he didn't want to end up in the same predicament.

"No, I think I can walk. I just need a moment." He scratched the back of his head, scanning his surroundings while the dwarves shrugged off their packs and stretched.

The breeze was warmer here, and the trees had thinned, revealing a bend where the road diverged into two. One went up into the hills, its path obscured by overgrown bushes lined with tree roots and stone slabs that resembled stairs. The other one headed down toward the sound of waves crashing against a shore. Though he'd never before left his home of Adolan, Alec recognized the sound of the sea, for his mother had let him listen to the inside of a shell she'd said carried the sounds of an ocean symphony.

Alec knew Ryne had taken the path to the water. If he followed the shore northeast, he'd eventually run into Aloa-Shay. Hopefully Ryne would make it safely to his destination, where he could find out why their glacier was melting. Alec only prayed that if he should cross paths with Ryne again, there would be no animosity between them. He didn't believe the dwarves had taken the stone. Where it had gone, he had no idea, but Ryne's companions had become suspiciously quiet while Ryne accused the dwarves of stealing from them. Why hadn't they spoken up in support of their friend? Did they know something Alec didn't? Either way, it mattered little now. He had chosen the dwarves over Ryne, and though it pained him to see the sadness in his friend's eyes, Ryne had left him no choice. Des's safety was worth far more to Alec than a stone, and he knew Des would be safest among the dwarves.

The boy came up to Alec, tugging on his tunic. "Are you going to live?" His eyes were red-rimmed and as wide as saucers. Had the child been crying?

He knelt beside the boy, grasping his shoulders. "Of course I am."

Des pointed at Alec's face. "But last time you looked this bad, it took my sister's magic to save you."

He didn't want to know what his face looked like, though just the act of breathing pained him. Damn Ryne for his imprudent temper. He shrugged off Des's concern. "I've had worse injuries than a broken nose."

Zier laid a hand on Alec's shoulder. "We need to be on our way, lads. We only have a few hours of daylight left."

Alec stood, stretching sore muscles. The fog in his head started to clear. "How long did I sleep?"

"A long time." Zier chuckled.

He gingerly pressed his fingers to his nose, wincing when the tender flesh throbbed with his heartbeat. "I suppose I needed it." He craned his neck toward the giant casting a shadow over their company. "Thank you, Gorpat."

But the giant didn't answer. She was too preoccupied with something on the horizon, her thick brows drawn down, nearly obscuring her eyes. She held a hand to her ear.

"What is it, my pearl?" Grim hollered up to his daughter.

She pointed toward the ocean's path. "Doggie coming."

Brendle took off with a loud yap, racing down the path, his tail spinning like a cyclone.

"Brendle!" Des screamed.

But then the dog raced back with Ryne's large mutt by his side.

"Tar!" Alec bent on one knee, petting the furry beast behind the ears. "What are you doing here?"

Tar bounced around, his frantic barks sounding more like the wails of a wounded animal.

"Where's your master, boy?" Alec asked.

Tar answered with a bark even more shrill.

He stood. "I think Ryne is in trouble."

"Of course he is, if they went that way." Zier gestured at the downward path and spat into the dirt. "That way leads to Siren's Cove."

What little moisture was left in Alec's mouth evaporated. "S-Siren's Cove?"

"Aye." Grim slung an axe over his shoulder. "'Tis where the sirens like to swim—and eat."

"'Tis true what I heard about them?" Des scooped Brendle into his arms, holding him close. "That they feed off human flesh?"

"Aye." Zier blew out a slow breath, shaking his head. "There's nothing to be done for your friends now."

Tar continued to frantically bark, spinning in circles. This excited Brendle, who squirmed and yelped in Des's arms. Zier and Grim's cousins removed their caps and bowed their heads, grumbling. Alec felt as if he was living in a dream—nay a nightmare. This couldn't be happening. Ryne and the others eaten by sirens?

Alec lunged for his pack, which was leaning against a nearby tree. He pulled out his bow and quiver and slung them across his shoulder before marching back to the others. Tar's wails were so loud and pitiful, his heart would have broken if he hadn't been so singularly focused on his mission.

"I can't stand idly by while they are eaten." Alec's voice cracked.

"Son, the sirens devour a human in a matter of moments." Zier smoothed his beard, his eyes dark with heavy shadows. "Your friends are long gone."

Alec's chest tightened. "I must see for myself." He refused to believe them all dead. What would he tell Markus when they met again in the spring? That he'd let Ryne run off and get eaten by demon fish? The dwarves had the same grim expressions, though Alec had no idea what they were thinking.

Grim turned to Alec, clearing his throat. "The dwarves will not risk their lives for those blue-skinned gnazes."

"I don't expect you to." Alec's heart constricted. He hadn't expected help, but he certainly wished for it. He struggled to find his voice. "I will go alone."

Grim's bushy brows lowered. "But young Des is depending on you." He motioned to Des, who'd gone eerily still, gazing at Alec with wide, watery eyes.

Alec's chest tightened even more. "And the Ice People are depending on Ryne's party." His limbs fell heavy, as if they were encrusted in blocks of ice. "Zier, should I not return, Dianna will come for her brother in the spring."

Zier pulled a trembling Des to his side. "I will keep an eye on the lad until then, but this is madness."

Alec squared his shoulders, summoning a confidence he didn't feel. "I will not let them see me. I have stalked prey for many a year." And he had, with Markus, though not often for he had a habit of spooking his brother's prey. He thought it best to leave out that detail.

Grim clucked his tongue, doubt in his narrowed eyes. "But this time *you* are the prey."

"I will not go up against the sirens if it is hopeless," he assured them, wishing his argument worked on himself, for his innards were twisting like a nest of starving serpents.

"Alec, don't go." Des threw himself at Alec, wrapping his arms around his waist and sobbing against his tunic.

Alec grabbed Des by the shoulders, forcing him away. Each second he dallied could mean the difference between life and death for his friends. "Des!" He didn't mean to sound so harsh, but he had to make the child understand. "You must be brave and mind Zier should I not return."

Much to Alec's surprise and relief, the boy stepped back and nodded, wiping snot off his nose.

Gorpat leaned down and blasted Alec with a nauseating wave of rancid breath. "Friend no go."

Alec patted the giant's arm. "I'm sorry, Gorpat."

"Son, this is a foolish quest." Grim threw his axe to the ground, stomping his feet as if he was squashing a nest of fire mites. "Your friends are dead by now."

Alec leaned down and grabbed his friend's shoulder. "Grim, I thank you for the kindness you have shown Des and me. You are truly a good friend."

Grim scowled and turned from him, swiping moisture from his eyes.

"Friend no go," Gorpat cried again.

Tar bit Alec's tunic, ripping the hem as he pulled him toward the downward path.

Grim's bulbous nose and cheeks were as red as two ripe apples. "Do you not understand the power of a siren's song?"

"Easy, boy." Alec jerked his tunic free of Tar's jowls.

"Here." Zier held up a leather cap with two fluffy muffs sewn onto the sides. "Put this over your ears."

He slipped the cap over his head, shocked when all sound was sucked from the forest, drowning out even Tar's incessant barking. He jerked the cap off his head. "I can't hear with it."

"Aye, 'tis the point. May the Elements protect you, son."

"Thank you," Alec said. Turning his back on his friends, he slipped the cap back on and took off after Tar, refusing to look behind him lest he lose his nerve, knowing full well this could be the last time he ever saw his friends.

DIANNA'S THOUGHTS RACED as she followed Sprout to the gardens, an underground farm even farther below the earth than her bedchamber, with rows upon rows of vegetables as far as her eyes could see. Though the cavern was dark, a generous amount of light was produced by hanging crystals. The gardens were flanked by fruit trees, some as large as the mighty *lyme* trees back home, with huge dangling pods that appeared to encase hundreds of smaller fruit. Though such trees didn't grow in Adolan, Dianna recognized the palma fruits. The trader Zier had brought a small pod with him to their hut years ago, and Dianna's father had exchanged a young stag for the succulent fruit. She and her family had eaten most of it that night, unable to control their appetites, it tasted so good.

She smiled when she thought of her brother and what his reaction would be to the rows of palma trees. Her smile faded when she realized he'd never be safe in the Shifting Sands as long as they sacrificed mortals to vicious little demons.

There were many workers in the gardens, picking fruit, pulling weeds, and watering plants. They shot Dianna sideways looks before continuing with their chores. They all had dark eyes and dark skin. Several guards flanked the perimeters of the gardens, gripping lances in their meaty fists. Dianna wondered why they were there. Was it because the people of the Shifting Sands still didn't trust her? A nearby guard leered at a young, pretty woman bent over a flowering plant, plucking large red beans and depositing them in her basket.

Dianna's stomach soured. The memory of Sprout's question about Dianna's brother echoed in her mind. *Is he your servant?* Because Des had been born without magic, Sprout assumed he was a servant. But did servants have to be watched with spear-wielding guards? The Kyanites born without magic were slaves, not servants. They weren't just assigned menial, grueling tasks, they were forced to do them, just like they were forced into becoming pixie sacrifices.

Though Dianna plastered on a smile as Sprout took her down a row of colorful plants, she felt anything but joy. The food she'd eaten that morning had been harvested and prepared by slaves. They wouldn't even look at Dianna as they worked, methodically filling their baskets. When she came upon a row of spiky plants, Dianna had to repress her tears. A young girl not much older than Des winced picking berries, her hands covered in cuts, dried blood, and old scars. No doubt the Kyanites had witches who could have healed her. Other slaves had scarring, too, and several had ears that looked as if they'd been chewed by mites.

They stopped at a long, low hut with a thatched roof and no walls, held up by a thick wooden pole in the center and a pole at each corner. Beneath the hut, women and girls sorted fruit, vegetables, and grain into barrels.

Their guards stayed outside, their stony gazes following the women who passed by carrying baskets on their heads, laden with the harvest.

Immediately upon entering, her attention was drawn to a young woman on a low stool in one corner, picking stems off fruit. The other women gave her a wide berth, moving away from her when she loudly sniffled. She kept her eyes on the basket by her feet, tears silently streaming down her cheeks. The woman's anguish pulled Dianna in, like their souls were tethered by an invisible cord. She knew she should look away, but she felt compelled to offer the woman comfort, for a dark, consuming grief shrouded her like an invisible cloak. She couldn't put her finger on it, but there was something strikingly familiar about the woman. Mayhap it was simply because Dianna recognized a kindred spirit. For many a night, she'd shed silent tears over the loss of her parents, too, afraid to let her baby brother see her grieve, lest her dark moods cause him to suffer as well.

Her attention was drawn back to Sprout when she pushed a slave girl aside without so much as an apology and grabbed a piece of bright purple fruit off the top of a barrel, handing it to Dianna.

"Cotulla fruit," Sprout said, grabbing a piece for herself. "You must try it."

Dianna tried to give the slave girl an apologetic look, but the child refused to meet her gaze, continuing to sort food into barrels. Though the idea of feasting off slave labor while the non-magical Kyanites were forced to work with no appreciation soured Dianna's stomach even more, she reluctantly took a bite, not wishing to insult their efforts.

When an explosion of sweet flavors burst in her mouth, she was compelled to take another bite. "This is delicious." She cast an appreciative smile toward a row of women sorting the fruit.

When none of them dared to look at her, Dianna's heart deflated, and she lost interest in eating. She was determined to finish it, or their efforts would have been in vain.

"I don't understand," she said to Sprout. "You have magic to grow plants but not harvest them? I thought you could make greens bend to your will."

"I can." The child bit into her fruit, heedless of the juices running down her chin, "but then the servants would have nothing to do."

"I see." Dianna smoothed a rough patch on her fruit. "And The Seven told you this?"

"Of course." Sprout dropped her half-eaten fruit on the ground, then kicked it under a bench made from a gnarled plank. "When the servants are idle, we have trouble."

Dianna picked up the fruit, dusting dirt off it before setting it on a table. She sat on the bench and patted the seat, an invitation for Sprout to join her. "What kind of trouble?" She did her best to keep her tone light, though inside she was seething.

Sprout flopped on the seat, swinging her feet. "Uprisings."

Dianna clenched her fruit so tightly, juices pooled around her fingers. "I would rise up, too, if The Seven wanted to feed me to the pixies," she whispered.

The little witch stiffened. "They try to be fair when selecting sacrifices."

Dianna wiped her hand on her tunic before placing the squished fruit on the bench. "What's fair about it?"

The child's eyes brightened. "They only pick those who disobey, or the sick and weak."

"Oh, heavenly Elements." She didn't know if she should be more upset by the Kyanites' barbaric practices or the fact that Sprout seemed unfazed by such brutality.

"Are you all right, Dianna? Your cheeks are turning red."

She clutched the girl's shoulders, intently searching her face for any sign of humanity. "You understand these people are slaves, not servants?"

The child struggled to break free of Dianna's grip. "What difference does it make? They have no magic."

Great goddess! This place was no sanctuary. It was a living hell. Dianna tightened her hold. "But they have souls." She ended on a shrill cry, not caring that she was causing a scene.

Sprout finally broke free and jumped to her feet. "My mother says they do not."

She stood, frowning down at the girl. "Well, she is wrong."

The child backed away from Dianna. "Don't say that. That's blasphemy."

Blasphemy? She felt sorry for the girl who had so easily been brain-washed. She stole a furtive glance at the slaves surrounding them, noting how several had moved so they stood between Dianna and the guards, humming while they worked. Could they be shielding her from their scrutiny?

Dianna bent down on one knee, taking the child's hand in her own. "Sprout, do you know who my mother is?" Again the child tried to slip away from her, but Dianna held firm.

Sprout's lip hung down in a pout. "Yes, the evil sky goddess."

She searched the girl's eyes, hoping she would find any sign of compassion in the sparkling gold depths. "Do you know what makes her evil?"

The girl's eyes narrowed. "She killed our benevolent goddess."

Dianna swallowed hard, unnerved by the assessing way Sprout glared at her. "She's killed lots of mortals, too."

"Oh." The child's voice faded like the remnants of a dream as she turned her gaze to her sandaled feet.

Dianna feared that whatever soul Sprout once possessed had been sucked dry, like a shallow creek bed during a summer drought. Dianna's soul wept for the monster these Seven had created.

She cupped Sprout's chin. "And what made your goddess benevolent?"

The child rolled her eyes. "She was powerful."

Dianna repressed a curse. Power and compassion were not synonymous, but these mages had led Sprout to believe they were. "Yes, but she was kind, too, right?" she pleaded, trying to keep the note of desperation out of her voice.

The child flashed a half-smile. "Right."

"That is the mark of a great ruler, one who is powerful *and* kind. Do you think Kyan would have fed her people to the pixies?"

Sprout shook her head and ripped free of Dianna's hold. "No, because she could control the pixies."

Dianna leaned toward the girl. "But even if she couldn't control them."

Sprout kicked the ground, and a ragged, angry weed grew beside her foot. "She was a goddess. Of course, she could control them."

"Sprout, listen. Sacrificing people and forcing them to do labor isn't kind. It is not the mark of a good ruler."

Dianna's heart clenched when the girl only stared blankly at her, another weed growing up beside her. Was this beautiful child, blessed by the Elements with such potent magic, destined to be cold-hearted?

Beware, the demons are coming! Sindri hissed in her head.

Dianna shot to her feet. "Demons?"

The ground beneath her shook, a slight tremor at first, but when baskets toppled, chaos ensued. The humans ran screaming, huddling behind barrels and ducking for cover.

"The pixies!" Sprout's eyes widened. "We must run."

A guard barreled toward them and picked up Sprout. "Follow me," he hollered above the din of frantic voices. Then he raced toward the crops with the child.

Dianna didn't follow. "Sindri," she whispered. "What do I do?"

Stop them.

But how?

The walls of the hut shook, and debris fell from the cave ceiling, pelting the humans as they raced for shelter.

Instinct fueled Dianna's movements as she ran toward a narrow exit at the far end of the cavern, dodging people who warned her to run the other way. A creature emerged from the hole, stumbling toward her, its arms flailing wildly. The creature was followed by a black, swarming cloud that reminded Dianna of a nest of angry hornets. It took her a moment to realize the creature was a person covered in vicious winged demons with razor sharp teeth. Blood spurted from his body as he fell to his knees with a howl. A woman raced past Dianna, hollering as she ripped biting pixies off him. The angry swarming ball that hovered over them shattered like ice and descended on hapless mortals. Guards swatted the pixies with large nets, cursing as the demons swooped down on them, ripping chunks of flesh off their heads and ears.

The stone in Dianna's pocket warmed and pulsed. She got over her shock long enough to realize everyone in the cavern would die if she didn't do something. She raised her hands, spinning a ball of magic between them.

"Stop!" she commanded, throwing the ball at the mortal covered in pixies.

A bolt bounced off the swarm and hit the ceiling, fracturing into millions of fragments of light. The cavern lit up like the sky during a brilliant thunderbolt storm as magic crackled and popped all around them. Then it dissipated, falling to the ground like rain. The air was heavy with magic and the smell of burning flesh. The soft glow of the few remaining lit torches illuminated the cavern enough so she could see pixie wings and body parts splattered on everything.

Dianna looked down at her legs, grimacing at a flopping pixie tail and smashed head stuck to her kneecap. She shook them off, then cringed when she stepped on the torso of another pixie, its guts spattering all over the soil. A low wail brought her to her senses. A woman hovered over the body of the mortal who just moments earlier was being eaten alive by the demons.

Dianna raced up to them, instantly recognizing the woman with the silent tears. Was this why she was crying? Had someone she loved been sent to be a pixie sacrifice?

Dianna nearly lost her breakfast when she saw the man lying supine and staring up at the ceiling with his mouth open. Several of his fingers had been chewed off, one eye socket was empty and gushing with blood, and guts hung out of a gaping hole in his stomach.

"Oh, heavenly Elements," she murmured. "I don't have enough magic to heal him."

I will help you, Sindri said. *We must try.*

Dianna fell to her knees and held her hands above him, not knowing where to start.

The woman pointed shakily to the entrails hanging out of him. "Start there," she whispered with a trembling lip. "Please," she begged.

Sindri's stone pulsed harder, infusing Dianna with its magical energy. She held her hands over the man's abdomen, feeling the warmth in her palms radiate outward, covering the man like a shroud. Closing her eyes, she concentrated on healing his wounds, calling upon the Elements to guide her. Her mind slipped away as if in a dream. She saw her brother Des. He was sobbing and being comforted by the bushy-bearded dwarf trader, Zier. Had something happened to Alec? She searched for Alec, then inwardly sighed in relief when she saw him crouching behind a bush with a strange set of thick muffs over his ears. The wheeze in his chest had returned, and he struggled for breath. What was happening?

That vision was interrupted by the image of Markus sitting cross-legged on a white fur, leaning against a girl who held him in her narrow arms, the silky curtain of her translucent hair falling over their shoulders. They both jumped up at the sound of a loud crack. The girl screamed when a wall of ice beside them split open.

Dianna's eyes flew open, and she sucked in a silent scream. Had she been dreaming or were her brothers in danger? She'd no idea how long she'd been in a trance, but when she looked down, the man's stomach had amazingly healed, and she could detect a heartbeat in his broad chest. His eye wound had healed, but the socket remained empty. He was missing almost all the fingers on his left hand as well, but the worst of his injuries had mended. She thought about trying again, but fatigue was already setting in. Such a deep wound took far too much energy.

"Thank you, Sindri," Dianna whispered.

Now the woman, Sindri said. The stone pressed against Dianna's chest throbbed like a heartbeat.

The young woman looked at her through a sheen of tears. That's when she recognized the woman's crooked, dimpled smile and long, thick eyelashes. This mortal woman looked like Simeon. Dianna knew they had to be related.

Before she could blink, the woman threw herself into her arms. "Thank you for saving him," she breathed against Dianna's ear. She pulled back just as quickly, bowing her head. "I'm sorry for touching you. I-I don't know what came over me."

"No need to be sorry." She turned the woman's hand over in hers, noticing the bloody gash in her palm. "You are injured, too."

"It's nothing."

It pains her, Sindri whispered.

"What is your name?" she asked, wordlessly running her hands up the woman's bloody arms, the heat of her magic sealing each wound.

"They call me Ghost." The woman flashed a soft smile, one that reminded Dianna too much of Simeon.

"Ghost?" She lingered on the woman's cool skin. "A strange name for a person who is not dead."

Ghost's smile vanished. "I am dead to my family."

Dianna's heart lurched. Just another reminder that those in power in this "sanctuary" were as hostile as its desert surroundings. The man beside them stirred, moaning. Dianna placed a gentle hand on his forehead, easing him back into sleep.

She turned back to Ghost. "I'm sorry."

"You have nothing to be sorry for." She folded her hands in her lap. "You are not responsible for the way the Elements made me."

Had this woman been born to witches and cast out because she lacked magic? How could Feira have let her desert sanctuary turn into this? Were not *all* of these people her descendants? As Dianna cupped the woman's shredded ears, letting the warmth seep into her skull, she realized why so many guards had chunks missing from their ears, and she couldn't help but resent the Kyanite witches who'd neglected to heal them.

The Seven approach, Sindri warned. *They are evil. Do not tell them about me.*

Dianna's head snapped up as seven robed figures walked toward her as if on a cloud. They were aligned in the shape of an arrowhead, a lone witch at the point, flanked by three figures on either side, their faces shrouded within the shadows of their capes. Only visible were their glowing golden eyes.

Ghost cradled the groaning man's head in her lap, bowing her head when the robed figures came to stand before them.

Dianna refused to bow. She stood, smearing dried blood on her white tunic.

The mage at the tip of the formation broke off, stepping forward and removing the hood, revealing a tall and beautiful woman with flawless coppery skin, whose age was timeless. Dianna squinted hard at her, trying to determine if she was young, old, or somewhere in between.

The witch scowled at Ghost, shrinking back as if she had stepped in a pile of dung. "I am High Mage Zephyra." Her voice was surprisingly rich and deep. "Who are you?"

She pulled back her shoulders, refusing to be intimidated. "I am Dianna, a guest of Feira's."

A golden-eyed man pulled down his hood, revealing a head that glistened like polished onyx. He pointed at Dianna. "Your face. I have seen it in the scrolls."

She flinched, looking away from him and instantly regretting it when she found herself buried under the weight of Zephyra's assessing stare. She fought to keep her gaze steady by focusing on the High Mage. "I have been told I look like my birth mother, though I am nothing like her."

Zephyra honed in on Dianna like a hawk targeting its prey. "You are Madhea's spawn?"

Guards and slaves formed a wide circle around them, standing behind an invisible line, as if they feared Dianna. Then she realized it was probably The Seven they feared.

She cleared her throat, raising her voice for all to hear. "Our faces are where our similarities end. I mean no harm to your people."

Zephyra raised a thin, smooth eyebrow. "Why have you come here?"

Despite the weight of seven judgmental stares, she forced a note of confidence into her voice. "She turned her ice dragon upon the people of Adolan. I had to take Lydra where Madhea couldn't control her."

"The ice dragon is here?" Zephyra said breathlessly. She stepped back, splattering a pixie beneath her foot, a pixie who wasn't yet dead, judging by the horrified squeal that ricocheted through the cavern like cannon fire.

"She's above with your healers, but she is well enough. The healers must see to the rest of the injured." She nodded toward the many injured slaves.

Zephyra cast a furtive glance at a weeping child, who had a gash in her shoulder so deep, Dianna could see bone. The High Mage turned up her nose. "We do not waste our magic on mortals."

Dianna clenched her fists in anger. "That is not true. It is Feira's magic that keeps her mortal husband alive."

Zephyra shared knowing looks with the other mages. The High Mage turned back to Dianna, her full lips pressed together and her face hardening to granite. "Yes, our deity thinks herself above the law because she is the daughter of Odu, but there are some of us who do not forget it was Odu and Dafuar's births that weakened our benevolent goddess's power and enabled *your evil mother* to turn her to stone." She sneered when insulting Madhea, a triumphant gleam in her eyes, as if she was expecting Dianna to be offended.

"You would blame babes for their mother's demise?"

The woman's golden eyes pulsed. "I would blame her love for her mortal husband. The same foolish love has weakened Feira's power and made us vulnerable to unwelcome pests."

Dianna had no doubt the mage was referring to her and not the pixies. This discussion would only frustrate her further. "Then I will heal them."

Zephyra shrank back. "You are the daughter of a goddess. Why would you do such a thing?"

"Because unlike my mother, I believe power should be tempered with compassion, a lesson I was taught long ago by Kyan's son, Dafuar." She flashed a triumphant smile. "The Seven should take a lesson from him."

The High Mage threw back her head and laughed gratingly. "Kyan's sons lost their minds centuries ago."

She narrowed her eyes. "Mayhap they have, but I can assure you, they have not lost their hearts."

Just then, the man she had healed let out a low, mournful wail, tossing his head from side to side. "Jae," he cried.

"I'm here." Ghost grasped his hands, crying.

Jae? That was Ghost's real name? How odd. That was the name of the girl the Elementals had switched with her at birth. The girl her mother had killed. Though Dianna had never met Jae, she'd considered her a sister, for she had been the true child of the parents who raised her.

"Guards!" Zephyra called. "Place him in the dungeon."

What! Though Dianna had healed the worst of his wounds, this man was far from well. He needed a warm bed and healing herbs, not a cell.

"No! He is still recovering." She jumped in front of the injured man, magic racing up her arms, stinging her flesh like the bites of fire mites. How badly she wished to strike down the seven evil mages.

Zephyra's head snapped back as if she'd been slapped. "He disobeyed the law. Had he not escaped the sacrifice, the pixies wouldn't have come here."

Dianna was so furious, her vision clouded. Magic encompassed her, turning her into a fuming ball of energy. "I'd disobey, too, if you tried to feed me to those flying demons." The deep tenor that boomed from her chest sounded like someone else's, momentarily startling her.

The High Mage's eyes widened, then narrowed. "Duly noted."

There was venom in the mage's words. "The pixies are not a threat now." She stalked up to Zephyra and ground her sandal into the small body of a dead demon. "There is no need to punish him."

Malevolence seethed beneath Zephyra's gold gaze. "Mortals need to learn their place in our society."

Before Dianna could stop them, two guards came up behind her and dragged the man away.

"No!" Jae cried. She turned to Zephyra and dropped to her knees. "Please, m—oh, High Mage. Please, I beg you to spare him."

Zephyra held up a hand, and the heat from the mage's magic rushed past Dianna, knocking Jae on her back.

Dianna threw her hands in the air. "This is madness."

"You may be the daughter of a goddess," Zephyra spat, "but you are a guest here and nothing more. Perhaps you need to learn your place, too."

The other mages whispered agreement.

Dianna focused on the most poisonous of the serpents. "Are you threatening me?"

There was no masking the menace in Zephyra's cold eyes. "The Seven do not make threats." She gestured to something beyond Dianna's shoulder. "Kyani, see our deity's guest back to her chamber."

"Yes, Holy One."

Sprout was behind Dianna, flanked by two guards. Fortunately, the child appeared to be uninjured.

Dianna held her ground, anger bubbling over in her brain. "I am not finished healing these people."

No, Dianna, Sindri warned. *The Seven will sense my presence if you use me.*

She cringed. The goddess stone in the hands of The Seven would be dangerous indeed.

She pulled back her shoulders, issuing Zephyra a challenging glare. "Fine, I'll take the injured with me." Without waiting for approval, she helped Jae to her feet. Even that small effort left her breathless. She wouldn't have enough strength to heal all the wounded anyway.

"Get the girl," she whispered to Jae. Dianna would heal the child with the shoulder wound, even if it took the last of her energy.

Jae wiped tears off her face and took the little girl by the hand.

Dianna stood in front of them like a shield, daring Zephyra with a look while magic continued to electrify her palms.

Get away from the mages, Sindri said.

Dianna glared at Zephyra once more before turning on her heel, pulling Jae and the injured child with her. She held her breath until her guards flanked her back, shielding her from the scowls she felt boring into the back of her head.

"What are you doing?" Sprout scolded as they hurried through the gardens.

She ignored Sprout, making a vow that she would instill compassion in the little witch no matter the cost.

THOUGH ALEC TRIED TO be quiet, he had no idea if he was making noise because of the thick muffs over his ears. All he could hear was the wild pounding of his heartbeat. Tired and breathless, he stroked Tar's back and watched the activity in the harbor from behind the safety of a thick bush. Tar's ears flattened against his skull, and Alec prayed the mongrel wasn't whimpering.

Though there was no sign of his blue friends, what he saw made his limbs turn to ice. There weren't just sirens in the water, but a ship that carried the symbol of the horned broot whale, much like the symbol on the shield he'd given back to Zier. There was only one army that used the symbol of that magnificent beast: Eris's army. Her soldiers, big brawny men with skin the color of polished oak and long, matted hair that cascaded down their backs like wild ivy, were leading a line of chained men to their massive vessel.

Their prisoners looked as if they'd come from the same seaside village. Many were without tunics, wearing simple sandals and loose-fitting trews.

Their sun-kissed skin like baked soil, they, too, wore their hair in long, matted braids.

Alec blinked hard when he saw an old man with a bald head and a scraggly beard, followed by a sobbing girl. The girl wasn't chained like the rest of the prisoners, and she appeared to be gliding, as if skating across ice. Alec blinked when the girl passed through one of the guards. Was she made of vapor?

She hovered above the guard like she was being carried on a cloud. "Let my father go!" she screamed in the man's face.

The guard laughed and swatted the air.

Great goddess! That girl was a ghost! Alec had heard tales of spirits, and there was a time or two when he'd feared he was being watched by his father's ghost, but never before had he seen a spirit, and so clearly.

When a guard cracked a whip at the prisoners, they filed up the ramp and onto the boat. The spirit followed. Odd how nobody seemed terrified of the girl. Alec wondered if ghosts were common among the seaside dwellers. Perhaps this explained the meaning behind Aloa-Shay, ancient tongue for "haunted waters."

After the prisoners disappeared below deck, he noticed the sirens lounging along the shoreline beside a pile of discarded bones, their tails aimlessly slapping the water. They were beautiful women from the waist up, with large tapered eyes and smooth, tan skin. But when they waved and smiled at the soldiers, Alec was horrified at their rows of razor-sharp fangs. The soldiers didn't appear to be concerned about the demon fish while they loaded goods onto the ship.

One of the sirens threw a bone at a nearby soldier. "More blue men, pleazzzz," she said with a sibilant tongue.

He answered her by smacking her tail with a whip. "Two is enough. The others are for our goddess."

The siren barred her fangs at the soldier before slinking back into the water.

Alec's heart clenched, and he had to bite his knuckles to keep from crying out. The remaining sirens picked their fangs with smaller bones. He'd arrived too late. Two ice dwellers had been eaten, and two were to be delivered to their evil goddess. He tried to determine which ice dwellers had become fish food, but the bones had been picked clean. He sent a silent prayer to the Elements that Eris would spare the two remaining ice dwellers. Though their fate was grim, at least they had a small chance of escaping.

Feeling a familiar vibration beneath his knees, he slipped off his earmuffs and looked around. Gorpat was barreling toward him. Tar barked wildly, hopping around on all fours. Oh, heavenly Elements! Every siren and soldier had to have heard the commotion.

Alec looked over his shoulder to see Eris's soldiers racing up the beach toward them, clutching harpoons big enough to kill full-sized broots.

Panic seized him, and he waved at the giant. "Run, Gorpat! Eris's soldiers."

The giant stopped as if she'd struck a brick wall. "Friend in danger." She picked him up, raising him up until he was level with her crossed eyes. "Friend come back."

Her breath hit him like an avalanche of rotting animal carcasses. He breathed through his broken nose. The soldiers were almost upon them. "Run, Gorpat! Run!"

She took off, Tar barking wildly as he cut in front of them and raced up the path. The giant let out a horrific scream before falling forward.

Alec had just enough time to jump from her hand before the giant hit the forest floor with an ear-splitting crash. He stumbled right into the chest of a beefy guard. He slipped out his knife and ducked under the guard.

Gorpat's face was planted in the mud, several darts sticking out of her legs. How had they brought her down with such tiny arrows?

When a dart hit Alec in the arm, and a rush of venom shot though him, he knew exactly how the soldiers had felled the giant—poison. His arm went numb, then it spread to his body. He fell to his knees, deep laughter ringing around him. Dazed, Alec looked into Gorpat's half-lidded eyes.

"Keep your filthy hands off my pearl!" Grim bellowed.

Siren's teeth! The dwarf had come, too! Would all of Alec's friends be captured?

Alec fell against the giant's arm before his world spun and darkness consumed him.

Chapter Nine

THE TREK BACK UP THE winding maze of tunnels seemed too long, as witches and mortals gathered to gawk at their entourage. Dianna stared straight ahead, ignoring whispers as she hurried Jae and the child along, putting as much distance between herself and The Seven as possible.

Once the tunnel spit them out, Sprout raced away without another word. Dianna would deal with the young witch later. In the meantime, she had healing to do. The noose of fear around her spine didn't loosen until they crossed the threshold to her chamber and shut the door on the outside world.

She marched straight to a table laden with fresh platters of food and juice and poured herself a tall glass of a frosty pink drink. She greedily drank it down, barely savoring its sweet and sour flavors, and poured another.

Jae and the child stood at the door, their gazes flickering between Dianna and the fare spread on the table.

"I'm sorry." She held up her glass. "Would you like food and drink?"

Jae flinched as the child turned into her, pressing her nose into her hip. "We are not allowed to accept food from witches," she said, stroking the girl's hair.

Dianna waved them over. "I will not tell. I need my strength if I'm to heal again, and I feel selfish eating alone."

Holding the child close to her, Jae took a hesitant step forward.

"Sit." Dianna shoved a slice of roasted meat into her mouth and slid a platter of food across the table. "I'll hurry, so I can work on her shoulder."

The girl sniffled, wiping her eyes. She stared longingly at the food.

"Please," Dianna begged.

"Thank you," Jae said and pulled up a chair, balancing the girl on her knee while cutting into the meat.

The girl took several greedy bites before gulping down a tumbler of juice. Dianna could tell by the sharp angles of her face that mortal Kyanites were not well fed. She reminded Dianna too much of Des that first winter they'd spent without their parents. She had just learned how to draw back a bow and rarely were her hunts successful. That winter had been harsh, but she was a fast learner, and by the second winter, Desryn had round, ruddy cheeks and a full belly.

After the mortal child had had her fill, Jae turned to Dianna. "Why are you doing this?"

She was taken aback by the mistrust in Jae's hooded eyes. Hadn't she already proven herself a friend to the mortals? She set her fork down with a *clank*. "Doing what?"

Jae's eyes met Dianna's for a brief moment before looking away. "Being kind to us."

Dianna rose and cautiously walked toward Jae and the child. "I was raised by mortals, loved by mortals. My brothers are mortal, too. I am not like The Seven."

Sindri's warmth pulsed within Dianna as she reached for the girl's shoulder. The child shuddered when Dianna caressed her injury. Closing her eyes, she channeled her magic into the girl's wound. She felt weightless, as if her spirit were floating between two worlds. She searched for her brothers again. First Des, who was clinging to his mangy mutt, Brendle, while the large hound, Tar, licked his face. The trader Zier sat beside him, staring solemnly into a flask. Next, she searched for Alec but saw only darkness. Gentle waves crashed in the distance.

She called upon Markus. He was standing beneath crystalline chandeliers in a large icy cavern in a sea of blue people. Children cried in their mother's arms while Markus argued with a much older man. Her brother was demanding they surface while the man said they must wait for Ryne's party to return. Dianna tried Alec again, to no avail. What had happened to him?

By the time her eyelids fluttered open, she was lying on the bed. How she'd gotten there, she didn't know, but the mortal child was lying beside her, smiling in her sleep. The only sign of her ugly shoulder wound was a bit of crusted blood on a dirty, ragged sleeve.

Dianna rubbed her eyes, sitting up when Jae sat on a stool across from her.

"How long have I been asleep?" Dianna asked.

"Not long."

She stifled a yawn and looked around the chamber, frustrated that she had no idea the time of day. "How did I get here?"

"You don't remember?"

"No." A chill swept through her. Something was wrong. She knew it. She just didn't remember what.

"You were crying for someone named Alec," Jae said. "Then you collapsed, and I helped you to bed."

She peered over the bed at the small table. A chair had been overturned, food splattered across the slick stone tiles.

"Thank you." She released a shaky sigh. Why had she been calling Alec's name? She vaguely remembered dreaming about her brothers. Had something happened to Alec?

"No need to thank me after all you've done for us." Jae motioned toward the sleeping child. "You are truly the sky goddess's daughter?"

She swallowed, knowing full well she'd be eternally judged for her mother's cruelty. "Yes, and though I have never met her, I assure you I am nothing like her."

A wave of relief swept over her when Jae offered a hesitant smile, but that relief was short-lived as a fragment of her dream flashed in her mind—the sound of waves crashing against a dark shoreline. What did it mean?

The door flew open, and Simeon raced inside. "Jae!" he boomed.

"Simeon!" Jae leapt from her stool and raced into his outstretched arms, sobbing as she fell against him.

They had the same full, tilted lips, high cheekbones, and sweeping brows. Could they be related? Simeon ran his hands down Jae's shoulders, kissing her cheek and whispering in her ear. How badly she wanted to strike them both with a bolt of magic and force them apart.

Easy, Dianna, Sindri said. *You are letting your jealousy get the best of you again.*

Her spine stiffened. Sindri was right. Magical charms or not, Dianna had to control her obsessive thoughts. She imagined building a fortress around her heart, shielding it from the effects of Simeon's devastating smile and penetrating eyes.

When Simeon helped ease Jae onto the edge of the bed, Dianna scooted back, pulling her knees to her chest. Looking from Simeon to Jae was almost like looking at reflections, so similar were their faces. She remembered Jae's words: *I am dead to my family.* Would Simeon's family have abandoned their daughter?

Simeon took the stool. Gone was that playful smile and mischievous gleam in his eyes as he locked gazes with Jae. "What happened?"

Tears bubbled over the rims of Jae's eyes. "Kerr was the sacrifice."

"What?" Simeon shot from his seat. "How did this happen?" He threw up his hands, the veins on his neck swelling. "I thought he'd been selected for the guard."

"So did I." Jae hung her head. "I only learned the truth this morning."

Simeon's gold eyes turned a dark shade of amber. "Why would Mother do this?"

Mother? So Jae *was* his sister. What a twisted family, throwing away their child simply because she'd been born without magic, and how odd they would both have mortal sisters named Jae.

Jae shrugged, her eyes rolling. "To hurt me, Simeon. Why else?"

Simeon's face fell. He dropped to one knee and grabbed Jae's hands. "I'm so sorry, sister." His voice shook.

She leaned into him. "He escaped, brother." She spoke with a breathy whisper.

"What?" He jerked back. "He lives?"

"The pixies swarmed the gardens." Her voice cracked. "Then Dianna saved us. She destroyed the pixies in the most stunning display of magic I've ever seen."

Dianna thought her soul was unraveling when Simeon pinned her with his swirling gold gaze. Oh, how she resented him for trying to kiss her, and how she wished he'd try again.

"Thank the Elements." He flashed a wolfish grin that both excited and made her uneasy. "I knew your magic was powerful."

Dianna suddenly felt hollow inside, as if the fire in her soul had flickered to embers, having been fueled by his smile. Dianna wanted to bang her head against the stone walls for being such a love-struck simpleton.

"Kerr was injured, and Mother sent him to the dungeons," Jae sobbed.

Had Jae said *her* mother had sent Kerr to the dungeons?

"The High Mage is your mother?" she blurted, unable to keep the derision from her voice. She wondered how Simeon and Jae could be related to such a woman, then remembered her own mother was more sadistic than Zephyra.

Simeon stood. "Yes, and Jae is my twin, the only one of my thirteen sisters born without magic."

"Sprout told me you had twelve sisters."

Jae winced. and Dianna regretted her careless words.

Simeon groaned, coursing fingers through the thick weave of his hair. "She doesn't acknowledge Jae. Our mother and the rest of The Seven have brainwashed my youngest sister." His boyish features hardened. "They have conditioned her to believe that non-magic Kyanites do not have souls."

Dianna played with the hem on her vest, ignoring the low pulses from the stone in her pocket. "Why haven't you taught her otherwise?"

"Don't you think I've tried?" The hopelessness in his voice sliced through Dianna's heart like a blade.

She shifted under the weight of his penetrating glare as the memory of his near-kiss played in her mind again and again. She smoothed the wrinkles from her breeches, willing the tremors in her hands to subside, though she felt anything but calm. "Mayhap now that I've destroyed the pixies, things will change."

Jae cleared her throat. "There are many who believe The Seven have possessed the power to subdue the pixies all along."

That made no sense. Why subject mortals to such barbaric sacrifices if the witches of the Shifting Sands had the power to control them?

Dianna's gaze flew from Simeon to Jae. "Then why haven't they stopped them?"

Jae swallowed, a knot visibly working its way down her throat. "This is how they control the non-magics—fear."

She shook her head. "Why would they need fear to control you?" Why, when the witches could use magic? Dianna had seen a child bind a dragon. Surely the witches of Kyanu could subdue a few mortals.

"Their numbers are far greater than ours," Simeon answered.

Dianna arched a brow. So far she'd seen mostly golden-eyed witches in Kyanu, with only a few dark-eyed servants and garden workers. "How great?"

"Kyanu runs deep," Jae said. "You have only seen a fraction of our levels."

Dianna straightened. From what she'd already seen of the mazes and tunnels, Kyanu was indeed vast. It was incomprehensible to imagine there were more. "How many levels are there?"

"Hundreds," Simeon said.

"Hundreds?" She gasped. "And the dwellers are all mortals?"

He nodded.

She couldn't conceive how there could be so many more caverns, tunnels, and levels. "What do they all do?"

"You have only seen one garden." Simeon paced the floor in front of them, his brow creased with lines Dianna hadn't notice before. "There are many more, plus there is a whole level dedicated to dying fabric and another for weaving." He held up his hands, counting on his fingers. "Then there are brothels, metal workers, carpenters, millers, miners, jewelers...."

"And they are each assigned to their own level?" Dianna asked.

"Yes, depending on their skills."

This society was sounding more like a prison. It had taken Dianna a considerable amount of time and careful traversing down treacherous steps to reach the level which housed her chamber. How long would it take her to reach the lowest levels? Days? Weeks?

She tried not to become unnerved by Simeon's continued pacing. "What level are we on now?"

"The third." Simeon pointed at the ceiling. "The ones above us are used for storage." He gestured at the floor. "With the exception of the servants, the non-magics live beneath us."

Dianna couldn't imagine living so far underground. "It must take them days to get to the top."

Jae said, "We are rarely permitted to leave our assigned levels, and we are not allowed up top."

Mortals were never allowed to experience the outside Elements? The child stirred in her sleep, striking out with her fist before rolling over. Dianna had almost forgotten the girl was there, but her heart wept when the child moaned for her mama.

Jae leaned into the girl, stroking her back and murmuring in her ear. "Sleep," she whispered. "You are safe here, Maya."

Watching the tender interaction between Jae and Maya, Dianna couldn't fathom how The Seven could convince other witches that mortals had no souls. Maya's mother must be worried about her daughter. Dianna had been so preoccupied with escaping The Seven, she hadn't thought about searching for the girl's mother when they'd left the gardens.

Dianna leaned over the bed. "We should return her to her mother," she whispered to Jae. "She's probably worried."

Jae looked at her with watery eyes. "Maya's mother was a pixie sacrifice when Maya was still a tot."

Her heart caught in her throat. She looked from Jae to Simeon through a sheen of tears so thick, 'twas as if she was looking through a sheet of ice. "I'm sorry." She wiped her eyes. "I wish I could help."

Simeon stopped pacing. "You can."

Dianna shifted, resisting the urge to disappear behind a tapestry. "How?" She regretted the question as soon as it left her lips, for she feared she wasn't going to like Simeon's answer.

The gleam in his eyes made her feel like a hapless mortal cowering beneath Tan'yi'na. "Overthrow The Seven."

Dianna's extremities numbed as she gaped at him. "Simeon, you would ask me to defeat your mother? This might not end well for her."

"I pray it doesn't." Storm clouds brewed in his eyes as he leveled her with a look so sinister, her soul quaked with fear.

He prayed for his mother's death? She didn't know what to make of it. She knew Zephyra was a prejudiced monster by how she treated mortals, but for her own son to wish her dead? She hadn't realized Simeon had such a dark side, and she wasn't sure she liked it.

She looked away from his penetrating gaze, toying with a stem of grass that was stuck to her breeches. "I-I don't know."

He knelt next to her, filling her personal space with the warm scent of his musk. His nearness didn't help clear the fog in her muddled brain. If anything, he made it worse.

"Do this for me," he pleaded, taking her hand in his, "and I will help you overthrow Eris and your mother."

"I can't ask that of you." For the first time, she thought of the ice witch as the woman who'd birthed her. Though she'd never wanted to consider the cruel goddess as her mother, the sand dwellers reminded her enough that she had her mother's face. Even if she somehow found the magical strength to destroy her mother, would her heart let her do it?

"Dianna, isn't that why you've come to the Shifting Sands?" Simeon batted impossibly long lashes, his expression shifting from grim to charming, as if he wore two completely different faces. "To find a safe haven for your people?"

She pulled her hand out of his grasp, instantly missing the warmth of his touch. "Well, yes."

Much to Dianna's chagrin, Simeon stood and wedged himself between her and Jae. She wanted to cry out to Jae to come back when the mortal crawled across the bed, lying down beside Maya and closing her eyes, making Dianna feel very much alone with Simeon. He reached for her hands again. Fool that she was, she didn't pull back.

"The world will never be safe as long as evil witches are in power." His voice was mesmerizing, as if he was speaking to her in a dream, luring her in with words coated in honey.

"But I am just one witch."

His mouth hitched up in that dimpled, sideways grin. "One very powerful witch."

"I think you overestimate me." She didn't want to tell him 'twas the stone that wielded most of the power. It had taken Dianna weeks to heal Alec's injuries, and the experience had been so draining, she'd had to rest in bed for several days. That was before Markus gave her the goddess stone. Without it, her magic was weak at best.

He squeezed her hands. "And you underestimate yourself."

She jumped at a loud banging on the door. Jae and Maya shot up from bed.

Grumbling, Simeon stood and marched to the door. He heaved it open, scowling as two beefy guards pushed their way inside.

A tall, dark man with hazel eyes stepped forward. "We have orders from The Seven to return the mortals to their levels."

'Twas then Dianna noticed the other guard remained silent, staring straight ahead, as if he was looking into a void. She had noticed earlier the eye color varied among the guards but until now hadn't made the connection that the guards were a mixture of witches and mortals. She wondered how these mortals had been elevated to positions of power.

Jae swung her legs over the side of the bed, standing with Maya straddling her waist. "I knew Zephyra wouldn't leave me here forever. I'm surprised she let me stay this long."

"Come." Simeon held a hand out to his sister. "I'll walk you down." He cast Dianna one last look when they reached the threshold. "We'll talk more when I return."

She shivered at the thought. She didn't want to talk. At the moment, all she wanted to do was fly far away and never come back. First, she needed to locate her brothers and ensure they were safe. Next, she had to find a safe haven for her people, not spur a war among witches and goddesses. Elements save them all should it come to that.

WHEN ALEC CAME TO, the first thing he noticed were the heavy chains weighing down his wrists, followed by rough wood chafing his legs. His tunic and soles were missing, and his body throbbed as if he'd just survived one of his father's brutal beatings. Though it was hard to move his sore neck, he cast a cursory glance at his surroundings. There were rows of benches with other men there, all chained like him, but they rowed with long wooden oars that disappeared under the wall's wood planks. He realized he was in the hull of a ship controlled by Eris's soldiers.

He looked up at the sound of soft feminine sobbing. A girl's spirit hovered over an old bald man who was rowing beside him. She was probably no older than Markus, with long wavy hair and luminous amber eyes. If she hadn't been dead, Alec would have thought her quite pretty.

Odd that he could make her out so clearly. His mother had told him tales of spirits and how they disguised themselves as whispers in the wind and movement in the shadows.

Like my father when he follows me.

Alec regretted the thought as soon as it entered his mind. His father wouldn't waste his time on him. Alec shut his eyes, resting his head against the wall until a guard approached.

"Why did you chain a sleeping man to the oars?" a deep voice bellowed. "We need every able body to tow the giant."

"He was only struck with one dart," a soldier with a scratchy, serpentine voice answered. "He will wake soon."

"Throw him to the sirens if he doesn't," the first soldier boomed. "I refuse to haul dead weight."

That was enough to make Alec open his eyes. No sooner had he grabbed an oar than he heard a loud crack, then cried out at the sting of a whip lancing his back. He stifled a curse and began rowing, which was no easy task. The oar was heavy, and his shoulders and back were sore.

"Thought you could fool us, boy?" Serpentine Voice sneered beside him.

Alec stole a glance at his captor. He looked part snake, with a twisted scowl and a bronze, bald head, save for one long braid that sprouted out of the top of his shiny skull and ran down his back in a tight weave. With one hollow eye socket where his right eye should have been and his left one covered in a white film, it was a wonder the man could see Alec at all.

He rowed harder as the reality of his situation hit him. The soldier had said they were towing a giant, which meant he and Gorpat were prisoners of Eris's soldiers. Two ice men had been captured as well. Grim and Tar had possibly been taken or killed. Alec hoped Des and the other dwarves hadn't followed him and gotten caught. He felt horrible enough for leading Gorpat into the fray.

Though it pained him to crane his neck, he glanced over his shoulder. He peered through the translucent skirts of the ghost beside him, who was still crying near the bald old prisoner. Surprise and relief washed over him when he saw Ryne and Filip rowing behind him. That meant Luc and Ven had been eaten by the sirens. Alec sent up a silent prayer to the Elements to guide his friends' souls into the light. He also prayed for the families of the fallen. They would need comfort when and if they ever learned what had befallen their sons.

Where the soldiers were taking them, he had no idea, but he suspected their fate would be grim indeed, as prisoners on a ship belonging to the malicious sea goddess. He thought about praying that Eris would show them mercy, but he had little faith in such a request. Instead, he prayed that the Elements would watch over young Des and keep him safe until Dianna's return.

The spirit hovering beside him cried harder. Her feet and hands were obscured like twirling wisps of smoke. "Please let my father go." She spun toward Serpentine Voice, who paced between the rows of benches. My father takes care of my crippled cousin. Tung will die without him."

The cruel soldier responded with a laugh, swatting her. "Good. Then the cripple won't be a burden anymore."

She hissed when the guard passed through her. "Curse you, son of a siren!"

His broad grin, revealed two rows of rotting teeth. "I'd rather be the son of a siren than the dead daughter of a slave."

Her pale eyes lit with the glow of twin suns. "And I'd rather be dead than serve a wicked sea witch."

"How dare you blaspheme my goddess!" He raised his whip and slashed through her translucent form.

She disappeared, then materialized a moment later, laughing as he struck her again and again.

With a wicked grin, the soldier turned to her father and whipped him across the back.

The spirit's unholy scream shook Alec to the marrow of his bones, drowning out all other sounds. The old man hunched over his oar, pain twisting his weathered features. The soldier repeatedly struck the old man as the spirit wailed, the sound ricocheting through Alec.

Finally Alec had had enough. He heaved the oar away and stood on shaky legs. "Leave him be!"

Serpentine Voice regarded Alec for a long moment before letting out a low and sinister chuckle, aiming the whip at him.

Alec stared into the soldier's one foggy eye, shrinking back in horror. That was no ordinary eye, for the fog swirled like a funnel cloud. Was the man's eye a sky-scape, a window into another world?

When Serpentine Voice raised his whip, Alec's knees weakened, and he fell back, bracing for the attack.

Crack!

Alec sucked in a curse, biting down on his lip when the whip tore open his flesh. He closed his eyes against the beating, thinking back to the days his father would pummel him for the simplest mistakes. He'd survived that. He could survive this.

The sting burned like hot pokers. His shirt was cut to tatters while blood dripped down his raw skin. He did his best to separate himself from the pain of his mortal body, a technique he'd learned to survive his father's brutality.

Alec fell against the oar, buckling over from the agony. He imagined himself floating high above the ship, looking down on its billowing sails, surrounded by the endless ocean waves.

If only.

"Stop! You're killing him!" the spirit cried.

A ghost pleading for his life. There was irony. He fought the urge to vomit as his flesh split open. Then the hull tilted, and the soldiers tumbled onto the benches across from Alec. The boat dipped and swayed before righting itself.

Serpentine Voice grumbled and cussed as other soldiers helped him to his feet. "What in the Elements is going on up there?" he bellowed. He cast one last glare at Alec before marching down the aisle and climbing a ladder into a hold above them, sparing Alec from any more torture.

Alec knew the reprieve would be short-lived. It always was with cowards. Alec let out a slow and shaky breath, trying hard to ignore the throbbing agony that felt like an army of fire mites burrowing under his skin. He grabbed the oars and heaved with a grunt, the gashes on his back widening with each stroke.

"Thank you," he thought he heard the ghost whisper.

Alec tried to answer the girl, but all that came out was a groan as he put all his energy into rowing. Out of the corner of his eye, he saw the ghost's father grab his oar, easing Alec's burden. At the moment, he considered himself fortunate to be counted among the living, a far cry better than the fates of

Ven and Luc. Now all he had to do was find a means of escape before their lives took yet another grim turn.

Chapter Ten

A Goddess Awakened

ERIS PULLED HERSELF up from the shallow edge of the lagoon and slithered across the smooth rocks until she reached her throne. She climbed onto her perch, sneering at a young servant boy who dared to step forward and offer assistance. Though she despised her fish tail, she was no invalid. She was a goddess and had more magic and might than a weak mortal.

Once seated, she ignored the cursed tail that twitched and slapped the stone slab. She peered into the swirling mists, frustrated and angry when the Elements, once again, failed to show her the progress of the expedition. She'd sent out her best men to retrieve the human called Khashka, knowing his daughter's spirit would follow. She desperately needed the child's soul to complete the ritual.

Had Eris known fifteen years ago, when she took the body of the mortal girl child, that it possessed great magic, she would have taken the soul, too, discarding it so she could claim the body as her own. Now the child had bloomed into a beautiful young woman with smooth skin, large, almond eyes, and two long, lean legs. She was perfect. All Eris needed to do was banish the spirit of the child to the Elements, cast her upon the foamy sea, where she would wash away and never trouble Eris again. Eris had tried claiming the body many times before, but the cursed vessel, sensing its true owner wandered the earth as a spirit, wouldn't allow Eris's soul to enter. Only after the child's spirit was no more, could Eris claim the girl's body as her own, freeing herself of her unsightly tail for good.

Oh how she despised the Elements for making her this creature. Her sister, Madhea, had been gifted with two legs and wings. She could fly to the heavens, untethered and free to explore the world. Their sister Kyan had been luckiest of all. The Elements had created her in the form of a mortal, so she could walk among them as their goddess. They built shrines and worshipped her. A handsome king had even pledged his love to her.

Eris chuckled when she thought of how Madhea had turned Kyan and her daughters to stone. How she wished she'd been there to see that—Kyan reduced to rubble while her handsome king was forced to flee with the two sons Kyan had bred from dark magic. Eris remembered seeing the king's image once in her swirling mists. How she'd been struck by his beauty: hair the color of sunlight, eyes a vivid blue, like summer waves under a cloudy sky. His bright features complemented Kyan's dark skin and golden eyes. In the mists, he'd been holding Kyan, kissing her and whispering words of love into her ear, their bodies melting into each other like daylight fading into night.

No man had ever looked at Eris that way. Or if he did, his admiration soon turned to horror when he caught sight of her tail. Because of her repulsive fin, Eris had no king, and the mortals who obeyed her did so out of fear, not love and admiration. Soon all that would change. Soon she would have a new body, and she would finally be free to walk among people. Perhaps she'd find a king of her own, and the mortals would adore her and build shrines in her honor.

Elements save them if they didn't.

DIANNA COULD NOT SLEEP in the soft, warm bed another night, knowing how the mortals of the Shifting Sands were forced to live in squalor. She also worried over her brothers' safety. Had the visions been real or just dreams? She'd obsessed over this most of the day, when she wasn't thinking about Simeon's dimpled smile.

It was taking too long to heal Lydra. After the healers went to bed, she'd go to the top and do it herself, hopefully with Sindri's help. She wasn't sure she could count on the stone, which had been suspiciously silent all day, despite Dianna asking her cousin for answers. Namely, what were the visions she kept having of her brothers, and why did Simeon make her heart flutter and her head throb?

She berated herself for her selfish obsession when others needed her. Mayhap she'd see another vision of her brothers if she healed Lydra.

After she'd declined Feira's invitation to dine with the other Kyanite witches, she ate alone in her chamber, eating her fill, for healing magic took much strength.

She'd just finished her meal when there was a knock at the door.

She was relieved to see Sprout, beaming at her as if the pixie battle from earlier had never taken place. She was accompanied by a cloaked figure. Dianna wasn't surprised to see Feira pull down her hood and shut the door behind her. Dianna had suspected she would receive a visit from the deity after her confrontation with The Seven.

Feira silently walked over to the table, leaned her cane against the chair, and grabbed a silver decanter, pouring herself a tall goblet of wine. Sprout skirted the perimeter of the room, decorating the stone walls with twirling ivy and flowers.

Feira downed the entire goblet before slamming it on the table and burping into her fist. She took a seat across from Dianna, running a crooked finger along the rim of the goblet, eyes averted. "I saw you meet The Seven in the swirling mists."

"Why didn't you warn me about them?" she snapped.

Feira shrugged. "I wanted you to come to your own conclusions."

"You don't want to know my conclusions," she grumbled. Feira wouldn't like what she had to say, namely that she was a coward for letting The Seven wrestle control of Kyanu from her. She eyed Feira intently. "What else have your swirling mists shown you?"

Feira looked at Sprout, who was creating a veritable flower garden on the wall. "The mists have been stubborn lately. Besides, they do not show outcomes, only possibilities."

She is withholding something, Sindri said.

Dianna suspected it, too. She feared Feira knew more about these mages than she was willing to admit. "Is it possible The Seven will come after me?"

When Feira silently nodded, Dianna was not surprised, though she was disappointed in Feira's reticence. This "deity" had become a coward in her old age.

"Can I count on you to help me?" she asked, her muscles tensing when the old woman looked away.

"I'm sorry." Feira held out her palms in surrender. "But all Kyanites are my children, The Seven included."

"When naughty children feed their siblings to demonic pixies," she said through gritted teeth, "it's time for the parent to intervene."

"I no longer control Kyanu. I am just someone they worship, nothing more. The Seven would have destroyed me long ago if they didn't fear a revolt."

Dianna didn't try to mask the disdain in her voice. "How could you have let this happen?"

Feira picked up a pale flower petal from the table and rolled it between thumb and forefinger, grinding it to shreds. "Do you know the story of our origins?"

Dianna folded her arms, aggravated with the change of subject. "Vaguely." Truthfully, Dafuar had told her about their origins many times, though his story continued to evolve.

Feira grabbed another flower petal, closing it in her fist. "In the beginning there was chaos: fires raged, wind howled, and seas churned. The Elements created the goddesses to bring peace to our planet. They gave all the lands to Kyan. To Madhea they gave the sky and to Eris the oceans."

"Yes, I've heard this part," she interrupted. "Many times, from Dafuar."

Feira flashed a weak smile. "Her sisters were not happy with their dominions. They were jealous of Kyan, who was worshipped by the mortals. When Kyan married my grandfather, King of the Shifting Sands, she gave him six daughters, but they were all born with Elemental magic and were in Kyan's likeness. The king asked his goddess to give him sons who looked like him, but it took a dark and powerful magic for Kyan to give her husband male heirs, a magic that compromised her own."

Dianna swallowed at this, for she knew the dark direction the story would take. "Again," she said. "I have heard this."

"After she gave birth to my father, Odu, and his brother, Dafuar," Feira continued, "Madhea took advantage of my grandmother's compromised magic and turned her and my aunts to stone, then seized her lands. When Eris fought Madhea for her share of the lands, they brought much death and destruction to the world, with powerful earthquakes and giant tidal waves."

Dianna drummed her fingers on the table. This story served no purpose, other than to make her feel guilty for her mother's actions. Perhaps 'twas Feira's point.

"Finally the Elements had enough of war and forced the goddesses to form a truce. They divided the lands among themselves, Madhea getting the mountains and Eris receiving the islands. My father and his brother were supposed to steward the lands between. They were given the magical stones of their mother and sisters. Though the dark magic which had made them gave them eternal life, it gradually robbed their minds of reason. 'Tis why they are so perplexing now. They are wise, yet unwise. Old and frail, yet immortal. Because of this, the Elements took their stones, hiding them in the recesses of the earth, and they gave power over the lands to Tan'yi'na. When he found me, he turned over the power to me until...." She picked grime out of her fingernails.

"Until The Seven took it from you?" she finished.

When Feira heaved a dramatic sigh, Dianna couldn't help but wonder if her show of pity was real or staged.

"Well, as you can see, because of the dark magic I use to keep Tumi alive, my power is waning." Feira threw up her hands in mock surrender. "The Seven feel we are safest from the likes of Madhea and Eris if they rule in my stead."

"And who will protect Kyanu from The Seven?" Dianna pounded the table, then lowered her voice when Sprout turned to her with a gasp. "They've grown even more cruel than Eris and Madhea," she whispered.

Sprout skipped over to Feira, leaning into her. "Grandmother, we must go. Mother wanted me to repair the gardens."

"I know, dearest." Feira stroked the child's face, kissing her cheek. "Look at what you've done here." She stood, hands clasped, surveying walls carpeted with brightly colored flowers. "Your magical talents know no bounds." She turned to Dianna, pride for the child in her bright eyes. "This was my grandmother's gift as well. She could make anything grow. The Kyanite's never wanted for food when Kyan ruled The Shifting Sands. In fact, much of our desert landscape was rich with vegetables and grains before it all turned to ruin." She paused, heaving an overly dramatic sigh. "How I wish she was still here with us."

Dianna read Feira's unspoken words loud and clear. *How I wish she was still here with us, but your cruel mother killed her.* If Feira wished to wound Dianna, she'd certainly succeeded, holding her accountable for something beyond her control.

"Grandmother." Sprout tugged on Feira's robe.

"Very well, child." Feira smiled down at the young witch and held out her hand. "Let us go. I must survey the damage as well."

She wasn't sure what to make of Feira's visit. Had she come simply to make Dianna feel bad or was it to warn her about The Seven's plans? Knowing she couldn't count on Feira to help her, should The Seven attack, was even more worrisome. Another reason to fly away from this cursed place.

IT WAS NIGHTFALL WHEN Dianna stepped outside. The sky was cloudy and vast, punctured with the occasional bright star. The full moon hung low, pressing against the horizon like a giant, bloated thumb. She lamented that she'd missed the feel of the sun this day. Then she thought of the Kyanu mortals who'd never been permitted to see it, and her bereavement paled in comparison.

Tan'yi'na wasn't there when Dianna found Lydra under the waterfall, ice crystals forming above her head as she blew out a curtain of what appeared to be diamond dust. The healing witches had gone, and the guards stayed within the recesses of the cave walls.

Lydra let out a howl, flapping her wings like a hatchling bird and clumsily skipping across the thin layer of ice that coated the pond. Tumbling to a stop, Lydra nearly crushed Dianna as she landed beside her, shattering the ice.

Soaked to the bone, Dianna wrung frigid water out of her hair. "I'm happy to see you, too, girl." Dianna playfully pushed Lydra's muzzle away but not before her dragon covered her head to toe in frozen slobber.

Lydra's wounds were almost completely healed. It wouldn't take much magic for her to finish, which meant she would be free to leave these cursed lands, their prejudiced witches, and menacing dragon. It also meant she'd have to leave Sprout, Jae, and Simeon, and that thought made her stomach churn.

Dianna couldn't express the gratitude she felt toward her dragon friend as she leaned against her, wrapping her arms around her neck. She needed friendship in this hostile world, for she wasn't sure who she could trust. She wished she could trust Simeon, but she couldn't see past the confusing mixture of attraction and annoyance she felt toward him. Lydra may be the only true friend Dianna could count on in the Shifting Sands.

Dianna stifled a curse when she felt a familiar heat on her back. She scowled up at Tan'yi'na. How had such a large, menacing creature managed to sneak up on her unnoticed?

What are you doing here? Smoke billowed out of Tan'yi'na's nostrils.

Dianna resisted the urge to fan her face. "I've come to sleep with Lydra." She didn't tell him her true purpose—to heal Lydra and leave.

His golden eyes narrowed. *What of your warm bed and soft furs?*

A low growl rose from Lydra's throat. Dianna pressed a hand to her cool scales. "Easy girl," she whispered. "I'd rather be with my dragon."

Are you afraid Zephyra will slit your throat while you sleep?

Word obviously traveled fast in the Shifting Sands. She plastered on an impassive face, hoping to fool Tan'yi'na, though Dianna had the unnerving suspicion he could see into her very soul. "That, too."

I heard what you did to the pixies. They were Kyan's pets, you know.

The accusation in his tone stirred a cyclone of rage. When Lydra issued a deep rumble, Dianna balled her hands into fists in an attempt to contain her fury.

"What I *know*," she snapped, "is that they were flesh-eating monsters."

He sat on his hind legs, licking his front paw. *What have you against monsters?* he purred, eyeing her through sideways slits.

She threw up her hands, flinging pent-up magic into the sky and wincing as sparks rained down on her. No doubt he'd been goading her. "I'm in no mood to fight with you, Tan'yi'na. I'm tired, and I need rest."

Against her better judgment, she turned her back on him, climbing under Lydra's wing, hiding beneath her pearlescent membranes and trying not to feel like a coward. She sent up a silent prayer to the Elements that he'd leave her be.

What will you do when Lydra is fully recovered? Will you fly away and forget about the cruel witches of Kyanu?

Dianna heaved a frustrated groan. "My brothers need me."

The people of the Shifting Sands need you.

Was he in earnest? After this brute had all but devoured her when she'd first arrived, now he wanted her to stay and help his people?

She crawled out of her hiding place. "I fear my brothers' situations may be dire." Though she wasn't certain, the only way to know for sure was to find them, especially Alec, whose dark world may have already consumed him.

And you do not think the situation here is dire?

"I did not realize you cared about the plight of mortals." It was an unnecessary jab, as the monster had never given her cause to think he was heartless, other than the unfair way he'd treated her.

I have always cared. My goddess was benevolent and kind. She would not have approved of the way her people have been sacrificed.

Dianna crossed her arms, impatiently tapping her foot. "Why doesn't Feira stop them? Why don't *you* stop them?" This world made no sense. The granddaughter of a goddess and a dragon should be able to overpower The Seven, and the rest of Kyanu would bow down to the victors.

The Seven would crush my deity, and she knows it. He sneered. *Her magic is not as strong as it once was, and you have seen what one child can do to me. Do you think I can go up against seven grown witches?*

Dianna looked into Tan'yi'na's golden eyes for a long heartbeat as his words settled in her stomach like a sack of stones. He and Feira were at the mercy of The Seven? How? Feira had mentioned the dark magic she used to keep Tumi alive had weakened her powers. Was it so diminished she couldn't defeat The Seven? Or perhaps they were stronger than she had surmised. In that case, how would she be able to defeat them?

"What makes you think they won't crush *me*?"

Because they don't have a goddess stone, he bellowed in her mind.

She instinctively placed a hand over it. How did he know?

He arched up, then bowed toward her, his serpentine neck swaying with the movement. *Don't try to deny it. I sensed Sindri with you the moment I met you.*

As if on cue, Sindri throbbed like a heartbeat. Curse the stone. She'd been silent almost all day, ignoring Dianna when she questioned her about the dreams she'd had about her brothers.

What good was saving Kyanu mortals from a nest of pixies if you are going to leave them in a den of wolves?

She flinched at the accusatory note in Tan'yi'na's voice. Curse the dragon. He was right. Still, what could she do?

"And what of the other witches of Kyanu? What of the guards?" she asked him. Even if she did defeat the evil mages, what of all the other witches? There had to be thousands in Kyanu. She couldn't defeat them all.

Most witches have mortal family, too, but they are too afraid to go up against The Seven. The guards are mortals born of affluent witch families. Only a few captains are witches, but even they do not possess great magic.

As if sensing her unease, Lydra nuzzled Dianna's back. She stroked her cold snout and smiled when Lydra rewarded her with a deep, satisfied purr. "I am but one witch."

One powerful witch with two goddess stones.

She spun around at that. "I have but one."

And I have another.

Her jaw dropped and her heart thudded. "Where?"

He arched a scaled brow, his lips pulling back in what appeared to be a fanged smile. *It is not far from here. Climb on my back, and I will show you.*

She did her best to still her shaking limbs, for she did not want the dragon to know how much the thought of riding astride him terrified her. He'd chastised her for riding Lydra like a pet, and now he offered his back? She feared their flight would end with her falling to her death or becoming a dragon snack. Why would he forget his grudge so easily and offer her another stone?

She pressed her back against Lydra's neck. "How do I know this isn't a trick?"

"It isn't." Simeon stepped out from behind Tan'yi'na and held out a hand. "We don't have much time. We must move quickly before The Seven discover our plans."

She shook her head. "I never agreed to anything."

Go with them, Sindri urged.

"Finally you speak to me?" She grumbled. "You don't get a say now."

The stone answered with an indignant huff.

Tan'yi'na raised his elongated neck until his massive head blotted out the moon. *With two goddess stones, you can defeat The Seven, then save your oldest brother from Eris.*

"My brother is with Eris?" She clutched her throat with a trembling hand. "How do you know this?"

My deity has seen it in the swirling mists, he answered, *but you cannot defeat the sea goddess with one stone.*

Realization struck her like a mallet to the head. They knew her brother was in trouble, yet they had kept it from her until they could use the information to their advantage. When she shot Simeon a dark look, he had the decency to look at his sandaled feet.

She glared at the golden dragon. "And you will not give me this second stone until I promise to first defeat The Seven?"

Finally, we come to an understanding. The dragon's low, ominous laughter echoed in her head.

"Well, what are we waiting for?" she snapped. Though she hated the feeling of being used, what choice did she have? She needed the other stone to defeat Eris.

When Simeon held out a hand to her, she turned her back on him. "I will ride Lydra." She grabbed her dragon's harness, climbing up on her back. Lydra's wounds had mostly healed, and Tan'yi'na said the stone wasn't far. She'd rather trust her fate with Lydra than the golden menace.

Once she was seated between her dragon's wings, she peered over Lydra's neck at Simeon, who'd already climbed astride Tan'yi'na.

She tossed her braid behind her back. "We're ready."

Tan'yi'na smirked. *Try to keep up, witch.*

She patted her dragon's scales. "Are you ready, girl?"

Lydra answered with a grunt.

When the massive golden monster launched, his wings beating sand down on their heads, her racing heart dropped to her stomach. Keeping up with Tan'yi'na was the least of her worries. She was more concerned with how she was to defeat seven powerful witches, then save her brother from the clutches of an evil goddess.

ALEC ROWED UNTIL HIS muscles cramped and he nearly passed out from exhaustion. A trio of guards finally unlatched his shackles and dragged him to a dank cell in the bowels of the ship. He fell face-first onto a straw pallet, too tired to roll away when someone kicked him in the ribs. He was only barely aware of a rodent squeaking beneath the straw and the shuffling of feet in the cell. He winced when someone flipped him on his back, sitting him up and forcing him to gulp down several ladles of water. Then someone pressed something hard and crumbly into his hand.

"Eat," a familiar voice whispered in his ear, "or you will not survive the next rotation."

His eyes flew open. In the flickering gaze of the low lamplight, he could just make out the hard angles of Ryne's face.

Alec looked down at the piece of bread he clutched, then shoveled it into his mouth, ignoring the throbbing from his injured nose. He barely had the strength to chew, but he managed to swallow the stale crumbs. Then he nearly coughed them back up, hacking into his fist until his lungs burned. A rattle coursed through his chest, one he hadn't felt since before Dianna healed him. He touched his forehead, hoping his damp skin was due to exertion and not fever. Eris's soldiers would throw him overboard rather than risk him infecting the whole crew.

Ryne scooped water out of a bucket and forced Alec to take several more gulps. Though the water was stale, it was cool enough to soothe his parched throat. After Alec's coughing subsided, Ryne found a spot in the corner to eat by himself. Filip sat in another corner, curled into himself, mumbling and crying. Alec squinted at several shadowy figures in a cage across from them. Most appeared to be sleeping, but one he knew to be his rowing partner, for the man's ghost child hovered nearby, softly sobbing while her father silently chewed his bread. The other figure looked like a lump and was so still, Alec thought it perhaps a mound of hay. When the lump moved and a bushy gray beard appeared, picking up stray strands of straw, Alec swallowed a curse. Though he was happy to see Grim alive, he'd hoped the dwarf had escaped. Then again, he couldn't imagine Gorpat's doting father abandoning his child.

Alec hung his head. This was all his fault. If only he hadn't chased after Ryne. At the sound of approaching footsteps, he looked up, peering between his fingers. He didn't recognize this soldier, but his face would be hard to forget. He had the beady eyes and wide nostrils of a boar, and his thick hair was pulled back in two matted braids. When the boar-faced soldier deposited a pile of sacks outside his cage, Alec thought he recognized his pack. The soldier plucked the string on Alec's bow before slinging it over his shoulder. White-hot rage shot through him. Markus had carved that bow for him, and now it was lost.

Grim pressed his face against the cell door, his bulbous nose and round cheeks molding around the bars like clay. "What have you done with my pearl?" he cried. "If you've harmed one hair on her pretty head, you will know the might of a father's wrath."

"Relax, pop." The soldier tossed a thick braid over his shoulder, puffing up his burly chest. "Your pearl is safe for now." His lips pulled back in a wicked smile, revealing a mouthful of rotten teeth. "Unless my goddess decides to use her for carnivus bait."

"Why you cowardly slog!" Grim kicked up straw and rattled the bars of his cage. "Open up and say that to my face!"

The soldier wagged a finger, clucking his tongue. "Do you take me for a fool? I've heard tale of a dwarf's strength."

He went through another sack, his eyes widening when he pulled out a pie.

"Hey!" Grim hollered.

The soldier ignored Grim's protests and shoved the whole pie in his mouth, making grunting, slobbery sounds while he chewed. Alec wonder if he was indeed part pig. The soldier cast the dwarf a smug look before climbing the ladder.

After their captor's boots disappeared above deck, he breathed a sigh of relief. But when that sigh turned into another coughing fit, Alec feared he wouldn't survive another day on Eris's ship.

"Are you okay?"

"I'm fine." Alec glared at Ryne, whose blue skin was ashen beneath the waning glow of the lamplight. Alec suspected he wasn't fine, but he refused to heap any more misery on his friends' backs. This was Alec's problem.

Ryne twirled a bent piece of straw between his fingers, so transfixed with its movement, 'twas as if he was staring into the swirling mists. "You shouldn't have come for me."

Alec couldn't help but gape at Ryne. "What was I to do?" he snapped. "Ignore your hound's cry for help?"

"Yes."

Alec wished he had the strength to march up to Ryne and pummel him. "It's a little too late for that now."

"Well, I'm sorry I got you mixed up in this." Ryne hung his head.

Alec had no response to Ryne's apology, especially as Ryne had much more to be sorry for. For one, his *brootish* behavior toward the dwarves.

"Aye, you should be sorry," Grim said from the neighboring cage, "and to more than just him. My baby girl is going to be carnivus bait, thanks to you."

Ryne's head snapped up. "No, thanks to your thieving, slog-faced cousin." He leaned against a bale of straw, narrowing his eyes in Grim's direction. "The only reason we took the wrong path was because he stole our damn stone."

"Slog-faced! Thieving!" Even in the dim light, Alec could see the dwarf's nose and cheeks turning red. "If I wasn't locked up, I'd throw your worthless blue hide overboard."

Ryne tossed back his head and laughed. "I'd like to see you try it, you stubby little slog."

Alec tensed at the shuffling of boots overhead. "Quiet," he hissed. "Someone's coming." He didn't know whether to be worried or relieved as the boarfaced soldier came back down the ladder, followed by Serpentine Voice.

The latter pushed Boar Face out of the way, yanking a sack from his hands. "Where'd you get the bloody pie?"

"I told you already, it was in one of these sacks." Boar Face kicked a sack, then let out an inhuman squeal, hopping around on one foot. He snatched up the sack and turned it upside-down, his brow furrowing as a stone rolled out.

Alec gasped, Ryne cursed, and Filip looked sheepishly at the stone as it rolled up against the bars of their cage.

The goddess stone!

Boar Face picked up the stone with a sneer. "Who carries a rock in their pack?"

Alec recognized the white leather pack the soldier held as belonging to one of the ice dwellers.

When nobody answered, Alec spoke up. "I do," he lied. "I'm a rock collector." He couldn't let Eris's soldiers know what it was, for he feared the outcome such a powerful stone would have in the hands of an evil goddess.

Boar Face scowled at him, his beady eyes crossing. "Is your brain made of seaweed?"

Alec didn't know which was worse, the soldier keeping the stone or deciding it had no value and throwing it overboard. He shrugged, feigning indifference, though his heart thudded when Serpentine Voice bent over the stone and picked it up. "I simply like smooth stones. That one is especially interesting, as I found it in a pile of troll poo."

The soldier grimaced, dropping the rock as if it was a scalding lump of coal. He kicked it across the floor, and it rolled into a dank and dark corner. Alec prayed the rats wouldn't scurry away with it.

After the soldiers ransacked everyone's packs, taking their food and weapons, they headed back up the ladder.

"Get some sleep," their foggy-eyed captor called over his shoulder. "You will be rowing again in a few hours."

After the muffled sound of their retreating boots died, Ryne raced over to Filip, repeatedly kicking him in the ribs.

Filip curled into a ball, crying out. "Stop! Please!"

"Why?" Ryne hollered between grunts. "Why?!" He kicked Filip again.

Filip rolled away. "Stop!" He shielded his face with his hands. "Or I'll scream for the guards."

Ryne lowered his leg, panting like a wounded animal. "Explain yourself," he said between gritted teeth.

"I had more right to it than Ven." Filip wiped his tear-stained face while cradling his stomach. "That stone should have been passed to *my* grandfather, the eldest son, not Ven's grandmother, who was my grandfather's youngest sister."

Ryne threw up his hands. "So you thought you had right to steal the stone because of a quarrel that happened three generations ago?"

"I was not stealing it." Filip sniffled, smearing a trail of snot across his dirty sleeve. "I was returning it to its rightful heir."

Ryne's face hardened. "Then why not tell us? Why let us think the dwarves stole it?"

Filip turned his gaze down to the straw beneath his bare feet. "Because I knew you wouldn't let me keep it."

"You *gnull's* hairy ass! Because of your greed, Ven and Luc are dead, and we'll be joining them soon." Ryne kicked Filip several times in rapid succession.

Filip curled into himself, whimpering but otherwise making no attempt to fight back.

When Alec thought he heard the crack of bone, he stumbled to a standing position. "Enough!" he growled. "Before Eris's soldiers throw you both overboard." Though he was also furious with Filip, an ice dweller with broken bones would do them no good. If they were to have any chance at escape, they'd need help from every able body.

Ryne stalked to the opposite corner of his cell, while his bloodied companion cried softly.

Alec glowered at Ryne, waiting for him to say something—anything.

Ryne looked at Alec through hooded eyes. "Why do you stare at me like that, land dweller?"

Alec nodded toward the dwarf in the other cage. "You owe Grim an apology."

"Gnull bollocks," Ryne answered, turning from them both.

Alec didn't know if he was angrier with Filip the thief or Ryne the fool. "You accused his family of stealing, and now they are prisoners, thanks to you."

"I didn't ask them to come for me," Ryne grumbled.

Alec arched a brow, rage threatening to boil over like a bubbling cauldron. "That is your response?"

"You heard the guard. We only have a few hours to rest." Ryne fluffed the hay beneath his head like a pillow before rolling onto his back and closing his eyes.

"You hard-faced son of a siren." Alec was having trouble breathing, much less talking. He coughed into his fist, summoning the strength to force out the words. "I'd like to apologize on behalf of this stubborn *broot*."

Ryne's chest rose and fell as if he was asleep. Though they were all sore and exhausted, surely Ryne hadn't fallen asleep that quickly.

Grim leaned into his bars with a sigh. "You don't need to, son."

"I do." Alec swallowed his tears. "If I hadn't been stupid enough to think his life mattered, we'd be on our way to Aya-Shay. I'm sorry."

"I'm sorry, too, son. I should've never let you go after this underserving slog. Lesson learned." Grim cleared his throat. "When the moment presents itself when we can escape, I will not risk our lives for him again."

"There is no escaping from the sea witch." The ghost's hollow words eerily echoed through the hull, as if she was speaking in a dream.

Grim frowned at the spirit. "We shall see about that."

The spirit disappeared like fading smoke, then reappeared again. "Even if you do escape her, there are still her dragon, sirens, pixies, and carnivus plants. Believe me, my father and I would have retrieved my body long ago if we didn't fear they'd sink our boat."

Alec couldn't help but gape at the girl. "Retrieve your body?"

"Eris keeps my body prisoner on her volcanic island." The the glow around her faded and reappeared like a flickering candle. "She took it when I was a tot, forcing my spirit to wander the earth."

Alec scratched his head. Was this ghost dead or not? "I don't understand."

The girl's father cleared his throat, piercing Alec with dark, haunted eyes. "As punishment for killing one of her broot whales, she took my daughter's body and discarded her spirit as a reminder to other hunters."

The room went eerily quiet, except for the occasional scurrying of the rats and the sound of splashing waves outside. Alec had heard tales of Eris's cruelty, but stealing the body of a babe and forcing her spirit to wander the earth in a state between life and death was harsher than even he could have imagined.

Alec finally spoke up, wishing to clear the air of the awkward silence. "My brother was cursed by Madhea for hunting."

The girl floated over to Alec. "I'm so sorry. What happened to him?"

Alec tried not to be unnerved by the ghoulish figure staring down at him and forced himself to meet her eyes. She was uncommonly pretty, with tapered eyes that gleamed like golden jewels, a pert nose, and long, black hair. Had she been flesh and blood, she'd have many suitors.

"My brother broke the curse," he answered.

The spirit gasped, her glow pulsing brighter. "How?" she begged, floating closer, the desperation in her golden eyes nearly enough to break his heart.

A thought occurred to him. "Tell me something, spirit. Are you able to pick up objects?"

She jerked back. "My name is not Spirit."

"Forgive me." With the exception of his mother and sister, he'd never learned how to talk to females. "It's been a trying day. What is your name?"

She floated so close he could feel a strange energy from her aura. Goose-flesh rose on his neck and arms. 'Twas the same feeling he'd gotten many times when he thought his father's ghost was near.

"My name is Mari. My father is Khashka." She indicated the bald old man in the other cage. "And no, I'm not able to pick up objects." She stomped the air like a toddler on the verge of a tantrum. "Are you going to tell me how your brother broke the curse?"

"'Tis a long story." Alec glanced at the corner where the rock had rolled. "But he had help from a stone much like that one."

When Mari turned toward it, it began to glow a soft white, like a wick had been lit from within.

Khashka clutched the bars of his cage. "How does it do that?"

"Magic," Ryne answered.

Alec glared at Ryne, who'd obviously been pretending to be asleep. The blue broot sat up and glared at him.

"It talks." Mari's voice sounded as if her words had been carried away by the wind.

"No, it does not talk," Ryne grumbled, irritated.

Alec wished Ryne would go back to sleep and spare them all his dark mood. "It talked to my sister, Dianna."

Ryne shook his head, snickering. "But she is a powerful witch. That is why she can hear its voice."

Alec held out a silencing hand when Mari floated over to the stone, her gaze transfixed on the pulsing glow, pulled to it as if by some unseen force.

"What does it say, daughter?" Khashka asked.

"It's a woman. She is asking me to pick her up."

Khashka let go of his bars. "Tell her you can't."

Mari looked at Alec, her lower lip trembling. "She is saying I can."

"Try it, Mari," Alec encouraged. "Try picking up the stone." He'd already seen one stone wield powerful magic, saving both his and Markus's lives. Could this stone help them escape?

The prisoners collectively gasped when the spirit lifted the stone with ease, holding the glowing orb in both hands.

"Oh, heavenly Elements!" Her eyes widened as she stared at her treasure. "I haven't held anything in a very long while."

Khashka rattled the bars. "Is she still talking to you?"

Mari nodded. "Her name is Aletha. She says she is the daughter of the fallen goddess Kyan."

Khashka's mouth fell open. "Child, you are holding a goddess stone in your hands."

"A goddess stone?" Grim clutched his bars while gaping at Mari, then at Khashka. "I thought those were only fable."

Khashka laughed. "Apparently not."

Mari floated toward Alec's cage, cradling the stone as if she held a newborn babe. "She wants me to press the stone against the bars."

Alec didn't know where he found the strength, but he got to his feet, scrambling toward her. "Do it, Mari."

When she pressed the stone against the bars, the metal melted like hot wax. Khashka scurried away from his cell door, waking the sleeping prisoners.

"Now ours, Mari," Khashka called. "Hurry, before the guards return."

Once the bars on both cages were melted, prisoners rushed toward their packs, removing blades from hidden compartments.

Ryne broke off a piece of partially melted metal from his door, slapping his hand with the long rod. "Can you melt off more bars, Mari?"

She broke apart several rods, and the prisoners gladly took their makeshift weapons.

Alec clutched a thick bar like a lifeline. 'Twas no bow and arrow, but it would do. "Now what?" he asked Grim.

The dwarf pulled a heavy hammer from his sack with a sinister gleam in his eyes and swung it over his head. "Now we fight."

Chapter Eleven

DIANNA HELD TIGHTLY to Lydra, relishing the feel of wind whipping through her hair. They followed Tan'yi'na across the sand. He flew low, the canopy of clouds overhead obscuring his golden hues, making him look like a shadow skimming across the ground.

Her limbs froze when they approached a crater in the earth. It appeared as if a giant arrow had punctured the sand, leaving a deep, gaping hole in its wake.

"No girl!" Dianna screamed, pulling back on Lydra when Tan'yi'na disappeared down the hole.

Her warning came too late. Lydra tucked her wings against her sides and dove after the other dragon.

She squinted against the onslaught of cool wind that rushed around her. They were falling down a black hole, descending into a pit which she feared was a trap set by Tan'yi'na.

"Oh, heavenly Elements!" she cried, struggling to catch her breath. "Lydra, where are you going?"

She heard a powerful boom below. Lydra opened her wings, flapping until she landed on the ground with a *thud*.

The rocky pit was lit with the soft glow of torchlight, and she saw clearly enough to discern they were at the bottom of a deep pit.

Simeon had dismounted Tan'yi'na and was walking toward Lydra. He didn't seem intimidated by her low growl as he held up a hand to Dianna.

"May I help you dismount?" he asked.

So shook up was she that she numbly let him help her down. Once she was safely on solid ground, she spun a slow circle, struggling to make sense of her environment.

The pit was attached to a low tunnel, barely large enough for two people to pass through shoulder-to-shoulder and certainly not big enough to fit either dragon. "Where are we?"

"The mines," Simeon answered.

Tan'yi'na nodded toward the tunnel. *You and Simeon must make the rest of the journey alone. Lydra and I will wait for your return.*

She warily eyed Simeon, who stared back at her with a grin so wide it was comical.

He held out an arm. "As I've said before, I won't bite." He leaned toward her, his whisper hot and heavy in her ear. "Unless you beg me to."

Dianna rolled her eyes. "I shall never beg for anything from you."

"Come now." The mirth in his eyes vanished. "It was only a jest."

She reluctantly took his arm, knowing she'd rather hold onto him than risk slipping on the slick rocks. "I don't find your jokes amusing."

"I'm sorry." He snatched a torch from its cradle. "We must hurry. We've quite a hike."

Refusing to rely solely on him for guidance, she grabbed a torch, too, though she wasn't looking forward to traversing the bowels of the Shifting Sands. Her fear of descending into the abyss almost overshadowed the butterflies swarming in her stomach as she dug her fingers into Simeon's smooth, bare skin, the hard muscles refusing to yield. The heat from his arm radiated through her fingers and flamed her entire body like wildfire.

Elements save her, this man's mere presence made her knees turn to porridge. She'd always considered herself strong and fiercely independent. She could only imagine the effect he had on weaker females, especially mortal girls. She did her best to clear her thoughts of him and focus on the rough terrain. The rocky tunnel they traversed was steep and slick. She nearly lost her footing numerous times. If it hadn't been for Simeon's hold on her, she would have slid down the slippery rocks, chafing her backside.

The air was cooler below, but it was also stagnant, making her strain to fill her lungs with each breath. This cavern should have lacked life so far below the earth, yet she knew people lived here, for she could see signs of them in the images of dragons and people carved into the walls.

The dark tunnel, lit with only a few distant torches, was made even more eerie by a low hum that reverberated off the walls, making her feel she was in the bowels of a musical pipe. As they traversed potholes and ridges, she had to cling even tighter to Simeon's arm. The silence between them was unnerving, so much so that she was forced to make conversation. She struggled for a topic, not knowing what to say to a man who both excited and aggravated her.

"How is it you have so much magic and your twin has none?" she finally blurted, then regretted bringing up a topic which probably pained him.

His silence was like an invisible wall between them. She cursed herself for asking such a personal question.

"There are some who say I stole her magic in the womb." The words tumbled out of his mouth.

"What a horrible thing to say." She chanced a look at him, hating the haunted expression in his golden gaze. "You don't believe it?"

When his eyes misted with a sheen of tears, she wanted to kick her own arse.

"My mother and father are powerful mages," he said, "and Jae is the only one of my siblings without magic."

She struggled for something, anything, to say. "There could be other reasons." She slipped on a rock and dropped her torch. It fell to the stones with a *clank*, its light extinguished. She breathed a sigh of relief when he caught her.

"I have spent too many years obsessing over those other reasons." The regret in his voice was palpable. "Do you know what Jae means in the ancient tongue? It means 'without light.' It is a common name given to non-magical children by their prejudiced, magical parents."

Dianna choked back tears as she thought of the girl Madhea had murdered. What a tragic life she must have lived while Jae's natural parents showered Dianna with love and adoration. Dianna welcomed the silence that followed, wishing she'd left well enough alone. She jerked Simeon to a standstill when she heard the familiar flapping of wings *swoosh* above her head. Sirens teeth!

She looked at Simeon, unnerved by the way his torchlight cast eerie shadows across his normally boyish features. "What was that?"

He shrugged, continuing down the tunnel. "Probably just a mine pixie."

"A pixie?" she snapped. Why hadn't he warned her about them?

"Relax." He chuckled. "The mine pixies are tame, a little mischievous, but they don't eat people."

So there were two breeds of pixies in the Shifting Sands? "How is it they are tamed?" She fanned her head as several squealing, dark objects darted past her. She didn't care that they were supposedly tame. Her chest tightened with fear.

"They obey Rení the Wise," he said, helping her navigate a large crater.

She tried to sidestep the hole without slipping. "He's a miner?"

"He's an earth speaker, an ancient one." He motioned for her to duck under a spiky column jutting from the ceiling. Such a jagged spike could drive a fatal hole through a man's skull.

"How ancient?"

"Some say he's older than Dafuar and Odu."

"And he lives down here?"

Simeon nodded. "He was cast down by The Seven years ago for siding with the mortals when the new laws were formed."

She'd heard of earth speakers from Dafuar. They were the bridges between mortal and magical worlds. The Elements gave them premonitions of things to come, which indeed made earth speakers very wise. Like all witches, though, earth speakers born below Ice Mountain had to be sacrificed to Madhea, so she had never knowingly met one.

"Rení keeps the stone hidden." He nodded toward a faint light at the end of the tunnel. "We must convince him to let you have it."

"Of course," she said, not feeling the slightest bit of confidence in her persuasive abilities. She certainly was no Simeon.

A cluster of screaming winged creatures flew past, one of them yanking a strand of hair out of her head.

"Ouch!" She swatted the menace away, then rubbed her sore scalp. "You're sure these pixies are not like the others?"

He shooed away a demon that buzzed his ear. "They've been cut off from their kin for hundreds of years."

She was confused. She'd thought all of the Shifting Sand's tunnels were connected. "This tunnel doesn't lead to the others?"

"No." He swatted another creature.

"Then how do the miners access food and water?"

"There are many springs down here." He pointed to a stream of water that ran down the stone wall beside him. "And they grow some of their food. The rest is dropped to them."

"Dropped? The way we came in?"

His boyish features hardened. "The only way."

Surely not even The Seven were cruel enough to banish an entire society to a stagnant pit. "So these miners are cut off from the rest of Kyanu?"

His golden eyes darkened. "They are born here, and they die here. Only the babes born with magic are allowed to leave, taken from their parents by The Seven. The rest are forced to become miners."

"How sad," she mumbled, not knowing what else to say. She couldn't imagine being born in a stagnant hole, never permitted to feel the sun's warm rays or smell fresh air.

They walked to the end of the tunnel in silence. When they arrived at a luminous cavern, she was filled with a mixture of shock and relief. The ceiling, at least thrice the height of Tan'yi'na, glowed with what appeared to be thousands of sparkling stars. The place was bustling with people dressed in crudely stitched breeches and thick tunics. Men, women, and children, all with grayish skin and dark eyes, worked at various stations. Some loaded golden rocks from heavy carts onto pallets, others weighed and counted sparkling gems, and a cluster of old men and women sat at low tables, examining each jewel through thick-looking glasses. These Kyanite's were shorter and thicker than those she'd seen above, and they all had a stoop to their shoulders. Some of the older miners were bent so low, they looked like they had broken arrows for spines.

When Simeon led her out of the shadowy tunnel and down the stone steps into the cavern, the bustle of the crowd died down as everyone turned to stare. Then the crowd broke into a chorus of low whispers.

She grabbed Simeon's hand, squeezing hard.

He squeezed back. "It's okay," he whispered. "They know you are a friend."

An old, toothless man hobbled up to them, bowing over his gnarled cane before Dianna. "Welcome, my queen, to the dragon's den."

She cast Simeon a wary glance and shifted uncomfortably as the rest of the miners followed suit. She hated the looks of pain and discomfort on their faces while they stared reverently up at her, as if she were the key to their freedom.

"Thank you for the warm welcome, but I am no queen. Please rise," she called.

The miners looked at one another as if seeking confirmation. A few of them stood, then helped others straighten. 'Twas then she realized, if she was able to defeat The Seven, she *would* be the key to their freedom. But Tan'yi'na had just asked her to fight the evil witches. Could the miners have known of their plan already?

The crooked old man scratched the back of his head, the lines around his eyes deepening as he squinted at her. "But you are a queen, for Rení the Wise has said so."

She vehemently shook her head. "He's wrong."

When the crowd collectively gasped, she feared she'd offended them.

"Rení the Wise is never wrong." The old man's mouth tightened. "You have the proud bearing of a queen and strong magic." He waved her forward. "He is waiting."

Dianna held tighter to Simeon's hand, feeling slightly self-conscious when her hand started to sweat, but she refused to let go.

"It all will be well," Simeon said. "I promise." When he slanted a sideways smile at her, it somehow emboldened her. She surprisingly believed him.

The crowd parted, opening a path toward another tunnel at the end of the cavern. Thankfully, this one appeared to be much wider than the one she'd just descended. Doing her best to keep her smile in place, she walked through the crowd. She was a head taller than most of the miners, though she suspected it was mostly due to their stooped postures. Were they all injured or had their spines grown that way, like a bent tree trunk twisting and turning toward the light?

She leaned into Simeon, taking comfort in the warmth and strength that radiated off him. "Why is this place called the dragon's den?"

"This was once Tan'yi'na's home." He alternated between smiling and waving at the miners, and speaking out of the side of his mouth. "Until The Seven closed off the north entrance."

"Why would they take away his home?"

"Because dragons are overly fond of gold and jewels, but The Seven are even more so," he said with a chuckle.

Realization washed over Dianna. The golden dragon had loathed her since she'd arrived in his desert home, then suddenly he stopped threatening her. Now he wanted her to defeat The Seven. Did Tan'yi'na care about the plight of the Shifting Sands mortals, or did he simply want his jewels back?

"Didn't Tan'yi'na fight back?" she asked.

"At first, but even Tan'yi'na knows treasure is no good when humanity is on the precipice of annihilation."

Or else Tan'yi'na knew he was no match for seven powerful witches. She felt momentarily guilty for thinking the dragon only cared about his treasure, even though he had been inclined to think the worst of her from day one.

"This way, my queen," the old stooped man called to them. "The Wise One is waiting."

Though the tunnel was much wider and brighter than the one that had led them to the cavern, she refused to let go of Simeon's hand. The crooked man walked at a slog's pace, finally leading them through a narrow archway into a narrower tunnel that dead-ended beneath a cloak of shadows. After the old man tapped his cane on the wall three times in rapid succession, the wall crumbled to the ground in a cacophony of rock and dust.

She coughed, choking and waving in front of her face to clear the smoke. The old man stepped over the rubble.

They followed him, and she found herself in a chamber not much bigger than her sleeping quarters. She jumped at noise behind her, surprised when the rocks and debris rolled back into place, sealing the gaping hole in the wall.

"An enchantment to keep this chamber hidden from The Seven," Simeon whispered.

Dianna recognized the mist that fanned across the floor, obscuring her feet. 'Twas similar to the swirling mists in Feira's chamber. They descended from a raised structure of stones in the center of the room that reminded her of a small, steaming volcano. A decrepit gray man sat on a throne carved of stone and jewels. He looked older than dirt and more frail than Feira's invalid husband.

Clothed in a sack-like robe, he was hunched over in his chair. White tufts of hair, wrinkly skin, and toad-like spots made him look as if he'd died there years ago. Even more unusual was that one side of his body was completely distorted, his features sliding downward like a melting puddle of wax. She wondered if he'd been injured by a vindictive goddess. Of one thing she was certain, Simeon was right—Rení the Wise was very old.

"Wise One." The crooked man, bowed. "I present to you Dianna, daughter of the Sky Goddess, Madhea."

Rení slowly lifted a hand with a feeble grunt, waving her forward. "Come." He rasped, his voice as rough as old wood. "Sit."

Dianna refused to let go of Simeon's hand, reluctantly sitting in a chair beside the earth-speaker while Simeon knelt beside her. She stared into the earth speaker's eyes, which looked as if they were covered in a thick haze of cloudy ice.

She tensed when the man took her face in a calloused hand. "Strong witch." Spittle flew from his lips as he spoke. "Strong magic."

She fought the urge to pull away as he traced the bridge of her nose and then her brows with the tip of a gnarled finger. He skimmed her shoulder and neck, stopping at the source of the pounding in her chest.

"Strong heart," he said. "Strong love for brothers."

She swallowed a lump of regret and fear at the mention of her brothers. How had he known?

Simeon cleared his throat. "Rení the Wise, our deity has seen in the swirling mists that Dianna will battle The Seven."

"I see, too." Rení pointed to the mists that swirled in front of him.

"But our deity says Dianna needs the sacred stone to defeat them," Simeon said.

Rení frowned.

Would Rení deny her the stone? She feared she couldn't save her brothers without it.

Simeon flashed her a knowing wink. "Wise One, she cannot hope to defeat The Seven without the sacred stone."

She shifted, feeling a strange tingling over her shoulder. When she looked into Simeon's eyes, she thought she saw starlight.

"Please let her have it," he begged Rení.

As the tingling intensified, blowing past Dianna's arm like a gentle breeze, she recognized the sensation. 'Twas magic. Simeon's magic. He was using his power of persuasion.

Rení sighed, then held out a hand. "Hold."

Simeon released her hand and nudged her toward the old man. She stared into the old man's cloudy eyes while reluctantly reaching for him.

It felt like she held onto a bird's wing, so frail was he, so she was not prepared for the blunt force of his magic shooting through her. She stilled, a prisoner in his grasp, unable to pull away.

"Heart kind," he said with a crooked smile. "But heart conflicted, too."

She flushed, fearing he was talking about her feelings for Simeon and wishing he'd let her go. "Oh, I-I don't think...."

"Love weaken magic," he interrupted, shooting Simeon a dark look. "Love may be undoing."

"I'll remember that," she said shakily. "But my brother is in trouble, and I can't help him without your stone."

Much to her relief, he finally let go of her hand, but she froze when he pointed a crooked finger at her.

"Must stop Eris sacrifice," he rasped.

Panic seized her chest. "Eris is going to sacrifice my brother?"

"No." Rení shook his head. "Eris sacrifice spirit."

She searched the old man's face. "I-I don't understand."

"Eris find new body. Eris become more powerful."

A new body? This "wise" man made no sense.

Simeon leaned forward. "Please let Dianna have the stone, so she can stop her."

Rení clucked his tongue. "Stone not mine to give."

"Then how does she get it?" Simeon asked.

Rení pointed up. "Ask stone."

She squinted at the ceiling, which appeared to be coated in diamond dust, like the cavern. "Where is it?"

Rení pointed higher.

Simeon stood. "He means it's up there."

She stood beside him, searching for any sign of the stone. There must have been thousands of little nooks and crevices in the walls leading up to the dazzling ceiling. The rock could be hidden in any one of them. "How do I get up there? I'm no climber."

"Pixies take you," Rení said, puckering his lips and blowing a breathy whistle.

She shrank back when hundreds of winged creatures emerged from the crevices and swooped down on them like falling debris. When they swarmed her like a hive of bees, she swatted them.

"Get off me!" she cried. "Simeon, help!"

Simeon tried to shoo the demons away, but there were too many.

"Pixies only way," Rení said.

"No." She buried her face against Simeon's chest. "Forget it." Relief swept over her when he shielded her from the monsters.

"Dianna, please," he soothed. "Let them take you."

"Are you in earnest? What if they drop me?"

He tucked a stray strand of hair behind her ear. "They won't drop you."

She got lost in his gold eyes for a moment before pushing away from him. "Don't use your magic on me."

"Stone not come down. You go up."

She glared at Rení. How could she trust him or his pixies?

"Look at me," Simeon commanded. "Calm yourself."

Perhaps he was right, and she should trust the pixies. "You promise?" she asked, though somewhere in the back of her mind, she suspected he was using magic to persuade her.

"Yes." He waved at the buzzing monsters that hovered over her head. "Please let the pixies take you to the stone."

She relented. On one hand, she was angry with herself for caving into Simeon so easily. On the other, she was relieved she would no longer have to continue this fight.

The stone in her vest pocket warmed and throbbed like a heartbeat. *My sister is up there. I sense her.*

"Ah," she mumbled, "so you're finally talking again." She wondered if Sindri didn't trust her or if she only made appearances when she had something to gain.

Before she realized what has happening, hundreds of winged creatures grabbed onto her vest and arms, lifting her off the ground. She was too frightened to look down as they ascended higher and higher, until they reached the ceiling. There was a shelf with a mound covered in what appeared to be green snake moss. She had seen snake moss in her village of Adolan. It was so thick and impenetrable, the only way to get rid of it was to burn it.

Not trusting the pixies, she grabbed onto the ledge and dug her feet into narrow crevices beneath it. Though the little demons still held onto her back, their wings buzzing angrily, at least she'd have something to hold onto should they tire of supporting her.

Neriphene, Sindri's cry echoed in Dianna's head. *My beloved sister, it is me, Sindri.*

The moss lit up in a brilliant emerald green. *Sindri, is it really you? I'd lost hope of ever seeing my sisters again.*

The stone in Dianna's pocked trembled like a feeble branch in a wind storm. *I am here.*

The moss turned from green to red, then faded to black. *This witch looks like the ice bitch.*

It is her daughter, Dianna, Sindri answered. *A good witch, as far as I can tell.*

"As far as you can tell?" she snapped. The crevice she'd wedged her foot in gave way, and she lost purchase. "What else must I do to prove myself?"

Saving the mortals from the voracious pixies was a start. Sindri's stone pulsed with each word. *I am simply being cautiously optimistic.*

"Neriphene," Dianna implored, "I need you to help us overthrow The Seven. They have imprisoned the mortals of the Shifting Sands, forcing them into slavery."

And you care about these mortals? Neriphene asked skeptically.

Another foot gave way, and she was forced to dig her knees into the wall. "I do."

There is something you aren't telling me, Neriphene accused. Her sister remained suspiciously silent.

"Eris has taken my brother captive," Dianna ground out, struggling to hold on while the pixies made sibilant hissing sounds. "I'm afraid she'll kill him if I don't stop her, but I can't do it alone."

And who is to say you won't wield our power for evil?

Gah! Neriphene was even less trusting than Sindri. "I won't." Sweat beaded Dianna's brow as her knees began to slide. "I swear it."

Neriphene pulsed a deep red. *I need a blood promise.*

Why didn't I think of that? Sindri giggled. *You were always so clever, sister.*

"A blood promise?" Dianna didn't like the sound of that. She shrieked when a pixie bit her ear. "Ouch!" Her hand flew to her ear, which throbbed with a vengeance. Elements curse that little demon!

Smear the blood across your heart and repeat after me, Neriphene commanded.

She rubbed her hand on her chest, then grabbed the ledge again, alarmed at the amount of blood coating her fingers.

I, Dianna, daughter of Madhea. Neriphene pulsed green, then blue.

She rolled her eyes. "I do not consider her my mother."

Say it!

She heaved an exasperated sigh. If the pixies didn't drive her to madness, the stones certainly would. "I, Dianna, daughter of Madhea."

Vow to only harness the magic of the goddess stones for the destruction of darkness and in the defense of light. I will not let my vanity or sense of self-preservation prevent me from protecting the innocent from harm. I offer the blood of my body to the Elements in recompense should I break my vow.

After she repeated the words, a tingly feeling originated in her chest and spread outward. She peered under her tunic, shocked to see a slight discoloration around the flesh where she'd smeared the blood.

"What happened to my heart?"

Nothing. Neriphene chuckled. *So long as you don't break your vow.*

Dianna stifled a groan. "Will you come out now?"

Yes, the stone answered. It pulsed red, then orange.

Dianna arched back when the snake moss caught fire, then disappeared in a cloud of smoke, revealing a pale stone that looked much like Sindri.

She fanned her face, choking on the acrid smoke before reaching for the stone.

Place me in your pocket beside my sister, Neriphene commanded.

When she slipped the stone inside her vest, they both glowed white, warming each other. She was slightly envious of the sisters and thought of the love she and Jae could have shared had her sister survived. Jae's death was even more reason for her to defeat The Seven and the goddesses, for she couldn't stomach the thought of another mortal dying at the hands of vengeful magic.

UNDER A CLOAK OF DARKNESS, Alec and the others tiptoed after Mari. She hovered above the guard sitting on a bench, going through a stolen pack. He stopped long enough to swat her, completely missing the dwarf who clubbed him across the back of his head with a sickening crunch. The soldier was right about one thing; dwarves were strong.

Alec grimaced as he slinked past the guard who had fallen face-first onto the floor. The back of his skull was split open, his brains oozing onto the wooden planks. He felt no remorse for the soldier. 'Twas the same boar-faced *broot* who'd called Gorpat carnivus bait. He knew Grim took paternal satisfaction in splitting him open.

Alec slipped his quiver out of the dead man's grip and strung his bow. He notched an arrow just as two burly guards came down the steps. Grim stepped from the shadows and clubbed one in the stomach. Alec unleashed an arrow, striking the second guard in the throat. *Markus would be proud*, Alec thought. Khashka and his men dragged the soldiers into the shadows.

"Save a few for me," Ryne grumbled.

Alec ignored him, notching another arrow as they silently crept up the narrow ladder.

When they reached the top, Grim cracked the hatch, peering out onto the deck. He quickly shut it. "There are too many."

Alec was not to be deterred. "We either die fighting them here, or we die when we reach Eris."

"No. They are wearing armor, and they outnumber us three to one. We need more men."

He pushed the others back and pointed to another ladder leading down. "I think that's where the rowers are. If we free them first, we have a better chance of defeating the soldiers above deck."

Alec and the others reluctantly agreed. "So what do we do?" Alec asked.

"I will go down and frighten them," Mari answered.

Grim shook his head. "They won't be frightened of you, child. They all know you exist." He held up a finger, looking as if the wheels in his brain were churning out a brilliant plan. "Fetch a dead soldier," he said to Ryne and Filip.

They walked away, mumbling, then returned with the man Grim had split open.

"Good," Grim said. "Now throw him down the ladder."

They tossed the body. Alec shuddered when it landed with a sickening *thump* and a crash, then cringed when he heard loud screaming, followed by the familiar sound of steel slicing through the air.

No sooner had the soldiers raced up the ladder than Alec and Grim disposed of them with clubs and arrows.

Grim called down to the rowers, and they answered back all was clear. After the rowers were freed of their shackles, they armed themselves with swords.

"Now we fight." Grim winked. "Stay behind me, boy," he said to Alec as they climbed back up the ladder.

The soldiers were already descending from above deck, no doubt alarmed when the vessel had slowed. Soon, all was chaos. Alec dropped his bow and arrow in favor of a club, doing his best to fight off the enemy, though he was no match for their strength. If it hadn't been for Grim, Alec would have succumbed to a number of soldiers. The dwarf was fast and powerful, clubbing their kneecaps with sickening crunches.

A platoon of soldiers poured into the hull, wielding giant axes and flaming arrows. He had barely enough time to defend himself against one enemy when another would attack, pushing him farther from Grim. Ryne and Filip had been backed into a corner, steel striking steel. Filip was losing strength, badly bleeding from a wound in his side.

When Serpentine Voice knocked his sword from his hand and forced him against the hull with his axe held high, Alec knew there was no escape. Grim was too far away to come to his aid, and Ryne was fighting for his life. Filip had slid down the wall with a sword protruding from his gut. Time slowed as his opponent charged, the axe descending toward Alec's forehead. Of one thing he was grateful: his death would be swift, for the gleaming metal was sharpened to a razor-sharp edge.

The ship tilted as if they'd struck a wave. An odd breeze tickled his nape when the soldier fell over a barrel that had come loose, his axe falling from his hand.

Fight, boy, the breeze whispered. Odd how that voice sounded like his dead father. His imagination had to be playing tricks on him.

Alec reached for the axe as the soldier jumped to his feet. When his opponent lunged for him, Alec ducked and swung the blade into the man's gut. He lurched forward with a grunt, then glared at Alec with that one cloudy eye. He jerked the axe out of his stomach, groaning as blood and guts spilled out. Alec fell back against the hull, screaming when his enemy raised his weapon, then buried it in the wall beside his head before falling to his knees. When he kicked the soldier hard, he fell on his back, gaping up at the ceiling, the swirling mist in his eye turning a cold, stale gray.

Alec snatched the axe out of the wall and rushed toward the fighting. The bulk of the soldiers had pushed back the group of islanders surrounding Khashka and his spirit child.

As the soldiers were about to reach her father, Mari cried out. "Stop!" Her eerie, hollow voice ricocheted in Alec's head and the walls and barrels rattled as if a giant shook them.

The soldiers flattened against the planks, dropping their weapons. Alec wiped sweat off his brow and exchanged a shocked look with Grim. How had she done that? He'd little time to contemplate what had happened before Khashka's group raced through the ship, driving their swords into the chests of the hapless soldiers. Though cries for mercy rent the air, the slaves showed them no compassion, cutting down every last one.

"Elements save their souls," Alec whispered, wiping blood on his tunic, and followed Grim above deck, unable to witness any more carnage.

Grim motioned for him to hide behind a pallet of crates while four nervous soldiers tried to wrestle a small boat off the deck.

"Ready?" Grim whispered.

"But they are leaving," Alec said. "Can't we spare them?"

"And risk them alerting the sea witch?"

He knew the dwarf was right, loath though he was to shoot a retreating man. He notched an arrow while Grim slowly snuck toward them. The soldiers' backs were to them. When Grim was in place, Alec fired off one arrow, then another, both hitting their marks. They dropped like baby sparrows, falling from a tree. Grim finished off the other two, clubbing them so hard, they were flung overboard from the blunt force.

"We need to find my pearl," Grim said as Alec joined him.

They ran around to the stern. The sleeping giant was being towed on a huge wooden barge, her arms and legs bound in thick chains, darts protruding all over her. So this was how they controlled her? By shooting her up with sleeping darts? Alec feared the giant would have a brutal awakening.

"I need to get to her," Grim cried. "Help me." He grabbed a cord of thick rope, twisting it into a noose around the ropes that had been fastened to the underside of a cannon, stretching from the stern to Gorpat's barge. Then he put his hands through the noose and tugged. "It's sturdy. Give me a push," he said to Alec.

He helped the dwarf onto the railing of the ship, then pushed him off. He sailed down the rope, landing on his daughter's foot, then began picking darts out of her legs. "My poor pearl," he bemoaned, flinging darts into the ocean.

The giant stirred but did not wake as Grim walked up the length of her body, plucking needles out of her, like Alec and Markus had once done when Alec found a stray hound that had been poked full of porcupine quills. The hound died of fever two days later. He sent up a prayer to the Elements that Gorpat would recover.

The other slaves came above deck. Khashka was clearly in charge, giving orders as if he'd been manning ships his whole life. Then again, Alec knew little about him. Mayhap he had.

The slaves alternated between hooting and hollering, patting Khashka on the back, and dropping bodies overboard. Alec fought the urge to cringe with each *thunk* and *splash*, as they bounced off the sides of the ship on the way down.

From the corner of his eye, Alec saw one of Khashka's kinsmen approaching. Though Alec knew him to be a man, his small, wiry physique and cropped hair made him look more like a child.

"Nice work with the arrows, son."

Alec shifted uncomfortably, feeling like a flower beneath the wilting heat of the midday sun under the man's assessing gaze. "Thanks. I had a good tutor."

"Thorne," the man said.

Alec took his outstretched hand, surprised at his firm grip. "Alec."

"Alec, I have heard from your blue companion that your sister is Madhea's daughter." He arched a thin brow. "Is this true?"

"Aye, 'tis true," His shoulders slumped when he thought about his sister, hoping her dragon protector was keeping her safe. "But Dianna's not like the ice witch."

Thorne arched back as if Alec had been infected with the plague. "You are brave to call your goddess a witch."

"Madhea is no goddess of mine," he grumbled.

Thorne eyed Alec closely. "Is it also true Dianna has flown Madhea's ice dragon to the Shifting Sands?"

He was forced to look away under the penetrating weight of Thorne's stare. "Aye, to find a safe haven for our people."

Thorne smiled, revealing a mouthful of decaying teeth. "May the Elements guide her to safety."

"Thank you, but she is a smart witch. I'm sure she will prevail." Alec was proud of his sister, not just of her magical abilities, but her kindness and compassion toward all mortals.

Thorne's gaze locked on Alec, his lips barely moving when he spoke. "What makes her so smart?"

"She provided for herself and our youngest brother through two harsh winters," Alec answered, suddenly feeling the need to put as much distance as possible between himself and this man.

"But she must have strong magic, too?"

"As strong as any witch, I suppose. Why do you ask so many questions about my sister?" Alec snapped, tired of the old man's prying.

"Curiosity is all." Thorne stepped back, looking contrite. "It's not every day I meet the brother of Madhea's daughter. I presume you have the same father and different mothers?"

"Aye." Alec spoke through gritted teeth.

Thorne nodded toward the bodies his kinsmen dumped over the side of the ship. "Those soldiers might have been children of Aloa-Shay."

"What do you mean?" Though Alec suspected he knew the answer, he prayed he was wrong.

"Where do you think Eris gets her soldiers? She steals them when they are boys, many from fishing villages like Aloa-Shay."

He swallowed. Eris was an evil goddess, which made him even more terrified to be stuck on her vessel. "Truly?"

"Truly." Thorne pulled down the neckline of his tunic, revealing an intricate tattoo on his shoulder. It was a horned whale, exactly like the one on Zier's shield. "Eris's marking," Thorne said. "I was stolen from Aloa-Shay when I was a child."

Great goddess! To have been captured not once, but twice by the evil goddess and lived to tell the tale! "How did you escape?"

"I had the Elements on my side." He flashed a sideways smile. "That, and I'm a damn good swimmer."

Alec's heart plummeted when he thought of all the soldiers he'd killed, especially those he'd shot in the back. What if they hadn't intended to return to Eris? What if they'd planned to reunite with their families? He'd spent most of his life fighting his brother's instinct to become a monster like their father, and now he was no better than a monster, killing fleeing men.

Thorne went to his kinsmen when they hauled up four of their own, wiping away tears and clutching each other's shoulders while they said their farewells, throwing their fallen friends overboard more gracefully. When Ryne hauled Filip up the ladder, Alec went to help him with the body.

Ryne laid Filip on a pallet and mopped sweat off his brow with a bloodied rag. He leveled Alec with a look so severe, the flesh on Alec's forearms and neck rose.

"Is it bad I feel no remorse for his death?" Ryne asked.

Alec was caught off guard. He hadn't been prepared for such a question. "I don't know how to answer you, Ryne. That is between you and your conscience."

Ryne nodded, his bloodshot eyes hollow and devoid of emotion. "Markus told me you were wise—and kind."

Alec swallowed a lump as he thought of the soldiers he'd shot in the back. He was too tired to tell Ryne he was anything but kind. Besides, he knew what was happening. Ryne had no kinsmen. Now that he was alone on his quest, he needed to befriend Alec again. But he had seen Ryne's ugly underside. As soon as they returned to land, he resolved to part ways with Ryne and follow Grim to Aya-Shay. Ryne wouldn't be welcome in the dwarf village. The ice dweller had ventured on his last quest by himself, and he would have to endure another solo journey.

Alec bowed his head. "We must say a prayer for him."

Ryne smoothed a hand down his face, the lines around his drawn mouth making him look far older than he'd appeared a few days ago. "I suppose he needs one, as he was the cause of Ven and Luc's deaths."

Alec wanted to remind Ryne that his foolish tantrum was also to blame, but he let it go—for now. Ryne had a lot to atone for, starting with an apology to Grim and the other dwarves.

Alec recited the same prayer he'd said at his mother's grave after he'd been left alone to bury her. "In life these dreams we make. In death our spirits wake. To the Elements we ask our souls to take. Amen."

Then he and Ryne hauled Filip over the side of the ship and watched his body spiral into the black abyss below. Alec reflected on how much his life had been altered over the past few days. He worried they wouldn't make it back to Aya-Shay, that they wouldn't find a safe haven for their people. He worried that Des was frightened without him and Markus wouldn't be able to escape Ice Mountain without catching Madhea's eye. He did not worry about Dianna's safety, for she had powerful magic and a mighty protector. He did fear for her heart. He and his sister had bonded this past winter. Would she mourn him if he didn't make it back? Even though they'd beaten their captors, they were still on Eris's vessel. If the sea goddess learned of their mutiny, she could send more ships or even her sea dragon after them. Elements save them if they had to go up against a goddess.

Chapter Twelve

AFTER THEY LANDED BESIDE the pond, Dianna stroked Lydra's neck. "Thank you, girl." She smiled when Lydra answered with a low purr.

She slid off her dragon, summoning the courage to challenge the golden dragon once more. Patting the stones in her pocket, she ignored Simeon's outstretched hand and marched up to Tan'yi'na. "I accept your challenge to defeat The Seven but on one condition."

The golden dragon snarled. *There are no conditions. You have already agreed to defeat The Seven in exchange for the stone.*

"I don't recall agreeing to anything."

The dragon reared back with a roar, shooting a stream of fire into the sky before hunching on all fours, growling at Dianna and blowing steam that dampened her clothes. *I should have known not to trust the spawn of the ice witch!*

Though Simeon tried to pull Dianna back, and Lydra growled behind her, she ignored them. "Help me defeat Eris, and I will help you defeat The Seven."

You expect me to fight a powerful goddess?

"No, not the goddess. I have heard tales that she has a water dragon, a powerful leviathan that spits venom."

She does.

Simeon cleared his throat. "And sirens, carnivus plants, and pixies, too."

A low, sinister chuckle erupted from Tan'yi'na's chest. *You expect me to fight all those monsters?*

She turned toward her dragon, whose red eyes were trained on Tan'yi'na. "Lydra will help you."

Tan'yi'na glared at Dianna for a long, tense moment. *And what is my motive for helping you?*

"I should think it obvious." She threw up her hands. "To prove you care about humanity and not just the treasure The Seven have stolen from you."

Simeon groaned, covering his face.

I never said this was about the treasure.

She folded her arms, impatiently tapping her foot. "Then what is it about?"

What it's always been about. Despite the heavy moon and brilliant stars which lit up the night sky, dark shadows fell across Tan'yi'na's features. *My one and only goal since your mother turned my goddess to stone is vengeance. I want to destroy the witch who shattered my soul over a thousand years ago.*

Though she hadn't been responsible for her mother's actions, she felt remorse for Kyan's death. "Help me defeat Eris and then we will take on Madhea."

The golden dragon rose to full height. *You would fight your own mother?*

"Madhea put a curse on my father's heart, turning him into a cruel monster. She murdered Jae, the girl the Elementals switched me with at birth, the true child of my adoptive parents. She cursed my brother and forced Lydra to murder hundreds of innocent people, including children." She took a deep, steadying breath. "I ask you, Tan'yi'na, what kind of mother is she?"

She is no mother at all.

She laid a hand against her chest, feeling the warm pulse of the stones, wishing she had a sister whose heart beat for her, too. "You do not know the guilt that weighs heavily on my heart. Had I not been switched at birth, Jae would still be alive. My adoptive parents gave me a childhood of love and happiness. What kind of life do you suppose Jae had? My brother Markus told me Madhea made her a servant."

Simeon wiped moisture from his eyes. "A mother who forces her child into servitude is no mother at all, and I understand the guilt, Dianna. I feel it every waking hour of my life. Though my twin was born without magic, we share a magical bond." His voice cracked. "I feel her suffering, her sorrow, her rejection as if it was my own." He wiped his wet cheeks.

"Oh, Simeon." Giving into an impulse, she hugged him. She stood on her toes, whispering into his ear. "I'm so sorry."

He wrapped his arms around her waist. "If you help us defeat The Seven, I will help you fight Eris and Madhea."

She pulled out of his embrace, instantly missing his warmth and hating herself for it. "Thank you, but I don't want you getting hurt."

"I won't." A wide smile split his face in two. "I have very persuasive abilities. Why, just recently I persuaded a powerful witch to trust her life to mischievous little pixies."

"You did." She couldn't help but smile back but reminded herself not to get lost in his golden eyes, though it was incredibly hard not to.

"And when this is all over, I may just persuade her not to slap me if I kiss her." The grin he shot her was so mischievous, she expected to see pixie wings sprouting from his back.

"If we survive a battle with seven witches and two goddesses, I will gladly let you kiss me." She wanted to mentally kick herself for her foolish promise, which both excited and unnerved her.

"Even more of a reason for us to win," Simeon said with a wink.

And that all of humanity is counting on you.

"That, too." Simeon laughed.

"So is it agreed?" She held out her hand. "We all battle The Seven and the goddesses together?"

He grasped her hand and squeezed perhaps too hard.

Tan'yi'na shrank back. *I cannot reach The Seven. Should I break through their tunnels, I will crush hundreds of innocents.*

"Fine, Simeon and I will take them on." She pointed at his scaly chest. "But will you help us defeat Eris and Madhea?"

Tan'yi'na nudged their joined hands with his snout. *If you defeat The Seven, I will gladly help you battle Eris and Madhea. I swear it.* He raised his head, gazing at something behind Dianna. *Something is wrong.*

A solitary cloaked figure approached them. She recognized Feira's gnarled cane and was surprised at how quickly the old deity moved.

Feira pulled back the hood of her cloak. "Come," she said to Dianna, holding out a hand. "We must hurry." The deity's expression was tight, guarded, though Dianna sensed a deep, disturbing chasm in the old woman's soul.

She looked to Simeon and Tan'yi'na, who nodded their encouragement. She said a quick goodbye to Lydra, rubbing her snout and promising a swift return. Then she took Feira's outstretched hand, looking over her shoulder as Simeon followed them. Knowing he was shadowing her brought Dianna comfort, even as panic jumped off Feira's skin in erratic currents.

The caverns and tunnels they traversed on their way to Feira's chamber were devoid of life, save for a few jumpy guards. 'Twas as if everyone had gone into hiding. Something had happened, and though she didn't know what, the prickles on the back of her neck and down her spine warned her danger was imminent.

Once they were inside Feira's chamber, Feira threw down her cane and chased away the few remaining servants, demanding in harsh tones that they leave, something unusual for the deity. Dianna halted beside the throne, her feet obscured by the fog.

Feira stared into the swirling mists. "Curse you!" the old deity swore, scattering the mists with a swipe of her hand. She fell back onto her throne with a guttural wail, burying her face in her hands.

"What has happened?" Dianna asked.

"Please tell us, Grandmother," Simeon begged, standing beside Dianna, his steady strength radiating off him in waves.

Feira lifted her head, staring at the scattered mists with red-rimmed eyes. "They've taken Tumi."

Shadows fell across Simeon's features. "The Seven?"

Feira wiped her eyes. "They came for him while I was inspecting the damage done by the pixies."

Dianna looked from Simeon to Feira. "Why?"

Feira absently twirled a worn metal band around her finger. "As punishment for weakening my magic." Feira clutched the sides of her throne. "The dark magic I used to keep Tumi alive has compromised my own. They say 'tis why I didn't have the strength to destroy you."

Dianna's knees weakened, and she stumbled back into a chair behind her. "Destroy me?"

Feira nodded. "As daughter of the goddess who turned our benevolent goddess to stone, they believe you should pay for your mother's sins."

"Ridiculous." Simeon punched the air. "Dianna killed the pixies and saved our people. She is clearly not like Madhea, and they know it."

Dianna cleared her throat, searching Feira's gaze. "Do you believe them?"

"Of course not, child." Feira waved her away with a shrill laugh. "Your mother's actions are not your own."

She swallowed hard, hating how parched her throat had suddenly become. "Will they come for me?"

"They are too afraid." Feira averted her eyes but not before Dianna read the guilt on the older woman's face.

She is hiding something from you, Sindri said.

She would not betray Dianna, Neriphene argued. *She has our mother's gentle heart.*

But her fear for Tumi has weakened her resolve, Sindri answered. *Can you not feel it?*

Sliding off her chair, Dianna knelt beside Feira, her legs disappearing beneath the blanket of mist. "They ordered you to kill me, didn't they? That's why they have Tumi, to ensure you do it."

When Feira looked at Dianna, tears streaming down her weathered face, her heart broke for the old deity.

"Yes," Feira whispered, then bit down on her knuckles and looked away.

"Grandmother!" Simeon's deep bellow echoed through the room. "You will not hurt Dianna!"

Feira reached for Simeon, patting his arm. "Of course not, my boy." She gave Dianna a watery smile. "You are our last chance for peace in the Shifting Sands. I will not take that from my people."

See sister, Neriphene chided. *Our mother's heart.*

I hope you are right, Sindri warned.

"Feira." She hoped Neriphene was right, and she could trust her cousin. "I will get him back for you." Her innards shook when she realized she might not be able to keep such a promise. What if The Seven defeated her? She'd no idea the strength of their magic.

"'Tis sweet of you, child, but he should have gone to the Elements long ago." She patted Dianna's hand, her smile affectionate. "I only wish for him to go on my terms, not theirs." Feira nodded toward Dianna's bulging vest pocket. "Did you recover the second stone?"

She slowly stood. "You knew?"

Feira pointed at the raised pool. "I have the swirling mists, as do The Seven."

Her heart thudded against her ribcage. What if they were ready for Dianna's attack? What if they had already laid a trap? "Do you think they know I have two stones?"

"The mists only reveal what they want us to see. I do not know what they have shown The Seven."

Feira scowled at the cloudy pool, and Dianna realized the old deity resented the swirling mists. Why hadn't they warned her The Seven would take Tumi?

"I need to strike now." The longer she waited, the more likely The Seven were to discover her plans.

Feira eyed Dianna's pocket. "Do you know how to use those stones of yours?"

"No." So desperate was she to recover Tumi for Feira, she hadn't thought that far ahead.

It's simple, cousin, Sindri said. *You will it and let our magic flow through you.*

She remembered flattening Tan'yi'na when she willed him to stop his attack against Lydra, but the second time she'd tried to subdue him, 'twas as if her magic had fled. "What do I will?"

Whatever you need the Elements to do, Neriphene answered.

She turned from Feira and Simeon, facing a cavern wall. "Fire," she breathed, holding out her hands. White bolts of flame flew out of her hands, burning the edges of Feira's tapestry depicting Tan'yi'na sitting regally among his jewels. "Sorry," she said sheepishly, though truthfully, she did glean a small amount of satisfaction seeing the smug dragon burn.

The old deity shrugged. "You are not concentrating hard enough. Watch me." She held up both hands, curling her fingers like cat claws. "Fire," she breathed, and flame burst out of each finger, striking the tapestry and making it combust into millions of tiny embers.

She gaped at the charred tips of Feira's fingers. "How did you do that without the stones?"

"Find that place between this world and the next." Feira gestured at the ceiling above them. "Give yourself over to the Elements."

"Like I did when I healed Jae?" she whispered to Sindri.

Yes, but don't lose yourself, Sindri warned. *Stay tethered to this world, or you may burn down all of Kyanu.*

"Siren's teeth!" she grumbled. "How am I supposed to do that?"

Focus, Neriphene warned.

She focused on a vase filled with brilliant young flowers, thinking about floating in that space between her world and the Elemental world. Bright bolts shot out of her hands, blasting the vase into a million fragments that sparkled like starlight.

"Whoa." Simeon swiped sparks off his arms. "Remind me to never cross you."

"Now you've got it." Feira flashed a feral smile, swatting the swirling mists, scattering wisps of cloud across the floor. "Let's go defeat The Seven."

Casting Simeon a wary look, Dianna stayed rooted to the spot. "I think I need more practice."

Simeon agreed. "She's still green, Grandmother."

Feira pulled her cloak tightly around her shoulders, her charred fingers flaking off on the fabric. "We are out of time. The mists have just revealed my Tumi strung up on a rope."

"Oh, heavenly Elements," Dianna cried.

"Do not call on them." Feira sneered. "Had they wished to help us, they would have revealed The Seven's plans long ago."

Dianna swallowed hard and took Simeon's outstretched hand. As they followed Feira out of the chamber, her legs felt heavy, weighted with a thousand stones. Somewhere in the distance was the steady pounding of a low drum, and she couldn't help but think she was marching to the beat of her own funeral.

SPARKS FLEW FROM THE bottom of Feira's cane every time it struck stone. More sparks flew off the old woman's skin, crackling as they dissipated in the heavy air. She moved with surprising alacrity. As Dianna followed Feira down the smoky tunnel toward the rhythmic drumbeats, her skin prickled with magic, too.

"Where is the smoke coming from, Grandmother?" Simeon asked.

The old woman's lips were drawn into a thin line. "You'll see soon enough."

Their journey felt interminable as they descended far into the bowels of Kyanu, farther than Dianna had gone before.

"Where are we going?" Dianna whispered to Simeon, trying not to inhale the smoke's fumes.

He coughed. "To the ritual chamber."

"It's so far down," she moaned. Being forced to battle a coven of witches underground was frightening enough, but so far below the earth, Dianna feared the world would crash down upon her.

Her eyes widened when they passed through a smoking archway carved in the form of Tan'yi'na's gaping maw. A blast of hot air hit her as they entered on the edge of a rocky slope, with a ceiling so dark and vast, she could not tell where it ended. Looking down into the cavern, her heart skipped a beat and then came to a sudden stop.

Below them was a seven-pointed, waist-high ring of fire, and in the center of that was a long platform where the seven witches stood, their hoods pulled back as they looked expectantly at Dianna with devious smiles. Behind them were two wooden posts connected at the top by a horizontal column on which hung two hooded people, ropes tied around their necks. They steadied themselves on stools. One figure was bent, misshapen, and eerily still as he leaned into the rope.

"Tumi," Feira breathed, clutching her throat.

The other figure fought her bonds to no avail. Dianna recognized Jae's tattered dress, which flapped against her legs in the smoky current. Had she healed Jae only to watch her perish at the end of a noose?

"Mother!" Simeon cried, falling to his knees. "How could you do this to your own child?"

Sparks flew from Zephyra's clenched fists. "That mortal is no child to me," she hollered, "and neither are you for siding with the spawn of our benevolent goddess's killer!"

Dianna offered her hand. "Please get up. We need to move closer."

He ignored her outstretched hand and jumped to his feet, rushing down the slope and stalking toward the fiery circle. "Mother," he boomed, his voice eerily similar to Tan'yi'na's deep baritone. "Release those prisoners at once."

Zephyra clutched her heart, swaying, then stumbling forward, her eyes widening as she walked toward the prisoners. "No, Simeon!" She pointed to her prisoner's nooses. "Don't make me do this!"

Dianna and Feira followed Simeon, but it took longer for Feira to navigate the steep slope. Though she wanted to run, she couldn't leave Feira to make the descent by herself.

Feira grabbed Dianna's shoulder, forcing her to stop when Simeon walked straight through the firewall, shrugging off his smoking tunic.

"Release them now!" he bellowed.

"Resist him, Zephyra," the other mages cried.

"Silence!" Simeon waved his fist at them, and they all fell to their knees, covering their mouths, frightened.

She was amazed at how the mages responded to Simeon, when she could not feel the strength of his words at all. 'Twas as if his magic was confined within the seven-pointed star.

Zephyra's hands shook as magical ropes twined around her fingers. She turned her face to the darkened cavern ceiling. "Kyani!"

Sprout emerged from a cloud of smoke, her eyes glossy with tears. "I'm sorry, brother."

Dozens of ivy strands burst from the ground. Simeon tried to run, but they caught his ankles, snaking around him and covering his mouth within a heartbeat.

"Simeon!" Dianna ran, but Feira caught her, forcing her back with a rope of magic.

"Stop!" she cried. "Do not go within the circle. It is a heptacircle. Their magic is contained there. Yours will be, too."

She watched helplessly as Simeon was covered in a cocoon of foliage, shrouding him completely with the exception of a narrow opening for his mouth. Magic crackled in Dianna's palms as rage threatened to split her skull in two. How could his own mother be so cruel as to turn her young daughter against her siblings?

"Sprout!" she cried, tears streaming down her face. "Do not do this! Zephyra will kill him!"

The child let out a strangled sob. Two of the seven mages came to their feet and led her back through the cloud of smoke.

Zephyra stumbled across the stage, pointing at Feira. "You had one job—kill the spawn of the bitch who murdered our goddess. Dianna trusted you. She wouldn't have seen it coming, but you couldn't even avenge your grandmother's death." Her face looked misshapen behind the smoke, as if 'twas a melting ball of wax. "Kyan would be ashamed of you."

Feira clutched her staff in a white-knuckled grip. "It is you she'd be ashamed of. My grandmother was a wise and benevolent goddess. She would not approve of the way you treat her mortal children."

Zephyra tossed back her head and laughed, a sinister chuckle that raced across Dianna's skin like a thousand tiny spiders. "It was her love of mortals that got her killed! Just like your foolish love is going to get you killed." She rested her foot on Tumi's chair.

When Feira raced through the circle, arcs of flame flying from her raised hands, Dianna chased after her.

Don't go in the circle! Sindri warned.

She ignored the stone. She would not let Feira battle the evil witch alone.

Zephyra looked over her shoulder with a smile, then raised her brows at Feira before knocking Tumi's chair out from under him.

The old man didn't even fight. His frail body fell with a violent snap, his torso and extremities detaching like a molting bug as his shrouded head swung in the noose, dripping blood on the ground.

Feira dropped her staff and fell to her knees. "Noooo!" She reached toward her dead husband before falling face first in the dirt.

Zephyra looked down on Feira with a snarl. "You are pathetic, crying over this old, drooling relic." She marched toward them. "You gave everything to this undeserving mortal—your beauty, your magic." She paused, raising her hands. "Your life."

When an arc of lightning flew off her curled fingers, rushing toward Feira with violent crackles, Dianna had no time to think, only act. She unleashed a bolt so bright, it lit up the cavern with blinding light. The other mages shielded their eyes, and Zephyra fell to her knees when Dianna's magic engulfed the evil mage's small bolt.

She felt as if she was floating on a cloud as she moved toward Zephyra.

The evil mage's eyes lit with panic as she bent beneath the force of Dianna's magic. "Do it!"

Two mages rushed to Jae's stool, and Dianna dropped her hands. "Do not touch her!" The command blew through the cavern like a wind storm, scattering smoke and flame and shaking the stage, causing the mages to tumble backward.

She threw bolts at them, driving them away from Jae. 'Twas why she didn't see the ivy snaking up behind her until it was too late. She screamed when it latched onto her ankles, knocking her to the ground. She struck the tendrils with bolts. They shriveled and retreated, their blackened tips falling apart and scattering. She scrambled to her feet only to see Zephyra knock out Jae's stool and keep her afloat by a tendril of flaming magic that snaked under the girl's feet.

Jae's shoulders shook. "It burns! Please, please stop!"

Dianna fought the urge to vomit when the smell of Jae's burning flesh hit her.

Zephyra turned to Dianna with a triumphant smile. "Throw down your stone, or I let the girl go."

No! Sindri cried. *Do not let her have a stone.*

"I can't let her kill Jae," Dianna whispered.

She will kill her either way, Neriphene predicted.

Simeon's cocoon shook like a hatching larvae, his muffled sobs piercing her heart. Feira lay on the ground beside him, unnervingly still, as if the life had drained out of her when Tumi died. Was she dead?

"She thinks I have only one stone," Dianna whispered. "I can defeat her."

No, you can't, Sindri growled. *There are too many mages. Look around you.*

She was indeed surrounded. A mage stood at every point of the star, including little Sprout, who was still sobbing, her eyes shining with regret. How cruel of Zephyra to do this to her children.

"I will release her on the count of three." Zephyra said. "Her brother is next."

Dianna fumbled with the button on her vest pocket. "I will give you the stone if you promise not to harm Simeon, Jae, and Feira."

The stones simultaneously gasped.

Zephyra smugly smiled as she held the sobbing Jae up with another rope of fiery flame. "I give you my word no harm will come to Feira and my children if you give me the stone."

"All your children," she said through gritted teeth, "including Jae." She couldn't believe she was giving a stone to the evil mage, but what choice did she have? She refused to let Simeon's sister die at the hands of a cruel witch, as her sister had been killed by Madhea.

"Very well." Zephyra heaved a dramatic sigh. "I will not harm Jae if you give me the stone."

Dianna, Neriphene chided, *you are a fool if you do this.*

"I will not let my own vanity or self-preservation prevent me from protecting the innocent from harm," she whispered the words of her blood promise. "I offer the blood of my body to the Elements in recompense should I break my vow."

When her cousins went eerily silent, Dianna pulled a stone out of her pocket. "Sorry," she murmured, "but I cannot break my vow." She dropped it on the ground.

An ivy tendril raced toward the stone, picking it up and snaking up the platform before dropping it in Zephyra's hand. With a screech and a maniacal laugh, Zephyra cut down Jae's noose with a bolt of magic. Jae fell to the ground with a *thud,* clutching her neck.

Zephyra kissed the stone and held it up, laughing and dancing, her eyes shining like golden gems.

When the ivy wrapped around her ankles again, Dianna fell with a curse, her head cracking against the floor. She tried to blast her bonds, but her magic had fled, leaving her feeling like a hollowed-out shell. It snaked around her quickly, binding her arms and legs so tight, her muscles screamed in pain. The last thing she saw before the plant wrapped around her face were Feira's lifeless eyes staring up at the sky, their golden flames extinguished.

Chapter Thirteen

ALEC THANKED THE ELEMENTS that the slaves were fishermen from Aloa-Shay and had sailing experience, though their vessels weren't quite as big as Eris's ship. Despite being feverish and tired, he refused to rest until he'd helped the others put the ship in order. He pitched in on all tasks, from mopping up blood to counting the food stores and even taking turns with the oars. It was early dawn by the time he stumbled above deck to check in with Khashka, whom their makeshift crew had elected to serve as captain.

Alec had thought 'twould be a simple matter of turning the ship around and heading back to shore, but then Khashka discovered a map in the captain's quarters, marking the carnivus waters. Carnivus plants were Eris's creations, man-eating monsters that rose from the seafloor, some as large as ships, with rows of razor sharp teeth. Alec had heard tales of them from Zier and Dafuar, and until recently had thought them to be fable. But once he'd thought giants and sirens to be only fable, too.

Because they were now on a tight path between carnivus waters, Khashka had said the only way to Aloa-Shay was to stay the course and loop around Eris's island before returning on the other side. Veering off course even slightly was too dangerous. This meant the journey would take almost seven days rather than a few. The men weren't too happy about having to spend extra time on Eris's ship, especially Ryne, who voiced his displeasure so much, Khashka threatened to throw him overboard.

Khashka's spirit daughter hovered behind her father like a shadow. Morbid curiosity had worn off, but Alec caught himself staring at her more often than he should. 'Twas her fair face that caught his eye. Heat flamed his face when she caught him looking at her, and she pointedly stared at him until he was forced to look away.

Alec went in search of Grim and found him on the stern, leaning against the railing and keeping an eye on his daughter, who had yet to wake.

"How fares she?" he asked before coughing. He worried his sickness would get worse before it got better, and he'd soon be forced to seek nourishment and rest.

"See for yerself." The dwarf pointed to his daughter's toe.

Alec squinted at the giant, the sunlight reflecting off her hair and ruddy cheeks making it hard to see much, but then a big toe moved, followed by another.

Grim beamed at him. "Not much longer, and my pearl will wake."

"That's wonderful." He patted Grim's back, forcing a smile, for he couldn't help worrying what would happen when the giant woke up.

He turned at a rustling behind him and was surprised to see Khashka, flanked by several men, heading their direction. His jaw dropped when he saw they were armed with spears and poisonous darts.

He nudged Grim. "Something's wrong."

The dwarf turned, bushy brows dipping low over his eyes. When he saw the approaching men, he grabbed his axe. "What's the meaning of this?"

Khashka stopped just out of striking distance, running a hand over his bald head. "Grim, I'm sorry, but the crew and I have had a vote."

The dwarf arched a brow. "A vote?"

Khashka nodded toward Gorpat's barge. "We cannot allow the giant to wake."

Several of Khashka's men pulled out narrow wooden tubes and loaded them with darts.

"Now you hear me!" Grim swung the axe above his head. "I will not allow you to poke my child full of needles again!"

When the men raised their darts, Alec grabbed Grim's shoulder. "Hang back, before they put you to sleep."

"Please listen to reason," Khashka pleaded, waving at his men to lower their weapons. "Her barge is tethered to us. She could become violent when she wakes and sink the ship."

Grim puffed up his chest. "I won't let that happen. I intend to be here when she wakes."

Khashka shook his head, the weather-worn lines tightening around his eyes. "She will still be in a dream-like state when she wakes. She may not be responsive to you."

"You cannot expect her to sleep for a week," Grim cried. "She will starve to death."

"That's another concern." Khashka frowned. "We do not have enough rations for the giant. The crew fears she will eat us when the food runs out."

"My pearl is a gentle lamb." Grim vehemently shook his head, his eyes filling with tears. "She wouldn't dream of eating people."

Khashka and the other men shared knowing looks. "And yet everyone knows the giant colony northwest of Werewood Forest has a reputation for eating humans," Khashka said.

Grim's face turned so red, Alec feared he was about to spew lava out his top, like Eris's volcanic island. "My pearl is more civilized than any of you sons of sirens!"

The anguish in the dwarf's eyes was more than Alec could bear. He stepped forward, hoping these men would listen to reason. "I have been traveling with the dwarf and his daughter for several days. Gorpat does have a gentle heart. I am confident she will not attempt to eat any of us."

"I'm sorry." Khashka let out a long breath. "The crew has already decided."

The crew? Alec was part of the crew and yet he had no say? "I did not get a vote."

"Your vote wouldn't matter, Alec." Ryne stepped out from behind Khashka, tightly clutching a dart tube. "The rest of us are unanimous."

Throughout their journey, Alec had been abused and mistreated by Ryne. His nose still throbbed from the break, yet that pain paled in comparison to the betrayal he felt at that moment.

A war cry erupted from the dwarf's throat, so powerful it shook Alec to the marrow of his bones. When he swung his axe at the crew's kneecaps, they ran for cover, screaming for Khashka to give the command to strike.

"Grim, please," Khashka begged, backing away from the dwarf and nearly stumbling over a loose plank, "I ask you to be reasonable."

Mari floated between them, glowering at the dwarf while shielding her father. "Put down your weapon, dwarf," she commanded.

"Everyone put down their weapons," Alec begged. "Let's talk this out."

"Get out of my way!" The dwarf sliced his axe through Mari's spirit, and she flickered like candlelight in a breeze. "I will cut the slog who dares shoot my pearl."

"Nay, dwarf." Ryne chuckled and raced behind a barrel. "We will simply shoot you first." He blew a dart, which Grim deflected with the head of his axe.

"You stupid blue gnaz!" Grim hollered. "You'll have to try harder." He gaped at something on the horizon. "Carnivus!" he screamed, pointing to the starboard side.

Alec followed the direction of Grim's gaze, but saw only clear sky.

"Think we'd fall for your dwarf trickery?" Ryne laughed.

The ship came to a violent stop. Alec was barely aware of the cacophony of terrified screams around him as he flew forward, smashing into a mast with a crunch. He fell on the deck and rolled onto his side, grasping his aching ribs and gasping for breath. A heavy shadow blotted out the morning sun, and all he saw were rows upon rows of razor-sharp teeth.

DIANNA HAD JUST ENOUGH magic to strike anyone who came near her cocoon, and so she did, zapping three mages when they approached her. Through the thin opening over her eyes, she watched two mortals drape a blanket over Feira's body, sobbing before carrying her away.

Simeon had chewed a wider hole through the foliage over his mouth, yelling obscenities at his mother and the other mages, who skirted the outside of the circle. Eventually, he was carried away, too, but not before he called to Dianna to burn off her bonds and fight.

Dianna had tried, but 'twas no use. The stone pressed against her heart had gone cold and refused to answer her pleas. She felt the mages' presence slip away as they left her in the flame circle. They returned only to put more kindling on the fire, otherwise, she was alone in her cocoon with her dark thoughts and fears. What would the mages do to her? Come back and end her life swiftly or leave her in the circle to slowly starve? What would happen to her brothers if she died? Simeon and Jae and the rest of the Kyanite mortals? What about those who lived beneath Ice Mountain? And Lydra, after saving the dragon from Madhea's cruelty—would Zephyra destroy her or use her as Madhea had once done, forcing her to terrorize mortals?

You should worry, Neriphene scolded. *Had you not crossed into the circle and given my sister to that cursed witch, you would not be here now.*

"Neriphene," Dianna pleaded. "Help me break the bonds."

Neriphene snorted. *The daughter of a goddess cannot break the bonds herself?*

She struggled against the ivy, and it responded by squeezing her tighter.

Why do you need my help? I, too, am the daughter of a goddess, and I am only stone. My magic is no stronger than yours.

"Obviously, it is," She grumbled.

Only because you lack confidence in yourself.

"I knocked Tan'yi'na on his back with the help of Sindri's stone." She blew out a frustrated breath. "I healed mortals in only a few breaths using a goddess stone. Before Sindri, it took me weeks to heal my sick brother."

Was it Sindri's magic that helped you or your belief in her magic?

She contemplated Neriphene's question but had no answer. It had felt as if Sindri's magic was flowing through her. Could it have been Dianna's magic as well?

"I have tried and can only manage a few sparks," she groaned.

Because that's all you think you can manage.

Could Neriphene be right? Was she as powerful as a goddess stone?

She closed her eyes and summoned a magic deep from within, letting her soul hover in the space between two worlds. When she was there, she was amazed to see a beautiful young woman standing opposite her. She wore jewels on her arms and neck, and a long flowing pale dress, a stark contrast against her smooth, ebony skin.

"Neriphene?" she asked.

The beautiful woman nodded. "It is I."

Dianna reached for her, touching her chest and surprised to find a warm, beating heart.

She was puzzled. Was this what her cousin looked like? "But you are not a stone."

Neriphene smoothed her skirt. "Here in the Elemental world, my body is free."

"Oh." Dianna held her pale hand in front of her face, pleased to see she was not translucent like a spirit. She stepped back and closed her fist, feeling each muscle tense as magical energy coursed through her.

Neriphene revealed a dazzling smile. "Do you feel the magic?"

She opened her hand and magic sparked off her fingers, floating through the air like thousands of tiny butterflies. "Yes. It's so powerful."

"It's always been strong." Neriphene chuckled. "You just needed to find it."

Warmth flooded her chest and then the magic flowed through her, gushing out of her hands like raging rivers. She flung it into the air, and it rained back down on her, prickling her skin.

"Oh, heavenly Elements," she breathed as her chest expanded with more magical energy. She looked at her cousin through a sheen of happy tears. "Thank you, Neriphene."

Neriphene nodded. "Just promise you will use your powers for good."

"You know I will." She wiped her eyes, sparks flying in all directions.

Neriphene closed the distance between them, clasping Dianna's shoulder. "You are not like your mother."

She sucked in a sharp breath, searching her cousin's golden eyes. "That's the nicest thing you've said to me."

When Neriphene smiled and held out her arms, Dianna welcomed her cousin's embrace, magic sparking all around them. Until this moment, she hadn't realized how desperately she'd needed to be held. She hadn't been so loved since before her parents had died. That feeling, and giving love in return, empowered her magic even more.

"Now go back and break your bonds," Neriphene whispered and pulled back.

She smiled at her cousin. "Oh, believe me, I will." Then she let her spirit fall back to the mortal plane.

When she awoke, powerful magic raced up her arms. Energy shot out of her like starbursts as she flung her arms wide, breaking her bonds with a violent *snap*.

She floated to her knees, smiling broadly at a lone mage who kept watch on the outskirts of the magical circle. She blasted a hole through the fiery barrier and latched onto the mage with a rope of magic, dragging him into the circle. She pulled him close, forcing him on his knees. "Did you think a silly circle could contain my magic?"

"Please, please, don't hurt me," he begged, sweat dripping down his gleaming bald head.

"Lead me to the High Mage." Dianna sneered. "Her reckoning has come."

A loud boom, followed by two thunderous roars, sounded overhead. She flung a magical barrier over her head as debris fell to the ground. A broad beam of light shone down from above, illuminating the smoky cavern. Two giant-winged creatures landed beside her with a deafening *thud*.

The mage rolled into a fetal ball, clutching his knees and crying.

Are you all right? Tan'yi'na asked, shocking her with his concern.

She brushed plant debris off her legs. "I am now, Tan'yi'na. Thank you for asking." She smiled broadly at both dragons. "And for coming. I could use a few extra friends down here."

Tan'yi'na sniffed the air before leaning over Dianna and inhaling her hair. *You've found your magic.*

She raised her palms, magic coating her hands like glowing gloves. "I did." She smiled triumphantly. "Now I'm ready to use it."

Tan'yi'na frowned. *I felt My Deity's distress cry, but now I do not sense her aura.*

Tears pricked the backs of her eyes as she mourned the loss of the old witch. Besides Dafuar and Odu, Feira had been the closest living descendent of Kyan, and she would be sorely missed. "I-I'm sorry. I believe her to be dead. After Tumi was killed by The Seven, she fell over, and her eyes were lifeless." Choking back tears, she was unable to continue.

The dragon let out a low wail, so dark and ominous, Dianna thought her heart would surely break. *If Tumi is dead, then so is Feira.* His golden eyes were luminous as a single tear cascaded down his snout. *'Twas a dark magic she used to keep him alive, one that tethered his soul to hers. If one died, then so would the other, just as one couldn't exist with half a heart.*

"Tan'yi'na, I'm so sorry."

The mage shook and curled into a tighter ball, urine pooling on the rocky floor beneath him when Tan'yi'na and Lydra's snake-like necks slithered down to his level, sniffing him with snarls.

Would you like to do the honors? Tan'yi'na said to Lydra.

When the ice dragon opened her icy maw, the mage let out a terrified screech and tried to crawl away. Lydra pounced in front of him and batted him back and forth between her paws. She bit the screaming mage in half, then gulped down his upper half, leaving his bloodied lower extremities on the ground. She let out a cold, rancid burp.

"Oh." Dianna gawked in horrified fascination as her dragon licked blood off her frosted lips. "That's one way to get rid of a mage, but he was supposed to take me to Zephyra."

"I know the way."

Dianna looked up to see Sprout walking toward them, tears flowing over red-rimmed eyes.

She stepped back warily as the young witch approached. "How do I know we can trust you?"

"They killed Grandmother." She sniffled, looking up at Dianna with watery eyes. "You are right. They are evil."

Dianna bent on one knee, grasping the child by the shoulders and searching her eyes for deceit. "Do you realize if you lead me to them, I will destroy them all, even your mother?"

The child nodded. "She's imprisoned Simeon. She says he is to starve to death in his cocoon." She let out a guttural sob. "It's all my fault."

"Don't worry, child." Dianna wiped tears off Sprout's cheeks. "I will free him."

Rage filled her when she thought about Simeon's own mother slowly starving him to death.

Elements have mercy on Zephyra, Neriphene whispered. *The goddess has awakened.*

ALEC COVERED HIS EARS as the deafening crack of cannon fire rattled the planks beneath him. The monster struck the ship's hull with such force, the ship nearly toppled on its side. Clenching his teeth against the burning pain in his ribs, he grabbed the mast, holding on for his life as men slid down the deck and right into the monster's open jaws. Another shot of cannon fire, and the boat tipped even farther. When Grim slid past him, Alec lurched to the side, grabbing the dwarf's vest by the collar.

"Don't let go!" the dwarf screamed, kicking his legs.

Feeling as if the cracks in his ribs were widening, Alec bit his lip hard, repressing a curse while hauling the dwarf up to him. Grim reached the mast, holding on beside Alec.

"Thanks, lad," he said, wiping sweat off his brow.

Alec could not look away as Ryne slid toward the plant, screaming and hacking it with a small blade as a leafy tendril wrapped around his leg.

"Why, I'll be a gnaz's hairy ass," Grim grumbled, letting go of the mast. He slid toward the plant with a warlike bellow and hacked off Ryne's bonds with his axe.

When the monster prepared for another strike, Alec screamed, "Look out!" But it was too late. The toothy maw landed on the deck, planks splintering, as the monster swallowed half the deck, along with Grim and Ryne.

Alec's world shattered when he realized he'd lost his friends.

The ship spun. His hold on the mast broke, and he was flung into the cold water. It rushed over him, sucking him down until he was submerged in the watery kingdom. Time slowed as beneath him, dozens of gaping mouths stretched toward him, coming within reach of his legs. Above him, the ship was completely flipped over, and terrified screams pierced the water. All the while, the slow, steady pulse of a beating drum throbbed in his skull. He pushed up into a gaping hole in the planks, gasping for breath when he surfaced in a pocket of air inside the dark hull. Seeing a flickering light, he swam toward it.

He blinked hard when he saw the light was the spirit, Mari.

"Help me find it," she cried.

He spit out a mouthful of salty water. "What?"

"The stone! The stone!" She flew in frantic circles. "I've lost it."

He dove back under the water, listening for the sound of the drum. For some reason, he just knew the drum was the stone. He thought he saw a flash of light underneath the heavy chest and swam down to it, cursing and grunting as he tried to lift the chest. His screaming lungs forced him back to the surface.

"It think it's down here!" he told Mari.

She dove into the water after him. He pointed to the chest. It rattled and throbbed as if it contained a living heart. He was barely able to lift it, giving Mari enough space to slip in.

She grabbed the stone, then swam away as fast a siren. Alec struggled to swim after her, traveling up the thorny neck of a beast that was twice as wide as Gorpat's waist. His stomach lurched when he heard men's screams coming from within the plant's throat.

As Alec reached the surface, he was struck by a blinding light. He shielded his eyes, then sucked in air seconds before a wave washed over him, throwing him against the side of the ship hard enough to break a couple of ribs. Paralyzed with pain, he was unable to move. As he sank into the abyss, Carnivus plants fell on their sides, floating in the current like dead, bloated fish.

Thanks, Mari, Alec thought, *but you are too late for me.*

Suddenly he was thrown onto Gorpat's wooden barge. He rolled on his side with a silent scream, pain shooting through him as he coughed up salt water.

The giant had broken her chains and was looking at him with crossed eyes. "Friend okay?"

"Grim," he gasped, finding the act of breathing, much less talking, to be unbearably painful. "In the plant." He pointed to the carnivus.

Gorpat jumped into the water with a splash, nearly toppling the barge. A wave washed over Alec, pushing him to the other side. He dug his nails into the planks to keep from sliding off.

The giant swam back to the surface, hauling the plant's bulbous head with her. She pried its mouth open wide enough for her to crawl inside, her head barely fitting through the tight opening. The dead plant's mouth closed, and it sank into the water.

Alec watched the surface with bated breath, praying to the Elements that his friends would return alive.

Khashka crawled onto the barge, heaving and vomiting water before flopping beside Alec with a groan. "My friends are all dead."

Alec's ribs hurt so badly, he had no strength to offer the man comfort.

The spirit floated beside her father, cradling the stone in her arms. "Thank you," she mouthed to Alec.

He answered with a nod, then rested his head on the barge, waiting for any sign of his friends. The water began to bubble and boil, then a great spout flew into the air, and the mighty plant was heaved above the waves, its jaw ripped in two.

When Gorpat climbed off the plant's fleshy tongue, cradling Grim and Ryne in her arms, Alec heaved a sigh of relief.

The dwarf affectionately patted his daughter's thumb, smiling at her as plant slime dripped off his beard. "I always knew you were a pearl."

Alec laughed, then regretted it instantly as his ribs screamed in agony. A cyclone of dizziness spun in his head, and light gave way to darkness.

ERIS FURIOUSLY JUMPED over waves and lava springs, pulling herself up on the edge of a jagged boulder that jutted from the sea. For too long her temperamental mists had been silent, no doubt punishing her for killing her Elementals. But what choice had she had? If her disobedient daughters hadn't secretly forged a truce with Madhea's Elementals, she would've conquered the winged ice witch. She did not mourn her disloyal daughters. In fact, she was glad they were gone, for they'd have disapproved of the child she'd stolen years ago, the child whose body would soon belong to Eris.

Her mists finally decided to reveal the status of her search party, only to show her that the ship had been destroyed by a carnivus plant. But how? She had gifted her captain with an enchantment to protect the ship from sirens and carnivus, a spell so potent, his eye had swirled with her magic. Rahn had been more than a captain to Eris. He'd been a lover, one of the few mortals who tolerated her repulsive tail. Now he was lost to her. Though he wasn't handsome by any means, he'd had a fine physique, and Eris loved strong men. She mourned his death, not because she cared for the man, but she loved how he'd cared for her, worshipped her, and made her feel less repulsive. Now she would have to content herself with her other lover, though he was scrawny and old, until she found a replacement for Rahn.

The mists revealed a glimpse of the survivors before fading to black. Had they only shown her these images to taunt her? She saw a giant, a dwarf, a blue man, another mortal, and Khashka with his spirit child. Thank the Elements that Khashka had survived, for the child's spirit would follow her father. The blue man intrigued her, for he was tall and lean with a muscular chest and hair so pale, it was almost translucent. She couldn't help but wonder what that hair would feel like slipping through her fingers. Perhaps after she possessed the young witch's body, she'd take the blue man as Rahn's replacement, unless, of course, he displeased her. Then she'd feed him to her sirens.

When the wind whipped her hair across her face, Eris tilted her head to the sky, listening for a word from the Elements. She shouldn't have been disappointed when they refused to speak to her. Curse the stubborn Elements! Because of their disobedience, she was forced to rely on spies, which had so far failed her. When she had Mari's body, she'd bend the Elements to her will, forcing storms to rage and cities to flood. They would not make a mockery of her much longer. In the meantime, she had to ensure the survivors made it to her volcano. She slapped the water with her tail in a familiar pattern.

When Naamaku ascended from the water like a tower jutting into the sky, his fangs dripping venom in thick pools on the surface and his aqua eyes glowing like twin stars, Eris's eyes rolled to the back of her head. She communicated a message to him. *Go find them, Naamaku. Bring the blue man and Khashka. Kill the rest.*

Her leviathan slithered underwater, darting through the ocean. Eris had no doubt Naamaku would eat his fill of the giant and the others, and return Khashka and the handsome blue man to her.

She rubbed her hands together when she thought of all the things she could do once she shed her unsightly fish tail, starting with destroying Madhea. Eris's soldiers had told her Madhea's glacier was melting at an alarming rate. Her sister's power was waning, no doubt because her Elementals had taken it for themselves. Soon, they and all the world would know the might of Eris's wrath.

Chapter Fourteen

SLAVES AND WITCHES scattered as Dianna marched with a singular mission on her mind—destroy The Seven. Actually, make that six. Lydra had already taken care of one mage.

Their heads scraping the low ceiling, Lydra and Tan'yi'na crawled behind Dianna and Sprout, growling at onlookers who were brave enough to stop and stare.

"Seek shelter," Dianna called to them. "And do not come out until it's over."

Much to her surprise, Sprout took them to a cavern with an underground waterfall and small pond. It was lovely, complete with a golden fountain in the center of the pond and shimmering cherubs dancing around the spout.

I get my treasure back when this is over, Tan'yi'na mumbled. *These witches do not need golden cherubs and fountains.*

Dianna didn't care about treasure, so long as the people of the Shifting Sands were free, and Simeon and Jae were unharmed.

Once they skirted the pond, Sprout pointed to swirling mists that poured out of a darkened tunnel. "They are in there."

She grabbed Sprout's shoulder. "Stay here."

The girl pouted. "Dianna, I-I'm sorry. I didn't want to bind you."

She cupped Sprout's face, kissing her forehead. "You're just a child. I do not hold you accountable for your mother's sins."

Sprout wordlessly nodded while tears streamed over her cheeks.

Dianna turned to the dragons. "That tunnel isn't big enough to fit you."

Tan'yi'na arched his long neck, ruffling his wings, reminding her of a graceful swan preparing for flight. *Step aside. I will show you that we can.*

She pulled Sprout behind Tan'yi'na, then watched in morbid fascination as Tan'yi'na puffed up his chest and released his flame with a roar. Within seconds, the tunnel walls came crashing down, sending smoke and debris into the air before it settled as a thick haze.

Six golden-eyed witches gaped at the dragons through the filthy air. They'd been dining at a table in the shape of a seven-pointed star, a feast large enough to feed dozens of men spread out before them. After all the death and carnage today, and after her twins had been imprisoned, Zephyra still had an appetite? Dianna was convinced that witch had no soul.

Zephyra pushed away from the table with a curse. Climbing over piles of rock, she stood on a mound of debris that brought her eye-level with Tan'yi'na. "What is the meaning of this?"

The dragon's golden eyes darkened. *What is the meaning of you killing my deity and her mate?*

"Feira betrayed her people and the memory of her grandmother by siding with the enemy's daughter." The witch fingered a pouch hanging from her neck, her iron-eyed gaze sliding from Lydra back to Tan'yi'na. "She left me no choice, and unless you and your dragon mate stand down, neither will you."

The magic in Dianna's hands became so heavy, it was as if she carried crackling leaden balls. She stepped out from behind Tan'yi'na. "No one else shall die by your hand, Zephyra."

The other mages screamed and ducked beneath the table. Zephyra straightened, her smile menacing. "You were no match against me before, and you are certainly no match now that I have the goddess stone."

Glowing balls of magic appeared in Dianna's hands as she pointed them at Zephyra. "Have you forgotten I am the daughter of a goddess, and there is more than one stone?"

The High Mage let out a bird-like screech and shot an magic arrow at Dianna.

She shattered the arrow and effortlessly threw a bolt at Zephyra. The witch ducked, tumbling behind the debris. The bolt flew past her and sliced the table in two. Mages scattered, though there was no other escape from the shallow cavern than past the dragons. The first mage that tried to run under Lydra's legs was met with the dragon's icy breath. Her terrified face froze in time in Lydra's impenetrable layers of ice. The next mage tried to run past Tan'yi'na and was burned to a pile of ash. The dragon's acrid breath filled up the small chamber, smoking out the rest of the mages, where they also met swift ends by ice and fire.

Tan'yi'na's laughter filled the smoky air. *Stoke a dragon's fury, and his flame burns hotter.*

Zephyra crawled out of the rubble, coughing and waving her hands in surrender. "Please," she begged. "You would leave my children motherless?"

More magic raced into Dianna's fingers. "What kind of a mother abandons her child, forcing her into slavery?"

"She's a mortal. It's the law."

Dianna stalked toward the mage, pointing an accusatory finger. "*You* create the laws. *You* subjugate your people."

"What would you have me do?" She crouched on all fours, snarling like a rabid animal. "The mortals outnumber the witches ten to one."

Wrapping magic around her feet, Dianna propelled herself up the mound of debris until she was staring down at the witch. "You could have ruled them with kindness and compassion, as Kyan had done."

Careful, Neriphene warned. *I see desperation in her eyes.*

"Kindness got her killed," Zephyra snarled before jumping up and grabbing Dianna's shoulders, wrapping her in a flaming ball of magic.

Dianna flung off the fire, sending Zephyra flying onto the cracked table with a crunch. "Cruelty gets you killed, too."

"Nooo!" Sprout screamed at Dianna. "Please don't kill her."

She caught the sobbing child in her arms. "Sh," she soothed, stroking the child's hair. 'Twas at that moment she knew Zephyra had won, for she didn't have the heart to kill Sprout's mother.

Dianna released the little witch and glared at Zephyra, lying motionless in a pile of splintered wood. She unspooled a magic tendril from her fingers and sent it after the pouch around the mage's neck, slipping it off her head and pulling it back.

Dianna slipped it around her neck. "Sindri."

I'm not speaking to you, the stone answered.

"Fair enough." She was just relieved to have the stone back. "Sprout, if you want me to spare her life, she must be tied up."

Sprout nodded and wrapped her mother in an ivy cocoon. When she finished, she fell to her knees with a sob.

Dianna picked up the child and handed her to Tan'yi'na, who cradled her in his jowls.

Where to now? the golden dragon asked.

"We need to find Simeon and Jae," she said.

When they emerged from the tunnel, witches and a few mortals came out of hiding, whispering behind their hands.

When Tan'yi'na laid Sprout down, a trio of young women rushed forward.

"She's our sister," the shortest of the golden-eyed girls said lifting Sprout into the tallest sister's arms.

"Take her." Dianna's voice shook, along with her hands, as she prepared to deliver the news about their mother. "Sprout has been through a trial and will need rest and comfort. The Seven are no more." She paused, swallowing hard. "Zephyra has been imprisoned."

The cavern broke into a cacophony of outbursts. Sprout shifted in her sister's arms, weeping against her chest.

The shortest girl shared looks with her sisters. "You did not kill our mother?"

Her shoulders fell. Though The Seven had been defeated, there were still thousands of other witches she had to contend with, and no doubt many of them were just as prejudiced as Zephyra. "No."

The girl glared at Dianna. "You should have."

That took Dianna by surprise. "The Kyanites will determine her punishment."

The girls exchanged glowers. "I can assure you," the tallest girl said, stroking Sprout's hair, "we will not be as kind toward our mother as you have been." They simultaneously turned their backs on Dianna. The crowd parted for them, then swallowed them like waves crashing over the sand.

Dianna recognized the guard with the gnarled ear as he bowed before Dianna. "Did you say The Seven are dead?"

"Six of The Seven are dead. The High Mage is imprisoned."

He fell down on one knee, tears falling on the ground. "Thank you." His voice cracked, then broke, as he bit his knuckles.

The rest of the crowd, mostly yellow-eyed witches, followed suit, thanking Dianna and falling down on one knee. She heard two thuds behind her.

When she turned, Lydra and Tan'yi'na were bent over as well. The golden dragon flashed her a knowing smile and a wink.

Looks like Kyanu has a new deity, Neriphene said with a chuckle.

It took all of her willpower to keep her legs from buckling. Oh, heavenly Elements! What had she done?

ALEC HAD A DREAM HE was lying in his old bed in his family's hut. In it, he ran his tongue along the roof of his mouth, wincing at the foul taste of spoiled food. He opened his eyes, expecting to see his mother with her healing herbs, and was surprised to see his bear of a father sitting in a chair beside him, his dark hair falling over sunken eye sockets.

"I'm sorry." Rowlen frowned at his hands, fisted in his lap. "I was not myself."

Alec struggled to move, but 'twas as if his arms and legs were bound to the bed. "I know you were cursed."

Hearing his father's apology made his throat swell with emotion. For so many years, he'd been beaten and ridiculed. For so many years, he'd loathed this man, finally ending his life with a blade in the back, only to discover his father's hatred stemmed from a curse put on his heart by Madhea.

He winced when his father reached for him, expecting a blow to the face. Instead, Rowlen placed a firm hand on his shoulder, his dark, haunted eyes shining with sorrow.

"They are trying to wake you." Rowlen gently shook him. "Be brave. I will be with you."

He awoke, his hand flying to his shoulder. He tried to recreate the feeling of his father's touch by squeezing hard, but 'twas not the same. He looked across the log barge to the endless ocean and then to Gorpat. She was in the water behind them, clutching the edge of the barge while she kicked up waves, propelling them forward.

Grim sat by his daughter, giving her words of encouragement. "That's my pearl. We'll be back on shore in no time."

When Mari floated over Alec, he was startled by her presence.

"How do you feel?" she asked.

He sat up on his elbows, amazed that the pain in his ribs and the throbbing heat that had penetrated his skin were gone. "Better." He heaved a sigh of relief, staring at the stone Mari cradled in her arms. "Thanks."

She held up the stone, smiling down at it as if 'twas her child. "I healed you with it."

He let out a slow, steady breath as he let himself get lost in the amber flecks in her eyes. "How can I ever thank you?"

Ryne nudged his side, handing him a round, furry fruit with a cracked top. "Drink this."

He scooted up, frowning when he saw Khashka and Eris's former soldier, Thorne, were sitting in the center of the barge, arguing over the map.

"I didn't know Thorne survived." Alec said to Ryne.

"He swam to the barge after you passed out." Ryne looked at Thorne, shaking his head. "How he dodged the carnivus, I have no idea. The Elements must favor him."

Grim and Thorne were surrounded by various goods, which had obviously been recovered from the ship. There was a barrel, a fishing net, and swords and clubs.

"Drink," Ryne reminded him.

He slowly sipped from the fruit, which was mildly sweet. "This is delicious."

"It's palma fruit." Ryne nodded toward a large bushel of pods beside them. "We were able to salvage one from the wreckage."

Alec greedily drank the rest. "It's so refreshing."

Khashka threw down the map and stomped over to them. "Don't drink it all, boy. We need to ration." He jerked the empty shell out of Alec's hands. "We have only one palma pod." He frowned at the shell, then threw it away.

Thorne stormed after him, waving at the map. "We wouldn't have to ration if you hadn't taken us this way to begin with! There's a break in the plants here." His tanned skin turned a bright fuchsia when he punched the center of the map. "It's a straight shot to Aloa-Shay."

Khashka threw up his hands. "Now hear me again, Thorne. Sirens patrol those waters."

Ryne stood and held out a hand to Thorne. "May I?"

After Thorne handed it over, the blue man examined the parchment for a long moment. "I'd rather take my chances with the sirens than the sea witch."

Khashka dragged a hand down his face with a low groan. "Have you already forgotten what the sirens did to your blue friends?"

"We don't have enough supplies to go around Eris's island," Thorne argued.

Mari paced, worry in her bright eyes and drawn mouth. "They've been fighting ever since you passed out," she said to Alec.

"Then we resupply on the island," Khashka answered through a frozen smile.

"Have you lost your mind?" Thorne groaned, the lines around his eyes growing long. 'Twas then Alec realized Thorne had to be nearly as old as Khashka.

Thorne struck his forehead with the heel of his palm, a string of curses pouring from his mouth. "Khashka, will you listen to yourself? This is like the broot hunt all over again."

Mari stopped pacing, and Alec and Ryne sucked in a collective breath.

Khashka waggled a fist in Thorne's face. "Take that back."

"I will not." Thorne's voice grew louder as he puffed up like a peacock. "Our kin are dead because of you! I don't know why we made you our captain after the broots. We should have learned then you've not a siren's sack of sense."

"Thorne." Mari waved wildly at the man. "I see something." She pointed to a bubbling in the distance that reminded Alec of his mother's boiling cauldron of soup. "Did you not say you were going to fish?"

"I did." He threw down the map and trudged over to the net, looking up at Khashka with a scowl. "We've already had a vote. We go through siren waters."

Once again, Alec didn't remember being included, though he did wholeheartedly agree. He'd rather take his chances with sirens than risk Eris chopping off his block or worse.

Whistling sharply, Thorne held out a hand to the giant. "Slow once we reach the boiling."

Gorpat slowed her kicks, eventually stopping as the barge cruised right next to the boil.

Thorne adroitly tossed the net into the water, then hauled in dozens of flopping colorful fish.

"Good work, man!" Grim said, racing to Thorne's side and helping him pull his catch onto the barge.

Thorne flashed a mouthful of rotting teeth. "He who casts the net never eats spoiled meat."

They dragged the net to the center of the barge and tossed fish into the barrel. Thorne laid a piece of driftwood across the top of it. Grim stood on a crate and hacked off heads and tails, throwing them into a bucket. "Waste nothing," he said to the others. "My pearl will eat the bones and skin."

"Yum, Dada!" she squealed, licking her lips.

Alec felt sorry for the giant, knowing a few remnants were not enough to sustain her.

Ryne pulled out a boning knife and helped Thorne filet each fish, tossing the bones and skin in Grim's bucket and the meat in a basket. Though Ryne and Grim didn't make eye contact with each other, Alec knew it was a good sign that Ryne was helping to feed Gorpat. He hoped the ice dweller would put pride aside and apologize to Grim, as well as thanking the giant for saving his life.

Khashka picked up the map and went to a corner, turning his back on the rest of the party.

Alec was left alone with Mari. Though he was healed, he was exhausted, but the awkward silence that hung in the air between them was more than he could bear. "I should go help them." He struggled to stand.

"No." Her command shook the air. "The stone says you must rest after a powerful healing."

He eased back down, realizing he was a lot weaker than he'd thought. "I never got to thank you for saving us."

"It was not me." She stroked the stone in the crook of her arms. "It was Aletha, but it feels good to be useful for once."

It took Alec a moment to remember Aletha was the name of Mari's goddess stone. He thoughtfully rubbed his chin while Mari flickered in and out of sight like wisps of smoke. She had done so much for him already. How he wished he could help her in return.

His sweet sister came to mind. She had healed Alec's infirmity, and she also possessed a goddess stone. Mayhap she knew of a way to help Mari. "My sister is a powerful witch. When we meet with her in the spring, perhaps she will know of a way for you to recover your body."

"Not unless she's powerful enough to take on a goddess."

Though Dianna was a talented witch, Alec doubted she was strong enough to defeat a goddess, and he did not wish her to, not even for Mari.

He pointed to the stone. "Hasn't it given you any ideas?"

"I haven't asked her."

"Mayhap you should."

"I will try," she mumbled, stroking the rock as if 'twas a living, breathing thing. "'Tis lonely as a spirit."

Alec's heart clenched. He couldn't imagine the aching sense of longing for just one touch, one hug. Before his mother died, she'd coddled him like a baby, which had angered his father even more. Though Alec knew her coddling was mostly to compensate for Rowlen's cruelty, there were days when he'd needed his mother's affection. Mari could probably use a gentle kiss and a warm hug, but she'd never get those things as long as Eris had her body.

"I'm sorry," he said, not knowing what else to say.

Her spirit faded out for a long moment before materializing again. "Not your fault."

He wondered where she went when he couldn't see her. Did she cross over to the afterlife? "Can you see other spirits?" he blurted, then regretted his question. What if she saw his father? Did he want to know if Rowlen was near? But there were times, not just in his dreams, when he thought he felt his father's presence.

"I'm caught in the veil between both worlds, so yes." She tilted her head, a dark curtain of hair falling over one shoulder. "Why do you ask?"

He looked at the endless sea of waves and the wispy midday clouds. "'Tis nothing."

"Does it have something to do with that large ghost who follows you?"

He froze, unable to speak for a moment. "A-A large ghost?"

"A big, burly man with dark features."

What little moisture was left in his mouth dried up as if he'd swallowed a mouthful of clay. "And—and he follows me?"

"Everywhere."

He stiffened, looking around as if Rowlen might be sitting beside him. "Is he here now?"

She pointed to an empty space beside him. "Yes."

He could scarcely believe her words, yet there was no guile in her eyes, and she'd described his father perfectly. "Can he tell you what he wants?"

"They don't usually talk to me. Like I said, I'm lonely."

His shoulders fell. "Oh."

"But I imagine he's protecting you. He was by your side through the battles with Eris's soldiers and the carnivus."

Alec's world threatened to spin out of control. "He was?" He thought back to the time when the ship tipped right as that soldier was about to gut him. And how had he managed to escape the hungry carnivus when so many others had been eaten?

Could Rowlen have been protecting him? He had to have known 'twas Alec who'd struck him in the back, even though he'd only done it to stop Rowlen from killing Markus. If Rowlen protected him now, did that mean he'd forgiven Alec for taking his life?

"Are you okay?"

It wasn't until he looked at Mari that he realized he'd been crying. "I'm fine." He wiped his eyes. "It's just, that ghost is my father."

"Oh!" Mari's hand flew to her mouth. "I'm sorry he's dead. I don't know what I'd do if I ever lost my Papa." She glanced at Khashka, who was still brooding in a corner.

"It hasn't been easy," he admitted.

She clutched the stone, smiling affectionately as she floated down to eye level with Alec, the rest of her disappearing under the barge's logs. "You have a kind father."

"I do?" he asked. He released a shaky breath, opening hands he hadn't realized were clenched. "He was unkind once, but 'twas a curse that made him so. I know it wasn't his fault."

She leaned into him. "Your guardian is smiling."

"He is?" Emotion flooded his chest.

She nodded. "It's the first time I've seen him smile."

"Thank you, Mari." A weight lifted from his chest, and for the first time in a long while, he filled his lungs fully. 'Twas then he realized how much the guilt of his father's death had weighed on his soul. "If I could hug you, I would."

When her pale cheeks colored, Alec thought he'd said too much, though he spoke the truth. How cruel fate had been to rob this sweet soul of her body.

"Lunch is served, lad." Grim laid a plank of raw fish fillets before him. "Sorry they can't be cooked, but you must eat to regain your strength." He picked up a fillet, slurping it down with a grimace. "See? Like this." He washed it down with palma juice.

Alec grabbed a fillet, hesitantly taking a bite. It tasted sour, almost spoiled—unusual for fresh meat. He quickly washed it down with palma juice, ignoring Khashka's scowls and grumbling that they were draining their reserves.

Grim slurped down another fillet, then held one up to Khashka. "Hungry? It's nothing like Dwarven meat pies, but it will have to do."

"Not I." Khashka waved the dwarf away.

Alec swallowed another bite, nearly retching it back up, then took another long drink of palma juice. He pushed the plank away. "I can't stomach anymore."

"I must feed Gorpat." Grim abruptly sank to his knees and fell over, his eyes rolling back.

Alec shot up. "Grim!"

He looked at Ryne and Thorne, who'd dropped their blades and were stumbling around the barge like drunks. Alec's tongue and limbs felt strangely heavy.

"Dada!" Gorpat screamed, knocking Alec back with her hot breath. "Dada sick!" She stopped kicking, causing Khashka to nearly tumble off the barge.

"You foolish broots." Khashka kicked over the bucket of fish entrails. "Those fish are somnus."

"Thomnus?" Alec mumbled, his heart slowing to a dull thud.

Swearing, Khashka dumped the guts over the side of the boat. "Don't eat these, Gorpat."

Mari floated down to Alec. "Eris's soldiers used somnus innards to make sleeping darts."

"Oh," Alec rasped, then slid down on his back, blinking up at the blinding sun, his eyelids getting heavier and heavier.

"Khashka!" Thorne cried. "I know why you want to go to Eris's island. 'Tis a fool's quest. Stay the course. Stay, stay...."

Alec heard nothing but the slow beating of his heart and the sound of his father's voice.

Fear not, dear son. I will keep watch.

THE GUARDS LED DIANNA to Simeon and Jae, who were wrapped in leafy cocoons in a small, dank cell. When she blasted the ivy restraints, they shriveled up and turned to dust, leaving Simeon and Jae gaping up at her like newborn babes. The scene was so comical, she couldn't help but laugh.

"What is so funny!" Simeon grumbled, stretching his arms and legs.

She wiped her eyes and fell beside Simeon. "I'm sorry." She took his hands in hers. "Now is not a time for merriment."

To her surprise, he sat up and pulled her hands to his mouth, feathering a soft kiss across her knuckles.

"There's always time to be merry," he said.

She jerked her hands back as if they'd been scalded by his lips. She was angry with herself for falling for Simeon's charms. After what happened with Feira and Tumi, Dianna never wanted to go through the pain of falling in love, only to cruelly lose him to old age and death while she continued on without him.

She got to her feet, wiping her knuckles on her breeches. "Zephyra is imprisoned, and the rest of The Seven are dead."

Jae sat up, brushing debris off her tattered dress. "Why didn't you kill my mother?"

Dianna blinked hard at the lack of emotion in Jae's words, though she could hardly fault her for hating Zephyra. "I couldn't." She turned away, unable to stand the look of disappointment in Jae's eyes.

"I could," Jae whispered.

"Do not worry, sister." Simeon grasped Jae's shoulders, searching her face. "She will face judgment."

When Simeon gave his sister a hard hug, Dianna felt like she was intruding on their tender moment, though she didn't look away. Instead, she watched longingly, yearning to be reunited with her brothers.

Simeon kissed his sister on the forehead, then helped her stand. He released her, then stepped forward, taking Dianna's hands in a surprisingly warm and strong grip. "Thank you for freeing Jae and me, and the people of Kyanu from The Seven's tyranny."

She nodded, feeling regret. Had she found her magic before they'd first fought The Seven, Feira might still be alive. "Feira did not survive." She pulled away from him, wiping her watery eyes.

"I know. She has gone to the Elements with Tumi. Do not cry." He wiped moisture from her cheek. "Tumi will be whole again, and they will be happy together."

"How do you know this?" Dianna sniffled.

"The journey of the afterlife is written in the scrolls," Jae said, "passed down from Kyan."

It is true, Sindri echoed.

Neriphene laughed. *I helped my mother write those scrolls.*

This made no sense. Feira kept her three-hundred-year-old corpse of a husband barely alive when they could have passed happily to the Elements together? "Then why didn't Feira and Tumi go to the Elements long ago?"

Simeon rocked on his heels. "I believe she was waiting for you to take her place."

"Oh." She didn't know if she was ready to accept Feira's role as deity of the Shifting Sands. Up until recently, she had simply been Dianna, big sister to Des, skilled huntress, and secretive witch. She'd been forced to flee with Madhea's dragon, an unwelcome visitor in a strange land. She did not wish to be anyone's deity. She simply wanted to keep her brothers safe.

Simeon arched a brow, his smile revealing the dimple in his cheek. "Have you found your magic?"

She stared down at her hands. Even now she felt the buzzing energy after striking down The Seven. "I have."

"Good." Simeon stepped close to her, so close, his fresh earthy scent wrapped around her senses. "Now we go save your brother."

Chapter Fifteen

ALEC KNEW HE HAD TO be dreaming, for Rowlen was dead, and yet he was back home in the family hut, sitting across from his father at the breakfast table. Father was drinking black coffee, saying not a word while penetrating him with those dark eyes. Their hut was slowly rocking as if 'twas a ship at sea. Alec stood and stared out the window, expecting to see his mother's herb garden. Instead there was a massive volcano jutting out from the ocean, waves crashing against its rocky shore.

Alec stumbled back when a great green beast with dripping fangs passed in front of the window.

He fell back into the chair, looking at his father. "What was that?"

"Eris's dragon," his father answered. "You must wake."

ALEC'S EYES FLEW OPEN, and he rolled over, gasping as he tried to stand.

"Easy, boy, before you topple off the barge."

Alec sat up and looked into Khashka's crinkled eyes through the haze obscuring his vision. "Where are we?" Wherever they were, the thick, soupy air was surprisingly warm, too warm.

The old man's gaze flickered away, then back to Alec, the smile he plastered on his face appearing to be carved of stone. "We are headed for Aloa-Shay." He latched onto Alec's arm. "Don't try to get up."

Alec shook off Khashka's grip. "Don't lie to me." He stumbled to his feet, weaving to the back of the barge where the giant was still kicking. The poor girl's droopy eyes looked ready to fall shut. Her nose and forehead were red from exertion or the sun, her lips chapped, and her fingers soaked, bloated sausages. "Gorpat, are you tired?" Alec asked.

"Gorpat tired." The giant heaved a sigh, her forehead folds handing over her brow. "Gorpat thirsty. Gorpat hungry."

He scanned the fog gathering on the water, so thick he could barely see a few paces in either direction. "Stop kicking. I think we're going the wrong way. I need to wake your father."

He bent down beside the dwarf, shaking his shoulder. "Grim, wake up."

Khashka hovered over them, wringing his fingers together. "I don't think that's a good idea."

He glared at the old man as an unsettling feeling washed over him. When he filled his lungs with the heavy ocean air, he was left with a bitter taste on his tongue, as if he'd eaten ash from a campfire. Though he'd never been to the fishing village of Aloa-Shay, he knew they were far from there.

Something was definitely not right. He shook the dwarf again, to no avail.

He looked up at Khashka with a scowl. "You knew those fish were poisoned. Why didn't you warn us?"

"I can't help it if Thorne is a fool." Khashka chuckled, rubbing a hand over his bald head. "He's a fisherman, too. He should've known better."

Alec stood, clenching his hands in anger. "But Grim and I are not fishermen."

"No matter." Khashka waved at a dark spec in the distance, though it was hard to tell if it was land or illusion, as thick as the air was. "We are almost to land."

"*Which* land?" When Khashka averted his eyes, Alec punched his shoulder. "You son of a siren! You brought us to Eris's island!"

"Alec, please." Mari floated between them. "It's a safer route."

"Is that what you believe, Mari?" Alec spat. "Or are you in on this plan to retrieve your body?"

The spirit winced, looking at Alec as if he'd struck her heart with a barbed arrow. "We are not here to retrieve my body."

"Aren't we?" He looked at Khashka, who turned his back on them both.

"Father!" Mari shrieked, floating after him. "Tell me you did not deliberately put these men's lives in danger."

Khashka walked to the edge of the barge, staring out at the water.

Mari moved in front of him, hovering above the waves. "Answer me!"

"I could not pass up the chance." Khashka threw up his hands. "Mari, we have a goddess stone!"

She shrank back. "Do you think I can defeat Eris with a stone?"

Khashka vehemently shook his head. "We present it to her as a gift in exchange for your body."

Rage pumped through Alec's veins, and he gaped at the man who may have just doomed them all. He advanced upon Khashka with a roar, pushing the man face-first into the water.

"No, Alec!" Mari shrieked, her aura flickering as she swam above the bubbling water in circles.

Alec was relieved when Khashka popped above the surface, grabbing onto the sides of the barge, if only for Mari's sake. He couldn't deny he felt bad for upsetting her, and he, too, wished there was some way they could retrieve her body, but tricking men into taking on the vindictive sea goddess was not the way to do it.

He badly wanted to kick Khashka below the surface for good. "And how do we know she won't just take the stone and kill us all?"

Khashka didn't answer, heaving himself back on the barge without Alec's help. Sitting on the planks, he wrung out his tattered pants. "It's a risk I'm willing to take."

Alec's vision clouded with red. He charged the man again, but Mari blocked him with the stone, sending him flying onto his back.

He shot to his feet, storming toward Khashka again.

"Alec, no!" she pleaded as he passed through her.

"Risk your own neck, old man!" He screamed in Khashka's face, spittle flying from his lips. "Not ours!"

Khashka was wise to scramble to his feet and back up a step. "You will not do this for Mari after she saved you twice and healed your broken bones?"

"No, he won't do it," Mari cried. "I won't let him risk his life for me. We must turn this barge around now!"

Alec's heart came to a violent stop when he went to give the giant orders to turn the barge around. Gorpat was gone!

The barge shook so violently, Alec and Khashka fell over.

"What was that?" Khashka rasped, the whites of his eyes standing out against his tanned, leathery skin.

"Leviathan!" Alec cried as memories of his dream came racing back. "My father warned me in my sleep."

"It's not a dragon." Mari pointed. "It's a broot. Look at all of them!"

A bulbous gray head with a solitary horn surfaced, blowing a spout of water before disappearing beneath their barge. Then another and another. They were surrounded by dozens of sea creatures! He fell to his knees when Gorpat surfaced with them, laughing and waving to Alec. "Big fish friends! Fish play with Gorpat!"

He cupped his hands over his mouth. "Gorpat, do not stray from the barge!"

But the giant was too busy laughing to pay him any heed.

"Great goddess!" Khashka's hands flew to the top of his bald head. "There must be over three dozen."

Indeed, there were so many, Alec lost count. They swam precariously close to them. He felt their low, guttural wails through his feet, yet none of them toppled the barge. Truly, they were gentle giants. He couldn't help but smile as Gorpat laughed and splashed with the horned beasts. She had found kindred spirits.

Mari floated over them, laughing when they sprayed her spirit with water. "I've never seen one up close." She turned to Alec, eyes sparkling. "Aren't they beautiful?"

"Aye," he agreed, though if he was being truthful with himself, he thought Mari far prettier than any whale.

"What's happening? Where are we?"

Grim sat up, rubbing sleep from his eyes. Alec bit back a curse, for once he told Grim of Khashka's trickery, the dwarf would start swinging his axe.

When Ryne and Thorne stirred, Khashka turned as white as his spirit daughter. He would soon face his reckoning.

"No, fishies!" Gorpat hollered. She swam back to the barge when the whales suddenly became violent, jumping out of the water and rolling over each other, bumping the barge so hard, Alec fell and slid to the other side, nearly careening over the edge.

Mari spun a fast circle. "Why are they acting this way?"

Alec pulled himself up once again, scanning the water. Despite the heated air, a chill raced up his arms.

Thorne sprang up like a rodent popping out of his hole, pointing to something in the distance. "Naamaku!"

"Dragon!" Alec cried, his knees buckling as two glowing aqua orbs raced toward them.

"Kick, Gorpat!" Grim screamed. "Kick!"

ONCE AGAIN, THE MOON was heavy in the sky. Thousands of Kyanites gathered along the bank of the pond, their numbers stretching into the dunes and beyond. For the mortals among them, this was their first glimpse at the world above ground. Though a few witches among the crowd seemed uneasy, most easily joined with their mortal kinsmen, linking hands and collectively bowing their heads.

Dressed in a long, black robe, Simeon stood solemnly before the pyre, holding hands with his sisters while reciting the prayer. "Through life these dreams we make. With magic, these blessings we partake. In death our spirits wake. To the Elements we ask our souls to take. Amen."

Dianna was surprised to find the prayer almost identical to the one she had recited for her parents, a prayer that had been passed down through generations in Adolan.

She leaned against Lydra, tracing the membrane of her smooth wing, pleased to see the healing magic she'd used on her after they'd freed Simeon had worked.

Tan'yi'na lit the pyre with his fiery breath. Simeon's sisters had taken much care wrapping Tumi and Feira in shrouds, and within the blink of an eye, they had been reduced to ash.

When the wind shifted direction, bringing smoke and ash, Dianna had to shield her face.

The leviathan attacks. Brother is in danger, the wind hissed.

"Wh-What?" Dianna spun in a circle to find the source of the warning.

'Tis a message from the Elements, Neriphene warned.

Dianna raced up to Tan'yi'na, her heart pumping so fast, she thought it would burst. The golden dragon was hunched over the debris that had once been his deity, his fanged face longer and more drawn than usual.

"I'm sorry," she said, "but we must leave—now."

What do you see?

"Eris's dragon is attacking my brother. We may already be too late."

The dragon's frown deepened. *Naamaku spits venom. I doubt we will make it in time.*

She did her best to quell her shaking limbs. "We have to try."

Chapter Sixteen

GORPAT GRABBED HOLD of the barge and pushed, then abruptly released, letting out an agonized wail when the leviathan drove his fangs into her leg. She turned, crying and shielding her face when the dragon arched back again, blood and venom dripping from his fangs.

A broot jumped between them, spraying the dragon's face with a stream of water. The monster let out a soul-shattering screech and dove for the whale, digging its fangs into its fleshy body. Blood pooled in the water, then the whale let out a shuddering breath and sank. Dozens of whales circled the dragon. Were they risking their lives for Gorpat?

Mari hovered between Gorpat and the serpent. "Stop!" she cried. The stone lit up like a starburst, then emitted spirals of light. The dragon slunk beneath the surface, water bubbling in its wake.

It wasn't until Alec released a pent-up breath of air that he realized he'd stopped breathing. "Is it dead?" he asked as Mari returned, the stone humming softly in her hands.

She shook her head. "I'm not sure."

Thorne squinted into the fog. "A leviathan as powerful as Naamaku doesn't die easily."

"My pearl!" Grim hollered as blood pooled around his daughter's leg.

"Leg burn!" the giant yelled.

Khashka wiped sweat and water off his brow. "She needs to push us to shore, then Mari can heal her wound."

"Aye, you'd like that, you stinking son of a siren!" Grim roared, swinging his axe at Khashka's kneecaps. "Right into the sea witch's den!"

"Grim, we don't have a choice." Alec gestured to the swirling water, where the monster had disappeared a few moments ago. "That dragon may not be dead."

As if to prove Alec's point, the whales scattered as the water began to boil again.

"Go, Gorpat!" Grim bellowed, his eyes widening to saucers. "Kick!"

She kicked up a mountain of water behind her, driving the barge on the edge of a rising crest. The barge continued to tilt forward, forcing Alec and the others to hang on to cracks between the planks, clutching what weapons they could while the rest of their salvaged supplies slid into the ocean. The air was punctured by Gorpat's heavy breathing and the occasional agonizing cry of a whale.

Great goddess, the dragon had awakened!

To Alec's amazement, the broots swam alongside them, coaxing Gorpat forward. Despite the terror which twisted Alec's innards, the gentle beasts brought Alec comfort, and he sensed they were purposely sacrificing themselves to impede the sea serpent.

Ahead, the volcano rose from the sea, shuddering and smoking like an angry god. As the crest beneath their barge grew, he feared they'd all fall into the water. More cries were heard behind them, followed by an angry and ominous roar. Gorpat kicked harder, faster, and just as he feared he'd lose hold of the barge, they were swept into a barren lagoon, its shore covered with black sand.

The leviathan screeched, circling and hurling venom at them, nearly hitting Gorpat's backside.

"Leg hurts," she complained, stumbling to her feet and pulling the barge up the beach.

"That's enough, my pearl," Grim jumped off the barge and ran to his daughter. "Mari!" he called as Gorpat plopped down on her arse with a *thud*.

She went to Gorpat, pressing the pulsing stone against the giant's leg and sealing the wound until it was nothing more than a faint scar.

Gorpat looked down at her father as a fat tear slid down her cheek. "Dragon scare Gorpat. Gorpat no like dragon."

Grim crawled up his child's leg, hugging as much of her as he could get his arms around—and let out a blubbery sob. "I'm so sorry, my pearl. So, so sorry."

Alec narrowed his eyes at Khashka. "You are not the only father who suffers for his child."

Khashka hung his head.

Ryne walked past Khashka, purposely jarring his shoulder. "We need to find food and shelter before more monsters find their way to us."

"Where's Thorne?" Alec asked.

"I don't know," Ryne said, scowling at the lagoon.

Khashka covered his eyes. "He fell off the barge."

Alec gaped at him. "Did you see him fall?"

Ryne circled Khashka with a sneer. "He probably pushed him."

"No." The older man protested. "I would never—"

"And we are supposed to believe the man who poisoned us, tricking us into retrieving his daughter's body?" Ryne jabbed Khashka's chest, backing him up a steep incline. "Tell me, was a venomous sea monster part of your rescue plans?"

Alec followed them. "We have to look for Thorne."

Ryne had Khashka's bony elbow in his grip. "No, *he* has to look for Thorne. I'm not going back out there."

"Nobody is looking for Thorne." Grim stalked up to them, chest heaving. "'Tis a fool's errand. There is no possible way he survived."

Alec's heart sank. Thorne had told him he was a good swimmer, but Grim was right. No mere mortal could have survived falling into the sea serpent's path.

Khashka pulled away from Ryne, running a shaky hand down his arm. "I agree with the dwarf."

Ryne advanced on Khashka again. "Nobody asked your opinion."

"They're coming!" Mari shouted, then fluttered away like a bird, disappearing up Gorpat's sleeve.

"Trespassers. In the name of Eris, drop your weapons!"

A row of at least three dozen beefy soldiers stood on the ridge above them, wielding spears big enough to take down full grown broots.

A team of soldiers rolled up a cannon, pointing it directly at Gorpat.

One soldier stepped forward. He was the biggest of them all and covered with patches of discolored skin ranging from pink to dark brown, as if the Elements had sewn him together, creating a human quilt from many different-colored men. Even his eyes were two different colors, one pale pink and the other dark brown. He wore a green breastplate that was similar to the sea serpent's scales and had the bearing of a military captain. "Drop your weapons, or we fire a cannon through the giant's skull."

"Curse the Elements!" Grim dropped his axe to the ground.

Alec threw his blade, and Ryne tossed a sword.

Khashka held up his hands. "Please take us to your goddess. We mean her no harm. We only wish to make a trade."

Patchwork Captain pointed his sword at Khashka. "What do you have that our goddess could possibly want?"

"What do we have?" Khashka cast Ryne a wary look and then stepped forward. "A rare and sacred treasure."

"No, Khashka," Alec hissed. "It belongs to the Ice People. It is not yours to trade." The man was desperate to retrieve his daughter's body, but that didn't give him the right to steal, not to mention a goddess stone in Eris's hands was dangerous.

"You would dare give away my people's stone?" Ryne's blue face turned an alarming purple.

Deep lines marred Khashka's brow. "Neither of you have children. You do not know the daily pain I suffer, having my child near but so far away, never being able to hold her in my arms, knowing she can never have a family of her own. I would give Eris my soul and all of yours if she would but give my daughter her body back."

A gasp and then a soft sob came from Mari, who was clearly distraught over her father's deception.

"Very well," the soldier said, whistling to the others.

They shot Gorpat full of darts. The giant stumbled, then fell on her arse. The ground shuddered under her weight.

"My pearl!" With a roar, Grim dove for his axe, then fell face-first into the black sand, a dart sticking out of his buttocks.

Alec raced to Grim, pulled the dart out, and rolled him on his back.

Before Alec could stop them, four burly soldiers had him in a headlock and were binding his wrists in heavy chains. They did the same to Khashka and Ryne before connecting everyone at the ankles with short lengths of chain.

"What will happen to them?" Alec whispered to Ryne, staring forlornly at Grim and Gorpat.

The leviathan still paced the waters like a hawk circling his prey. "The giant and dwarf? They'll probably be fed to the dragon."

Alec glared at Khashka. "See what you've done?"

He had the decency to stare at his feet. "I didn't intend for anyone to get hurt."

"I think you did." Ryne's grumble sounded like Tar's low growl. "You just didn't care."

DIANNA HELD TIGHT TO Lydra as they flew low across the water. Beside her, Simeon rode Tan'yi'na. Simeon had been solemn since he'd said goodbye to his sisters and the people of Kyanu, leaving them in the capable hands of Rení the Wise. The old man had graciously accepted the role as Kyanu's new deity, though he insisted the position was only temporary.

When a brilliant burst of fire lit the sky, Dianna looked over at Tan'yi'na, who flashed a fanged smile. *It feels good to fly over the ocean again.*

Simeon fanned his face when Tan'yi'na's cinders and smoke blew over him. His dour mood was out of character, and she knew he feared not returning to his family. Though she'd begged him to stay behind, he'd insisted on accompanying her. She prayed that his charms would work on Eris. She would never forgive herself if the sea goddess took her wrath out on him.

*Hurry. You mussst stop the sssacrifice, t*he Elements whistled in her ear.

"Sacrifice? What sacrifice?"

The sssea witch will have all the power.

She leaned over her dragon's neck, peering at the ocean waves that moved like a blur beneath them. Lydra had never flown this fast before.

"This is as fast as we can fly," she said to the wind.

Not fassst enough, the Elements hissed. *We'll help you.*

She looked over her shoulder and saw a sideways funnel of wind stretching toward them like a giant finger.

"Brace yourselves!" she screamed. "The Elements are coming!'

When Simeon looked behind them, his mouth fell open. "What in Elements' name is that?"

Dianna didn't have time to answer as she hunched over Lydra and faced forward.

The dragons roared when the wind tunnel caught them, but the sound was sucked into the vortex. She held tight to her dragon's reins as the wind propelled them at mind-numbing speeds. Islands and ships passed in a blur, and they streaked across the sky like falling stars. Not much longer, and Dianna would face down a goddess.

Chapter Seventeen

Sacrifice of the Sea Witch

ERIS'S SOLDIERS LEFT Grim and Gorpat behind and marched Alec, Ryne, and Khashka across the hostile volcanic landscape for what seemed like hours. The sweltering heat made Alec's legs go weak, and he stumbled across scalding rocks that bloodied and bruised his feet. He alternated between crying out in pain, worrying over Grim and Gorpat, and dreading his meeting with the sea goddess.

Every so often Alec caught sight of Mari behind a bush or boulder, ducking when the soldiers looked in her direction. Many times he tried to signal her. Why hadn't she used the goddess stone to save them?

By the time they arrived at a cave high above the shore and at the base of the smoking volcano, the blisters on Alec's burned feet ached so badly, he feared they were infected. When the soldiers unlocked their ankle chains and led them to a shallow pool deep within the cavern, collective sighs and moaning ensued as everyone fell to their knees, drinking the water.

Alec nearly passed out from exhaustion while splashing his face. Despite the difficulty of working with bound hands, he managed to palm several scoops of water, spilling most of it down his bare chest, trying to wet his blistered lips. He sat back and took in his surroundings, wincing when the cracks in his heels split open, though he was too tired and terrified to dwell on his feet overly long.

The cavern was eerily beautiful, with huge crystal spikes rising from the ground and similar dripping spikes hanging from the ceiling. Some of them appeared to be lit from within, illuminating the cavern with a pleasant, soft glow. On the other side of the pool was a stone throne with a raised, steaming pool in front of it. Mist swirled from the top of it, fanning down the sides and out across the surface of the water, making it look like a miniature volcano.

Alec jerked at the sound of a soft splash and saw Mari in the water.

"Mari," he whispered. "Do something."

"I can't," she said. "Aletha will not help."

He bent over her, unable to keep the note of desperation out of his voice. "Why?"

"She's angry that my father deceived us."

Alec fought back the urge to punch the water. Now was not the time to hold grudges. "Tell her if she doesn't help us now, we will all be captured by Eris, including her."

Mari's spirit faded in and out like a blurred dream. "She is trying to get me to flee the island and take her back to Ice Kingdom."

"And risk Madhea capturing her?" When a soldier passed behind him, Alec dropped his voice to a low whisper. "Tell her if she helps us, I will persuade Ryne to take her to the Shifting Sands."

Ryne knelt beside Alec, jabbing him in the ribs. "Eris!"

Alec looked up, his breath catching in his throat at the sight of the beautiful woman whose head had surfaced at the other end of the shallow pool. Long, black hair clung to her back in sodden waves as she gracefully rose above the water, swimming past them as if propelled by magic.

When she struggled to pull herself onto the rocky bank, he was compelled to look away but not before he saw the awkward fish tail and gills. Spying from under his lashes, he observed her slither across the slick stone floor before pulling herself up on a throne covered with carvings of broot whales. Her deep blue tail twitched as it slapped the slab beneath her. He kept his head bent while Eris's assessing look swept over the row of prisoners.

She steepled her fingers, regarding Ryne for a long moment. "Who speaks for you?"

Ryne and Khashka answered simultaneously, "I do."

Eris scowled at Khashka, waving him away with a flick of the wrist. "I would hear from the blue man." She offered Ryne a fanged smile, her gaze roaming the length of his body. "What is your name?"

"Ryne Nordlund," he answered tersely, stiffening.

"Ryne?" She toyed with a strap on a flimsy leather top that barely covered her chest. "What magic has turned your skin blue?"

"I'm not sure." His voice was emotionless, as was his expression. "It's how I've always been."

She licked her lips and shifted in her seat. "Where are you from?"

"Ice Mountain."

"Madhea's mountain?" The goddess leaned forward, her tilted eyes narrowing to slits. "Do you serve her?"

Ryne puffed up his chest. "I serve no one."

"No?" She tossed her wet hair over a shoulder, laughing. "Soon you will be serving me."

Ryne turned as pale as Mari's inert stone.

"Oh wise and beautiful goddess." Khashka waved his bound wrists at her.

She bared her fangs with a hiss. "I didn't give you leave to speak."

He hung his head, his cheeks coloring. "Forgive me, but I have an urgent message for you."

"Urgent?" She arched a thin brow, drumming her fingers on the armrest. "Well, spit it out then."

Khashka released a shuddering breath. "Fifteen years ago, you took my daughter's body from her, leaving her spirit to wander the earth. It was a lesson well learned for killing your beloved broot whale." He wiped the sweat off his brow. "I have since learned the error of my ways, and I vow to never harm another broot again." He struck a prayer pose, his hands shaking so hard, Alec feared the man was about to seize. "Please give my daughter's body back to her, and in return, I will give you something more valuable."

Ryne jumped to his feet, chest heaving as he bore down on Khashka, his bound hands raised. "It is not yours to give, old man!"

"Oh, Captain?" Eris drawled, pointing to Patchwork Captain.

He swiped Ryne's legs out from under him, and he fell to the hard ground with a crack and a groan.

"Bow before your goddess!" the captain hollered, the pale parts of his patched skin turning bright pink.

Ryne slowly came to his knees, shooting the captain a look that could melt metal.

"Enough!" Eris held up a hand when the captain advanced upon Ryne again. Her lips pulled back in a sinister smile, the wicked gleam in her eyes more threatening than her sharp fangs. "What could be more valuable than her two beautiful, long legs and pretty smile?"

"We have recently discovered a goddess stone, and I offer it in trade for my child's body."

The sea witch bolted up and flung herself into the pool. She swam the short distance between them, climbing up the rocky embankment and sidling up to Khashka with an inhuman growl. "The Elements hid those stones far below the earth centuries ago. How did you come by one?"

A bead of sweat rolled down his brow. "It belonged to an ice dweller, who has since been eaten by your sirens."

"The stone belongs to the Ice People and is not available for trade," Ryne bellowed, then fell over when the captain clubbed him on the back of the head.

"Do not kill him!" Eris spat. "Put him in the dungeon."

"Yes, my deity."

Alec's heart felt as if it would implode when two soldiers hauled Ryne's limp body away. Despite all the trouble the ice dweller had caused, Alec feared he'd never see him again.

Eris slithered between him and Khashka, her twitching tail nearly slapping his knees. He slowly scooted back, the dark aura which radiated from her soul shrouding him like a poisonous fog.

"Let me see it," she whispered in Khashka's ear.

The old man trembled. "Only after you return my child's spirit to her body."

She dragged a fingernail across his bald head, inspecting him as if he was a cut of meat. "I will do no such thing."

"I'm sorry." His voice shook. "I cannot give you the stone then."

She tilted back her head and laughed, her high-pitched squeal hurting Alec's ears.

"You are a funny man." She toyed with his ear, tracing a pattern down his neck. "Where is your spirit daughter?"

"She is here somewhere."

When the goddess batted her long lashes, Alec easily saw through her attempt at kindness, for the chill that radiated from her eyes reminded him of a serpent preparing to strike her prey.

"The chalice!" She snapped her fingers, and the captain brought forth a wide bronze goblet intricately carved with broot whales on the sides and matching lid. She palmed it in both hands, and the soldier removed the lid. Swirling mists poured forth.

"Have her put the stone in this chalice,"—she held it above her head—"and I promise you her beautiful body will rise, and you can hold her once again."

"Thank you, my goddess."

Khashka let out a blubbering sob, and Alec couldn't help but feel pity for him. Though stealing the stone was wrong, loving one's child was not. What he wouldn't have given to have been loved like that by his father.

"Mari!" Khashka called. "Come out."

"No, Father. The stone is not mine to give."

Alec searched the cavern, but didn't see Mari.

"Mari!" Khashka's face reddened. "Do what the goddess says."

"The chalice is a trap. She intends to banish my spirit to the Elements and take my body for herself."

Time grounded to a halt as Alec slowly processed Mari's words. Banish Mari! Fear pumped wildly through his veins.

"W-What?" Khashka stammered.

"That has been her plan all along."

"Silly spirit." Eris handed the chalice back to Patchwork Captain. "Where did you hear such nonsense?"

"The goddess stone told me."

Eris tensed, let out a screech, then dove into the water, disappearing in its depths.

Alec's innards quaked with fear when she resurfaced, pulling herself up with a snarl. When she turned to them, he nearly vomited. Her eyes glowed an unnatural aqua, like the color of snake moss in the sunlight.

"Foolish stone!" she shrieked at the ceiling, her voice shrill. "You ruined my surprise!"

Alec hunched when the hanging spikes trembled above his head. Should they fall, their sharp points would surely pierce his flesh.

Eris motioned to Alec and Khashka. "Throw them over the cliff to Naa-maku."

Great goddess!

Khashka slumped against Alec. "What have I done?"

"No!" Mari screamed, appearing, the stone pulsing in her hands.

Eris hit the spirit with a bright bolt, knocking her back and twisting a rope of energy around her. "The chalice!" she hollered, and Patchwork Captain rushed over with the open goblet. Mari shrieked when Eris dragged the soul toward her using the magic rope and laughed. "Think a mere stone could take on a goddess?" She tossed Mari into the chalice and slammed the lid shut. Holding her prizes in her hands, she laughed maniacally, bolts of electricity dancing around her.

Alec's tenuous grasp on hope slipped away. Mari's spirit was to be banished, lost to him forever. He wanted nothing more than to let Eris banish him, too.

The sea witch turned her ghoulish gaze on Alec and Khashka.

"What are you waiting for?" she sneered to her soldiers. "Naamaku needs to be fed."

THE SUN RELENTLESSLY beat down on them while Alec trudged back across the treacherous terrain with a heavy heart. What a fool he'd been to leave the safety of the dwarves to go after Ryne. Now everyone he loved was about to die, and Eris had a goddess stone and would soon have human legs. Her increased power meant trouble not only for Madhea, but for the rest of humanity as well—perhaps even Dianna and the people of the Shifting Sands. But what made Alec's soul weep was knowing that Mari's sweet soul would be banished forever. She had not asked for any of this. She'd been an innocent when Eris took her body, and she was an innocent still. Had Khashka been able to retrieve her body, she might have lived a long, happy life. Perhaps Alec would have courted her, for she had a gentle spirit in her beautiful smile. How could the Elements have designed a goddess to be such a heartless monster?

Alec's battered feet left a trail of blood across the hot black stones, and his strength faltered many times. He tripped, skinning his knees and bringing Khashka down with him. The old man didn't complain. Alec barely flinched when Eris's menacing soldiers swore and struck them with whips. Soon it would all be over. Markus, Des, and Dianna would lose a brother, and the world would lose hope. The thought of never seeing his family again made him sway on his feet. Heartbroken and exhausted, he struggled to keep his eyes open while slipping in and out of awareness. He feared dying a miserable death on this cursed island.

Alec stumbled when a soldier applied a whip across his back.

Do not give up, son. The wind that whispered in his ear sounded too much like Rowlen.

Visions swam before Alec's eyes. Were they illusions, or did he see the shadow of his father's ghost?

"I have no strength left to fight, Father," he murmured, staring blankly at the backs of two burly soldiers. True, there were only four, two leading and two behind, but they might as well have been twenty. Alec had not the will to take on one soldier.

I will be your strength.

Alec stilled, held up by some invisible force that then moved him forward, as if he was being carried on the wind.

"Thank you, Father," Alec whispered, a lone tear sliding down his cheek. Whatever monster Rowlen had been when he was alive had died when Alec drove that blade into his back. "I know 'twas not your fault."

A shadow flickered before him. *Do you forgive me?*

"Aye, Father." Alec blinked back more tears. "I forgive you, though there is nothing to forgive. Do you forgive me for killing you?"

You didn't kill me. You freed me from the monster. I will do what I can to free you, too.

Alec stumbled when he heard a roar in the distance. "I hope so, Father."

THE SOLDIERS LED THEM up a steep hill toward the edge of a cliff that overlooked the black-sand beach where they'd first landed. The sirens' laughs below were punctured by the earth-shattering roar of the dragon. Gorpat was still sleeping on the beach. She and Grim were surrounded by about a dozen soldiers, who were debating the best way to get the giant back in the water.

Grim paced circles on top of his child's belly. Somehow he'd gotten hold of his axe, and he was threatening to cut off the bollocks of any soldier who drew near. How Alec wished he could break free of his chains and save his friends, but he'd failed them all.

"Shoot him with a dart!" Patchwork Captain called to them, his one pink eye fading to a milky white and then back to pink.

"We would, captain," another soldier responded, "but we are out."

"Why doesn't he shoot him with a spear?" a soldier grumbled, sweat darkening his matted locks.

The captain laughed, his pale pink spots turning a dark crimson. "You know Naamaku likes to kill her food." He tossed a leather sack to the other soldiers.

They hollered and hooted, pulling out several darts and tubes. Grim deflected three darts with his hatchet before one finally struck his arm. The dwarf quickly jerked it out, tossing it to the ground with a curse, then his eyes rolled back, and he fell on his daughter's chest. Eris's soldiers dragged him off the giant and up the hill.

Gorpat let out a shuddering breath. "Dada," she mumbled.

"Hurry, before the beast wakes!" Patchwork Captain called down.

This was Alec's one and only chance to warn Gorpat. He groaned while lifting his arms weighted heavily with rusty chains, then cupped his hands around his cracked lips, and despite a parched mouth managed to holler, "Watch out, Gorpat! Eris's soldiers have your father!"

The captain spun on Alec with a roar, both eyes turning as black as coal. "Silence!" He raised his whip as if to strike, then stumbled back as a gust of wind hit him in the face. "Help!" he cried, tripping backward.

Alec sighed. "Thank you, Father."

The captain would have fallen off the edge of the cliff if two soldiers hadn't caught him at the last moment.

"What in Elements happened?" a soldier asked Patchwork Captain.

The captain pointed at Alec. "Earth speaker."

The captain advanced on him, and Alec stepped back, then stumbled over his chains and fell on his arse, taking Khashka down with him.

They all turned at the blood-curdling screams coming from the beach below. Alec stumbled to his feet and watched with fascination and horror as Gorpat tossed soldiers into the sea, right into the leviathan's open maw. When she grabbed the two soldiers who were hauling Grim up the hill, they begged and pleaded to no avail. She tossed them as if she was skipping rocks, skimming across the surface before the dragon snapped them in two.

The captain and his three soldiers ran to a cannon positioned between blocks on the edge of the cliff. The gears made loud grinding noises as they turned the barrel toward the giant's back.

"Behind you!" Alec screamed.

Gorpat spun around and plucked two of the soldiers from the cannon, tossing them like pebbles into the sea. Two hungry sirens grabbed one soldier, shredding his flesh from his bones in a matter of seconds. The leviathan took the other.

The captain and the last remaining soldier abandoned the cannon and sprinted down the hill, emerging with a sleeping Grim in their arms.

"No!" Alec yelled. Despite the fatigue which had turned his bones to clay, he summoned strength from deep within and stumbled to his feet, swaying while yanking on Khashka's chains. "Get up, old man." No sooner had Khashka stood than Alec was yanking him toward Grim's captors. They stumbled into a run, but they were no match for the burly soldiers, whose long legs were double Alec's stride.

The soldiers released Grim over the side of the cliff as Alec and Khashka came upon them. Alec ran into the captain full force, butting his backside with his head and sending him careening over the edge. Khashka kicked the legs of the other soldier. The man spun around in horror, grabbing for Alec's chains, but a sudden wind pushed him back. He slid down the cliff face and fell on a rock below, dying instantly. Sirens made quick work of him, leaving behind nothing but bones. Grim floated in the current, face-down beside them. If Grim didn't drown, surely he'd be eaten.

As the leviathan dove for Grim, Gorpat raced into the water, latching onto the monster's tail. The sirens shrieked and swam away when the monsters fought, the leviathan pulling Gorpat farther from her father.

Do not go in the water, the wind whispered in Alec's ear.

"Sorry, Father." Alec heaved a groan, then jerked on Khashka's chain. "I hope you're a good swimmer."

"I am," the old man said, gaping at the scene below. "This is the least I can do for the dwarf after the fool I've been."

Together they jumped off the cliff. They screamed all the way down and hit the water feet first. Alec instinctively curled into a fetal position, sinking past long tendrils of seaweed while flaming arrows of pain shot up his heels. Great goddess! The water's surface had been as unyielding as a block of ice. He opened his eyes, struggling to swim to the top, but Khashka was motionless below him, sinking like a stone and pulling them both toward a watery grave.

Alec shook the old man's shoulder, then saw they were falling into the open jowls of a carnivus. He shook the old man harder. The plant reared up and swallowed Khashka, its jagged teeth snapping the chains that bound Alec to the old man.

He had no time to mourn Khashka as he swam away from the monster plant's reach to the surface.

The waters around him were in turmoil, and he nearly slammed against a crop of sharp-edged rocks as he made for Grim. The dwarf had flipped on his back and appeared to be slipping in and out of consciousness. He grabbed Grim's hand and tugged him toward the beach while Gorpat and the dragon fought.

The leviathan turned on Gorpat, biting the giant's arm. She let out a wail and slammed him against the side of the cliff. He landed in the water, creating such a large wave, it sent Alec and Grim into the middle of the lagoon. Another wave pushed them under. The dwarf thrashed wildly against the current. Alec was kicking toward the surface when he saw rows of snapping carnivus teeth within striking distance of his feet.

Alec hauled Grim against him, then swore when he saw a trio of pretty female heads bobbling close to shore. He wouldn't stand a chance against the sirens.

"Come clossser," they hissed, crooking long fingers at Alec. A wave splashed over his head, filling his ears with water just as they broke into song, thank the Elements, for they were far enough away that their seductive music was muffled and indecipherable.

His options were to swim back out into the ocean, where no doubt carnivus plants would be waiting for their next meal, risk trying to get past the voracious sirens, or swim toward the cliff where Gorpat fought the leviathan. He spied a shallow cave in the cliff face. If he could get around the monsters, they could wait out the battle.

"My pearl needs help," Grim sputtered.

"Are you awake now?"

"Aye," Grim said. "Take me to my pearl. I cannot swim fast enough with these stubby legs."

Alec held Grim's hand and kicked off toward the cliff. "I doubt there is much we can do against a dragon."

Grim spit out a mouthful of water. "Never underestimate a father's determination."

They fought wave after wave, swimming through and under them until they reached the cliff. Gorpat was losing strength. Though she held the serpent in a headlock, he'd managed to puncture her arm with sharp fangs, her flesh around the wounds sizzling like frying bacon.

"I'm coming, my pearl!" Grim cried, hopping up on a jagged boulder with surprising speed. He soared to the cliff wall with a grunt, then began the ascent up the side as if he was part goat.

Breathless and fatigued beyond imagining, Alec slumped on a large rock, his dangling chains rattling as he watched the dwarf climb ever higher until he was above the serpent. Grim lifted a boulder over his head and hurled it at the leviathan's mouth. It bounced off one of the beast's teeth, cracking it in two before tumbling into the ocean. The leviathan released his hold on Gorpat. The dwarf made a quick retreat up the side of the cliff, barely avoiding the serpent's strike. The leviathan cried out again as another tooth broke off.

A loud rush of water startled Alec. The lagoon appeared to be draining at an alarming rate, the water rushing out to sea. Carnivus tipped on their sides, fish flopped in pockets of water, and sirens disappeared.

What was happening?

Gorpat released the leviathan, clutching her sore arm as the water drained down to her knees. When the dragon chased after the current, Gorpat scooped up Grim and Alec, smashing carnivus plants while trudging to shore. She fell on the black sand with a deep boom, Alec and Grim tumbling out of her hands.

"My baby pearl!" Grim wailed. "You are injured."

Alec's chest tightened with panic at the number of bloody and festering gashes covering the giant's body. The skin around the wounds was turning gray, and Alec worried the giant would succumb to the venom.

Gorpat fell on her back, staring up at the sky. "Gorpat save Dada."

He climbed up her dripping hair. "Yes, you did, my pearl." Tears flowed down his ruddy cheeks as he planted a kiss on the tip of her flat nose. "You shall always be Dada's heroine."

She smiled at that, then lifted a bloody hand. "Dragon hurt Gorpat." When she turned her hand over, Alec cringed at her three missing fingernails. "Gorpat no like dragon."

Grim patted her cheek. "Me neither."

Alec surveyed the lagoon, fearing 'twas no coincidence it was nearly drained. Hundreds of upturned carnivus plants, ranging from smaller than Alec's foot to as large as Gorpat's head, made sickening wheezing sounds while struggling for breath. Two sirens, surrounded by mounds of human remains, flopped in shallow puddles, calling out for Alec to save them. Their shrill screams made Alec wish Eris's soldiers hadn't taken his bow and arrows. One rather large carnivus caught Alec's eye, for it had a familiar chain hanging from a spiked tooth.

Alec raced through the marshy lagoon, dodging the razor-sharp teeth of smaller plants. He cautiously stepped up to the monster plant, which heaved and shuddered, its mouth falling open with a final wheeze. He tugged hard on the chain, pulling with all his might until Khashka slid off the monster's gray tongue.

With a groan, he heaved the old man onto his shoulders, stumbling through the muck as he carried him to the beach. Grim helped him get Khashka off his back.

Alec fell beside Khashka and turned him on his side, knocking water from his lungs.

"No, like this." Grim pushed Alec aside and pumped the old man's chest, stopping to blow air into his mouth. The dwarf felt the vein on Khashka's neck, then placed an ear to his chest. "He's barely breathing."

"Ahhhlec," Khashka whispered before a stream of blood poured from his mouth.

Alec leaned over him. "What is it?"

"Mari. Save her."

How he wished he could save the pretty spirit from banishment, but he was no match for the sea goddess. Khashka heaved a shuddering breath, and his mouth dropped open.

Grim shut the man's eyes. When he bowed his head, Alec joined him in reciting a prayer for Khashka's soul.

The afternoon sun had fallen midway toward the horizon, as they carried Khashka to the top of the hill, laying him beside the cannon and covering him in a tarp they'd found in the soldiers' supplies. Gorpat was leaning against the side of the hill when they descended, her snake bites, oozing blood and puss, far worse. Alec feared the giant would soon succumb to her wounds.

"Dragons, Dada!" Gorpat hollered, pointing to two winged silhouettes circling overhead.

"Elements save us! More bloody dragons!" Grim squinted at the darkening sky.

Alec's heart plummeted, then raced when he noticed one of the dragon's iridescent wings looked all too familiar. A woman leaned over the dragon's neck, her long blonde hair flowing behind her, reminding Alec of the ethereal scrolls picturing Madhea in flight. She wildly waved her hands, then both dragons nose-dived right for them.

When Grim grabbed his hatchet, grumbling, Alec placed a hand on the dwarf's shoulder. "It's okay." A deep, rich burst of belly laughter sprung from him for the first time in what felt like many moons. "We're saved."

Chapter Eighteen

"BROTHER, YOU ARE ALIVE!" Dianna jumped off Lydra and leaped into her brother's arms.

He flinched and drew back. "Sister? What are you doing here?"

"We've come to save you." She shuddered when she saw his shredded feet. Oh, heavenly Elements! Her poor brother. What torture he must have endured.

And defeat the sea witch. Tan'yi'na added.

She touched Alec's cuts and bruises, effortlessly healing them, then looked around. How had the marshy lagoon been drained of water? Was Madhea's power strengthening? The setting sun glared through the clouds, making it hard for her to see how far this drought stretched. Behind her a mountain marred by rivers of lava loomed, smoking and spitting ash and radiating heat over the entire island.

"You've come to battle Eris?" A dwarf with ruddy cheeks, slapping an axe in his palm, leaned against the leg of a giant sleeping girl. "Are you mad?"

"Perhaps." She shrugged.

"I didn't know your magic was so strong." Alec flexed his fingers, then looked at the smooth soles of his feet.

"Neither did I." She chuckled. "I seemed to have discovered a deep well of magic."

"Then there is hope you can save Mari?" Alec's words were hopeful. "Eris is going to banish her spirit to the Elements and steal her body."

"Is Mari your friend?" she asked.

"Aye."

When her brother's cheeks colored, she suspected Mari was more than a friend. Even more reason for her to defeat Eris. "Don't worry, Alec." She grabbed his hands. "I will do all I can for her."

"Thank you." He took her in a fierce hug, then gestured at the dwarf and giant. "This is Grim and his daughter, Gorpat. They've saved my arse more times than I care to count."

"Thank you for keeping my brother safe." She smiled warmly at Grim, curious as to how he'd come to be the father of a giant.

"It was my pleasure. He's a good lad who's bravely saved me, too." Grim wiped misty eyes before glancing at his child. "Think your magic is powerful enough to heal a giant? I fear my sweet pearl may not make it...." The little man let out a strangled sob.

Her heart clenched as Grim's pain became hers, shrouding her with his sorrow. She walked the length of the giant, who laid supine, breathing heavily. Gorpat was covered in oozing bloody welts, each the width of a dragon's bite. Only one creature could have inflicted such injuries: Eris's sea serpent. She prayed Gorpat had defeated Naamaku before succumbing to her injuries.

Start with the heart, Sindri whispered, *before the poison reaches it.*

She threw a tendril of magic over Gorpat, then climbed up the rope and onto the giant's chest.

Gorpat's eyes were shut, her breaths torturous. Kneeling, she placed a palm on the giant's chest, alarmed at her slowing heartbeat.

"I fear the poison has already spread to her heart."

Hurry, Neriphene urged.

Shutting her eyes, she summoned her healing magic, traveling to that place between this world and the next, then going farther still, knowing she needed to draw on the full strength of her magic. She flew over Neriphene and Sindri toward a bright and brilliant sun, basking in its glow.

Come back, Dianna, before you go too far, Neriphene called.

She threw out her arms, shuddering a breath of surrender, then fell back, back, past her cousins to the mortal plane. When she awoke, she was snuggling in Gorpat's arms, and the giant was sitting up and smiling down at her.

"Pretty girl save Gorpat." The giant sniffled, then smeared Dianna's hair and arms with sticky fingers. "Gorpat like pretty girl."

She smiled back. "I like Gorpat, too." She looked down at Gorpat's arms and legs, pleased to see the welts were no more than faint scars.

"You saved my pearl!" Grim hobbled up Gorpat's arm, yanked Dianna down to his level with a surprisingly firm grip, and wrapped his stubby arms around her shoulders. "I owe you my life!" He sobbed into her hair.

"No." She pulled back, offering the dwarf a warm smile. "You've saved my brother many times. Now we're even."

"Just like your brothers said." Grim sniffled. "'A good witch.'" Then he fell on his daughter's arm. "My sweet baby pearl!" he spoke through a blubbery snort. "Dada was so worried!"

Dianna slid down a rope of magic, right into Simeon's embrace. Heat flamed her cheeks when she backed away.

Simeon scowled at his hands. "You're covered in something."

Dianna shrugged. "Just giant boogers." She couldn't help but laugh when Simeon frantically brushed his hands down his pants.

"Alec," Dianna said. "This is Simeon, a distant grandson of the Goddess, Kyan, and this is Tan'yi'na." She pointed at the golden dragon. "He served Kyan when she ruled the Shifting Sands."

Greetings, mortal, Tan'yi'na said haughtily.

Simeon held out a hand to her brother. "I can't tell you how relieved I am that you're alive. Your sister feared the worst."

Alec jerked Simeon toward him, violently shaking his hand. "I can assure you I'm well. And how *well* do you know my sister?"

"Uh...." Simeon looked like a lamb at slaughter. "We're merely friends. Good friends."

"That's *good* to know." Alec continued to shake Simeon's hand, squeezing so tight, Simeon jerked back with a grunt to free himself.

Dianna had to bite back a laugh. She'd never seen this protective side of Alec before.

Mortals, Tan'yi'na asked, *how long has this lagoon been empty?*

"Only a few moments," Alec said. "The water rushed out unexpectedly."

I saw this happen a millennia ago, when Eris and Madhea were at war. The spice traders named it the ocean's kiss, Tan'yi'na said.

"Sounds beautiful." Dianna shrank back when Lydra's nostrils flared, and she let out a high-pitched wail after sniffing the air.

Get to higher ground! Tan'yi'na boomed, snatching Simeon in his jowls and tossing him on his back before jumping into the air.

Dianna swung onto Lydra's back and held a hand down to her brother. "Come with us!"

Alec stepped back as Gorpat stumbled to her feet. "I'm not leaving my friends."

"What in the Elements is that?" Grim stood on his daughter's shoulder and pointed an axe at something in the distance.

Dianna's heart hit her stomach when Lydra lurched into the air. It took her a moment to realize a wall of water twice the height of Gorpat was barreling down on the island.

"Monster wave!" Grim screamed.

Oh, heavenly Elements! Alec and his friends would perish!

Tan'yi'na flew above the clouds. Gorpat raced up the beach with Alec in her fist and Grim clinging to her hair. Dianna yanked on Lydra's rope. "Hold, girl. We must stop it!"

Dianna's spirit flew to the place between two worlds and summoned the deep magic. "Stop!" Her command was a boom that rent the air like a crack of thunder. The wave froze, suspended. Magic pulsed through her fingers and her chest heaved as she struggled to push the wave back. She did not know how long she could hold it. As if sensing her distress, Lydra flew under the curved monolithic shadow of the stationary wave, blowing out a curtain of ice and solidifying the water.

When they emerged, Dianna released her magic with a groan. As tension slowly unwound from her neck and sore muscles, she was pleased to see the wave holding steady as a giant glacier. She patted her dragon's scales. "Good work, girl."

With the catastrophe momentarily averted, Dianna only had to worry about taking down the goddess who'd created it, for no mere witch could harvest such Elemental power.

Lydra landed on a cliff overlooking the lagoon. Gorpat's footsteps made the ground thunder beneath them as she climbed up the side of the hill.

Alec climbed onto Gorpat's other shoulder and let out a low whistle. "Eris must know you're here."

"No, not Eris!" A shrill voice called down from atop the glacier, his profile a shadow against the setting sun. "Do you think the sea goddess is the only one who can bend the Elements to her will?"

"Thorne?" Alec was surprised. "You're an earth speaker?"

Alec knew this earth speaker? She squinted at the shadowy man. Even from this distance, his golden eyes sparkled like twin suns. A misguided descendent of Kyan, no doubt.

Dafuar and Odu have spread many seeds across this earth, Sindri said, *leaving their magical roots to grow untethered and unchecked.*

And unhinged, Neriphene added wryly.

"My goddess says I'm the most powerful earth speaker who's ever lived." His maniacal laughter echoed across the lagoon. "Once I finish destroying your witch sister, and Eris claims a new body, we will rule the world together."

Tan'yi'na flew down to them, with Simeon perched between his wings. A low chuckle reverberated from the dragon's chest. *And you believe that lying witch?*

"Do not dare blaspheme my goddess!" Thorne shrieked, a deafening crack rending the air.

Dianna jerked back, expecting the ice wall to shatter.

Tan'yi'na shook his head, a cloud of smoke blowing through his flared nostrils. *Eris and Madhea have a truce. The Elementals will not let her break it.*

The earth speaker floated down to the edge of the cliff as if he rode an invisible cloud, boldly coming within striking distance of Tan'yi'na. Dianna was struck by his plain appearance. He was thin and only about a head taller than her young brother, Des, the lines framing his tapered eyes and slight peppering of gray in his cropped hair revealing he was around the age of her deceased father. 'Twas hard to believe such a small and simple man wielded so much power.

Thorne tilted his chin at Tan'yi'na, his lips pulled back in a snarl, revealing a mouthful of rotting teeth. "Eris killed her Elementals years ago."

Dianna gasped, sharing horrified looks with Tan'yi'na. "She killed her own children?"

Thorne shrugged, then looked at her with a demonic gleam in his eyes that rivaled the meanest pixie. "They were worthless and disobedient."

Tan'yi'na's chest expanded, his fire lighting his lungs with an eerie glow. He blew out the flame with a roar. The earth speaker held out a palm, his expression one of boredom as he deflected the fire. Lydra howled, releasing a curtain of ice as flames arched off the earth speaker and fanned her legs.

"Stop this!" Dianna waved wildly at the dragons. "You cannot fight an earth speaker with Elements."

Both dragons backed away from Thorne, Tan'yi'na shaking icicles off his scales and Lydra stomping out fire beneath her. Simeon, clinging to Tan'yi'na's back, shivered uncontrollably.

Dianna climbed off Lydra and stalked up to Thorne. "Hear me now, earth speaker!" She spat the words as if they were made of venom. "I did not defeat seven powerful mages and travel all this way simply to be bested by you."

Thorne threw out his hands, knocking her back with a wind so powerful, she flew against her dragon with a sickening crunch. Dianna cried out, placing a hand over her cracked ribs, summoning her healing magic while straining for breath. After her bones mended, she let out a shaky exhale, then rolled up her sleeves and marched back to the earth speaker.

Another loud crack rent the air, and water poured from a gap in the ice. Thorne's wicked smile faded when she threw a bolt of lightning at him. He grabbed it, palming it as if he was molding clay. Then he hurled it back. She jumped when the bolt struck between her legs, cracking the earth.

A loud snap came from the glacier, and she knew the entire structure would fall at any moment. She threw more bolts, but he captured them all and returned them.

"What do I do?" she asked the stones.

He is not as strong as you, Neriphene answered. *Keep wearing him down.*

"I don't have time for that!" She threw a bolt and then yelled at her friends. "Get out of here before the glacier collapses."

"I'm not leaving you!" Alec called. He climbed down the giant and stood behind her.

Curse her brother! Didn't he realize he was making her job harder?

"Neither are we!" Simeon yelled from Tan'yi'na.

Speak for yourself, Tan'yi'na grumbled before launching into the air despite Simeon's protests.

More cracks were heard. The lagoon was rapidly filling with water. She threw another bolt at the earth speaker, and he returned it with a victorious squeal. "I can do this all day!"

Gorpat's foot crashed down beside Thorne so suddenly, Dianna's heart leapt into her throat. The earth beneath the giant's foot began to buckle. She leaned down and slapped the earth speaker as if she was swatting a bug off her arm. He went careening through the air, his screams fading into nothingness, followed by the sound of a distant splash. When the hole beneath her foot widened, Gorpat backed up as a chunk of earth detached from the cliff and fell into the sea.

"Bad man not nice to pretty friend," Gorpat said.

"No." Dianna agreed. "He wasn't. Thanks."

Grim balanced himself on Gorpat's shoulder. "My pearl is as gentle as a lamb, but even lambs have their limits."

Dianna was grateful for those limits. She secretly hoped Gorpat's slap had been enough to kill Thorne, though she had no time to find out. They had to make their escape before the ice wall crumbled.

Dianna didn't give her brother another chance to argue. She wrapped a magical rope around his waist and tossed him on Lydra's back, then flew to a spot behind him and grabbed Lydra's reins. "Go, girl!" she screamed. "Run, Gorpat!" she called to the giant.

Lydra soared over the blackened landscape toward the massive puckered crater in the center of the island, Gorpat skipping behind her like a herd of wild elk on a rampage.

When the ice broke, water rose to Gorpat's waist, pushing the giant across the island.

Her father climbed up on top of her head, pointing to a wooden barge being pushed by the current. "Swim to the barge, Gorpat!"

Dianna heaved a sigh of relief when the giant pulled herself up on the barge, but her relief was short-lived when a fanged beast with slick, shimmery scales wove through the current toward them.

Naamaku. Tan'yi'na's growl echoed in Dianna's head. The golden dragon soared down to Gorpat's barge, releasing Simeon before diving for the leviathan.

"Lydra!" Dianna cried. "We must help them."

Lydra flapped backward, hovering over the barge. Alec slid off the dragon, falling into Gorpat's outstretched hand.

Lydra flew to the side of the mountain which bubbled with lava. She landed beneath the crater, dancing as her claws landed on the molten surface.

Then she plucked Dianna off her back, depositing her on the branch of a lone tree, its blackened skeleton stripped of its leaves.

"Lydra, no!" she screamed, but her dragon had already flown off to fight Naamaku without her.

ERIS SLITHERED UP TO the girl lying supine on the stone slab. She brushed off the last remnants of snake moss; it had been used to nourish and shield the body from the Elements. She closed her eyes, running a hand down one long, lean leg. Those pretty legs would soon belong to her. She would be able to walk on land with ease, and her lovers would gladly take her to bed without looks of repulsion upon their faces. She licked her lips, thinking of that blue man waiting in a cell for her. He would not have the strength to turn her away when he looked upon her beauty.

The ritual chamber was prepared. Eris knew she should wait for the next full moon, when the connection between this world and the Elemental world would be strongest, but she was out of time. The swirling mists had finally spoken to her, and what they revealed was troubling indeed.

Her sister was here! She'd seen Madhea's ice dragon deposit her on Eris's volcano. Though the Sky Goddess no longer had wings, Eris would have recognized that fair face and pale blonde hair anywhere. Besides, who else but Madhea could control Lydra? Had she come to stop her from obtaining human legs? Was she the only goddess allowed to shed her immortal defects?

When the Elements revealed the flood raging across Eris's island, fury had nearly split her skull in two. How dare Madhea! The ice witch would pay for destroying her island home. If she had come to turn Eris to stone, as she'd done to Kyan, she was in for a surprise. Eris now had the power of a goddess stone, her niece Aletha. Though Aletha was unwilling to bend to her will, Eris's magic was stronger. Besides, she knew Aletha harbored a grudge against the goddess who'd turned her family to stone and wouldn't pass up the chance for vengeance. Tonight, not only would Eris get her legs, she'd trap the Sky Goddess, giving her complete control over the world and its people.

Elements save them all if they didn't bow to her. A scorned woman's revenge burns hotter than a pyre. The vengeance of a goddess is more destructive than a thousand fires.

ALEC'S KNEES CRACKED when a wave knocked him over, and he fell on a log. He dug his fingers into the uneven surface, clinging for his life as the barge was knocked about by more violent waves.

The water boiled and bubbled. Monster tails slapped the surface as the golden dragon and the sea serpent surfaced and then went under again. Lydra dove into the water like a suicidal bird. She latched onto the leviathan's tail and launched into the sky. Alec crouched and rolled when the monsters flew above him, the leviathan's open jowls dripping burning venom on the barge, leaving blackened holes on its deck. The vessel, such as it was, shimmied before breaking down the middle. Alec and Simeon went one direction, Gorpat and Grim going another.

"No, friends!" Gorpat fell in the water and lunged for the barge. Her head bobbed above the surface while she tried to steer the two halves away from the fight.

Tan'yi'na surfaced, sprouting a flaming geyser, trying to flap above the water with a torn wing. Lydra dropped her catch into the path of Tan'yi'na's flames, but not before the leviathan bit her. Tan'yi'na lit the leviathan on fire. The sea monster writhed on the water's surface, its green scales blackened and oozing blood.

When the wind changed direction, Alec fanned his face, the heat from the golden dragon's breath making him feel like he'd fallen into a flaming pit. Tan'yi'na blew more fire on the water dragon, and the leviathan let out a shriek, the rancid smell of its burning flesh causing Alec's stomach turn over. Tan'yi'na reared back and bit the leviathan in two, its halves pouring greasy blood into the water before it sunk.

Flopping into the water, Lydra cried out then breathed ice on the bloody wound beneath her wing. Tan'yi'na struggled to help the ice dragon keep her head above water while staying afloat himself.

The current slowed. When Alec and Simeon hopped over to the other barge with Grim, Gorpat steered them toward the two dragons. Lydra climbed into Gorpat's arms, wrapping her wings around the giant's shoulders with a shudder. Then the current retreated, taking them back across the island to the volcanic center jutting above the water.

When they reached the volcano, Gorpat helped the injured dragons move to higher ground before securing the barge to a rock. When Alec, Grim, and Simeon climbed onto the rocky soil, Alec hopped from foot to foot, wishing he had boots to protect his newly healed feet from the scalding ground. He waved to his sister, who was running down the side of the mountain toward the dragons, jumping over streams of lava with ease.

Dianna was almost upon them when an enormous hole opened up in the earth. With an ear-shattering scream, she was sucked down into the mountain.

"Dianna!" Alec and Simeon simultaneously hollered, running over, but the hole had sealed shut. Rocks and dirt rolled back into place, leaving no trace of her. Alec fell to his knees, pawing at the dirt, but 'twas no use. His sister was lost, and he knew without a doubt the sea witch had her.

Chapter Nineteen

DIANNA GAGGED ON A mouthful of dirt while falling through the crude tunnel that collapsed above her, pushing her farther into the bowels of Eris's mountain. She landed with a *splash*, wading waist deep in a murky pit. She pushed through the sludge toward a wall made of several large stones, each the breadth and height of at least two men, that rose high above her. Blue flames lined the top of the wall, their embers rising into the darkness. She spun in a slow circle, noticing how the flaming wall encompassed her. Its seven distinct points glowing because of massive torches. A seven-pointed flame wall.

"Sindri, Neriphene," she whispered. "Where am I?"

You are in a heptacircle, came Sindri's reply, *a seven-pointed magic circle.*

Her knees weakened at the thought. The Seven had created this to trap her magic. Had she unwittingly fallen into Eris's snare? She licked her dry lips. The cracks between the stones were wide enough for her to see a watery cavern on the other side.

"Like the one The Seven created?"

No, Neriphene answered. *This one is far stronger.*

Siren's teeth! Dianna had to get out of there. Lydra was injured and needed her help. She summoned her magic. Arcs of flame flew off her fingers but bounced back when hitting the firewall above the stones. She still had magic, but it was restricted to the circle. What good did that do? She couldn't escape if her magic couldn't penetrate her prison walls.

"How do I break the circle?" she asked the stones.

You don't, Syndri said solemnly.

"What do you mean, I don't?" Dianna threw up her hands, kicking something hard in the sludge. A human skull floated to the surface of the muck, bobbing in smelly seaweed.

"Does she intend on killing me down here?" she hissed.

Those bones belong to one of Eris's Elementals. Neriphene said. *This was where they perished.*

"Oh, heavenly Elements!" She quailed at the thought of suffering a slow death inside Eris's prison, the same prison where Eris had murdered her children. She leaned against the wall for support. "This could be my fate then."

Let us hope Eris isn't that lucky, Sindri answered, but she didn't sound reassuring.

TIME SLOWED TO A CRAWL as Lydra and Tan'yi'na frantically dug holes in the mountain. Alec and Simeon had to keep moving away as the dragons threw mounds of black dirt large enough to bury them. The sun had dipped low behind the horizon, leaving behind only a few rays of light. Soon it would be too dark to see anything. After several interminable heartbeats, the dragons finally uncovered two narrow tunnels lined with stones and blackened moss, one a few paces above the other.

Tan'yi'na arched a scaled brow at Alec. *Which one did she fall into?*

He examined the holes, all while trying not to be intimidated by the magnificent winged beast whose breath rivaled the sulfuric smell cascading from the top of Eris's volcano. "I don't know."

"The top one," Simeon said, "if she was running down the hill."

Are you sure? Tan'yi'na asked.

Simeon scratched his head. "No."

Alec heaved a groan, knowing he was ten times a fool for going back into Eris's volcano, but what choice did he have? His sister was in trouble. "Only one way to find out. I'll go in the top hole," he said to Simeon. "You go in the bottom."

Simeon frowned. "I'd rather go in the top hole."

"Of course, so you can be alone with Dianna," Alec snapped.

He already suspected something between Simeon and his sister, just by the way Simeon had been looking at her like a love-struck pup.

Simeon's eyes went cold. "All I care about is saving your sister."

You're wasting time. Both of you go in the top hole, Tan'yi'na grumbled. *The dwarf can explore the bottom. Lydra, Gorpat, and I will find another way into the mountain.*

Grim blanched as he stared into the blackened tunnel. He turned to his daughter, who was leaning against the side of the mountain, her feet submerged in the flood. "Stay with the dragons, my pearl, and let them do the fighting."

The giant eagerly nodded. "Yah, Dada." They exchanged heartfelt good-byes.

Grim looked up at Alec with a tear-stained face. "Elements save you, lad."

They hugged. "And you as well, my friend."

Grim crawled into the tunnel, cursing as he squeezed his broad shoulders through the narrow opening. Alec and Simeon pressed against Grim's backside until he finally slid down with a *pop*.

Simeon peered into the top tunnel and let out a low whistle, his dark skin turning pale olive. "You first."

"Coward," Alec grumbled, though he somehow felt compelled to obey. After all, his sister needed him. He jumped into the hole, refusing to give his actions a second thought. When a jagged rock stuck to his tattered breeches, he had no choice but to pull them free with a violent rip. He slowly eased into the hole, then the wind was sucked from his lungs when he suddenly dropped through the tunnel as if he had fallen into a deep well. Too terrified to scream, he flailed in the blackness as he fell down, down, down into the abyss. He yelped when he hit something smooth and unyielding, causing his head to spin. His eyes rolled into the back of his head. Then silence.

ONE OF ALEC'S EARLIEST memories of him and his father was when Alec was a tot, and they had gone fishing at the Danae River. This was back before Madhea had put the curse on Rowlen's heart, making him hate Alec. He vaguely remembered Mother picking herbs along the riverside while Father helped Alec haul in their catch. Alec was weak and sickly even then, but his father had loved him so, patting his head and affectionately holding his hand while teaching him how to put a worm on a hook.

"The key is to lure them out with this worm," Father had said. "Then snatch up the hook and pull in your line."

Father wasn't fishing now. He was sitting on the riverbank, a backdrop of thick pines behind him, gazing into the water. A small wooden raft floated nearby, carried downstream by the current. The raft reminded him of Gorpat's barge, and the black soot of the riverbank was eerily similar to the sides of Eris's volcano.

Rowlen poked the dirt with a stick, revealing hundreds of tiny mite tunnels. "Your sister is trapped in a seven-pointed star."

Alec looked at him, then at the tunnels. Dirt fell away beneath them, revealing a network of mazes. In the center of that maze was a flaming circle with seven points. A solitary pebble was in the middle of the circle. The pebble symbolized his sister.

"What does that mean?" Alec asked.

Rowlen flicked the rock with his stick, but it did not budge. "It means she will not be able to escape unless a powerful witch from the outside frees her."

Great goddess! How was he supposed to save Dianna? "Where do I find such a witch?"

"You must free the spirit."

Mari? But Eris had imprisoned her spirit and was going to banish her to the Elements.

"But how?" Alec asked, unable to mask the panic in his voice.

Rowlen pointed to another room in the maze with two solitary pebbles. "Seek Simeon's help." Then he pointed to another room farther down. "After you free Dianna, you will find the ice dweller and the dwarf there."

Ryne and Grim were trapped in the same cell! Alec hoped he freed them before Eris killed them, or worse, before they killed each other.

Rowlen squeezed Alec's shoulder harder, so hard, Alec flinched. "You must wake before you drown."

ALEC AWOKE WITH A GASP, swallowing a mouthful of thick, warm water. He sprung to his feet, coughing up sludge as a shadowy figure approached him.

"Alec, is that you?"

"Aye." Alec coughed, more sludge dripping out of his nose. "Is that you, Simeon?"

"Yes," he grumbled. "I can't see a damned thing."

Alec found a pinprick of light in the darkness. "Over there!" He pointed, then realized Simeon probably couldn't see him. He grabbed Simeon's arm. "Follow me."

They trudged through waist-deep water and muck, bumping into boulders until they reached a solitary sconce hanging on a stone wall covered in black algae.

Simeon smoothed a hand down his face. "Why did we think this was a good idea?"

"We didn't." Alec frowned. "It was the *only* idea." He scanned the shallow watery cave. The jagged ceiling was so low, it almost scraped the top of his head. He cupped his hands around his mouth. "Dianna!"

"Hush!" Simeon snapped, grabbing his arm. "Do you want Eris to hear you?"

Alec noted how Simeon's hand trembled. He shook Simeon off with a growl. "I'm not letting *your* fears prevent me from finding *my* sister."

"I want to find her, too," Simeon snapped. "I just don't want anything else to find us first."

Alec froze when he heard feminine laughter, followed by a splash. He and Simeon simultaneously backed up, climbing onto a boulder and pressing against the cave wall.

Alec swallowed a lump of panic when he saw a dark form attached to a long fish tail swimming beneath him. "Siren," he hissed. "They eat people." He frantically searched for a weapon and picked up a jagged stone, squeezing it so tight, blood pooled in his palm.

A pretty female head popped out of the water, so close to Alec, she could have bitten off his toes. She looked much like Eris, with tapered eyes and long, black hair. Alec knew her exterior beauty was a façade. When she smiled, she revealed razor-sharp fangs.

"Hello, mortals." She hissed like a snake, nostrils flaring. "You smell so delicious."

Alec lifted his primitive weapon. "I can assure you, we are not delicious, and we're plagued with disease."

She bit her bottom lip. "I do not smell disease, do you?"

Another pretty female popped above the water. "No. Just two ripe, delicious men."

"Very delicious men." A third voice echoed behind them.

Oh, holy Elements! How would they fight them all?

"I found them." The first siren turned to the others, baring her fangs. "I get pick of the choicest cuts."

"Now hear me, sirens!" Simeon boomed, his golden eyes glowing. "None of you are going to eat us. Do you understand?"

A strange feeling washed over Alec, and he felt compelled to obey Simeon as well.

The sirens stared blankly at Simeon. "Yes."

Simeon folded his arms, looking down at them as if they were wayward children. "You are going to help us escape this cave."

"Yes," they answered again.

What was happening? How was Simeon able to make them do as he asked? Were these sirens going to help them escape? If so, where would they take them? Memories from Alec's dream came racing back. Dianna inside a seven-pointed flaming circle, and Mari was the only one who could save her.

Alec nudged Simeon. "They need to take us to the spirit." When Simeon eyed Alec through narrow slits, Alec clutched his rock tightly in both hands. "My father's ghost speaks to me. He said Mari is the way to save Dianna."

Simeon looked down on the Sirens, his command slicing through the room like a blade through butter. "Take us to the spirit."

The sirens shared quizzical looks. "We don't know of a spirit."

Alec leaned forward, hoping they wouldn't rip open his throat. "The one Eris is using for her ritual."

"You wish to go to Eris's chamber?" the first siren asked.

"Yes," Simeon said. "Take us there." Then he turned to Alec. "I hope you know what you're doing."

So do I, Alec wanted to add, but then a siren let out an ear-splitting screech and clawed at Alec's legs with sharp nails, dragging him down into the water and pulling him through the muck with a strong arm around his throat.

Elements save him! The siren was taking him to Eris's chamber or pulling him to a watery grave. Either way, he feared the outcome.

Chapter Twenty

ERIS GLARED AT THE pale ice witch through a crack in the wall. She was sitting on a stone slab, crying and cradling an Elemental skull in her hands. No doubt the tears were a ruse. She would never cry over Eris's murdered children. Or perhaps she realized she'd soon share the same fate.

Eris swam to another crack in the stones, smiling as she got a clearer view of Madhea's backside. No sign of her wings at all. How had she done it? Surely she'd used dark magic to rid herself of them.

Eris flexed her tail and pulled back her shoulders, clearing her throat. "I see you've become reacquainted with my children."

"Yes, I have." Madhea set down the skull, her back going rigid. "Such a tragic way for children to die, murdered by their own mother."

"Yes, indeed. Such tragic deaths, trapped in a heptacircle, unable to use magic to break free." Eris forced a laugh, repressing that uncomfortable ache in her heart when she thought about her dead daughters. If only they'd been loyal to her and hadn't created a truce behind her back, she wouldn't have had to kill them. What choice had she had? The only way to break the truce, sealed by a blood bond, was to kill the Elementals. They should never have put their mother in such a position. "No matter. I will have new children once I get my human legs."

Madhea turned, glaring at her between the cracks. "You're lacking the motherly instincts required to birth more children."

"Motherly instincts?" Eris jerked back as if scalded. "I've been feeding and taking care of a mortal child since she was a tot."

The Sky Goddess slowly rose, pointing at Eris with an accusatory finger. "You've been keeping her body warm so you could steal it."

Eris shrugged. "This child's father murdered my beloved broot whale, and my *motherly instincts* demanded retribution."

"Then he should be dealt with." Madhea threw up her hands, sloshing through the water toward her. "Leave his daughter out of this."

Eris couldn't help but laugh at Madhea's mock concern. "Oh, look who's suddenly turned compassionate. Is that why you decided to flood my island?"

Madhea clucked her tongue. "You can blame your earth speaker Thorne for flooding your island. I had nothing to do with it."

Fury overcame Eris. She should have killed Thorne long ago, as she'd done with all the other witches given to her in sacrifice. What a fool she'd been to trust the earth speaker after he'd pledged his heart to her. She'd given him the sole task of ensuring the spirit was delivered to her, and he'd taken it upon himself to wreak destruction on her home. How many broots had he killed with his foolish display? Fortunately, her ritual chamber was on higher ground, or else all would have been lost in the flood. If the spirit had been swept away, Thorne would have suffered greatly, though Eris would still ensure he was punished for his rogue behavior.

"Why did you come here, if not to destroy me?" She still didn't entirely believe her sister, though Madhea wasn't to be trusted anyway, and rightfully so after what she'd done to Kyan and her daughters.

Madhea walked up to the stone, resting a pale hand between the cracks. "I came here to stop you from taking an innocent life."

Madhea had to have gone mad. "And why would you care about an insignificant witch's life?"

Madhea let out a slow, long exhale. "Because her life is not yours to take."

"It is the only way I can rid myself of this hideous tail."

"Hideous? The Elements made you that way for a reason."

Eris had had enough of her sister's duplicity. No doubt she'd come to Kyan the same way, pretending to care for the fate of humanity and then striking down her sister when she least expected it.

"Says the hypocritical witch who's shed her wings!" Eris's tail slapped the water erratically. "Do you honestly think I'd believe any of your sentimental drivel? You knew I was using dark magic to perform the ritual, and you thought to turn me to stone as you did our sister!"

"No," Madhea cried, looking far too innocent. "I promise I do not wish to battle you, so long as you agree to respect innocent lives."

Ha! What good was a promise from Madhea? "As if I'd believe your promises. Well, sister, our visit has been fun. If you'll excuse me, I have a ritual to perform."

"Wait, please!" Desperation punctured Madhea's words. "You can't just leave me here."

"If I can trap my daughters in the heptacircle to slowly starve to death, surely I can do the same to my two-faced sister. Oh, and don't bother trying to douse the flames." Eris laughed, remembering how her children had tried to splash the circle's magical fires with their tails, only making the flame rise higher. "I have placed enchantments over the entire circle."

"Wait! Wait!" she screamed. "I'm not Madhea!"

"I've grown tired of your lies. Goodbye." She swam away from her sister for the last time.

Now that her sister was trapped, Eris thought perhaps she'd wait until the next full moon to take her mortal body. Then she thought of that intriguing blue man waiting for her in a cell. The sooner she received her human legs, the sooner she could visit her new prisoner. She was itching to feel his shimmering hair. She imagined the translucent strands cascading through her fingers like water while he lovingly looked up at her with those mesmerizing silvery eyes. Yes, she would complete the ritual tonight and claim her new body. With Madhea safely locked away, there was no one to stop her.

ALEC VOMITED WATER and sludge as he crawled to the edge of the shallow pool. He recognized Eris's chamber, for the guards had taken him here earlier that day. The sirens swam away at Simeon's command. Alec still couldn't believe Simeon's power to compel the voracious creatures to do his bidding. It made him wonder if the sand dweller had used such magic on his sister. Simeon sat beside him, wringing water out of his matted locks of hair.

"How many times have you used your persuasive powers on my sister?"

Simeon had the nerve to smirk. "Only a few times and only for her own good."

Alec's blood was ready to boil over. "I'm sure you think so." How badly he wanted to strike down the sand dweller, but now was not the time. He had to focus on saving his friends from an evil goddess.

Simeon stood, offering Alec a hand up. Alec reluctantly took his hand, rising on wobbly legs.

"You there!" Two soldiers rushed them with swords drawn.

"Go!" Simeon held out a staying hand, his booming command shaking the sweltering air. "Leave us in peace, and do not tell your goddess we are here."

The guards lowered their weapons and marched away without another word. Simeon certainly had incredible persuasive powers. The thought of him using them to take advantage of Dianna made Alec's chest seize with anger. Again, he forced himself to put it out of his mind and focus on the task at hand. They had to find the chalice and free Mari's spirit.

His gaze was drawn to the swirling mists. Then he spied a small chamber behind Eris's throne aglow with pulsing red lights, as if the very earth was on fire. He trudged toward the chamber, his legs feeling as if they were weighted with a thousand stones. Lying on the stone slab in the center of the chamber was a beautiful young woman. Though her eyes were shut in sleep, he'd recognize that sweet face anywhere.

He gingerly touched one tanned arm, her warmth prickling his skin. He traced her thick eyelashes and full lips, hardly believing this was Mari, the spirit who'd selflessly saved and healed him. At that moment, he realized he'd give his life to return the favor.

"Mari," he whispered. "How do I return your soul to your body?"

He heard a muffled scream above him. Alec looked up, his jaw dropping when he saw the chalice suspended above Mari, floating in a magical swirling sphere that appeared to be made of mist.

Alec looked over at Simeon. "I can't reach her spirit. It's too high."

Simeon picked up a rock and threw it at the chalice. The stone disintegrated to ash when it hit the sphere.

A light breeze tickled his nape, and he watched with fascination as an invisible force dented the sphere. "Thank you, Father," Alec whispered.

The chalice tipped, and Mari's soul streamed out, floating down to earth. "Alec!" She thew her ghostly arms around him, tickling the hairs on the back of his neck with her aura. How he longed for a real hug from her.

She looked at Simeon. "Where's my father?"

Alec's heart caught in his throat. If only he'd reached Khashka sooner. "I'm so sorry."

Her smile faded, and her eyes dimmed. "What happened?"

"Carnivus," Alec said solemnly, the tightening in his throat making him unable to say more. Though it was Khashka's deception that had brought them all to this island, he couldn't fault a father for wishing to save his daughter.

"I see." Mari turned from him, her shoulders shaking, and covered her face with her hands.

Simeon cleared his throat. "We need to get to Dianna."

Alec scowled at the sand dweller. He knew that. He was desperate to free his sister, too. "Mari, I'm sorry about your father, but time is wasting, and we need you to help us free Dianna."

She dropped her hands, her eyes shining like stardust, as she stared sorrowfully at her sleeping body. "And then we must flee. I do not want anyone else dying for me."

Alec clenched his hands, determination hardening his jaw. "I will not leave this island until your spirit is inside your body once more."

"Thank you, Alec." She offered him a watery smile, so sweet and pure, his heart broke all over again. "But enough people have already died on my account."

"Mari, listen to me. We have come all this way, and I will not let their deaths be in vain." He badly wanted to grab Mari and force her to listen to reason. "My sister is a powerful witch. After she defeats Eris, we will find a way to put you back in your body. I swear it."

"We don't know if she can defeat Eris."

The tension in Alec's neck and back wound so tight, it felt as if he'd been beaten by the plague. "Yes, she will," he insisted.

Dianna *had* to defeat Eris. It wasn't just Mari's soul at stake. It was all of humanity.

WHY HAD DIANNA THOUGHT pretending to be Madhea would be a good idea? She'd hoped Eris would back down if she thought Dianna was a goddess. She heaved a sigh, burying her face in her hands. She supposed it didn't matter who Eris believed her to be. If the vindictive goddess could starve her own children, she'd not hesitate to do the same to her niece. With a groan, she climbed up the stone slab, pulling her knees to her chest, hoping to air out her water-logged feet.

She had to think of a way out of here before Eris turned her wrath on her brother and friends. She'd already tried and failed to put out the magical blue fire surrounding her. She'd scooped water into a hollowed-out skull, throwing it at the fire, only to watch hopelessly as the flames rose ever higher. She'd never forgive herself if Alec and her friends perished at Eris's cruel hands.

She coursed her fingers through her hair, clenching the roots while struggling for ideas. "There has to be a way out of here," she said to the stones.

If there was, don't you think the Elementals would have escaped? Neriphene answered.

You must wait on your friends to find you, Sindri echoed.

"Then what?" Dianna asked.

The heptacircle spell has trapped you within the stones, Sindri explained. *It is a spell similar to the one Madhea used when she trapped my mother, sisters, and me in rock.*

Because we are already trapped, Neriphene continued, *we should be able to pass through the heptacircle if a mortal carries us out.*

Dianna wiped tears from her eyes, her insides trembling. "What if my friends don't find me? What if Eris reaches them first?"

Then all the world will perish, Neriphene said darkly.

Chapter Twenty-One

ALEC LED THE WAY THROUGH the dank and humid tunnel, relying on dim torchlight. He recalled images of the maze from his dream. All they had to do was reach the center, and they'd find Dianna. He halted when he heard a rustling above him. He looked at Mari, who floated beside him, then turned to Simeon. The sand dweller gaped at the tunnel's low ceiling.

Alec looked up. Hundreds, mayhap thousands of creatures no bigger than Alec's palm were nestled in holes lining the top of the walls. A few were grooming themselves, licking their red scales, but most were sleeping, their horned heads tucked under their wings.

Simeon put a finger to his lips. "Pixies."

Alec had heard of these winged demons. Though Madhea's pixies had delivered Markus safely to Adolan, Alec had heard tales of them stripping away human flesh as fast as sirens.

Alec tried to tread lightly, then winced when he accidentally kicked a pebble, sending it across the tunnel. His heart hammered, his gaze flying to the demons above. A few shifted, but thank the Elements, none of them attacked.

Alec's shoulders slumped in relief when they reached a watery cavern with flaming stones. He recognized the magic seven-pointed circle from his dream. He pointed to the walls, a barrier lit with torches. "She's in there," he said to Mari. "Her magic is trapped inside."

Simeon trudged through the muck, banging on the stone walls. "Dianna! We're here to save you!"

Alec grumbled. Of course, Simeon had to reach her first, no doubt to take credit for the rescue.

"Simeon," she cried, her green eyes wet as she peered at them through a crack in the wall. "Is that you?"

Alec nudged Simeon aside, forcing a smile as he peered at her. "And Alec and Mari."

"You can't put out the fire. It's fueled by magic. You need to find a giant or a dragon to tear down the walls from the outside."

It could take days for the monsters to claw their way down to Dianna. By then it would be too late. "We don't have time for that." He nodded at the beautiful spirit floating beside him. "Mari can do it."

Dianna peered at Mari. "Are you the spirit?"

"I am," she answered, her soul flickering like lamplight. "But Eris has my stone."

"Can you fly over and get one of Dianna's stones?" Alec asked.

"No!" Dianna shrieked. "She'll be trapped here, too. The circle imprisons magic."

Simeon rubbed his chin. "Then Dianna's stones are trapped, too."

"Mayhap," Dianna said, then whispered, "The stones are saying someone without magic can come and get one of them."

When all eyes turned to Alec, he threw up his hands. "How am I supposed to climb over the wall?"

Simeon held out a hand. "Get on my shoulders, and I'll give you a boost."

"Come, Alec," Dianna pleaded. "I'll catch you with my magic on the way down."

He peered up at the tall stone slab he'd have to mount. Even if he could climb over it, what about the flames on top? They'd light him up like a pyre. Still, what choice did he have? He was the only non-witch among them, and his sister needed to be freed before Eris discovered them.

Alec took Simeon's hand and climbed onto his shoulders, wobbling while trying to balance himself.

"Hurry up," Simeon snapped. "Your bony feet are killing my back."

Alec seriously doubted that. Simeon was twice Alec's width and at least a head taller, and his shoulders were as solid as marble slabs. He latched onto the top of the stone wall but flinched when the flames scalded his fingers.

Simeon shook beneath him. "Just do it," he hissed.

Mari floated up to him. "Jump through as fast as you can. Dianna will catch you on the other side."

Though Alec was not a big man, like Simeon or his father, he feared Dianna would not be able to hold his weight.

"Hurry up!" Simeon shifted, glaring up at Alec.

Alec tried to mentally prepare himself for the ascent. He flattened his palms against the wall, amazed when a strange buzzing sensation rippled through him. He looked down. "What is that sound?"

"Pixies! Hurry!"

Alec grabbed onto the ledge, cursing when flames burned his skin. Simeon pushed Alec up and off his shoulders, and he scrambled to the top, crying out as fire burned his chest. He pulled himself through the flames, then tumbled down the other side, screaming as he fell. An invisible force caught him, suspending him in the air.

He was slowly lowered to the ground and into his sister's arms. "Here." She kissed his cheek, running a soothing hand down his burned chest before placing a stone in his hands. "You must hurry."

Alec sucked in a scream as he was moved back to the wall. Again he scrambled through the fire and fell off the wall into a swarm of pixies. "Mari!" he screamed, holding the stone tight while the demons tried to pry open his fingers.

The spirit's warmth encompassed him as she took the stone from him. "I've got it!"

"Ouch!" Alec struggled to sit up, swatting pixies off his head while they ripped chunks of flesh from his ears and scalp.

"Stop!"

A blinding light washed over him. When he opened his eyes, the light had faded to a dull glow, there were pixie entrails hanging off his tattered clothes, the heptacircle walls had toppled, and Dianna was standing before him with a smile. The smell of burned flesh hit him like a punch to the gut, and it took him a moment to realize the nauseating smell 'twas his flesh. When his sister leaned over him, her soothing hands were a balm to his soul. He smiled up at her before feeling his world slip away.

ROWLEN WAS SITTING in the shade of a mighty lyme tree beside two soft mounds of dirt. Alec recognized his parents' graves and wondered why his father had brought him here.

"I'm proud of the man you've become, despite your traumatic childhood." Rowlen smiled at the gravesite. "Beloved mother" was etched into the smooth slab of wood. "You have a gentle heart, just like your mother did."

He struggled to speak around the lump of emotion in his throat. "Like you, Father, before your heart was poisoned."

"Aye, before it was poisoned." His smile faded. "Mari is a beautiful soul. She will be lost without her father. You must protect her."

He nodded, not realizing he'd desired his father's approval of Mari until this moment. "I will, Father."

Rowlen grasped Alec's shoulder. "Tell Markus and Dianna how proud I am of them, and that I love them."

He tried to hold back tears to no avail. "I will."

"I love you, son." Rowlen's eyes softened, saddened. "It was my love for you and desperate fear for your life that made me climb Madhea's mountain."

"I know." Alec's voice shook with emotion. "I love you, too."

Rowlen's dark features hardened. "You and your sister must face a final trial with Eris. Beware, her earth speaker approaches. Be strong, and I will do my part."

"Your part?" How would a ghost help defeat a goddess?

"Son." His father shook his shoulder. "I will pass to the Elements soon. You must wake. Your friends need you."

ALEC SAT UP AND LOOKED into his sister's soulful blue eyes. "Dianna, the earth speaker is coming."

"How do you know?"

"Father told me."

"Father?"

"Aye," Alec said. "His spirit has been visiting me in my dreams."

The cavern was dimly lit by a few torches that had been pressed between fallen stones and the walls. When he reluctantly let Simeon help him up, he tasted bile when he saw they were standing knee-deep in water bloodied by pixies. Wing pieces and pixie heads floated in the warm, murky water. A few tiny torsos were still twitching while their lifeblood drained out of gaping holes where their legs used to be.

Alec checked his hands and legs, pleased to see they'd healed so quickly. Even his scalded stomach no longer pained him. Had Dianna healed him while he slept? Her powers had indeed strengthened.

Simeon touched Dianna's shoulder. "We need to leave before Eris finds us."

"Leave?" She shook her head. "I can't leave until Eris is destroyed."

"Listen to reason." Simeon waved at the crumbled circle that would have trapped her forever is she hadn't given a stone to Mari. "You've already felt the power of Eris's magic." There was no mistaking the concern in the sand dweller's eyes. Perhaps he did care for her.

Alec stepped forward, resolve hardening his spine. "We're not leaving without Mari's body."

Mari protested. "It's my fault we're on this cursed island in the first place. I will not have you jeopardize your lives again."

Alec was determined to make her see reason. "We didn't come this far only to turn away without your body."

"He's right." Dianna brushed Simeon's hand off her shoulder. "Besides, if we leave now, Eris may retaliate by destroying your body. Then your spirit must pass on to the Elements."

"It's fine." She gazed at the hem of her flowing gown. "I will join my father in the afterlife."

"But I'd miss you, Mari." Alec forced out the words, despite the anvil striking his heart.

"Alec," she said and sniffled. "I couldn't live with myself if anything happened to you."

He took a step forward, losing himself in her pretty golden eyes. "I feel the same way about you."

"Mari," Dianna argued. "This goddess murdered her own children. She would not think twice about destroying all of humanity. She must be stopped."

Mari hung her head, translucent tears stained her face. In that moment, Alec knew he could not fail her. She had suffered too much for too long. He would end her suffering or die trying.

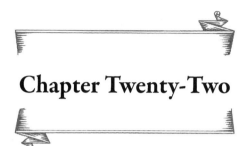

Chapter Twenty-Two

ERIS LEANED AGAINST her throne, her tail gleefully slapping the stone slab, watching her soldiers prepare the girl's body for the ritual. Her first task as a human would be to kill the foolish earth speaker who'd flooded her island. Her second would be to visit the blue man in the dungeon. Her final objective would be to take over the world. If her blue man pleased her, perhaps she'd spare his Ice People when she flattened Madhea's dominion. If he did not, she'd smite every last person he'd ever loved.

"Eris, my love, I have returned to warn you." Thorne floated up to Eris from her pool, flaunting his Elemental magic, bubbles trailing in his wake. He truly was a gifted speaker, his power over the Elements stronger than any witch Eris had ever known. Too bad she would have to kill him.

"Warn me of what?" she snapped, snarling at the scrawny man like a rabid animal. "That you've destroyed my island with your foolish flood?"

He floated next to her, bending the knee and reaching for her hand. "I had no choice, my love."

She snatched her hand away. "You take liberties without permission. I never gave you leave to call me *your love*!"

He flinched as if she'd struck him. Was he such a simpleton? "But we are lovers."

"I have many lovers." She waved him away with a dismissive flick of the wrist. "And none as bothersome as you."

He floated upright without asking permission. "Forgive me, but I thought you should know Madhea's daughter, Dianna, is here, and she's brought dragons and a giant."

"Madhea's daughter?" Eris shot up, panic icing her limbs. "What does she look like?"

"Like her mother but without wings," he answered. "She is half mortal."

Dragon's blood! She'd been fooled!

"That witch deceived me. I thought I'd trapped Madhea in the heptacircle." She nervously drummed her fingers against the stone armrest. "Madhea is probably waiting for me to do the sacrifice. It requires dark magic. I will be vulnerable then, and she can turn me to stone."

"What will you do?" Thorne asked, looking too much like a lost lamb.

She leaned forward, slapping the swirling mists that fanned out in thick clouds. The mists parted to show her Madhea's ice dragon frantically clawing her way inside Eris's mountain. What was that behind the beast? Could it be the giant and another dragon? The shapes were blurry, but it appeared Madhea had brought a monster army, and Naamaku was nowhere in sight. If Madhea had hurt her leviathan, the Sky Goddess would feel Eris's wrath! Next the mists revealed the magic heptacircle, or what was left of it. It was flattened like trampled grass, and floating around the stones was a carnage of shredded pixies. She bit down on her knuckles, stifling a scream. Madhea had to have freed Dianna, for none other than a goddess could break through Eris's magical barriers and destroy her nest of pixies. Though troublesome devils, Eris had grown fond of her little pets. That Madhea would take them away from her made her blood boil.

"Her monsters are trying to find a way in, and Dianna is freed." Eris thought for a long moment and then an idea struck her. "I will perform the ritual and put the girl's spirit back in her body. Madhea will destroy the girl, thinking she's me, and then together we will surprise Madhea and take her and her monsters down."

Thorne gasped. "But you need the girl's body. Surely you do not wish to stay tethered to your tail forever." Eris didn't miss the nuances in his expression, which soured as if he'd drunk rotten wine. "Uh...." He looked away long enough that Eris knew he was formulating a lie. "Not that I don't think your tail is beautiful."

She had no time to be offended—not when she knew the sky goddess was waiting to strike. "Silly earth speaker." Despite her annoyance with Thorne, she forced a laugh. "Once Madhea is dead, I will take her daughter's body as my own. Do not destroy the young witch if she comes to fight with her mother." She rubbed her hands together, licking her lips as she recalled the girl's tight breeches hugging long, shapely legs. Yes, Madhea's spawn would do just as well. "She is young and beautiful, too, the daughter of a goddess. She has more magic than *that* body."

She scowled at the freshly-cleaned body two guards laid back on the slab before quickly taking their leave. If the ritual proved a success, she would not only retain her magic, she'd inherit Dianna's magic as well. That would please her immensely, since that cursed goddess stone had gone cold, it's magic fleeing like a deer before a wolf. She kicked the stone at her feet, and it rolled into the pool. No matter. She didn't need it. With Dianna's magic, she'd be unstoppable!

"Yes, she is quite beautiful, with pale hair and green eyes. You will be lovely." A slow smile spread across Thorne's face, as if he expected her to make him her lover once she stole Dianna's body.

"I will be lovely?" She snarled. "As opposed to now, when I'm tethered to this repulsive tail?"

He backed up, nearly tripping over his own feet. "I didn't say that."

"You do not need to say it." She jabbed his side. "I can tell what you think."

He clasped his hands together, dropping to one knee. "Forgive me, my goddess. I did not mean to offend. "

She forced herself to restrain her anger. She needed Thorne to help her defeat Madhea. After that, she'd discard him like old bones. "Grab the chalice with the girl's spirit. We must act now before Madhea strikes."

"OH, NO! WHAT WILL SHE do when she finds my spirit is gone? I may have missed my only chance to return to my body," Mari whispered to Alec as they observed Eris and Thorne from a darkened tunnel leading to the chamber. Behind Alec lay two sleeping guards, knocked out by a rope of Dianna's magic. Dianna and Simeon were crouched in front of them, waiting for the best moment to strike.

When a wind blew by his nape, Alec grabbed Dianna's shoulder and he bent to her ear. "Father."

She shrugged him off, a look of skepticism in her eyes. "Really?"

"Yes, really," Alec answered. "He's helping us."

When Thorne reached for the chalice, it fell out of his grip as if some unseen force had knocked it away. It clanked across the stones before coming to a stop, its lid falling off as it rolled back and forth on its side.

"Foolish man!" Eris hollered, her tale wildly slapping the slab. She pointed to the dark blob that circled above and then behind her. "Capture that spirit!"

"Go, Mari!" Alec urgently whispered.

Mari swirled into the chamber.

"There you are, child." Alec's breath caught in his throat when Eris struck Mari with a magic rope. "Do not fret." The sea goddess smiled wickedly. "I've had a change of heart. You are going back inside your body."

Eris flung Mari's spirit in the air. It hovered above the supine body like a thick fog over a midnight tide. The sea witch swayed, her tail slapping the ground in time with a low hum that reverberated off the walls. Her humming grew louder as she shut her eyes and turned her face to the ceiling.

"Elements of fire and flame

Hear me speak your name

Make this mortal whole

Bind her flesh and soul

Elements of earth and light

Hear my plea this night

Deliver this spirit to her skin

That she may rise again"

The earth trembled when the soul sank into Mari's body, and a brilliant light lit the room, then fractured into myriad crystals of sparkling color.

Alec held his breath for several interminable moments, waiting for Mari to wake. Finally, she flung an arm across her eyes with a groan. Thorne raced to her side, helping her sit up.

"There, there, my child," he soothed. "Come sit down while you adjust to your body."

Eris slithered into the water while Thorne carried Mari to her throne. Mari seemed disoriented, gaping at her hands as if they were not her own. Alec's heart pounded so wildly in his ears, he could barely think. What if Mari tried to run, and Eris punished her? Or worse, what if Mari got caught in the middle of the fight, recovering her body only to sacrifice her body and soul?

Mari thanked Thorne when he handed her a goblet of wine. She greedily drank it as if 'twas her last drink. Then Alec realized it was her first drink in fifteen years.

"Thank you for your kindness," Mari said to Thorne, "but my legs feel numb. Maybe I should try walking."

"No, no." Thorne held her down when she tried to stand. "You rest a while."

Eris slipped farther into the water, until she was nearly submerged.

"I can't wait any longer," Dianna said through gritted teeth and jumped to her feet.

Alec's world spun on its axis as his sister left.

DIANNA BLASTED THORNE first, knocking him back against the wall. She turned to Mari. "Run!"

Mari slid off the throne, landing on her arse. "I've forgotten how to use my legs."

Dianna had no time to help the girl. She spun and blasted Eris, who was swimming away, striking her tail and reeling her in like a fish.

"Thorne!" Eris screeched, flopping around. "Stop her!"

Something struck the back of Dianna's head. She was about to tumble face-first into the water when a strong wind flipped her around, and she fell on her side instead. Pain shot through her ribs, and she winced.

She thought she saw a familiar set of dark eyes sweep past. "Father?"

Duck, child!

She dodged Eris's magic rope, which then shot across her shoulder, striking the swirling mists. They exploded with a bang, the clouds scattering and fogging Dianna's sight.

She was barely aware of Alec racing past and sweeping Mari into his arms before stumbling away. He'd almost made it to the darkened tunnel leading to the chamber when Eris caught him with a bolt, holding him suspended. He then fell to his knees, an agonizing cry escaping his lips.

Mari tumbled out of his arms, screaming. "Stop, please! You're killing him."

Desperate to save her brother, Dianna staggered to her feet but was struck again. She touched the back of her head. It was wet and sticky with blood. Had Thorne whacked her with thunderbolts?

"Don't kill her, you fool!" Eris released her hold on Alec and swam to the edge of the pool. "I want her body! Save your strength for Madhea."

Get up and fight, Dianna! Sindri said.

Our sister Aletha is near you, Neriphene pleaded. *She has powerful healing magic. She can help you.*

Dianna's vision cleared.

"So pretty." Eris stroked Dianna's leg. "So long and lean." She looked at something beyond Dianna's shoulder. "Put me in her body now, before Madhea comes."

"This witch is dying. You must heal her first," someone said.

Was she truly dying? No! What would happen to her brother and her friends? Blood poured out of the back of her head. She felt it. She smelled it.

"Fool!" Eris screeched. "I told you not to harm her."

A slow, deep clap broke through Dianna's confusion. "Well done, my deity. Well done."

Eris slithered across Dianna's legs like a snake. "Who are you?"

"Who am I? My beautiful goddess, you don't recognize me?" Simeon strutted toward them like a peacock.

Sparks arched off Eris's fingertips as she slunk back into the pool. "I do not."

"I am Simeon." He slapped his broad chest, stepped into the pool, and walked past Dianna. A moment later, something solid rolled against her leg. Could it have been a goddess stone?

"Descendant of Kyan and Orhan," Simeon continued. "I followed Madhea here in hopes I could be the one to destroy her and her daughter for turning my benevolent grandmother to stone. Even now Madhea is restoring your heptacircle, where she hopes to ensnare you."

"He lies!" Thorne hissed, advancing on Simeon. "He is with Madhea's daughter. He must be destroyed!"

"Do not hurt him!" Eris implored, no doubt already taken by Simeon's charms.

Dianna touched the smooth stone. "Help me, Aletha," she whispered. The stone pulsed.

Aletha, Sindri said. *She is not like her mother. Help her.*

Simeon chuckled, tossing a braid over his shoulder and sneering at Thorne. "You lie, because you know I'm a far superior lover. My reputation precedes me wherever I go. Surely you've heard of Simeon the Strong."

Simeon flexed his muscles.

Eris gaped at Simeon's arms as if in a trance. "No, I have not."

"Do not trust him, my love," Thorne cried.

"This scrawny man is your lover?" Simeon's deep, rich bellow echoed off the walls. "Surely a goddess as beautiful and powerful as you can do better."

Eris bit her lip, batting long lashes, her tail playfully slapping the water. "He is not my only lover."

"Once you have been with me, I can assure you, you will want no other." Simeon's smooth baritone coated Dianna's nerves like a bath of warm honey. No wonder this man had so many admirers.

Though she knew it to be an act, the thought of him as Eris's lover made her so angry, all she could think of was flattening Eris's island. Her strength returned, and the dizziness subsided.

"Thank you, Aletha," she murmured.

You're welcome, spawn of Madhea. I only healed you because my sisters begged me to.

Dianna repressed a chuckle. She'd have to convince Aletha to trust her another time.

A jolt of power surged through her. She jumped to her feet. "Duck, Simeon!" she hollered, striking Thorne with one bolt and Eris with another. Energy poured from both hands with such brutal force, she cried out as her fingertips split open. She pushed more energy through her, smiling when both forms writhed and then shriveled, until nothing was left but ash.

She pulled back with a hiss, her retracting magic scalding her already charred fingers. The bolts dissipated, and she fell to her knees with a strangled sob.

Dianna curled her battered fingers around Aletha's stone, tears of relief on her cheeks as her wounds healed.

Simeon steadied her with a hand beneath her arm as she stumbled over to Alec. She felt for a pulse, alarmed when she felt none. "Alec!" she screamed.

ALEC WAS HOME AGAIN, curled up in his mother's lap in front of a warm fire. He sank into her loving embrace... and was amazed to find his father holding him.

"I used to hold you like this before Madhea cursed my heart," Rowlen said in his deep tenor.

Alec looked into his father's dark eyes. "Am I dead?"

Rowlen pushed a lock of hair out of Alec's eyes. "No, you are resting, but you need to go back to your body soon, and I need to pass to the Elements."

Alec laid his head against his father's chest, sorrow and regret threatening to split his heart in two. If Madhea had never cursed his father's heart. If Alec had never stabbed his father in the back.

Rowlen rocked Alec in his arms. "No regrets, son. I can depart this world, knowing I have your forgiveness, and you can return to the world knowing I will always love you."

Alec hugged him once more, and then his warmth slipped away like water spilling through his fingers.

Chapter Twenty-Three

"ALEC!" DIANNA THREW her arms around her brother's neck. "I thought I'd lost you." Indeed, she would have if it hadn't been for Aletha boosting Dianna's healing strength.

"Father has gone to the Elements." Alec sobbed into her shoulder.

"Has he?" She caressed his hair, once feather soft and now wet and sticky with filth. "He helped me when I was battling Eris." She recalled seeing her father's eyes and then hearing him tell her to duck. If not for him, Eris would have roped her with magic and possibly banished her soul. She was forever indebted to the man she'd once believed to be a monster.

Alec sniffled, tears watering over his eyes. "He loves us."

"I know."

The ground shook so violently beneath them, Dianna fell into Alec's arms.

"What was that?" Simeon cried, holding Mari close.

"Eris's volcano." Dianna jumped to her feet, giving Alec a hand up.

"The Elements sound angry," Alec said before his jaw slackened and he gaped at Simeon, fire brewing in his pale eyes.

"She can't walk," Simeon explained, handing Mari to Alec and looking sheepishly at Dianna. "What was I supposed to do?"

MARI WRAPPED HER ARMS around Alec's neck, snuggling against him. "He has no power over me," she whispered. "My heart has already surrendered to another."

263

Alec's heart soared as he held her close. She smelled like fresh moss and sage, and was as light as a bird. She felt so right in his arms, he never wanted to let go.

The ground quaked again, and Alec fell against the cavern wall, holding Mari as if she was more valuable than dragon's gold.

"We need to leave!" Dianna waved them toward the tunnel.

"Not without Grim and Ryne."

Alec ignored Simeon's groans, pushing ahead of them while he pictured the tunnels from his dream. Though he'd no idea why he was risking his neck for Ryne after all the ice dweller had done, he'd never forgive himself if he escaped Eris's island without trying. As for Grim, Alec would drown in a pit of lava before leaving his friend behind.

The tunnels shook, raining debris on their heads. Alec shielded Mari as best he could as they raced against time to save their friends. Dianna lit the way by holding up a glowing goddess stone.

By the time he came upon the solitary dungeon at the end of the tunnel, they were already chest-deep in warm, filthy water. Though the air was humid and stifling, Mari clung to Alec's neck, shivering in his arms. He knew 'twas from fear and not a chill, and he hated himself for endangering her.

Simeon yelped. "Be careful. There are hot springs beneath us."

When Dianna blasted the bars off a cell and shined a light inside, Alec's heart hit his stomach, and he had to bite down on his lip hard to keep from laughing. Ryne was standing neck deep in muck, with Grim perched on his shoulders.

"Well, this is an unexpected sight," Alec chuckled as Simeon held a hand out to Ryne.

"I couldn't very well let him drown," Ryne grumbled, wading toward them. "After all, it was my foolish pride that got him captured."

Alec shifted Mari in his arms, unable to repress a grin. "So nice of you to finally acknowledge it."

"Indeed it was." Grim chuckled. "Now let us leave this island and put all this bickering behind us."

Dianna led the way, Simeon at her side, while the others followed.

"I've had plenty of time to contemplate my stupidity in this muck." Ryne dodged a burst of steaming water. "I have already apologized to Grim, but I owe you an apology as well. I have behaved like a slog to you."

"Apology accepted," Alec answered with a grin. Indeed, Ryne had been a slog, but life was too perilous to hold grudges. Besides, Alec could hardly recall old quarrels while he had a beautiful girl in his arms.

Simeon waved them forward. "How about we save the making up for later and get out of here before this volcano explodes?"

THEY WERE LOST.

Alec had led them through the maze of tunnels only to run into a dead end at each turn. A river of lava had completely overrun one hall and crumbled walls blocked several others. Eris's soldiers proved no help. Dianna had to blast the few they'd encountered after they'd charged them with swords drawn. When they found themselves back in Eris's chamber, Dianna worried the volcano would erupt before they found their way out.

"There is an exit this way." Alec circled the pool.

The volcano heaved, filling the chamber with sulfuric smoke. She and the others gagged and coughed, following Alec up a steep slope, slipping on loose gravel. They were running out of options. If they couldn't escape, she would have to blast a hole through the mountain, which could compromise the entire structure. She swore when she saw the exit had been buried under an avalanche of rocks.

"Stand back while I try to blast through it." Her throat was more parched and raw than when she and Lydra had gotten lost in the Shifting Sands. She shone a light on the obstruction and was startled when when one boulder moved, a bulbous eye blinking at them.

"Gorpat found friends!" the giant boomed.

"My pearl!" Grim clambered over loose rocks to reach his child.

"Go back, Dada." The giant's command echoed through the chamber, causing a wave of debris to fall on their heads.

Dianna turned into Simeon's arms when the giant's fist shot through the tunnel, blasting dust and soot all over them.

As she climbed out of the tunnel and into the humid night air, Dianna had never felt more relieved. Alec was alive, and Eris was dead!

Grim wobbled up to his child, holding out his arms. "My sweet pearl!"

She pulled Grim against her like he was a stuffed toy, coating the top of his head in slobbery kisses. Fortunately, the dwarf didn't seem to mind.

The ground shook, and Dianna tumbled back, landing in a pair of strong arms. "Thank you." She expected to look up into Simeon's eyes and was surprised to see icy eyes in a blue face. She struggled to remember his name. *Rhine? Rhes? Ryne!*

"The least I could do after all you've done for us," Ryne said with a wink. Beneath the light of the nearly-full moon, she hadn't realized until this moment how striking his features were; a long, straight nose, an angular jaw, and the most intriguing hair, so pale it was translucent.

Simeon loudly cleared his throat. "Dianna, we need to go."

"Of course." She pulled out of Ryne's embrace, absently rubbing her arms where he'd touched her. "Where are Lydra and Tan'yi'na?" she asked the giant.

"There." Gorpat moved aside, pointing to the two dragons nestled beside an angry stream of lava. Lydra was on her back, her charred wings flat against the scorched earth while Tan'yi'na licked a gaping bloody wound in her side.

"Oh, heavenly Elements!" Dianna gasped, ignoring the sweltering heat that plastered her hair to her face as she raced to her dragon.

There you are. Tan'yi'na looked her over with a deep scowl. *We'd almost given up hope.*

The mountain shook again, and this time Dianna tumbled into Simeon's arms, not realizing he'd followed her so closely.

The mountain is angry, Tan'yi'na boomed.

Simeon puffed up his chest, beaming. "Because Dianna killed its goddess."

Splendid, the dragon said wryly. *Only one more goddess to go.*

Dianna pressed a hand against Lydra's charred scales. The dragon let out a low wail.

"I'm sorry, girl," she breathed, letting her healing magic soak in.

Do not ask me for help, Aletha chided. *This dragon served the witch who turned us to stone.*

Dianna repressed a groan. "Lydra was under Madhea's spell. She follows me now."

'Tis true, sister, Sindri answered. *Dianna has proven herself to be a good witch and nothing like her mother.*

Warmth flooded Dianna's chest when Neriphene agreed. "Thank you, cousins," she whispered.

Very well, Aletha sighed. *Let us heal this beast and get out of here before we're all turned to ash.*

Channeling Aletha's powers, Dianna was able to rapidly heal Lydra as well as a tear in Tan'yi'na's wing before the volcano rumbled and spit out a geyser of angry lava.

Lydra howled, ducking beneath Tan'yi'na when a flaming boulder barreled toward them. Tan'yi'na burned it to a crisp before it struck the ground.

Alec raced toward them, swearing and hopping from foot to foot. "We need to go."

Dianna helped Alec and Mari climb up on Lydra, and they launched into the air ahead of a steaming geyser of lava that singed the tips of Lydra's wings.

Simeon helped Ryne scale Tan'yi'na's back. Gorpat put her father on her shoulder and waded into the water. The flood had subsided, sloshing Gorpat's shins, but the water was mixed with lava, and the giant yelped, racing across the island. She found half of the broken barge floating in the lagoon and fell on it, kicking it into the ocean. Many of Eris's soldiers were huddled on an embankment, trapped between the flood and erupting lava.

When Dianna saw the other half of Gorpat's barge stuck in the embankment, she said to her dragon. "Help them, please."

Lydra swung around and picked up the splintered logs in her talons. Then she flew past the soldiers, dropping the broken barge nearby.

They hollered their thanks and piled on the barge moments before a raging river of lava washed away the earth behind them.

Dianna prayed that wherever the Elements took them, they'd live the rest of their lives honorably, passing on the mercy they had been shown.

Alec peered over Lydra's wing as they flew over the lagoon. "Could we land on that cliff?" he asked, pointing to a lone cannon. Beside the cannon, a white shroud was illuminated by the moonlight.

A large chunk of mountain slid into the water below. "It's not safe."

"Please," he begged.

She knew why Alec wanted to land. With a groan, she relented. "You must be quick!"

"We will be," he agreed.

Even as Dianna asked Lydra to land, she was having second thoughts. More geysers sprang up, turning the landscape into an inferno. Great goddess! Why had she given in to her brother? She prayed she wouldn't regret it.

ALEC WAS GRATEFUL WHEN his sister helped him lift Mari off Lydra's back, as his hands were numb from the chill radiating off the dragon. He stumbled when the ground shook, but with a few long strides, he was at the cannon.

"Is that my father?" Mari whispered, her words shaking like a leaf in a winter storm.

"Yes," Alec murmured. "I thought you'd want to say goodbye."

Mari cupped his cheek, her eyes brimming. "Thank you."

Alec set Mari beside her father and pulled back the shroud. He'd hoped Khashka would stir, having miraculously recovered, but his body was already stiffening, just like his parents before he'd buried them.

Mari wiped her eyes, though it did no good. Her tears fell in torrents. "I never got to hold him."

Alec placed a hand upon her shoulder. "You can hold him now."

Mari fell on top of her father's body, sobbing against his chest.

The ground shook again before splitting in two, a large chunk of the cliffside falling into the ocean.

"I'm sorry, Mari." Alec scooped her up in his arms and ran back to Lydra. "Farewell, Father." Mari buried her face in her hands.

The cliff split again, and Khashka fell into the sea.

Mari sighed. "I didn't get to say a prayer for him."

He held her tight when Lydra lurched into the air. "Grim and I did."

"Thank you," she whispered.

Alec was too choked up to answer. He looked over his shoulder one last time. Lava gushed from the volcano, and the whole structure receded into itself, melting into the ocean.

"DRAGONS NICE." GORPAT leaned over her narrow barge and splashed the water. "Dragons play with Gorpat?"

Tan'yi'na floated aimlessly, shaking water off his wings. *I'm too tired to play.*

Lydra let out a slow chuckle and sent a flurry of snowflakes at Gorpat, who squealed and smashed the crystals between her palms.

Dianna smiled. Gorpat's playfulness made her miss Des, and she couldn't wait to reach Aya-Shay and hold her young brother in her arms again. Tan'yi'na had flown ahead, circling back to tell them they'd reach Aya-Shay by the morrow. Thanks to Sindri and Neriphene teaching Dianna how to manipulate wind and water, she'd been able to create a wave strong enough to push the barge across the ocean, with Gorpat hanging on the side and the rest of Dianna's friends on a small fishing vessel they'd found adrift at sea, preferring the cramped boat to riding on the backs of dragons. They had stopped occasionally to rest and hydrate. Lydra made everyone icicles to suck on, and Tan'yi'na had roasted a few carnivus plants. The plants were not as tasty as venison, but no one complained.

Brrrr. The water is cold. Tan'yi'na shook again, splashing Dianna with frigid water. *I thought the air would be warmer here.*

"That's odd." She leaned over Lydra's side and dipped her toe in the ocean. "It *is* unusually cold." Though the Elements didn't normally bother her, she was disturbed.

She looked at Alec, who was resting with Mari in his arms. Dianna wanted to be appalled at the way the two were cooing and nesting like love-struck birds, but her brother was content, and that was all that mattered.

She cupped water in her hands and threw it at her brother.

He startled. "By the Elements, that water is colder than your dragon!"

Grim and Ryne dipped their fingers in the water, sharing dark looks.

The dwarf scowled up at Dianna. "Methinks 'tis a bad omen."

Simeon sat up. "But what could it mean?"

Tan'yi'na leveled Simeon with a look. *It means, now that Eris is dead, Madhea has all the power.*

Dianna's innards turned to porridge as she fell against Lydra's scales. "Elements save us."

The End

Dear readers, I hope you are enjoying my fantasy saga. Be sure to read *Scorn of the Sky Goddess*, the conclusion to my *Keepers of the Stones* trilogy,

Blessings,
Tara West

Scorn of the Sky Goddess

Scorn of the Sky Goddess, Keepers of the Stones, Book Three

With the balance of power shifting, the young witch Dianna must destroy the Sky Goddess, Madhea, before the world turns into a frozen tomb. First she'll need to convince the Ice People to give her their goddess stones, making them vulnerable to Madhea's wrath. Next she must face an army of dwarves and giants to retrieve the final and most powerful stone. Only then will her magic be strong enough to take on the sky goddess. But even with all the stones, she can't fight Madhea alone. Forced to rely on the two men competing for her love, she must convince her rivals to work together while ignoring her pining heart.

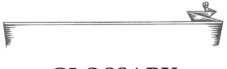

GLOSSARY

ADOLAN – A VILLAGE below the glacier, and far below the peak of Ice Mountain.

Alec – Brother to Markus and Dianna.

Aletha – One of Kyan's daughters turned to stone.

Aloa-Shay – A seaside village, several weeks' journey from Adolan.

Aya-Shay – The dwarf village by the sea.

Bane Eryll – Oldest son of Elof Eryll. Vindictive and selfish, he constantly pesters Ura to marry him. Their clan is the most powerful in Ice Kingdom.

Brendle – Desryn's little dog.

Broot – A large horned whale

Carnivus – Man-eating plants created by Eris that grow beneath the ocean.

Dafuar – Ancient prophet and son of the fallen Goddess, Kyan. He dwells in Adolan and his twin brother is Odu.

The Danae – A stream beside Adolan. It branches off from The Danae River, which flows beneath the glacier.

Desryn (Des) – Younger brother to Dianna, the witch huntress.

Dianna – A young witch, secret daughter of Madhea and half-sister to Markus and Alec. Dianna is a foster sister to Desryn, whom she has cared for since their parents died.

Dragon's Den – The mines in the Shifting Sands.

The Elementals – Daughters of the Elements and of the goddesses. Six Elementals serve Madhea and six serve Eris.

The Elements – The creators of Tehra, and the source of magic for the witches and Goddesses.

Eris – Goddess of the Sea. Also known as the sea witch, she is Madhea's sister.

Feira – Granddaughter to Kyan and daughter of Odu. She rules the Shifting Sands in her grandmother's absence.

Filip – An ice dweller traveling with Ryne.

Gnull – Large predatory ice creatures (think prehistoric walrus) that are very dangerous and a threat to the Ice People. However, they are prized for their blubbery oil, which is used as candle tallow. Gnull fur is used for clothing, and their bones are used for weapons and crafting boats.

Gorpat – The dwarf Grim's giant daughter.

Grimley (Grim) – Gorpat's dwarf father.

Ice Kingdom – City within the glacier.

Ice Mountain – A towering column of ice that stretches beyond the Heavens, built by Madhea as a shrine to herself. She dwells at the top of Ice Mountain with her daughters, the Elementals.

Ingred Johan – Council member and Elof's cousin. Her son is Ven Jonan.

Jae (Ghost) – Simeon's non-magical twin.

Jon Nordlund – Kind ice dweller, and father to Ura and Ryne.

Kerr – Jae's betrothed.

Khashka – Mari's father who killed a broot whale, resulting in Eris stealing Mari's body and discarding her soul as punishment.

Kicelin – Village at the base of Ice Mountain.

Kraehn – Fanged fish that dwell beneath the icy river. They devour just about anything, even people, in a matter of moments.

Kyani (Sprout) – Simeon's witch sister who can spontaneously grow and manipulate plants.

Luc – An ice dweller traveling with Ryne.

Lydra – Madhea's (now Dianna's) dragon, which breathes impenetrable ice.

Lyme tree – A tree large enough for a gathering hall to be built within its branches. Found at the base of the mountain and surrounding the village of Adolan.

Madhea – An evil goddess sometimes referred to as the Sky Goddess or the ice witch.

Mari- The young spirit girl whose body was taken by Eris.

Markus – The hunter who brought on The Hunter's Curse. He is the son of Rowlen and brother of Alec and husband to Ura.

Naamaku – Eris's leviathan who spits venom.

Neriphene – One of Kyan's daughters turned to stone.

Odu – Ancient prophet and son of the fallen Goddess, Kyan. Twin brother to Dafuar, he dwells in Ice Kingdom.

Orhan (O-Ran) – Kyan's mortal husband, and father to Odu, Dafuar, and their six daughters.

Pixies – Small, flying, fanged creatures with razor-sharp teeth, long claws and red eyes. They have a penchant for creating mischief and an appetite for blood.

Rení the Wise – An ancient and wise earth speaker who lives in the mines of the Shifting Sands.

Rowlen Jägerrson – Alec and Markus's father.

Ryne – Ice dweller who tries to convince his people that the ice is melting. Jon's son and Ura's brother.

The Sacred Stones (Goddess Stones) – Seven stones, each one possessing the spirit of the fallen goddess, Kyan, and her six daughters.

The Seven – Seven evil mages who rule the Shifting Sands.

The Shifting Sands – A land with a hostile, dry climate, which serves as a sanctuary from the goddesses.

Simeon – A handsome Shifting Sands witch who has the magical power of persuasion.

Sindrí – One of Kyan's daughters turned to stone by Madhea.

Sirens – Man-eating mermaids.

Slog- A creature who eats mites. Think of a sloth.

Tan'yi'na – Magnificent golden dragon and guardian to the fallen Goddess Kyan.

Tar – Ryne's loyal dog companion. Think of an Alaskan Husky.

Tehra – Their world.

Thorne – A powerful earth-speaker.

Tryads – The three goddesses.

Tumi- Feira's corpse-like husband.

Tung – Mari's disabled cousin and Khashka's nephew.

Ura – Ice dweller. Jon's daughter and Ryne's sister. Also, Markus's wife.

Ven Johan – Ingred's son who travels with Ryne.

Werewood Forest – An enchanted forest, halfway between Adolan and Aloa-Shay.

Zephyra – Head mage of The Seven.

Zier – The dwarf trader.

Books by Tara West

Eternally Yours
Divine and Dateless
Damned and Desirable
Damned and Desperate
Demonic and Deserted
Dead and Delicious
Something More Series
Say When
Say Yes
Say Forever
Say Please
Say You Want Me
Say You Love Me
Say You Need Me
Dawn of the Dragon Queen Saga
Dragon Song
Dragon Storm
Whispers Series
Sophie's Secret
Don't Tell Mother
Krysta's Curse
Visions of the Witch
Sophie's Secret Crush
Witch Blood
Witch Hunt
Keepers of the Stones
Witch Flame, Prelude

Curse of the Ice Dragon, Book One
Spirit of the Sea Witch, Book Two
Scorn of the Sky Goddess, Book Three

About Tara West

TARA WEST WRITES BOOKS about dragons, witches, and handsome heroes while eating chocolate, lots and lots of chocolate. She's willing to share her dragons, witches, and heroes. Keep your hands off her chocolate. A former high school English teacher, Tara is now a full-time writer and graphic artist. She enjoys spending time with her family, interacting with her fans, and fishing the Texas coast.

Awards include: Dragon Song, Grave Ellis 2015 Readers Choice Award, Favorite Fantasy Romance

Divine and Dateless, 2015 eFestival of Words, Best Romance

Damned and Desirable, 2014 Coffee Time Romance Book of the Year

Sophie's Secret, selected by The Duff and Paranormal V Activity movies and Wattpad recommended reading lists

Curse of the Ice Dragon, Best Action/Adventure 2013 eFestival of Words

Sophie's Secret, iBooks Breakout Book Award

Hang out with her on her Facebook fan page at: https://www.facebook.com/tarawestauthor

Or check out her website: www.tarawest.com

She loves to hear from her readers at: tara@tarawest.com

Made in the USA
Las Vegas, NV
22 January 2021